THE PURGE OF DISTRICT 89

THE PURGE OF
DISTRICT 89

A GROWER'S WAR
BOOK 1

D.J. MOLLES

Text copyright © 2017 D.J. Molles

ISBN: 1542345758
ISBN 13: 9781542345750

CHAPTER ONE

Quiet moments were the worst.

How very un-Chinese of him to think it.

Captain Kuai Luo sat in the back of the guntruck, and the world passed him by to the whisper of the miles that moved beneath his feet, beneath two inches of armor plating, and under the knobby tires of his guntruck. And under that crust of asphalt was soil that three generations of his family had fought and died on.

Kuai had lived almost his entire adult life here. His grandfather came back speaking fluent English with a southern-American twang, just like he'd learned it. And now Kuai was deployed to the very same region that his grandfather and father had fought on, trying to stabilize these people, these restless, rebellious people.

Kuai could talk like them so easily that it made him feel an alien amongst his own people. If you couldn't see his genetically-modified stature and the heavy armor plates he wore, the chest-plate emblazoned with the flag of the People's Republic of China, you would think you were talking to a person born and raised in North Carolina.

He looked out the thick ballistic window at the countryside flying by. He felt that familiar dichotomy in his chest, and he didn't know whether he hated this place, or loved it.

This place that would probably, one day, kill him

Here in Agrarian District 89 (abbreviated as AD-89 and often written shorthand as simply 8089—even the locals called it "Eighty-Eighty-Nine"), he was surrounded by great swaths of open land. Here, the fields were the lush green of winter wheat, just beginning to send up its heads of grain as spring warmth drew it out of the soil.

The green was so thick that he could barely see the tractor rails and hydroponics lines that he knew striped through that field. In another two months, these would be the famous "amber waves," but now they were still young.

On other tracts, the land was bare, but pregnant with possibility.

The bare fields had been pumped with the chemicals that dissolved the stalks of the previous crop, and then pumped with the chemicals that would condition the soil for the new crop. As the weather warmed, those chemicals would run off and create the algae blooms that would turn the Rocky River as orange as a pumpkin for a good part of the late summer.

But right now, in April, the Rocky River was still running clear, and the planting tractors were out. Great, beastly machines that sat astride the tractor rails like a giant, splay-legged spiders, ready to begin planting the spring crop.

Corn, Kuai guessed, since it was April.

Love or hate?

Difficult to say.

Kuai's Personal Device chirped.

He shifted around inside his armor, straightening slightly, and moving his battlerifle to the right a bit. He fished the PD out of a pouch on his chest. It was a thin, black rectangle, smaller than his palm. The Americans had theirs biometrically attached to the inside of their wrists at fifteen years old. The Chinese didn't prefer this, as they believed it created dependence and weak minds.

But, if you were going to talk with Americans, you had to have a PD.

The Americans had theirs issued by their government—and China's tenuous ally—the Fed.

His was purchased black market.

Kuai swiped his finger across the little black rectangle. The screen jumped into the air, then adjusted to his viewpoint with a little shakiness. Older model. But it still served its purpose.

He read the new message. Closed the projected screen with another swipe of his hand. Put the PD back into its pouch.

"They're waiting for us," he said in Mandarin.

He glanced to his left. His lieutenant nodded along. A Uyghur. More American-looking than Chinese, really. Lieutenant Qasim adjusted his grip on his own battlerifle. He did not like these meetings. He said there was no honor among thieves. He did not trust the Americans. Not the Fed troops, and certainly not the people they were about to meet.

Kuai couldn't blame him.

Qasim was a first generation soldier, and this was only the third month of his first deployment to America. All he knew of the Americans so far was that they wanted to kill him. And those that weren't trying to kill him looked like they certainly wouldn't mind if he died. And even the ones that were supposed to be friendly—the Fed troops and the loyalists—even they seemed resentful most of the time.

Kuai didn't blame any of them.

No one wanted to live under the thumb of another. But that is the nature of these things. That is the nature of history. One people represses another people, only to be repressed themselves. It is the never ending cycle, and there was nothing that could be done to stop it. It had begun the day human beings wanted what someone else had, and it would never go away.

Kuai was just another little cog in this giant machine.

So was Qasim.

So were the people they were going to meet.

What they did in these strange, tumultuous years would be remembered for a short time, but it was really all quite worthless in the end. All that truly mattered was connections. Connections with others. With wives. With family. With friends. Everything else was just…intermission.

Yes, these quiet moments were the worst.

Quiet was time to think. Time to reflect. Time to receive clarity on your place in the world and the miniscule nature of your efforts. How your life could be given for something as silly and inconsequential as the bartering of medicines to garner local favor in a country an entire world away from anything you actually cared about.

And that wasn't good.

These were not the things he should be thinking about.

Not if he ever actually wanted to make it home.

Only five more years, he told himself. *Just twice what you've already done. And then you can go home, permanently.*

All the time and money they spent to turn a mere mortal man into a New Breed soldier—that investment had to be recouped, you know.

He smirked ruefully to himself.

He'd thought his wife would enjoy the body mods. The increased stature. The thick neck. The slabs of lean muscle that appeared almost overnight. And...other things.

She'd covered it well, but he'd been able to tell that she was slightly frightened of him.

Ah, well.

She knew what she was getting into when she agreed to marry him. He'd been slated for soldiering the minute he came out of the womb. It was only the change that frightened her. She would eventually forget about his pre-modded form—his gangly teenaged state—and accept what he had become.

Kuai leaned forward in his seat, pointing out the windshield at the fork in the road coming up. "This is the turn," he said to the driver, Sergeant Jen. "Stay to the right."

Ahead of them, the convoy stayed left—a supply truck, a personnel carrier, and two more guntrucks. Captain Kuai Luo's guntruck was at the rear, and then it simply veered off onto the other road that cut through this Agrarian District, heading now for the Town Center.

To his left, Lieutenant Qasim clipped his battleshroud into place. It covered everything from the bridge of his nose down to his clavicle. Only his blue eyes looked out, suspicious of this foreign countryside.

Kuai watched him for a moment more, feeling his own stomach turn a bit. He left his battleshroud undone. He had to project confidence. Not only with his troops, but with the people they were about to meet. It would not do to appear frightened. Cautious was okay—everyone appreciated caution. But no one wanted dealings with a coward.

Still, Qasim's feelings were not wrong.

If something were to happen, it would be now, when they were split from the protection of the convoy.

"We're alone now," Kuai said to the other three occupants of the guntruck. Qasim, Jen, and a new private by the name of Zhang. It was obvious, but it bore repeating: "Keep a sharp eye out. We're easy prey for opportunists."

Kuai turned his attention out his own window again.

They passed another planting tractor. This one close. Facing them. From the bubble of the cab, high in the air, he could see the two faces looking down at them. He looked back, knowing they couldn't see him through the tinted ballistic glass of the guntruck.

He wondered if they would hop on their PDs to tell some friends that a lonely guntruck was heading up the highway.

Another few minutes brought them to the edge of the Town Center.

It was still early morning. What cars there were on the road got out of their way. They knew the drill. The guntrucks didn't stop, didn't wait for anything. If you got in the way of a guntruck, you'd be not-so-gently tapped in the rear bumper until you moved.

They skirted around the eastern edge of the Town Center, not actually going into it where the stores and the bars and the entertainment hubs were. They kept to the outside, which was mostly a grid of hangars to store tractors and planters. Pumping stations for the hydroponics. Large, cement yards where the workers parked and where farming implements sat, waiting for their season of use.

Kuai directed Sergeant Jen, and they took a right on a service road that led away from the Town Center. No cars on this road. It was abandoned. Here were the harvesters. Locked up behind chains and razor wire fences. There would be nothing to harvest for another two months, and so until then, this place was a ghost town.

A good place for a meeting.

Or an ambush.

"This one, here," Kuai said, pointing to a gate that was unlocked and open. Beyond the gate stood a two-story hangar and several acres of pavement. Parking spots for workers cars that stood empty. A few rows of grain-harvester attachments.

Jen slowed the guntruck and turned in.

"Drive around to the back of the hangar."

Lieutenant Qasim checked the bolt on his battlerifle. Brass glinted. He snicked it back into place. His breastplate rose and fell with a deep breath.

In the front, Private Zhang buckled up his battleshroud. Shifted around, nervously.

Without the sound of the road moving under their tires, Kuai could hear the little movements of the anti-sniper cannon, scanning. Small, electric noises. Servo motors whirring back and forth over his head.

"Qasim and Zhang," Kuai said, keeping his voice calm and level. "You're with me. Keep an eye out. Don't watch them. It won't be them that does anything. Watch everywhere else. Jen, you just stay ready to drive us out."

"Yes, sir," the private said.

The lieutenant and the sergeant just nodded.

They drove around to the back of the hangar.

Two black, compact GUVs waited for them. No markings on them, but he could see the strobes in the grill.

On the roof of the guntruck, the anti-sniper cannon kept scanning.

"Stop here," Kuai said.

The guntruck stopped, just behind the hangar and out of view of the road. They faced the two black GUVs.

Kuai, Qasim, and Zhang stepped out quickly.

Kuai kept his hands near his battlerifle, but not on it. He didn't want to look too aggressive. These were delicate times. He stepped to the front while Qasim and Zhang flanked him, looking out everywhere but at the two trucks, as Kuai had instructed.

The three New Breed soldiers stopped a few meters in front of their guntruck.

The doors to the GUVs opened.

Two men in green uniforms stepped out of the drivers' sides. They wore softarmor—not the heavy plating that Kuai and his men carried. They were not soldiers. They were not body-modded. Twenty kilograms of armor plating would be too much for their normal frames to carry all day, every day. They wore no helmets or battleshrouds. One of them had a subgun strapped to his chest and a pistol on his leg. The other only carried a pistol.

Across the chest of their softarmor was the boldly printed English word: SHERIFF.

The two men in green uniforms met Kuai's group in the middle.

"Captain Luo," the man with the subgun said in English.

Kuai nodded to him. "Sheriff Honeycutt."

Sheriff Honeycutt was tall for a normal man, though he was still a head shorter than Kuai and his men. Dark hair cropped short with the beginnings of gray at the temples. He had dusky, suntanned skin that crinkled like worn leather at the corners of brown eyes.

Sharp eyes. Canny eyes. They jumped between Kuai and his men, assessing them, gauging them. Not much fear for a man so outsized and outgunned.

But that was good. They weren't here to fight. If the sheriff had had fear in his eyes, it would have been a bad sign.

"The medications?" Honeycutt asked.

Good. Right to business.

Kuai nodded. "In the back of the truck."

"How much?"

"Two cases. One hundred and twenty doses apiece. Each case will treat five people."

Honeycutt's lips twitched. "Ten people total, huh?" He looked out at the fields far beyond the fenced-in parking lot. "Out of how many that are dying?"

Kuai nodded, almost sympathetic. "If all goes well, there will be more."

Honeycutt smirked, coldly. "Of course." He seemed to brush off his offense. "Well, let's do the business then." He extended his hand.

Kuai glanced at the hand. He was not in the habit of shaking hands with these people. He did not intend to start today. He shook his head once and looked up from the hand to Honeycutt's face. "Nothing personal, sheriff…"

Honeycutt's eyes.

The small drop of perspiration at the corner of his right temple where the hair was gray.

Kuai felt it. Felt the weirdness of the moment hanging there.

He started to pull back. "Sheriff—"

zzZZWHACK

The sound of lightning.

Out of the corner of his eye, Kuai perceived one of the black GUVs shudder and shimmer, like a mirage.

Not lightning.

Kuai knew the sound.

It was a directed EMP.

The cannon…

Kuai was already moving by the time his brain made the connections. He pivoted sharply, swinging his hips, rotating them, and sent a hard boot straight into Honeycutt's chest, launching the smaller man off his feet.

In the same motion, Kuai grabbed his battlerifle…

A noise—actually two noises, very close together.

Bullets on flesh.

Even as the sheriff was still falling.

Even as Kuai was still bringing his rifle up.

Even as the directed EMP was still crackling, disabling the anti-sniper cannon.

He saw Qasim and Zhang, pitching backwards, almost synchronized, red ribbons spinning from the small gap between their battleshrouds and their helmets. Their eyes were no longer visible. No longer there. Exploded into pulp.

All in a single second.

Kuai didn't even have time to register fear.

In a strange and disconnected way, his brain—modded to think faster in less time—was able to appreciate that this was a very well-executed ambush. It was expertly timed. Those two bullets had to have been fired nearly simultaneous with the activation of the EMP. Otherwise the anti-sniper cannon would have turned the snipers into bits of gristle.

What fine-tuning!

He righted himself and brought his rifle up, just as Honeycutt was hitting the ground, flat on his back. He was going to shoot Honeycutt first, and then the deputy, and then address the sniper problem. He already had that prioritized.

He aimed reflexively for the sheriff, but out of the corner of his eye, he saw the deputy moving. He saw the deputy's arm outstretched. And suddenly his brain decided that the deputy was the more immediate threat, and so Kuai pivoted in that direction, changing his decision in the span of a few hundredths of a second.

But for all his body and brain modifications, it was not fast enough.

Something struck his face.

Sharp pain arced through him.

He felt his body lock up against his will.

He pitched forward with a groan.

Hit the concrete.

Thinking, *So fine-tuned.*

And, *I should have worn my battleshroud.*

CHAPTER TWO

It took a bit of finesse to guide a 150-foot span planter onto the tractor rails. For all of its multiple tons of weight, the controls were surprisingly sensitive. And of the 1,775 inches that Walter Baucom currently had it spanned for, his margin of error was about two inches per tread.

Not a lot.

He sat in the operator's chair, his feet on the pedals, his hands on the leveraging and spanning controls, and his eyes flitting back and forth between the monitors. The windshield was a broad bubble of reinforced glass and the cockpit of the giant tractor was nearly thirty feet in the air. From that vantage point it seemed that he could see everything from there.

How to describe an Agrarian District to someone that had never sat in this seat? Never looked out across the endless rolling landscape? Seen the breathtaking expanse of those croplands and the clarity and the hugeness of the sky with nothing around to block your view? All those fields so evenly lined with gray hydroponics lines and tractor rails?

He guessed that any grower you asked would give you a different take on it.

To Walt, it was this, right here.

It was the smell of diesel fumes, and the grainy scent of the seeds in the hopper. The pungent odor of the soil conditioner that had been piped into the fields the previous week. It was the feeling of warm air from the span planter's vents, and the cool brace of the April morning coming in through the open window of his cockpit. The air so clear that he could see seven hills away.

It was a tickle of familiarity, almost like déjà vu. Something that came with the changing of the seasons.

But then again, Walt tended to try to focus on the positive.

There was another aspect to it. One that he didn't like to entertain, because there just wasn't shit he could do about it. And that was just the perfect *utility* of it all.

Sometimes all he could see was the cold practicality in it, and he could almost picture the Chicoms and Russians drawing up the plans for all this farming infrastructure. How to maximize the farmable land. How to make soil-hydroponics large scale so that people like Walt could grow more food, and faster.

Because if you kept people busy, if you kept them focused on their work, then they would just keep making you money, and their opportunities to rebel would shrink.

He could see their efficiency in this, if he chose to look at it.

But instead he chose to keep his head down. That was what his Pops had taught him to do.

There was a saying that the growers had. It went, "So the wind blows, and the seasons go, and the seeds grow."

In other words, "There ain't shit you can do about it."

It was an invocation of the complete futility of trying to fight unstoppable things. And long, long ago, the Coalition—or "CoAx" to their detractors—had become another unstoppable thing, right up there with the blowing of the wind, and the changing of the seasons, and whether or not a seed chose to germinate and grow into a plant.

"So the wind blows," they would say, and shrug off life's inequities.

And it embodied the apathy of a population with no power over their lives.

Keep your head down. Do what you're told. It's easiest that way.

Walter could have a wife. He could work. He could have the satisfaction of a job well-done. He could have a quiet life. And there was nothing wrong with that. There was a beauty, a peace to it. And he was okay with the fact that it was small. Small dreams were good enough for him.

Walt stretched his back a bit and refocused himself on the two vidfeeds.

One from the right strut. One from the left strut.

He was operating a 2.7 million dollar machine, attempting to guide it onto a 1.4 million dollar rail system. He knew those numbers because SoDro Growers Group saw fit to remind him on a somewhat regular basis—probably about once a week. So he was well aware that any error on his part could be very costly, and there was an applicant pool of nearly a thousand qualified growers who were stuck on maintenance trucks that would love to have his job.

So he focused. And he was very gentle with the controls.

Steady as she goes.

He'd operated that machine for the last five years. When he'd first started, he'd been a nervous wreck. Now, it was just another day at the office. Every once in a while, the reality of it would hit, and he'd get that little jump-start in his chest. But then he'd be lulled by the normalcy of it, the every-day nature of it. This was nothing special, really.

That was how you had to think about it.

To his right, his partner, Merl, sipped coffee from the planter's seat. Feet on the dash, making his section of the cab muddy. Walt's side was pristine.

"Careful now," Merl said. "Don't want my taxes going up."

It was a long-running joke. Hardly worth laughing about, so Walt just ignored him.

When the first tumults of war had hit the Districts, it had left the hydroponics systems damaged so much that the Fed raised taxes on land ownership to an extravagant level to pay for the repairs. Of course, everyone clamored that it was a punitive tax designed to punish the growers, because the Agrarian Districts had harbored so much of the resistance.

The Fed didn't even try to deny it.

"You break it, you buy it," was the tongue-in-cheek response.

The old joke struck a little closer to home for Walt, though. The acreage he'd been contracted to plant had once been owned by previous generations of his family. An old birthright that had never had the chance to be passed on. Now it was owned by the government, leased by SoDro Growers Group under five year contracts, and Walter Baucom was paid his paltry commission to work the land that his fathers once owned.

So the wind blows.

The Baucom family had tried to hang onto it for a while. They'd succeeded a little longer than some of the other families in the area. But little by little the land had been bled away from them, as it had from everyone else. They couldn't keep scrounging the money up to pay what they owed on it.

He'd been a kid when his Pops had finally made the decision to sell out. The Land Patronage Act made sure that the Baucom family received a tax subsidy for working the land they once owned. Walt guessed that was supposed to salve any resentment. Maybe it did, maybe it didn't. At the end of the day, he supposed they were better off financially.

He got the right strut lined up, then focused on the left. That was how you had to do it. Power to the right, then to the left. Kind of wiggling the big beast of a machine up into place, until both of your running struts were about six inches from contact and perfectly lined up.

His eyes shot back and forth between the two monitors. Judging the pictures from the vidfeeds. Making sure that they were mirror images of each other. If he didn't, there would be a cracked strut, or a damaged rail, and he would have much explaining to do.

Everything looked right.

The feeds were both reporting near-identical measurements.

The ramps were steep. He had to feather the power just a bit to get the multi-ton planter up onto the rails. Couldn't just stomp on the gas. That would be disastrous.

Five years ago, he would have been "sweating in his creases," as Merl put it.

But today, he just wanted to get the damn thing on the rails and get to planting. He had a shit-ton of acres to plant, and he really didn't want to work on his day off. Carolyn's day off was finally due to sync up with his, and if he screwed that up, he wouldn't hear the end of it. She'd been excited about their day off together for a month.

Walt smiled through his concentration. Fiddled the controls a bit.

Merl took another long sip of coffee. He leaned over and saw where Walt had positioned them, and he pulled the cup away from his face, knowing what came next.

Walt feathered the power. The planter started to rock back and forth.

"Easy now," Merl said again, mainly because he knew it would get on Walt's nerves. Then he began making sudden noises every time Walt tapped the power, as though Walt had made some terrible mistake: "Whoop! Oop! Watch out!"

What a bastard.

Planters thought it was all fun and games. The computer did all their work for them, and if by some insanely improbable happenstance, the coulters struck a hydroponics line, it'd be a measly few thousand in repairs. Not enough to get them shit-canned.

Walt kept the planter rocking back and forth, making a little more progress onto the ramp. Little by little. A little more…

He felt the resistance give way and the giant bulk of the machine made it onto the tractor rails, moving just a bit too quick. The planter jerked around and made a nasty groaning sound.

Hot coffee splashed on Merl's leg. "Fuck!" he yelped. "Come on, man!"

Walt immediately loosened his grip on the controls, letting the rails guide the tracks of the planter. He took his foot off the power, allowing the machine's own inertia to slow it down. Then he gently applied the brake.

He looked over at Merl, smiling.

Merl glared back. "Smooth, y'knocker. How long you been doing this now?"

Walt scoffed. "We're in there." He moved his hips, suggestively. "Little rough, but that's just what she likes."

Merl rolled his eyes and took another swipe at his coffee-stained tans. He stowed his cup of coffee and took his feet off the dash. A few taps of a few buttons. The computer scanned the ground beneath them.

Walter watched his partner's body language with the unconscious ease of a natural born talent, and confirmed that Merl was just blustering at him. There was no true anger there.

But Merl was an easy read. Not only had Walter been partner's with the man for a few years now—goodness, had it been that long?—but Merl didn't know about Walter's abilities, and Walter didn't advertise them, so Merl had never tried to hide his body language.

All Merl knew was what everyone else in District 89 (and in the casinos in the city) knew: you don't play poker with Walter Baucom.

Poker was the game that Walter had squandered his talent on, earned himself money with, gotten the shit kicked out of him over, and eventually abandoned, because no one would play with him. Or, in the case of the casinos, they didn't *allow* him to play.

But Walter was an enterprising young man. He'd found other ways for his abilities to make him money. Other, much more dangerous ways. And soon he would learn just how much danger he was putting himself in, but for now he was just a grower getting paid a pittance to operate this giant piece of machinery.

Walt felt the huge planting arm lower down as Merl activated it. It came through as a slight vibration in his feet and a dip in the tachometer. The agitators in the giant hopper full of corn seed started whirring, making the planter rock slightly.

Then a thunderous roar.

Which was not normal at all.

"Shit, what…?" Walt looked at his readings, his gauges, his hands instinctively removed from the controls. But then he recognized the sound for what it was.

Merl was already leaning forward, looking up into the sky through the viewport.

Three gunships went overhead, flying low and fast.

Walt caught the markings on their tails.

One Fed. One Chicom. One Russian.

"Oh, look," Merl said, flatly. "It's the Three Brothers."

Fraternity Flights, the growers called them. No real purpose but to fly over, slow and showy, and demonstrate to any insurgents on the ground that the Three Brothers were still united, still holding hands, still ushering this country into the new era of safety and security, and they'd better get the fuck on board, or else.

Except this didn't seem like a Fraternity Flight.

Walt squinted at them as the three gunships hung a hard right and began circling around, heading for the Town Center area. "I dunno. Those looked like they were goin' somewhere fast."

Merl watched them silently for a moment, lips pursed in thought. Fast and low.

That wasn't how the Fraternity Flights went.

Merl knew Walt was right. Those gunships were heading to something. And the thought of that filled the cockpit with an uncertainty. Both of the growers leaned out a bit and looked in the direction of the Town Center, and Walt knew that they were both looking for the same thing: smoke trails.

These were violent times. It'd been almost docile for a while. But something had happened. Something in the last few months, and the rumors were flying.

Some said it was another country that had come in to aide the resistance. Others said it was a portion of the Fed military that had defected. Still others said it was a prison break from one of the DTIs—Domestic Terrorist Internment—out west.

According to the grapevine, it was any one of a dozen different things.

But whatever it really was, the Fed-controlled newsfeeds weren't saying, and in all the silence, they were seeing more gunships, more guntrucks, and more patrols than they'd seen in previous years.

And everybody knew somebody who was involved in one way or another.

Somebody who could die in the violence at any minute of any day, on one side or the other.

Merl sat back in his seat. He swallowed and frowned at his controls. "World's goin' to shit."

For a fleeting second, Walt wondered if he should call Carolyn, check in on her, make sure that she was okay. Make sure that some wingnut resistance group hadn't detonated a bomb too close to the dining hall where she worked...

Walt shook his head.

You couldn't live your life in fear.

It would be fine. Everything would be fine.

"She's ready," Merl said, in an almost subdued voice. He opened the feed tubes from the hopper to the coulters. "It's on you."

Walt took a calming breath and focused on the good things. The familiarity. The beautiful view. He let himself at least *try* to feel satisfied as he throttled up the power to the planting arms and pulled the speed down to a solid ten-feet-per-second.

Steady as she goes.

———

He went with Merl to the tavern after work, because Merl offered to buy him a beer and they'd actually finished their acres ahead of schedule. Carolyn wouldn't be home from the dining hall for another two hours. He wouldn't be missed.

Nothing on the news to tell them what the flight of gunships had been going towards. Nothing to alert them to anything out of the ordinary, although they did pass two separate patrols on their way in. One Chicom. One Russian.

The days were lengthening and it wasn't quite dark when they got there. The tavern was tucked into the back corner of their Town Center—pronounced "*tan sinner*." To most everyone that grew up as a grower, it was the center of their universe, the only commercial space allowed to exist inside the borders of their District. You could go into the city if you were feeling ritzy, but it was a rare occasion when driving an hour and half each way to be sneered at by a bunch of urbies sounded like a good way to spend your night.

Their Town Center was a sprawl of brownstone buildings that had been constructed damn-near a hundred years ago. Stuffed into all of those old buildings was a collection of small businesses, a lot of them owned by SoDro Growers Group. Hardware stores, grocery stores, liquor stores, rec centers, mess halls, a few restaurants, a smattering of apartments, and of course, four pubs. All four were nearly identical. For some reason Walt and Merl had long ago chosen Brown's Tavern as home base.

Driving into the town center, Walt saw the usual run of people. Old, beat up trucks just like his own, carrying old, beat up men and women fresh from the fields and pump stations, their tans still smudged with dirt and purple regulator cleaner, all heading to a bar, or a mess hall to cash in on their meal ticket—generously provided by their gracious employer, SoDro. They were the first shifters, of which Walt considered himself lucky to be one.

Parking was a bitch, which was about average for shift-change. Walt followed Merl's pickup truck mindlessly, letting the other man figure out where to park. Merl circled around Brown's Tavern three times, like a dog trying to find a comfortable spot to lay down. They finally found a pair of spots and pulled their trucks in, close enough that the mirrors scraped.

The two of them edged out of their half-open doors, cursing and mumbling half-heartedly. They met at the back of their trucks with a pair of smirks, and then walked the block to Brown's. Walt zipped up the front of his tans. The evening was as crisp and clear as the morning had been.

Walt turned the corner to Brown's and almost stopped walking.

He caught himself at the last second and covered his hesitation with a cough.

Outside of Brown's, three guntrucks were parked. A few soldiers—Russians, it looked like—stood around the big vehicles, their battleshrouds undone, talking and smoking.

Merl took a glance at him, evaluating his partner.

Walt just looked straight ahead. But not directly at the soldiers. Off to the side a bit, while he clenched his teeth. It was best not to make eye-contact. He felt the heat, the resentment, rising up in his chest, but he pushed it down and went for the door to Brown's, hoping that the rest of the soldiers weren't inside the tavern.

The Russians were known to take drink breaks while on patrol. Sometimes they hung around the taverns after-hours. Some of them were nice. A lot of them weren't. And nice or not, they all knew that they commanded a level of fear, and so the barkeeps pushed free drinks at them and hoped not to get on their shit list.

If they're in there, I'm walking right back out, Walt thought bitterly.

The two of them pushed through the old, white doors and into the tavern.

A bit of peeling white paint clung to his palm. He brushed it off on his tans.

The place was dark and musty. It smelled like growers that had worked all day, and stale beer drying and re-fermenting on the floor mats. One could make the case that it was a bad smell, but it long ago stopped being offensive to Walt. Now, he associated it with the feeling of finally being free of work, and the taste of a well-deserved beer.

The interior was lit by advertisement lights and the monitors of people's PDs. A few dim recessed fixtures struggled to be important but weren't offering much.

Walt glanced around the dimness, looking for the soldiers. But it was just growers.

He let out a low breath of relief.

The tavern was crowded. It was payday. So, naturally, the first bill to be paid is to the barkeep. SoDro Growers Group, who leased 90% of the land in 8089, had come through again with their meager weekly salaries. It wasn't much, but when your balance is always so close to nothing, a $9,500 jump makes you feel like a rich man.

Of course, it would all be gone by Thursday, without a doubt. A week's groceries alone would take about a third of it—a gallon of milk for $80, a loaf of bread for $65, oh the joys of fifty years of runaway inflation. Then there was utilities. And rent. Both of which were paid directly back to SoDro, who owned their house, so paying that bill was always darkly amusing.

Walt flipped up his PD monitor and traced his eyes over the transparent blue glow. His balance sat at $9,437. Walt opened his mouth, coughed rudely, standing there in the middle of the tavern entryway.

"What the fuck?" he snapped.

Merl looked at him. "What's the problem?"

"We got shorted," Walt said back. "Or at least, I did. Did you get shorted?"

As he said it, his fingers scrawled across the projection, opening the itemized deductions list. He scrolled through all the taxes that he already knew and expected—property, income, energy usage, grocery (yeah, that was a good one, considering he grew the damn groceries to begin with), vehicle ownership, healthcare, charity, roads and infrastructure.

There were a few subsidies, too. Credits made back to him for keeping his head down and doing what he was told. Walter Baucom had two subsidies, and he knew damn well that without them his financial ends would not meet, no matter how much creative stretching he and Carolyn could do. There was his Land Patronage subsidy, and his Best Career subsidy—for sticking to farming, because that's what his Aptitude Test said he'd be good at.

Scrolling through all of this, Walt stopped and jabbed a finger at something he hadn't expected to see. "Ecosystem Recovery Act?" he looked up at Merl. "The hell is that?"

Merl just shook his head and continued into the bar. "Come on, y'knocker. You ever read your corporate mail?"

Walt walked after him, only half-paying attention to where he was going. Mostly focused on that culprit of his missing money. "Ayuh," he murmured. "When I get around to it."

Merl grabbed a seat at the bar. "Close that shit. I'm fuckin' parched."

Walt snapped his PD shut, but didn't sit.

Merl looked up at him. "SoDro sent the memo about that shit. Fed's twisted their arm into—" he put up air quotes "—'revitalizing the ecosystems damaged by chemical runoff.' Our hydroponics, basically."

"And we have to foot the bill?" Walt grumbled to himself.

"So the wind blows." Merl propped his elbows on the bar. "Relax. It's only two-hundred and thirty-four bucks."

Walt made a raspberry noise. "Easy for you to say, Moneybags. I only got two in my house. Pops's retirement barely counts."

Merl was married, his pops was still working, and his grandpa had not been "disappeared" like Walt's. He was a five-income house, which was pretty normal. Walt's was only a two-income house—just he and Carolyn. Walt's father's income barely contributed because he insisted on living alone.

Independent, he called it. Like people used to live.

And nearly every penny of his retirement subsidy went to paying his rent.

It hadn't always been like that.

Life had dealt its blows. It had taken much.

Merl cleared his throat. "No moneybags here. I got two chaps."

Walt nodded silently. Didn't have a reply to that. It never failed to feel like a jab in the gut, and Walt tried like hell to hide his change in demeanor—squinting at the beer taps, or looking away. The moment was there and then gone, just a small, unconscious reaction that Walt mitigated as quickly as possible. Because in the end, he shouldn't begrudge Merl his kids, even if he and Carolyn couldn't have their own.

Merl realized he'd tread himself into sensitive areas. He raised his hand. "Good God. Can two guys just grab a beer and quit talking about this shit?"

Walt gestured to his PD. "You sure you're good buyin' me a beer? That deduction ain't gonna put you in the red?"

"Naw, man." Merl waved him off, then raised his hand to the bartender and requested two beers.

Walt took a seat at the bar. It burned a little bit. He knew damn well that Merl had offered to buy him the beers because he knew the deduction from SoDro would likely have put him and Carolyn too close to the edge this month.

Growers could be stubborn. Especially about accepting kindness from others.

21

But…they were also a close community. Money troubles were no stranger to them. And there was a delicate social dance that they all knew that allowed them to help each other out in the leaner times without making each other feel beholden. It was a small thing, an understanding. Today, Merl was the one with a few extra dollars. Next week, it might be Walt.

No tally was necessary.

Merl knew Walt would get him back when he could.

The bartender placed the two beers in front of them. Caps already removed. And by then it was too late to refuse, even if Walt had wanted to. And right then, that sweating cold beer looked like he didn't want to.

They took their bottles of beer.

Merl raised his. "Cheers. To a good planting."

They clicked bottles and drank.

Walt remembered the night that the Baucom house had lost one of its own.

It hadn't been the first time. But it was the time that he remembered the most. Before that time, it had been his Grandpa Clarence that they'd come for, but he'd been young when that happened, and he only remembered the absence, and not the incident itself.

This time, he'd been there when it happened.

It had been evening. Late in the evening, because he remembered it was summertime and it was dark out. So it had to have been after nine. It was the summer before his senior year in high school. He was seventeen and spent most of his time in the evenings glued to his PD because it was still relatively newfangled to him.

The days he spent learning the ropes as a knocker—a bottom of the barrel, know-nothing rookie—on the hydroponics maintenance rigs, and, occasionally, begging a tractor operator to let him ride along to absorb some of the tricks.

That summer, his brother, Roy, had butted heads to the point of fists with his Pops over how vocally anti-CoAx he was. But even after all of that, Roy took his Aptitude Test and it told him he would be working on software maintenance for the planting tractors. And in a strangely defeatist way, Roy accepted his fate. He'd met a girl named Shana, and he spent most of his time with her. Walt and his family rarely saw him anymore. There was a strange distance there.

But on that one, late-summer evening, Roy had come back to them.

This was after a month or so when none of them had seen or heard from Roy and they'd all assumed he was out with Shana. So it was a nice surprise to see him show up at their door that night, just before dinner, and Walt had almost been giddy to help set an extra place at the table.

The house was very boring by himself with no one to convince him to get into trouble.

Roy seemed different that night, but in a good way. Gone was the resignation and the bitterness. He seemed to have found some sort of purpose in his life again, and it didn't seem like he held anything against Walt, or Mom, or even Pops. He seemed happy to see them again.

"How's Shana?" Walt ventured as they were finishing their dinner plates and Pops was rooting around the pantry for moonshine.

Roy smiled. "She's good, man. Real good."

"What's she doin' with herself?"

"She's workin' at the Barn."

"Really?" Walt was surprised. "I never see her."

"She works first shift hours. Parts Requisitions."

"Ah." Walt nodded. "I'm third shift on the maintenance rigs right now."

"I heard." Roy gave him a look that said he was *almost* proud of Walt. "Helpin' Mom and Pops pay the bills?"

Walt nodded. "Just a little bit. Crossing my fingers for the Aptitude Test."

Something dark passed over Roy's face. "Ayuh."

Pops reappeared with a mason jar of moonshine. He set it onto the table with a flourish. "Now, there it is." He motioned for Roy. "You missed the last batch. Go ahead. Guest of honor."

Walt glanced into the kitchen and Mom was sipping coffee, shaking her head at them, but she had a smile on her lips. Good to see the boys back together again. It was nice to pretend that everything was okay. To hope that everything would be smooth sailing from there on out.

Roy was looking down into the clear liquid in the mason jar, and Walt could tell that he was struggling with whether to say something or not. There was a slight frown across his eyebrows, and his lips twitched just a bit with unsaid words. He seemed not to want to ruin the moment.

Pops slapped him on the shoulder, gave it a squeeze. "Good to have my boys back under one roof," he said.

If Roy had been close to saying anything, that pulled him back. The look of hesitation left him and he forced a smile that, after a moment, became a little more natural. He lifted the mason jar. "Ayuh, Pops. It's good to hang out with you guys."

Then he drank and passed the jar to Walt.

They sipped and laughed and even Mom joined them for a few nips.

An hour passed, talking about childhood memories when Walt had followed Roy around to getting in trouble in nearly every corner of the damn District. Talking about when Roy was going to pop the question to Shana. It went back and forth between the subjects of Roy's future and Pops's imminent retirement—still a few years away, but for which he fervently looked forward to. And eventually the conversation came back to Walt, and to his hopes, and his nervousness about the Aptitude Test, and Mom and Pops's nervousness about whether Walt might test out.

Without Grandpa Clarence, they were down to two incomes. Roy still helped, but if he married Shana there was a good chance he would join his finances to her family. And Walt was barely helping out—his twenty hours a week paid for maybe one or two of the smaller bills. They would never tell him to fix his test scores, but if he managed to test out, and Roy combined finances with Shana's family, then their parents were going to be living very close to the red.

Not that it really mattered, as Walt observed.

Growers didn't test out very often.

But Walt remembered his brother looking at him, holding that jar of moonshine in one hand, and Walt knew he was buzzed, but his eyes were sharp nonetheless. He pointed at Walt with an index finger from the hand that held the jar.

"You listen to me, little brother. Those tests?" he paused, mason jar hovering in the air, and his eyes grew watery and he looked away from Walt with a small shake of his head. "We're smarter than they think we are. We could be better. But they won't let us."

"Roy," Pops intoned, warningly. "Do we have to?"

Roy set the jar down decisively. "No. I'm sorry. What were we talking about?"

Those were the last words that Walt ever heard his big brother say.

In that moment, at about ten o'clock, Walt heard the sound of rotors. He heard how they reverberated the house, how they shook the dishes in the cabinets, clattered the pots and pans. And for a half-second, he felt annoyance, because their house sat underneath a very common route for the gunships, so this was not an abnormal thing to hear them roar overhead.

But then he saw the look on Roy's face, the sudden, clenched terror in it.

And then it became very clear that the rotors were not passing *over* them.

They were hovering.

And then the spotlight hit.

The windows were suddenly bright.

Pops looked at Roy, their eyes coming together with some unspoken knowledge.

"Go!" Pops hissed.

And Roy went.

He shot out of his seat and ran for the back door. Walter remained sitting, not knowing what to do or what to say or even what to think. His mind was blank, hanging open like a door left unlatched in a storm, letting every horrible thing of that moment in without filter.

Huge, concussive explosions, one after the other, from the front and the back of the house. Bright, buzzing light that seared his retinas like he'd been looking into the sun. His ears rang like church bells. His dazzled eyes watched Roy's silhouette shoulder his way through the back door. He ran full-tilt, his arms up to shield his eyes from the light.

The front door exploded in.

Walter's Mom began to scream.

Faceless men in hardarmor and battleshrouds bellowed over her screams, telling them to get on the ground. Mom couldn't hear them, or didn't register what this nightmare was. She just stood there. And Walt watched one of the New Breed soldiers grab her by the back of her neck and slam her face-first into the floor. He watched her face mush into the wood, her eyes closed tight, her mouth open even as the scream was cut off by a knee being driven into her back.

Pops didn't even try to move. He watched Walt's Mom taken down with a sort of sad resignation, and then he was swept to the ground as well. His chair flew out and clattered to the other side of the kitchen table.

Walt felt rough hands across his body, searching for weapons, and there was the sound of boots flowing smoothly and efficiently through the house. Commands were called. Rooms cleared.

All in just a few seconds.

Walt turned his head to see out the open back door.

He could still see Roy running, across the backyard like they had when they were kids, escaping into the cornfields, escaping the boredom of a summertime stuck with Grandpa Clarence and his bottle of whiskey. He watched the spotlight from the gunship shift, tracking with Roy, and black shapes came out of the cornfields, moving swiftly onto him, driving him to the ground.

The rotor wash kicked dust and debris off the small back porch and into Walt's face, but he couldn't close his eyes, couldn't avert them, and he watched as the gunship lowered down, and his brother's hands were yanked behind his back, and a black sack was placed over his head and he was hauled into the back of the gunship with four soldiers.

Then the gunship lifted off, and Roy was gone.

Disappeared.

CHAPTER THREE

Walt hung at the bar for about an hour. Merl bought him another beer because he saw that Walt was nursing the first and it apparently irritated him. Walt was just starting the second beer when his PD chirped at him.

He checked the preview monitor and saw the text of the message, and who had sent it. It simply read: **Need help. Now.**

Walt felt something creep up the back of his throat, like nervous bile.

Shit. Tonight?

He leaned away from the bar so Merl could not see, and then he pulled up his full monitor and stabbed out a quick response: **standby 5.**

He closed the monitor and leaned onto the bar. Clutched his beer in fingers that had gone suddenly cold and bloodless.

Shit, shit, shit.

He realized he was gripping his bottle hard. He forced himself to relax. Breathe.

You gotta do it. For Carolyn. For both of you. This is the only way.

But, he didn't want to be rude. Merl had spent his hard-earned money on that beer in his hand, and just because he had five in his house didn't mean he could afford to be buying Walt drinks. Like Merl pointed out, he had two kids.

So Walt finished the second beer over the course of a few minutes, even though his nerves made the beer taste flat and over-cold, almost painful on his empty stomach. Merl offered to buy another, but Walt refused, citing early bedtimes and wife expectations. Merl nodded understandingly and raised his bottle again.

"Good work today," Merl said. "More next week."

"Always." Walt smiled. Convincingly, he felt.

They were commissioned for 2,500 more acres next week.

"Night," Merl said.

"Night."

Walt managed to edge out of the bar just after 8 o'clock. He felt guilty about lying to Merl. Even worse about lying to Carolyn. He would tell Merl that he was heading home. And he would tell Carolyn that he'd been at the bar with Merl. The two of them didn't exactly talk to each other much, so Walt could only cross his fingers and hope the truth didn't come out.

Outside, the Russian patrol was gone.

The wind had picked up. He pulled the top of his worn tans closed and zipped it up as he walked along the street. Two men were walking toward Brown's. More growers in their stained tans. One of them raised a hand to him in greeting. A younger guy with tight, skeletal features. Walt recognized him. Another regular at Brown's, though he didn't know the guy's name and had never really talked to him outside of occasional sports commentary.

"Hey, man," the grower said.

"Hey." Walt smiled, kept walking.

"They got checkpoints up on the roads out," the guy said as they drew abreast of each other.

Walt stopped and turned slightly to face him. "Really?"

"Ayuh."

"Why?"

The guy shrugged. His friend was nodding along.

"No idea," the younger guy said. "Doin' their own thing, I guess."

"Aigh' then."

"Be careful."

"Thanks."

Walt kept walking. He stuffed his hands in his pockets. Felt the little piece of news settle on him like a brick in his gut.

Checkpoints on the roads out.

All the roads?

He clenched his hands together in his pockets.

He made it back to his old truck and climbed inside. The vinyl seats were cold. Torn and leaking batting in places. He started his truck and turned the heat on. He flicked his PD monitor up and looked at the message again.

Need help. Now.

He had no reason to think that the closing of 8089's borders was connected to this request for help. But he couldn't help thinking that it was. And that ratcheted up the stakes in Walt's mind, almost to an unacceptable level.

But…he needed the money.

And cashing in on his peculiar talent was getting harder and harder.

Shit. Walt, what are you getting yourself into?

He glanced around him, but there was no one around. Even if there had been, they wouldn't have been able to read his monitor while he was sitting in his truck. But his heart was beating in that hard, fast way that it did when you were a kid and you knew you were on the threshold of getting in *Big Trouble*.

He blew air out of pursed lips, and keyed out a message with his right hand.

On the way. Where?

The reply was almost immediate. They were waiting on him.

Same place. ETA?

He keyed back: **10**

He backed out of his parking space and drove slowly out of the town center. On the main drag, a pair of guntrucks roared by at their usual breakneck speed, darting in and out of cars that were trying to shuffle out of the way like scared sheep.

Something was going on.

He pulled out onto the main drag, heading the opposite way as the guntrucks, and then hung a left at the next intersection. This road was quiet. Two lane. He accelerated up, but didn't break the speed limit.

He felt a tension in his District, in the night, in the movement of these gunship and guntrucks, everyone scrambling around for something, for some reason.

"What the fuck have you got me into now?" Walt whispered to the dark.

———

The place was a small, dark, double-wide trailer out in the middle of nowhere. And the fact that Walt thought it was in the middle of nowhere meant something.

To an urby that spent his or her life in the city, the Agrarian Districts were all *the middle of nowhere.*

When a grower considered it *the middle of nowhere,* then it was truly the boondocks.

He'd been to this location before, but prior to that the location had changed twice. They never explained why they changed locations. Perhaps the previous locations had been found out. Or maybe they just switched it up for the sake of obfuscation.

They did not confide in Walt. And he didn't ask many questions.

He needed the money.

He had a skill that they wanted. And this was at least a *bit* cleaner than getting his ass kicked for fixing poker games. Cleaner, but the consequences were much higher for what he did now, so that he felt like he was walking a tightrope. He knew he *could* walk the tightrope, but the consequences if he fell—or was found out—would be death.

Or being disappeared, which was close enough.

Rather die than DTI.

He pulled his truck up to the trailer.

This place was tucked back off the road, at the end of a gravel path nearly a half mile from the road. A single light shown from inside. There was no exterior illumination. An old streetlight sat atop a powerline pole off to the side, but it was overgrown by vines and its bulb was dark and dead.

Walt's headlights swept across the front of the trailer, and he quickly switched those off.

In the brief flash of Walt's headlights before he cut them off, he saw a man in a green uniform, standing at the bottom of the front steps.

Walt put his truck into park and killed the engine.

He stepped out. His boots crunched on dirt and dry grass just beginning to come back from winter. The place was overgrown. He supposed they preferred it that way.

He walked in darkness towards the figure on the front steps.

The window with the single yellow light seemed brighter now in the darkness.

A few steps closer and he was before the man at the front steps. He could just barely make out the man's features in the gloom. The stern face. No smile of greeting. This was all business.

"Walt," the man said, quietly. "You check your six?"

Walter nodded, shoving his hands in his pockets again. They were cold. Cold from nerves and cold from the wind. "Of course. No tail."

Sheriff Virgil Honeycutt didn't look out to the road over Walt's shoulder to confirm this. Instead, he looked skyward. He held an object in his hand, a monocular, and he raised this to his eye, and then slowly twisted around, scanning the entire sky around them.

A thermal scope.

The drones didn't give off much heat, but Walt knew their electric motors could make little heat spots in a night sky, particularly on a cool evening like tonight.

After a moment, Virgil lowered the monocular and slid it into a pouch on his side. He still wore his softarmor. The subgun he usually carried on his chest while on duty was not there, but he had a pistol strapped to his leg.

He nodded to Walt. "Alright then. Come on."

Walt followed him inside the trailer.

When Virgil had the door closed, Walt withdrew his hands from his pockets and almost blew into them, but didn't want to appear overly-cold, or overly-nervous.

"What the hell did you guys do?" he said under his breath to Virgil.

Virgil locked the door behind them, then turned to Walter with a raised eyebrow.

Walter waved an arm in a nebulous direction. "They're running around like ants on a kicked nest out there."

Virgil looked briefly tired. He raised a hand and rested it on Walt's shoulder, leaning in a bit closer, the way you would with a close friend or family member. "Walter…"

Here we go. Walter clenched his jaw and just barely avoided rolling his eyes. He knew what was coming. He'd heard it before.

"I promised Roy that I'd *try* to look after you," Virgil said, evenly. "But if this is getting too much for you, you can always go back to the casinos."

Virgil knew damn well that Walt wasn't allowed within fifty yards of a casino entrance. He'd been banned by three of them, straight up, and the others knew his face.

"We're fighting a war," Virgil pressed on. "And wars are dangerous. If you'd rather walk and let the CoAx do their thing, then you're free to do so. I won't stop you. But I can't help you much either. You want the pay, you do the work. Just like with anything else."

Walt sucked his teeth. "Right. I got it."

"You walkin'?"

"No."

"So can we get back to work?"

"Yes."

"Good." Virgil gave him an amiable pat on the shoulder. Amiable, but always a bit condescending.

Virgil had been Roy's friend all through childhood. The two of them, thick as thieves. Walt had been the tag-along, the little brother that insisted on coming along. No matter how many years passed, no matter how the age gap shrunk—now Virgil was thirty-two and Walt was twenty-seven—it would always be big brother and little brother.

"Come on," Virgil said over his shoulder as he walked out of the entryway and through a rundown living room with no furniture but a single folding chair. Beside the folding chair, choosing to stand, was a man in greens that Walt knew damn well wasn't one of Virgil's deputies.

To Walt's knowledge, all of Virgil's deputies were loyalists.

The fake deputy nodded to Walt as they passed by.

Walt nodded back. He recognized the man from previous times, previous safe houses. He was one of Virgil's *snatchers*. One of Virgil's tight-knit team that did to the CoAx what they did to the resistance.

Took their people. Snatched them like the bogeyman.

Disappeared them.

Virgil had tried time and time again to get Walt to simply drop out of life. Abandon everything. *Poof* into nothingness and become one of them. Ghosts that haunted the CoAx. People that existed, but didn't really exist.

Resistance.

Walt had a skill, and that skill could be useful to them.

But Walt knew it meant leaving everything behind. And he simply wasn't willing to do that.

He was no loyalist. But his Grandpa Clarence had spoken out, and he'd been disappeared. And his brother had spoken out, and he'd been disappeared, too. Before that, two generations of Baucom men had died in the first outbreaks of this bloody, protracted conflict.

Walt knew the costs. And he didn't want to pay them.

What he wanted, what he fervently wished for, was to be left alone.

Not loyalist. Not pro-CoAx. Not pro-Fed. Not pro-resistance.

Just pro-Leave-Me-The-Fuck-Alone.

Virgil stopped in the hall that led from the kitchen down to what would be the master bedroom. They stood beside the open door to the laundry room and the back door. There was no washer or dryer unit. Just the plugs, some dust bunnies, and a lonely water tube hanging down to the floor next to an old water stain like a guilty puppy that's peed the floor.

Walt faced Virgil. "Aigh'. What're we dealing with?"

Virgil nodded to the closed bedroom door. "Chicom. Captain. Name's Kuai Luo."

Walt's mouth twitched, but he said nothing. He kept watching Virgil's face.

Chinese could be a challenge. Their body-language was not quite as easy for Walter to interpret accurately. He had to think about it, whereas he could read an American like an open book, without thought, everything coming through subconsciously.

But…Walt had done it before. He could do it again.

What he really didn't like was the look on Virgil's face, the slightly pursed look, that was saying *I'm not telling you something—I'm holding back a big piece of info.*

Walter didn't say anything else. It was one of those moments where he knew that he should allow the information to come to him, rather than push for it. So he stood there and watched the other man with a pointedly-raised eyebrow.

Virgil shifted. Finally met Walter's gaze, and accepted it with some careful consideration. Then he appeared to make a decision, and he said the thing he'd been holding back: "It's a New Breed."

Walter stared. He pulled his head back. Then he frowned. "What?"

Virgil only nodded in response, a little twinkle of something like savage happiness in the background of his otherwise stoic features.

The import of the words settled on Walter, not suddenly and harshly, but gradually. Like the slow but inexorable pressure of a trash compactor. He reached up and rubbed his temple, realized his hand felt shaky. He slid it down over his face and his skin felt insensate.

"Oh, Virgil…shit." Walter spun away, then spun back. "What the fuck were you thinking?" he hissed.

Virgil looked towards the closed door again. "Things are very complicated right now, Walter. There's movement in the different factions of the resistance, and we're unsure where it's coming from, and what the end goal is. Some faction—we don't know who—has already been kidnapping New Breeds."

Walter was flabbergasted by this. "Been kidnapping them? How? And why?"

Virgil shook his head. "We don't know. But I mean to ask. If the Fed or the CoAx knows who's been kidnapping their super soldiers, I think our captain in there might have an inkling."

The irony was not lost on Walt. This resistance was so fractured and the factions all so contentious with each other, that vital information was easier to obtain by capturing and interrogating enemy soldiers than it was to get from the people that were supposed to be on your side.

But the bigger issue at the moment was the fact that they had a New Breed in custody. An officer, no less. And all of the sudden it was making perfect sense why the CoAx troops were running around 8089 and blocking off the exits.

"How?" Walter breathed. "How did you do it?"

Virgil shook his head yet again. "It was a one-in-a-million opportunity—to get this guy separated from the pack. We had to take it. And we did it. With very careful planning, and some very expensive equipment. And probably with a lot of luck, too. Even then this one almost took us out anyways. I have no idea how that other faction has managed to capture *multiple* New Breeds. And I don't know why they're doing it. But the powers that be are very interested. And that's why we're standing here right now."

Walter swallowed thickly. "Shit. What if the body language is off? I've heard their brains are…different."

Virgil bit his lip, thoughtfully. "They're just people, right?"

Walter made an unsure sound.

"They're just people," Virgil repeated.

"Is your team okay?" Walt asked.

"Ayuh," Virgil nodded. He put a hand to his chest, almost subconsciously. "Fucker kicks like a goddamn mule. And I almost got shot in the face. But I figure we got off pretty damn easy."

"Jesus," Walter breathed. "Anything else I should know?"

Virgil shook his head. "Nope. You ready?"

Walt took a steady breath, then nodded.

He followed Virgil into the room.

CHAPTER FOUR

The first thing you do is watch.

You absorb.

As much as possible in the time allotted. Sometimes it wasn't much. In Walt's case, it never was.

Everyone was unique. A scratch of the ear could be meaningful. A twitch of the mouth. The way the eyes zipped in another direction, almost too brief to catch.

Or…they could just be the ticks of a nervous person. And everyone had their ticks. But eventually the patterns began to emerge. And it wasn't that Walt was so special that no one else could see these things, but the patterns just made sense to him far quicker.

The ability to read people could be taught to anyone.

It was just that Walt had never had to be taught it.

For him, it was simply a talent.

Often the things that he picked up on were so slight that he could not articulate them if he tried. But even when he couldn't put it into words, his subconscious brain knew the truth of what he saw, and it produced a feeling in his gut that was simply beyond positive.

Sometimes explaining what he observed was like trying to explain the color red to a person born color blind. You couldn't really explain it. It simply *was*. But Virgil had long ago stopped questioning the veracity of Walt's gut feelings. They'd proven to be accurate.

His brother had recognized his abilities early on. And, as brothers will do, he figured out how to capitalize on his tagalong brother. Roy and Virgil made it a point to start dragging ten-year-old Walt to their little penny-ante poker games, and the games went from penny-ante to dollars and up, and for a while they were the kings.

But then, of course, people stopped wanting to play with Roy and Virgil and their annoying tagalong brother.

Eventually, the poker games went by the wayside as Roy and Virgil got involved in other things that dominated their time, such as adulthood and working actual jobs. When it was Walt's turn to start earning money, he hadn't returned to it. Not until a few years after marrying Carolyn.

But that didn't last long either.

And so here he was.

In a dim and unfurnished bedroom, in a dilapidated double-wide that sat in one of the many dark corners of their Agrarian District. Because Roy was gone, and it was just Virgil, and Virgil carried the torch, and he'd found another way to capitalize on Walt.

And Walt needed money.

And here in that bedroom, Walt waited, and he watched.

Captain Kuai Luo sat in the center of the room, taped to a sturdy chair. His arms behind his back. Wrists secured. Ankles taped to the legs of the chair. A dark red mark on his left cheek where they'd hit him with a stun-round to incapacitate him.

He was a giant beast of a man. Even sitting down, that was apparent. He filled the room the way a tiger filled a cage. A tiger that was restrained, but you couldn't help staring at it with a certain dread-filled awe, wondering if it was going to break free somehow, wondering if you could stop it from killing you if it did.

Behind the Chicom captain, two more of Virgil's snatchers stood. One was a small man with a rat-like face—large, round ears, a long, pointed nose, and large front teeth that became apparent whenever he opened his mouth. The other was a woman with a slight build and short-cropped black hair and kind-looking doe eyes that didn't match with the large rifle strapped to her chest.

These two did not wear the guise of deputies. They wore old camouflage fatigues. They'd cleaned their faces, but Walt saw the vestiges of face paint close to their eyes and ears and under their chins. Their hair was matted like they'd been wearing hats. Bits of foliage still clung to their fatigues.

Virgil never introduced any of his crew. Despite Walt's involvement, he was not considered a member of the resistance. He'd long ago learned that any requests for extra information were usually brushed off by Virgil as "need to know."

He was there for his ability. He was not a part of the team.

Walt turned his attention back to the Chicom. He'd positioned himself off to the prisoner's right-hand side, and a little forward so that he could see most of the man's face, but wasn't in the center of his view. He did not want the man's attention on him.

Virgil stood directly in front of the prisoner. Close to him. Well inside what you might call "personal space." Looking down at the seated and bound man, as Walt was sure he was not used to being looked down on.

"You must be thirsty," Virgil said suddenly. He looked to the rat-faced man. "Get me a water, please. This gentleman is thirsty."

"No," Kuai said.

Virgil smiled. "Of course you are."

The rat-faced man stooped and plucked a bottle of water from a case of it, lying at his feet. The case already had several missing bottles. They were empty and crumpled up, piled up to the side of it. Four of them, that Walt could see.

The rat-faced man handed the bottle to Virgil, over top of their prisoner's head. Virgil took it and held it in front of Kuai with a cordial smile. He twisted the cap off. The pop of the seal breaking. A little hiss of air pressure.

"Fresh water, I promise you."

"I'm not thirsty."

"You need to stay hydrated," Virgil insisted. He brought the bottle up to Kuai's face, placed it almost tenderly against his lips, and tilted it gently back.

Kuai locked eyes with Virgil. He took one gulp into his mouth. Then he ripped his face away and spit it out. "Enough. I don't need any water."

"Yes, you do," Virgil said, the way you might encourage a stubborn child to take their medicine. "You've been through a stressful thing today. You have to flush out the toxins." He looked over the top of Kuai's head to the rat-faced man, and then nodded.

Rat-face grabbed Kuai by the shoulders and heaved backwards.

The chair tilted, toppled. Crashed into the floor with a loud bang and a grunt from its occupant.

Virgil walked around, still holding the bottle and its cap. "Hold his head still. He needs to drink more water."

Rat-face knelt and put his knees on either side of the prisoner's head, clamping it between them.

"Nose," Virgil said, calmly.

Rat-face grabbed Kuai's nose in a harsh pinch.

Kuai writhed and growled. But he was bound so tightly to the chair that he wasn't able to get much movement. He tried shaking his head, but Rat-face had his legs battened tight. He looked down at the prisoner with steady eyes and a steady face. He did not enjoy this. Nor did he shrink from it. It was almost…clinical.

Virgil knelt down at Kuai's side. He put the bottle to his lips and upended it again. "Drink."

Kuai tried shaking his head again. Water dribbled down his cheeks.

Walt fidgeted, uncomfortably. The woman with the doe-eyes glanced up at him, a quick evaluation, as though curious why Walt would feel his bones getting itchy with the desire to not be in this room at this moment. Walt avoided her gaze. Watched Kuai's face. That was his job, after all.

"I got a whole case of water," Virgil said. "If we run out, we'll just refill them and continue. Just drink the water. That's all I want right now."

Kuai was trying to resist, but he was running out of air.

He had to open his mouth eventually.

And he did. The water went in.

Kuai coughed.

Rat-face released his grip on the nose.

Kuai sucked a breath in through his nostrils and it sounded wet and ragged.

Rat-face let him get about half of a lung-full, and then clamped the nose again.

Kuai growled, but started drinking.

The water bottle in Virgil's hand crackled and collapsed in on itself. "Good," he said. "Very good." He held out a hand. The woman quickly grabbed another bottle of water and put it in Virgil's hand. "One more, okay? One more, and then you can be done."

Kaui stared at the bottle, almost afraid of it.

Virgil took the empty bottle from his lips.

"Stop!" Kuai demanded.

"Ssh." Virgil frowned at him. Uncapped the bottle. Pressed it to Kuai's lips. "Drink."

Same process. Kuai holding out. Needing air. Opening the mouth. Water goes in, Rat-face released the nose, a bit of a breath, then clamping down again, and Kuai drank. He drank the bottle empty. Coughed halfway through, stifled it, and kept drinking, and when it was empty, Virgil pulled the bottle away and Kuai gasped for breath. A mist of water and spit erupted from his mouth.

Virgil stood. Pitched the crumpled bottle into the pile with the others. "Good job."

Then he knelt and helped Rat-face haul the chair upright again.

Walt thought he could actually hear the sloshing of water in Captain Kuai Luo's stomach. He looked off to the pile and counted them again. Six bottles now. And he knew what Virgil was doing.

He'd seen it before. It wouldn't work on a Russian, and in Walter's Western-thinking mind, it seemed a bit absurd. But on a Chicom who came from a deeply-entrenched shame-honor culture, it had proven to be effective more than once.

Virgil walked around and stood in front of the captain, looking down at him again.

Captain Luo's dark eyes remained heavy-lidded, almost drowsy. Calm, one might think. A pretty good veneer. But like any veneer, if you looked close enough…

Virgil backhanded him across the face. It was an almost casual motion.

Walt stifled his urge to wince. He focused on the man's face.

Captain Luo's skin reddened, but not just where he'd been slapped. He blushed across his entire face. His jaw muscles bunched rapidly. For the briefest of moments, his eyes shot open wider and looked up murderously at Virgil, and then they were calm and half-lidded again.

Virgil smirked. He put his hands on his hips. Nonchalantly pressing his crotch forward. Then he relaxed and leaned over the man in the chair. "Should I be recording this?"

The man didn't meet Virgil's gaze.

A tiny tremor across the right side of his mouth.

"Maybe we record it," Virgil said. Lazily. "Beam that shit back to China. Let your family watch me whip out my cock and piss on you. Be the talk of the town. You'd be a goddamn celebrity."

A few blinks. Stillness.

"Isn't that how it works?" Virgil asked. "You get body-modded into a super-hero for the People's Republic, they throw you a ticker-tape parade, and you get shipped out here to earn glory for China and your family?" Virgil shook his head. "Mm-mm-mm. What if they could see their glory boy now? All those other generations of soldiers in your family would be disgusted."

Still no response from Captain Luo, but Walter wasn't buying that.

His gut was telling him, no matter the stillness in the other man's face—and perhaps *because* of it—that the picture Virgil was painting was now lodged firmly in Kuai Luo's brain.

Virgil bent down a little further, trying to force his face into the path of Captain Luo's gaze. But the captain just moved his eyes away again. Virgil snapped his finger. "Hey. Hey. Look at me."

The man did not want to look at him. He stared off to the side now, at some point that was not in this room. Maybe trying to think of something else. Trying to imagine another place.

Virgil slapped him again. Not hard. An upwards slap across his face, like a harried mother might do to the back of her disobedient son's head. Just an insult. Nothing more. The subtle message was that

Captain Kuai Luo didn't warrant much harsher abuse than that. He was little more than a child.

"Look at me."

Captain Luo wouldn't.

Two quick slaps. Back and forth.

The captain's nostrils flared. His breathing quickened. Lips tightened.

"Look at me, or I turn on the cameras."

A small request. Such a simple thing. Just to make eye-contact. Why would you make that your stance? Why would you draw the line there?

Captain Luo looked at him.

Looked away.

Then back. Held the gaze.

Virgil smiled without humor. "Good boy. What's your name?"

The man in the chair swallowed. Chewed on that for a moment. Then said his name: "Captain Kuai Luo."

"Kywo?" Virgil squinted and sneered, like the name sounded gross to him.

"Kuai…Luo."

"Okay. Kuai, then," Virgil waved it off. There was no way in hell he was going to call the man by his rank. Walt already knew that. He'd seen enough of these to know how the game was played. "Kuai. What happened?"

Kuai's eyes stayed fixed on Virgil's. Now it was a challenge *not* to look away. Virgil held the gaze unflinchingly. If he had any fear about the tiger-in-the-cage, he didn't show it. Not to an average person, anyways. But even while Walter was not paying attention to him, he could tell that Virgil was nervous.

Virgil waved a finger in the air, conjuring clarity to his question. "The thing? The big thing that nobody is talking about?"

Kuai remained still. Quiet. Like a statue. Walt thought maybe he was holding his breath.

"DTI break," Virgil said, matter of factly. "Yeah, we know. It's fine. I want you to tell me about it."

"I don't know about that," Kuai said without much inflection.

"Sure you do," Virgil replied. "Rumors spread around. There's been talk. You've heard something about it. That's all I'm asking for. Just what you've heard. The word on the street, as we say."

Kuai swallowed. His lips drew tighter. "You think they tell us everything they know?"

"What have you heard?" Virgil repeated, his voice less conversational now.

"I haven't heard anything."

Virgil grunted, then walked around the back of the bound man, so he stood out of view. Without Virgil there to resist, Kuai slumped slightly. But then he tensed, knowing the man was behind him.

Virgil looked at Walt.

Walt swallowed hard, felt his gummy wad of spit barely making it down his throat. His hands were in his lap, clutched together, fingers cold, the lightest little shake in them that he was trying to hide.

Walt looked at Virgil, just a quick glance, subtle, so as to not draw Kuai's attention. Walt gave him a slight shake of the head.

Kuai was being deceptive.

That was all you could really say.

You could never say that someone was lying for sure. All you could do was observe their behaviors. You accumulated the behaviors in your mind, and you began to see clusters of oddities around certain topics. And the topic of the alleged DTI break was throwing up some red flags for Captain Kuai Luo.

Maybe he didn't know everything, but he knew more than he was telling them.

Virgil continued on, all the way around, circling Kuai, and then back to standing in front of him. He looked down. "Who's taking you guys?"

Kuai looked briefly confused.

The expression was a sham.

"Someone has been kidnapping New Breed soldiers," Virgil stated.

Kuai's head faced the wall, but his eyes were off to the side, watching Virgil. He knew a thing or two about this topic. He was a well-informed captain.

"Who is it?" Virgil asked.

"Not you?" Kuai asked, but the tone said he already knew it wasn't them.

Walt kept quiet, but his head swam violently with these things. These new revelations. God, but Virgil kept him in the dark. He felt like a voyeur, like he wasn't supposed to be seeing or hearing all of this.

A break out of DTI? That was unheard of.

And New Breed soldiers being kidnapped?

What was going on out there?

What the hell was happening in the resistance that was causing all these fault lines to suddenly appear? What had been going on under Walt's nose while he minded his own damn business and got busy planting the spring crop? What forces were maneuvering just out of sight, in the shadows?

"The kidnappings of your New Breed soldiers and the DTI break. Are they related?"

Kuai clenched his jaw. Looked away again. "I don't know."

"Hm." Virgil walked around to the back of Kuai again.

He looked to Walt.

Walt shook his head again.

Virgil pointed to the woman. "Get the camera."

Walt watched Kuai's face. A few rapid pulsations of his jaw. His head rocking back a bit, then forward, almost sternly. The summoning of will-power.

Where was all that water sitting in his guts, now? Those last two bottles were probably mostly still in his stomach. But the other four? They were probably further along now.

The woman produced a small, handheld recorder. She stepped in front of Kuai, where Virgil had been standing, and held the recorder up. She tapped the side of it with her other hand and a projection monitor sprang into the air. She reversed the image so Kuai could see it.

Virgil was standing over Kuai. "There. Now you can see what everybody back home will see." He nodded to the woman holding the recorder. "Start recording."

Virgil knelt down behind Kuai.

On the monitor, you couldn't see Virgil behind Kuai's bulk.

Walt could, though. He could see Virgil pull out a staple in every line-knocker's toolbox: a set of pipe-cutters. He opened them, the cold steel blade moving aside, and then he grabbed hold of Kuai's hand and slid his index finger into the little space where a hydroponics line would usually go.

Walt's mouth was dry. He tried to work some spit up. Forced his eyes to Kuai, who was still staring at himself in the monitor, trying to look brave for the folks back home. Trying to save face.

"Kuai," Virgil called. "Who was broken out of DTI?"

Kuai stared straight ahead. Surely he felt the metal on his fingers. Surely he knew what was about to happen. Did he think they were bluffing?

In the privacy of his own mind, Walt was urging the man, *Just tell them!*

A moment of silence passed.

Snip.

CHAPTER FIVE

Walt stood on the far side of the living room, fists clenched, guts knotted.

There had to be a better way to earn cash.

He closed his eyes.

He breathed out slowly.

His back was to the kitchen, to the hallway, to the master bedroom door that lay in the darkness. And the quick-moving, nauseating sounds of plastic bagging, like a man was so much trash to be thrown away.

"Hey."

Walt opened his eyes. He glanced to his left, where the snatcher in the deputy's uniform stood. He didn't look much like a cop. He had wild, unsteady eyes. Or maybe Walt just *knew* he wasn't a cop and so the uniform hung on him like a cheap costume-store fake.

The man was holding out a pack of cigarettes. He already had one in his lips.

Walt stared at the cigarettes for a moment. Then shrugged and took one.

"You know," the guy said, mumbling slightly around his cigarette as he sparked a lighter and lit it. "How many times you done this for us?" He passed the lighter to Walt.

Walt took it and lit his own. The smoke was nice. Acrid at first. But then...mellow. It burned in his throat and lungs, just slightly. It'd been a while since he'd had one. He looked at the cherry which glowed brightly in the dim interior of the trailer. "Seven times."

"Shit." The man smiled. "Seven times. You got a helluva conscience if this still bothers you so much." He dragged. Blew out. Still looking at Walt. "Good for you, man."

Walt flicked ash. Didn't quite know how to respond to that.

In the back bedroom, the sound of quiet voices now. The thump of a limb.

"My brother," the man said, conversationally. "He's a loyalist. You know…doesn't know what I do. But knows my opinion. Gadamighty, but we argued about that shit for a long time. Now it's just a given. Doesn't bother me. I do what I do. He does what he does."

What are you even talking about?

Walt drew smoke. Felt a little lightheaded. But it was nice.

"You mind me askin' you why it bothers you so much?" The man looked genuinely curious. Shifted positions, pointed his cigarette at Walt. "And why, if it does bother you, do you keep doing it?"

Walt cleared his throat. Glanced in the direction of the bedroom door. "I got no love for the CoAx," he said, slowly. It wasn't an answer. It was the beginning of a list of facts. That moment that you don't know the answer, so you start saying the things you do know, and hope an answer somehow germinates from that. "I don't want them here. I've had members of my family disappeared. My brother. My grandpa. My Pops is dying of cancer from the chemicals in the lines. That's how my Mom died. How most of the people I know died that didn't die of violence during the war. Probably how I'll die." Walt sucked on his cigarette and thought, *well, this is funny, huh?* "I've got no reason to pity that man. No reason to want him to live."

The man in the deputy's uniform nodded along, familiar with the story.

He waited for Walt to continue.

Walt wasn't sure he had anything else to say.

So he just shrugged.

The man smiled again. Shrugged himself. "Well. Maybe you don't really mind it that much," he said. "Maybe you just *think* you should mind it, and you don't, and maybe that's really what scares you. Huh?"

Walt looked at him sharply. Irritated. He threw his cigarette onto the floor of the trailer. Squished it with the toe of his boot. "It's not a *scared* thing."

The man gave one, slow, exaggerated nod, as if to say, *Sure, buddy. Whatever you say.* "Good for you again," he said, amused. "Rock solid conscience *and* fearlessness. That must be awesome."

Walt turned away from the man. Faced the bedroom door, as if to prove to himself that he wasn't scared, he didn't need to hide from the truth. It was what it was. And had any other time been different?

Well. Maybe a little.

This time had been...extreme.

The first finger had been a surprise to Captain Kuai Luo. Maybe it took a moment for the pain to hit him, or maybe he just couldn't believe it. But he didn't seem to understand what had happened until Virgil tossed the man's index finger on the floor.

Then there was a lot of heavy breathing and some low sounds in the back of his throat—screams that were trying to get out, but the Chicom captain wouldn't let them. He just kept looking up at the camera. And Walter knew that he wasn't seeing a camera, but his family. The people he knew. All of them watching him, judging him, judging his worth.

He lasted through another two fingers before breaking.

Though it wasn't the fingers that broke him.

It was when he peed on himself. It was when the urine started to dribble onto the floor, slow at first, and then steadily, as his bladder released. And who could really blame him? Force-fed six bottles of water and having your fingers snipped off...the body had certain reactions to things that you just couldn't overcome.

And it was when the doe-eyed woman with the camera started to point and jeer at him, that he broke, and Walt watched it with a sort of lurid fascination, the way you first felt when you saw something die, maybe an animal squirming in the road after catching a bumper.

The woman's sing-song, schoolyard voice: *He pissed his pants! Look at this pants-pisser! How'd you even make it past selection, pants pisser? You see how much he's pissing? Jesus, stop pissing! You can't stop! He can't stop pissing! He's so scared!*

After that Captain Kuai Luo answered the questions. Some of them he didn't know the answers to, but he told the truth the entire time, and Walter never had to shake his head at Virgil to tell him that the captain was lying again.

After that, it was cleanup.

Virgil made it clear that Walt should excuse himself.

The last thing Walter saw and heard before closing the bedroom door behind him was Virgil standing over the weeping giant with his hand on the man's shoulder, speaking softly to him and saying, "We'll delete those files. Your family will never see them. They will believe you died with honor."

And now Walt stood in the dim living room with a man he didn't know, who apparently, despite not knowing each other, wished to have some sort of heart-to-heart, and he stared at the door to that master bedroom, and he listened to the sounds of a man's body being wrapped in plastic for disposal.

The door opened, and Virgil stepped out. He didn't make an effort to close the door. Didn't make an effort to hide what was beyond it, but still, in the dimness, Walt could only just see some pale plastic sheeting in a roll, and a pair of boots sticking out of it.

Virgil walked briskly down the hallway to Walt. He had a cloudy look on his face. It had settled over him the second that Kuai had started talking. He'd been asking the questions, and Walt had been assuring him the answers were legitimate, but he hadn't liked anything he'd heard.

Virgil stepped off to the side as he entered the living room. He appeared distracted. Preoccupied in his thoughts.

In the corner of the living room there was small stack of cardboard crates with generic, industrial labeling on the sides. Most of it was in Chinese.

Virgil picked up two of these boxes, which was more than an armload, and he walked to Walt, very businesslike, and shoved them into his arms.

Walt looked at them with a frown. "What the hell is this?"

"Payment."

Walt's eyebrows went up. "Payment?"

"It's cancer meds." Virgil planted his hands on his hips and didn't look at Walt. He looked at the other two crates of meds. "The shit that actually works. The shit that the Fed won't approve."

Walt had a million questions in that instant, but he shook his head like he was trying to get a cloud of gnats to stop buzzing in his ears, and glared at Virgil. "What am I supposed to do with this shit? I thought the deal was for money."

Virgil finally looked at him. "Each cycle goes for almost four thousand on the street. And there are one hundred and twenty cycles in a box." He lifted his arms in a *sorry-not-sorry* gesture. "We're not exactly flush with cash right now. And besides, your help was minimally necessary today."

Minimally necessary? Really?

Walter knew for a fact that his ability to tell a lie from a truth had turned a potentially long interrogation into a short, perfunctory extraction of information. He had saved them time, in a situation where time was worth their lives.

But suddenly, saying any of this seemed useless.

Walt stared at the boxes in his arms. Mouth open. He closed it.

A sinking, frustrated disappointment. The feeling of knowing you're being cheated, and simultaneously knowing there isn't shit you're going to be able to do about it. Was he going to lodge a formal compliant? Take Virgil to small claims for unpaid criminal labors?

"Motherfucker," Walt mumbled, more to the world and all its shitty circumstances than to Virgil himself.

So the wind blows.

"Ayuh, well..." Virgil trailed off.

Walt stared at him.

Virgil seemed to have already forgotten about Walt. His eyes were staring at nothing, thinking, computing, turning things over in his head.

"Who are the Eudys?" Walt ventured.

Virgil looked at him like Walt was a statue that had suddenly moved and talked.

He sniffed loudly, wiped under his nose, then shook his head. "Nobody. It doesn't concern you."

"Of course not."

Virgil's expression softened a bit. "Look, man. You don't want to be a part of this. You've said that from day one. So I'm trying to keep you from *being* a part of this. Do you want to be a part of it?"

Walt rolled his eyes.

"Do you want to be a part of it?" Virgil said, more sternly. "Because I'll take you on in a heartbeat. I'd love to have you. We could use you. But you know the cost. You know what it takes. And you've already made it clear that you're not willing to pay it. So don't treat me like the asshole, alright? You want in, you can be in. But then you're in all the way. You can't straddle the line." He moved his hands from one side of his body to the other, a clear delineation of *this here, and this here.* "If you're in, you're in. If you're out, you're out."

Walt nodded. "Right. I know."

"And you're out." It was less of a question, and more of a confirmation of what was already known.

"Ayuh," Walt turned himself for the door. "I'm out."

He opened the door, and then stopped himself. He stood there for a second or two, staring out into the darkness outside, and he thought about the CoAx troops, the convoys racing to and fro, the flights of gunships going fast and low over the skies. The blocked exits.

All of it created an undefined fear in his stomach.

He turned to look over his shoulder at Virgil. "The purges. Are they real? Or are they just rumor?"

A dark rumor. Something whispered about, but it was treated like a conspiracy theory. Someone knew someone who knew someone who had been in a district when it had been purged. But there were no videos of it, no pictures of it. No proof that it had ever happened.

In fact, Walter felt silly asking the question.

Virgil shook his head. "No, Walt. The purges are just rumor and hyperbole."

Walter watched the other man's face for a moment and read perfectly easily the reality that was hiding behind Virgil's overt expression. He nodded curtly to Virgil, and then went out the door and closed it behind him.

But as he walked through the crisp night air to his truck, the thing he'd seen hiding in Virgil's tiny facial cues troubled him.

Virgil was being deceptive.

Walt's Pops lived in an old duplex that he'd moved to not long after Mom breathed her last breaths, laying in a utilitarian hospital bed in the Fed-run cancer clinic just outside of their Agrarian District. They did "all that they could." Which wasn't enough.

"All that they could" didn't include using medicine that had been proven to work elsewhere in the world. Such as the box of meds that now sat in the back of Walt's truck cab.

And what was a family of growers supposed to do about it? Buy tickets to the UK? Pay for that treatment out of pocket? It was a thing so far outside of the realm of their financial possibilities that they'd hardly considered it, except to look bitterly up at it, like one might look at a mountain that you know you can never climb, but which, at the top, lies all the answers to your problems.

So she died in the bed. As she knew that she was going to when the second and third lines of defense didn't stop the rampaging "red lung" from spreading out from her chest to other vitals and organs. She died, just like Walt's Pops knew she was going to. Just like Walt knew she was going to.

Just like all the others.

So the wind blows.

And soon after, Pops signed the lease of Walt's childhood house over to him and Carolyn, and moved out to a duplex that was dirt cheap because it was barely habitable, but he insisted. Said it was Walt and Carolyn's turn to make a family. He remembered too well the unpleasant memories of raising his own family with Grandpa Clarence ever-present.

Pops had still been working then. And the duplex left him enough money to help Walt and Carolyn maintain the rent on the old house until they got better secured on their feet. Eventually, Walt went from being a line-knocker on a maintenance rig, to an equipment operator, and Carolyn pulled a supervisor spot at the Town Center messhall, and they were able to pay their own way, although it was still tight.

After that, Pops took his Retirement Subsidy, which allowed him just enough to pay for his duplex, plus food. He lived a very quiet, very lonely existence, Walt thought.

A year after he'd taken his retirement, he'd been diagnosed.

He'd refused treatment. Knew it would be ineffective, as it was with most. Knew it would only steal his last few years away from him, sinking them into constant sickness worse than the cancer itself, and all his days spent inside doctor's offices, those medical staffs becoming his new family while his last remaining son passed by like a short, pleasant dream when he had time, which would not be often.

That was not how he wanted to go.

Pops was a stubborn man. He wanted to go on his own terms.

And, Walt wasn't so sure that he didn't just *want to go*, period.

Which was why he harbored no great hope when he put the box of meds with the Chinese writing on them under his arm, and he climbed the short, rickety wooden steps to his father's front door and knocked.

He could hear the TV.

The news. Always the news, rambling on and on about the same old shit presented in new and not-so-exciting ways. Pops was addicted to it.

Walt got no response from his first knock—probably couldn't be heard over the TV, or maybe Pops was napping in the glow and babble. He knocked a little harder.

"Pops. It's me," he called through the door.

A hack. Cough.

"What?" The voice on the other side was irritated. "Who is it?"

"Walter." He looked down at the box under his arm. Then felt the need to clarify: "Your son."

A grunt. Then another racking cough that sounded a lot like his mother's racking cough, except for just a touch deeper in pitch.

That was the way of it all, wasn't it? You live, you work, you pro-create, then you get sick from the shit they force you to be around and you die.

What a wonderfully purposeless life. Like a crane fly. Those poor bumbling insects that popped up around this time of year, lived for a few days, just to fly clumsily around, mating with each other and then dying. The whole of their existence to provide food for predators, restart their species' life-cycle, and then pass on.

So the wind blows.

"Walt?" the voice said, coming closer to the door.

"Yeah, Pops."

The door opened.

Walter Lawrence Baucom II stood there in the doorway, looking at Walter Lawrence Baucom III.

Pops was a shorter man, just like Walt was a shorter man. Until recently, they'd stood at about the same height. But sometime in the past few months, almost so fast that Walt started to find it hard to recognize him, Pops's shoulders had rounded, and his thick chest and sunken in, and he'd become *stooped*, as it seemed all old men became eventually. Like they could no longer bear the mantle of their lives. The years like burdens that drove them steadily into the ground.

He had clear blue eyes, but he was the only one in the family. Walt's Mom had been a brunette with brown eyes, and both of their children favored her in this aspect. But where Roy had also inherited Mom's softer features, Walt had taken his father's hawk nose and his thin lips, and his angular cheeks and jaw.

Those same features looked back at him now, but they seemed... melted.

Pops smiled, but there was hesitation in it. He was pleased—painfully pleased—for the company, but this was not Walt's usual time to drop by. In fact, it was getting a bit late in the evening. And unannounced drop-ins at later hours were usually omens of unpleasant things to come.

"Walter!" Pops said, and reached out, grabbing his son around the shoulders with arms that still had a lot of strength in them, but were a far cry from what they'd been only a year before, and the soft, trembling embrace broke Walt's heart.

"Hey, Pops," he said, hugging his father back. He let himself be drawn into the doorway, and Pops swung it closed with a surprising *bang*, and locked it with the suddenness of someone who thinks the enemy is lurking in the shadows outside.

Pops turned and looked at him, bushy, graying eyebrows up. "It's kinda late," he observed, then waved the statement away. "Not that I mind. Shit, I can't sleep for anything these days. Usually don't doze off until two in the morning. It's good to see you. Just surprised."

Walt forced a smile. "How are you feeling?"

Pops grunted again, and Walt heard a slight wheeze in the exhale that came after. The older man moved passed him, smirking with one side of his mouth, an expression without much real humor. Perhaps a little irony was all.

"Like ten pounds of shit in a five pound sack, Walter." Pops moved into the living room where the big blue screen continued to flicker, the volume now turned down to almost nothing, just a faint trickle, like someone had left the water on in the bathroom.

The living room was about all there was to this place. An attached kitchen. A bathroom. A bedroom. The duplex was tiny. And it smelled.

It had smelled when Walt had helped moved his Pops in, and the odor had not improved. He didn't think it was his father, who had always been almost prissily clean for someone who spent nearly twenty years on the line rigs before moving up to a tractor. And he was still getting around good enough to take care of himself.

No, the place just stank. As houses went, this one was a rotting corpse.

Walt wondered, and not for the first time, if the duplex might be exacerbating some of his father's symptoms.

Pops found his chair again—the very same, ancient faux-leather recliner that Grandpa Clarence used to commandeer for the better part of every day, with a whiskey bottle in his lap and an unused tumbler sitting on a table, a pointless affectation of restraint.

"Sit down," Pops said, pointing at the only other seat in the living room, an old wooden chair that looked like the missing piece of a dining set. Another little piece of furniture with ancient memories attached to it, these ones of Walt when he was small enough to crawl under tables, the image, the feeling, of clambering through the legs of that chair, a secret tunnel, a little burrow for his wondering young mind.

Walt considered refusing the seat, but then...what the hell? He was tired. Mentally. Physically. He wanted to sit. He sat down slowly, feeling his age, which was silly, because it wasn't much of an age, he was still young. Should his knees ache like that? Should his back?

Maybe the first whispers of red lung, echoing through his body.

He put the box of meds on his lap. When he looked across at Pops, the older man's eyes were on the box, a question in them, but then they went up to Walt's face, and his father smiled, more congenially, and chose the route of small talk.

"How's Carolyn?"

Walt smiled politely. "Good. No complaints."

"Still no chaps on the way?"

Walt sucked his front teeth. "Come on, Pops." He looked away. "You know the situation."

"Eh." Pops sneered. "Fuck the situation." He chuffed. Made a series of other, wordless sounds of indignation. "It's ridiculous. Insane. I would've never imagined it'd be like this, Walt. Never would have imagined." He jabbed a finger at Walt. "And they can't tell you what to do like that. They can't."

Walt shrugged with his eyebrows. "They can, Pops. And they do. And they have. For pretty much my entire life."

This conversation had happened before, between each generation of Baucoms, and Walter knew it. Between Walter Lawrence Baucom I and Grandpa Clarence. And between Grandpa Clarence and Pops. And now between Pops and him.

Each telling the other that their hindsight was truly clear, and that things had gotten out of control.

But to the generation being told it was just...life.

When Grandpa Clarence had been an adult, the CoAx had just come stateside to stabilize the faltering republic. And it seemed to be the end of all things to Grandpa Clarence. But to his son, it was just life.

Pops grew up seeing CoAx patrols on a daily basis. He grew up with this war all around him. And when Walt had been a kid, all the other countries had pulled out and it was just Russia and China that remained, and by the time he was a young adult, the Sino-Russian influence on American politics was not anything to gawp at, it was just life.

The Russians and the Chicoms run my life—Ayuh, so the wind blows.

So while laws and regulations and taxes and subsidies that guarded and ruled almost every aspect of human life seemed to chap the ass of Walt's Pops, to Walt himself, it was just life.

This was just the way of things.

Walt had once heard that if you throw a frog in a pot of boiling water, it'll jump out. But if you put a frog in luke-warm water, and then slowly turn up the heat, the frog will sit there and let itself be boiled alive.

Walter didn't think people were so different.

Now, Pops sat in his old chair and regarded his son with misty eyes, his lips parted as though he were about to speak, his fingers rubbing together as though he were nervous about something. No, not nervous. Regretful.

"Maybe," Pops said softly. "I should have fought. Maybe your Grandpa Clarence was right. Maybe Roy was right. But I didn't want to fight. I wanted to be comfortable. I wanted to live. And so I didn't fight. But now I think...now I think I should have." His eyes blinked rapidly as they looked at Walt. "I feel like I done you wrong by not."

Walt shook his head, dismissing the notion. "Come on, Pops. If you woulda fought they woulda disappeared you and Mom both. Just like they did Grandpa. Just like they did Roy. And then what?" Walt pointed to himself. "I'da been a ward of the state. Just like Carolyn was. No childhood. No parents. Raised by some ward mother. Probably moved out to some strange District in Iowa." Walt shook his head more emphatically. "It's best to stay quiet," he said pointedly. "A smart man told me that once."

Pops made a sound like a chuckle, but there was no smile on his lips.

Walt held his father's gaze for a moment more, then looked down at the box in his lap. "Look. Maybe I can come by later this week. But Carolyn's probably already off work, and it's our first day off together in a while. So I should get home and see her. But…I wanted to get this to you."

"What is it?"

Walt looked at his father from under his brow. Gaze a little more intense than it had been. He knew the stubbornness of this man. Knew it quite well.

"Listen," he started. "Just listen for a minute and don't argue with me. That's all I ask."

Pops grimaced, but remained silent.

Walt patted the top of the box. "I got meds. Not the shit from the clinic that they gave Mom. The shit that they use overseas. The shit that works."

Pops twitched, started to speak, started to rise out of his chair.

A flash of anger went across Walt's face. "Would you shut up?" he snapped. "Seriously, you ornery old bastard. Listen to me. These meds could save your life. I know you don't give a shit, but I do, okay? I care about you living. I care about you being around. So don't argue with me about this. It costs you nothing to take these things. The side effects aren't supposed to be that bad. And they have a much higher success rate. Like eighty percent, or something like that."

"Walter," Pops scooted to the edge of his seat and pointed a bony finger at the Chinese characters on the box. "You think I can't read that shit? I ain't takin' no Chicom meds. Not sure where you got 'em, but I don't want that shit in my veins, you hear?"

Walt had to take a breath. The anger really had been very sudden.

He clutched the sides of the box. Looked at the ground. Almost afraid to look at his father. Afraid of how angry it was going to make him. And he didn't want this night to end in blows, or even in shouting, both of which were possible, and had happened in the past.

"Pops," he said, choosing his words deliberately. A man walking a tightrope and on either side the open drop of a lost temper. Walt had never had a great temper. Neither had any of the other Baucom men. "This wasn't a handout, if that's what you're worried about. If it makes you feel any better about it..." Walt toyed with how much to say here. "This was *taken* from the Chicoms. It was taken from them, and now I'm giving it to you. And you're going to take these doses, because they are going to keep you alive, and that's what I would *really* like for you to do."

"Why?" Pops demanded.

"Why?" Walt finally looked at him. "'Cause you're my Pops. Is that really a question you need to ask?"

Pops leaned back in his chair again and his eyes went up and down—the box, then Walt, then the box, then Walt again. He made a sound of uncertainty, like a dog who isn't sure whether they've heard a suspicious sound or not so they're just going to lie there, grumbling under their breath.

Walter stood up. He put the box of meds on the seat he'd just vacated. Then he turned to his father. "You're going to take those meds, Pops." It wasn't a command. More like speaking in faith. In hope. "And they're going to kill this thing inside of you. And you're going to buy yourself another twenty years. And it's going to be worth it, okay? It'll be worth it, I promise you. But you have to trust me. Just trust me."

"How'd you get the meds?" Pops asked, quietly.

Walt shook his head. "Don't worry about how I got them. They're yours now."

Pops looked at him. Then he looked around, as though there might be someone else in the little duplex that he hadn't realized was hiding in some dark corner, eavesdropping on their conversations. Back to Walt, with a whisper. "Are you fighting? Are you resistance?"

Walt stood there in his father's shitty living room, looking down at the older man, but seeing a gray plastic tarp rolled up, a pair of boots sticking out.

But Walt hadn't pulled the trigger.

Walt hadn't snatched him.

Or any of the others that he'd helped interrogate.

He'd just...*helped.*

Not for idealistic reasons. Just because he needed the money.

"No," Walt shook his head. "I'm not a part of the resistance."

CHAPTER SIX

Walt drove on old two-lane roads, back to his home. In the darkness of the cab of his truck, the white cardboard of the remaining case of meds seemed to glow. He looked over at it, once or twice, thinking about the astronomical number that Virgil had told him the doses were worth.

And, at the same time, knowing damn well that he wasn't going to sell it.

He wasn't going to see a red cent of what it was worth.

How the hell was he supposed to go to dying people and charge them money for their lives? He only knew a few people in the immediate circle of friends that he trusted not to dime him out for having stolen Chicom meds. Of those people, three of them had family members with early onset symptoms of red lung. The meds could be the difference between life and death.

And he would not be willing to charge any of those people.

He let out a frustrated sigh. Gripped the steering wheel harder.

His personal account—the one tied to his PD, tied to Carolyn—it was always hovering in the lower-income margin of $10,000-to-$0, and every once in a while, overdrafted, which was probably the source of damn-near every argument he'd had with Carolyn in the span of their five year marriage.

But Walter had a second account.

An illegal account. Tied to a fake identity. Which was pretty much the only way you could accumulate money through illegal measures— every other source of income went through the Fed. But in a small lockbox, in the glove compartment of his old pickup truck—old being important, because no one would be likely to break into it—he had a datajack. A little piece of equipment that he just plugged into his current PD, and everything he ever was or earned or did or searched simply disappeared and he became a man that never had actually existed, a man called John Tapper.

And in John Tapper's accounts, there was $55,778.

He should've added several grand to that for today's services rendered. But all that potential money had taken the form of a white cardboard box with Chinese characters that was supposed to be worth so much, but in the end would be worth nothing. Not monetarily, anyways.

Could you put a price on life?

Walt laughed, grimly.

Yes. He could. Or, at least, John Tapper could. And to John Tapper, the value of saving those lives was exactly $0.

There would be other opportunities. Other jobs.

He was so close. So close, and yet it seemed like the last twenty grand would be the hardest to get his hands on. But it would happen. It would require patience, and then, one day, that fictional account would have enough money in it, and everything would be made right.

Walt thought about how excited Carolyn would be, the day that he could finally tell her.

He would never be able to tell her *how* he got the money. No. Of course not. Not in a million years. But he didn't think she'd press the issue. He didn't think she'd demand to know where the money came from. She'd be so excited that she wouldn't care.

He didn't like sneaking around behind her back, but if he told her his plan, she would make him stop. She would make him promise. She would work him, just as she'd always been able to do. And he would cave. No matter how important the *purpose* of the money was. He would cave because she would be miserable if she ever found out.

This way, she didn't have to worry about it.

And in the end, Walt thought that she'd forgive him his deceit.

He had met Carolyn the first day of his last year in high school. She'd been sitting in the back row of his classroom when he walked in. He was a sullen seventeen-year-old, depressed from a summer of living in a family torn open by its second disappearing.

First, it'd been Grandpa Clarence. And then it had been Roy.

Now their house seemed empty and quiet. Dead inside.

There was an insidiousness to the disappearings. It was not like death, where things were final—you had a funeral, you grieved, you put a body in the ground, and you celebrated a memory. There was no ceremony to mark when a loved one had been disappeared, no way to get closure.

Because there was this ridiculous, futile hope that maybe—*just maybe*—one day they would just...drop that person back off. And everything could be normal again.

But Walt knew he would never see his Grandpa Clarence again.

And he knew he would never see his brother again.

Because nobody that got disappeared ever came back.

Nothing was sacred. Nothing was safe. Every part of your life was disposable, according to the whim of people you did not know, and whether they deemed you to have crossed the often-shifting lines of what it was to be considered a "domestic terrorist."

That was the mindset that Walter Lawrence Baucom III had settled into when he walked into his senior homeroom, and he saw Carolyn in the back of the class, sitting there with her head down, much in the same manner as he was holding himself.

Walter's innate abilities had not been forcibly exercised in years. The poker games that Roy and Virgil used to drag him to so that they could be kings for a night were a thing of the past now. But the ability remained, and whether or not Walter knew he was doing it, he could *feel* other people. Poignantly at times.

And when he saw Carolyn in the class that day, he felt her very clearly. And there was something in the familiarity of seeing someone suffer what you yourself are suffering. Some sense of sudden commiseration, a camaraderie that connects two people, even if they don't know each other, because they know that they have been through the same thing.

And, of course, it hadn't escaped his notice that she was pretty.

He was seventeen. Pretty girls *never* escaped his notice.

Her hair was a dark, earthy blonde. Almost brunette if the sun hadn't brightened it. Her skin was tanned from being outdoors all summer, maybe working one of the vegetable farms where things still had to be harvested by hand. It struck him that her skin and her hair were almost the same color, and he thought that was interesting. But her eyes stood out starkly, a bright color of hazel. Delicate features. Generally, a kind of delicate manner about her.

He'd never seen her before. Which meant only one thing.

She was new to the school, and people did not just show up to a new school for senior year, and certainly not a school in an Agrarian District. Growers didn't move around from District to District. Not unless something bad had happened.

Walt took a seat next to her in the classroom. He realized the he'd been staring at her and that he was walking unconsciously towards her. When he realized what he was doing, he was already standing next to the seat adjacent to her, and at that point it was either introduce himself or play it off and take his seat—act like he had been going there all along.

He took his seat. Tried to play it cool. Of course. When you're seventeen, you always have to be cool.

She caught him looking one or two more times that day.

She didn't crack a smile.

Walt figured he was irritating her.

At lunch, she sat alone. Walt couldn't help himself. Didn't want to be that guy who just kept silently staring at her from across the room, but then he couldn't quite stop staring, so he decided to nut up, so to speak, and he walked over to her.

He stood there across the lunch table, holding his own brown bag, wondering what the best words to say were to break this icy silence.

And yes, it was icy. That was something Walt would always remember. But even then, even in his relative inexperience with women, he sensed that the ice was very thin, more of a skin, more of a defensive measure than anything truly significant.

Walt gave his best smile—well aware it was not *the* best, just *his* best. But he'd always been comfortable with himself, at least. He had that going for him. "Can I sit here?"

She looked up at him. Seemed to be studying him. He wasn't quite sure what he saw, besides the obvious: another lanky-limbed grower boy, still wearing his tans for the third time since they'd been washed, the sides of them streaked with grease and stained with purple regulator cleaner. Really, pretty much a wreck. But if one took a moment to look around, one could see that he wasn't out of place. Not around here anyways.

"Sure," she said.

Walt was almost surprised.

He sat. Quickly, like he thought she might change her mind.

"I'm Walter," he said, not bothering to extend his hand or anything like that. He wasn't sure why. She seemed like such a clean, delicate thing, like she didn't belong in an Agrarian District. And here he was, this colossal wreck, with his stained fingers and dirt under his fingernails and his dirty tans. Perhaps he felt *unworthy* to touch her.

"Carolyn," she replied, still eyeing him. "Hartsell."

If for no other reason to escape her evaluating gaze—Walter always felt awkward when someone looked at him like that, always had the sneaking suspicion that he was coming up short somehow—he opened his brown bag and began pulling out his lunch, wondering what he'd gotten himself into, and what the hell he was supposed to say next.

He was drawing a bit of a blank, and he had twenty-five minutes of lunchtime left.

"I saw you looking at me," she stated.

Once again, he was taken by surprise.

That was…quite a bold statement.

And unexpected from her quiet voice and soft demeanor.

Walt looked up at her, his hands frozen in the unwrapping of his sandwich. She had her elbows up on the table, a fresh tomato perched between her slender fingers. Nice fingers, delicate, like the rest of her—and lo and behold, what was this under her nails but a bit of dirt?

She had one eyebrow up, awaiting his response to this charge.

Looking back on that moment, Walt was pretty sure that was the moment that he fell for Carolyn Hartsell. Because suddenly and inexplicably, he felt okay. Unlike every other interaction with girls so far—pretty much just sexually-charged verbal jousts—he felt weirdly comfortable. Relaxed. And it was nice. It was very good to feel the warm, slackening of tensions in himself.

"Yes," he said. Then he smiled.

"Why?"

"Why what?"

"Why were you looking at me?"

She knew the answer. She wanted *him* to say it.

He opened his sandwich. It was white bread with a slice of cheese product. Pretty typical lunch fare. His Mom tried to go light on lunches so that they could afford better dinners. Maybe once he started working full time they'd do both.

He looked back up at Carolyn.

"Because you're new," Walt said. He watched her expression, saw just a shade of disappointment, because that was not what she'd wanted to hear, but obviously, she wasn't going to go fishing for it. And strangely, Walt felt immediately averse to being the source of her disappointment—something that would carry through to nearly every aspect of their relationship from that moment on—so he told her what he knew she wanted to hear, and it also happened to be the truth: "And because you're pretty."

Honestly, he was very impressed with himself. Roy had always been the bold and reckless one. Walt got into his fair share of tight situations, but it was less because of his own nature, and more because he followed Roy around. It was not his usual way to be quite so straightforward. He was more likely to sit back and allow things to take their own course.

She began to slice her tomato with a piece of plastic cutlery. She cut the tomato carefully. Then she stabbed two thin slices and held them out to Walt. "Here," she said. "Your sandwich looked boring."

Later, that would become a running joke. How the way to a man's heart was through his stomach, but Walt must've been desperate, because she won him over with two slices of tomato.

Walt accepted her offer, of course, and had the best tomato-and-cheese sandwich that he'd ever recalled having. And for twenty-some-odd minutes, he forgot about his unpromising future, and the disappearings, and the CoAx, and the Fed. He was focused on Carolyn in those minutes, and it seemed like, despite everything else, things were going to turn out okay.

It wasn't for another two weeks and several more lunches of small talk that he dared to ask the more personal question that had been pestering the back of his mind since the first day he saw a new girl sitting in the back of his homeroom.

"Can I ask you something?" he said, almost with a cringe, thinking, *here you go, here's where you blow it to pieces.*

Sometimes people in Carolyn's "situation" were sensitive about their past. But Walt had met many more that actually *wanted* to talk about it. And what little read he could get off of Carolyn, she struck him as perhaps wanting to get it off her chest.

And in that moment, it seemed like she knew what was coming next. He watched her straighten up a bit, as though bracing herself.

"Sure," she said, a little stiffly.

"Are you a ward of the state?" he asked, studying her face.

She looked down at her place, then nodded. "Yes. What gives it away?"

Walt shrugged, tried his best to communicate that it wasn't a big deal, to make her comfortable with it, let her know that he accepted it. "The fact that you're here," he said, gently. "No one transfers out of their home District. Not unless the state moves them."

"Hm," was all she said to that.

Walt poked at his food for a bit. "I, uh..." he needed to give her something here. He'd just pulled off a scab. Exposed her. Here they were at lunch, busy forgetting about how shitty things could be, distracting each other, really, from the reality outside those school walls. And here comes Walt, making it all real, all present, all *right now*. "I've lost two," he said with decisiveness. "My grandpa and my brother. They were both disappeared."

She looked up from her plate.

And just like that, they had something in common. Something besides the surface bullshit with which they'd filled their lunchtime conversations for the last weeks. Something that was not just about music and entertainment and other meaningless things that were bound to change. This was something that went hard, like a vein of some unwanted, poisonous ore, down through the crust of them and into the core of who they were.

A shared pain. The fellowship of misery. Of sleeping at night, wondering when the boogeyman might throw a diversionary grenade through your door, leave that crescent-shaped scorch mark on your floor, just like it had with your brother, with your grandfather, and maybe this time they were there for you. Or even worse, for the precious few family members that you had left.

But...if Carolyn was a ward of the state, then she had no family left.

"Both my parents," she said. "Taken on the same night."

Damn. Walt kept the word from exiting his mouth.

Her whole life. Destroyed in one swipe. One minute a happy family, and less than sixty seconds later, she was an orphan, a ward of the state, and everything she thought she knew about her future was gone, changed. She was suddenly someone else, living someone else's life.

They didn't say anything else about disappearings that lunchtime. They just stayed quiet for a bit, then finished up with more insignificant small talk about what they had planned for the weekend. She had to work, and so did Walt. If they weren't studying, they were doing their paid internships, because every household needed the extra income, and even if you were just a ward of the state, it was always best to show SoDro Growers Group that you were serious about your work and secure yourself a full-time position when you graduated high school.

As though they could really do anything else.

As though if Walt decided to do something else with his life besides farming, he wouldn't live the rest of his life broke and hungry, relying on Fed handouts simply to subsist.

That was how they got you. That was how they beat you. That was how they eventually learned to engineer the society that suited them. How do you make a free people beholden to their government, and not the other way around? Slowly. In small ways. In little taxes here, and little rewards there, making success a measure of how much you stayed in line with the government's plan for your life.

Frog in the pot of boiling water.

But they'd been boiled to slag a long time ago.

That's what Grandpa Clarence used to say. And Roy after him.

But Walt did his best to keep his head down.

Do what they told him to do.

Let the wind blow where it may.

Lunchtime ended and Walt and Carolyn separated, but not before he figured out what time she got off work on Saturday, and when she was expected to be back at the foster home. Then he showed up to her work in his ancient, rusted pickup truck that had once been Grandpa Clarence's, and then Roy's, and finally his. She spotted him sitting there at a rumbling, creaky idle, just outside the gates to the hangar where she worked, and he watched her break into a big smile.

He drove her out to a place where nobody was, because their whole lives were surrounded by others. There in those rural Agrarian Districts, supposedly the least-populated in the country, where civilization was kept to a minimum in order to increase the amount of untouched, farmable land, they somehow managed to never be alone. They lived in small, crowded houses, and they went to small, crowded schools, and after work they sat in small, crowded bars and drank their sorrows away.

Not tonight, Walt thought.

He took her down to the old Rocky River Bridge, and it was empty and forlorn and clear, and you couldn't tell that the water was a murky orange color because it was just liquid blackness that trickled moonlight. He parked his truck on the side of the road where an old checkpoint used to be stationed to keep all the mischievous kids at bay, and he led her down to the water.

They passed old graffiti, and new. Most of it angry young folks, ranting about the Fed, or the CoAx, or both. Some of it scrubbed away, or whitewashed over. More painted over the fresh canvas of whitewash.

At the water's edge, they stood and threw rocks in the quietude of the moving river, and they simply enjoyed this moment of solitude in the darkness, in the presence of a kindred spirit.

It was in that long, quiet moment, that Carolyn became still and stared out at the darkness all around them, and Walt could see her eyes were wide in the moonlight. She held a rock in her hand. Then she looked at him.

"What happens if you yell?" she asked, barely audible over the water.

Walt scratched his toe in the clay, unsure of the question, or the answer. "If you yell?"

"Yes," she nodded, quickly. "If I scream."

Now he was even more confused.

She clarified: "If I was to scream something, would anybody hear me?"

Walt looked around. "Uh…I guess not." He scratched the back of his neck. "I mean…hell…closest house has gotta be about a mile away. At least."

She raised her head to him. "Yell something."

"Me?"

"Yes, you. Yell something."

He laughed at her. "Like what? What do you want me to yell?"

Carolyn considered this, tossing the stone up in the air and catching it. "I don't know." She pointed to the columns of the bridge supports. "Imagine those are the CoAx. Look at that. There's three of them. That could be the Three Brothers, right there. Imagine that it's the Three Brothers standing there, but you can't get in trouble for anything right now. What would you yell at them?"

He stared at her, the curious smile falling away from his face. He looked out then, and imagined all three of them standing there, big, body-modded men in their bulky armor and their thick battleshrouds that covered everything but their cold, cold eyes. Stubby black rifles strapped to their chests. Standing there. Still and silent. Waiting for him. Waiting to hear what he had to say.

"I want my brother back," he suddenly blurted, only slightly louder than the river itself.

He looked at Carolyn, wondering what her judgement was of this.

She didn't judge the fact that it came out so quiet. She looked at him from behind a curtain of her dark blonde hair, twisting around in the wind. Then she turned, shaking the strands of hair out of her face and she took a deep breath.

"Fuck this place!" she screamed at the top of her lungs.

It made him jump. He almost laughed from sheer surprise, but there was a certain gravity to it that killed the laugh before it came out.

From the sandbar where they stood, Carolyn reeled back and hurled the stone at one of the columns. Walt watched it glide through the air and *clack* off the face of one of the columns, then splash into the water.

"Fuck you!" she screamed again, fists clenched at her sides, veins standing out on her neck as she yelled it out. "Fuck this place!"

Just like the first day he had met her, Carolyn's boldness emboldened Walt. He watched her thrusting her face out into the windy darkness and yelling, and he felt that he should have yelled louder at those fantasy enemies made of old concrete. So he stooped down quickly and he scooped up a stone and he flung it hard at the nearest column.

"I want my brother back!" he yelled at the column.

Carolyn threw another rock. "I want my parents back!"

"I don't want to live here for the rest of my life!"

"I don't want to be afraid anymore!"

Then they stood there in stunned silence as the moonlit ripples were caught and obliterated in the never-ceasing current, and the wind carried the echoes of their voices away, and their throats burned with their secret rebellion. They looked at each other then, needing to see another person in the darkness, as though they both suddenly felt how small and insignificant they were in this great, violent scheme of things.

Just two more little worker bees.

Just two more little cogs in the machine.

Their existences were inconsequential.

They held hands on the way back up to his truck.

CHAPTER SEVEN

He asked Carolyn to marry him when he was nineteen. She said yes, and they weren't wasting time. He had asked in March, and they planned the wedding for July. Walt didn't have a large family, and Carolyn didn't have a family at all. It would be a small affair. They planned to host it at his parent's house.

Then, in April, a giant train-wreck of a bill called the Social Recovery Act passed through its necessary channels and was force-fed to them as the law of the land. The reality of it came crashing down on their heads and smothered their tiny dreams.

The "Two Child Rule" had been enacted when Walt was a young child, when his parents were past their child-rearing years. He'd grown up with the reality of it, and so it seemed normal. And it wasn't that, bad, really. They weren't saying you *couldn't* have more than two children. This was America—you were free to do what you wanted. But the Federal Government had let the Chinese and the Russians in, and it was like the old tales about vampires: if you invited them in, you would have no power over them.

They'd never admit it, but behind closed doors, they'd let the CoAx have control. He who had the gold made the rules, as they say. And under the guidance of the Chinese, the Fed decided that they would allow their citizens to use healthcare to pay for only two children—one girl, and one boy. And because the Fed provided the only healthcare available, the alternative was simple: You can have the amount of children you were told you could have. Or you could somehow scrounge up the $75,000 to pay for the medical expenses on your own.

Which was, of course, virtually impossible for most.

And don't even think about having it at home, using "natural birth" or some other old-fashioned thing. Natural births were considered felony child-endangerment. The punishment was severe.

But…this was all old news.

Walt had grown up with this. It had chapped his parents' ass to no end, but they hadn't been all that outspoken because they were already done having children and so it didn't affect them really, so why rock the boat about it?

It was just a fact of life.

So the wind blows.

The Social Recovery Act was a new punishment. Supposedly so that the Fed could "limit the healthcare expenses associated with hazardous genetic matches," and "relieve the taxpayers of an unnecessary burden."

From the date of the bill and onwards, anyone that wished to have children had to first be tested for genetic compatibility, to ensure that their child would have the best chance of coming out without some sort of mental or physical defect that might put a strain on the healthcare system.

Walt and Carolyn were shell-shocked, but they stayed hopeful.

Stupidly hopeful.

Like the good citizens they were, they went to get tested, hand in hand, not yet married but inextricably committed to each other. Small hopes, small dreams, held close in their chests. The audacity just to do what they thought they were allowed to do—accept their prescribed careers according to the APT, stay in the District, pay their taxes, have their two children, and live quietly with their heads down. Those were the big plans.

They were not a match.

———

He went down to the river again with her, the afternoon they found out that they were not a match. That their genes were "incompatible."

How incompatible? They had asked them that question.

8% incompatible, was the frank, pragmatic answer.

"Does that mean that we're ninety-two-percent *compatible*?" Carolyn had demanded of the technician at the clinic. And, sitting beside her, Walt could hear the volume of Carolyn's voice going up.

The technician blinked, a little nervously. "Yes."

"So there's still a ninety-two-percent chance that we'll have perfect, healthy kids?" Carolyn's chest was rising and falling quickly, her pulse quickening in her neck, her tan features flushing. "And that's not good enough? Ninety-two-fucking-percent?"

The technician glanced at Walt, like she hoped that he would be the voice of reason.

But he didn't trust himself to speak. He felt a big black hole in his gut. He felt beaten down. Cheated, really. He had played by the rules. He had kept his head down. He had done what they'd wanted him to do, hadn't he? Was it too much to ask that he had the two children that they'd told him he could have, with the woman that he loved? He didn't want a giant house or nice cars. He wasn't going to buck the system and try for a career outside of the one they'd recommended for him. He didn't fight back over the fact that foreign soldiers patrolled the streets of his hometown.

What else did they want?

Why could he not have this one thing?

"The cutoff is six percent," the technician said, carefully. Then she closed her folder and drew herself up. "I'm terribly sorry about this. I don't make the rules, you know. They are what they are."

They are what they are.

It is what it is.

So the wind blows.

Right?

So they sat, down at the river, him next to her, but uncomfortably distant for some reason. They would usually sit so close. Now there was space between them. Carolyn sat with her knees drawn up to her chest, her chin resting on her knees, and her arms wrapped around her legs. He wanted to give her comfort, but he wasn't sure she wanted him to touch her.

This is how it is when nothing is sacred. When you are not secure in anything—not your house, not your property, not your person. Not even your choices. When there is no security to anything, you distance yourself from everything. Because it all has teeth, it all bites, it all stings.

And Walt remembered thinking to himself that maybe he wanted to jump out of the pot of water now. Or was he too boiled already? Boiled into paralysis? Boiled to slag, just like Grandpa and Roy used to claim?

He looked out at the big, wide ribbon of glistening orange that floated past them. All that chemical runoff from the hydroponics in the nearby fields, blooming that orange algae, season after season.

Blooming that red cancer in their lungs.

He wondered, if his parents had been tested, would they have been compatible?

"Listen," he said, and he disliked the coldness of his tone. "If you don't want to marry, I'll understand."

"What?" she asked, quietly.

Walt figured that she'd heard him, so he didn't repeat himself.

She turned her head to look at him. "What did you just say to me?"

"I said..." he wasn't quite sure of his footing here. He didn't really mean the words that he was saying. It just seemed like the...*honorable* thing to do, he guessed. But it was a damn nightmare. The thought that she might actually say "okay" and then get up and walk away from him seemed like the worst thing that could possibly happen.

It *was* the worst thing that could possibly happen.

But what the hell did he expect?

They couldn't have kids together. They couldn't have the family that they both wanted. Their dreams were crashed before they even started. Did he expect her to just stick around for the hell of it?

"I heard what you said," she snapped at him, suddenly.

She'd been angry at him only a handful of times.

He didn't like it. It made his spine prickle, and he disliked it in one aspect, because he didn't want to let someone else have that kind of control over him, but he also recognized that that ship had sailed quite a while ago. That was what a relationship was, right?

He clenched his jaw. "Well...why'd you ask, then?"

She reached across and slapped his shoulder. Not in the friendly way she would sometimes do. This one was hard. A whip. He could see how angry she was by the set of her mouth. She was not joking with him. "How *dare* you say that to me!"

Walt spread his arms out, taken aback. "What do you mean? I'm trying to give you the choice here!"

She slapped him again. "The choice?" And again. "The fucking *choice?*"

He grabbed her wrist to keep her from slapping him again. "Stop."

She twisted her wrist out of his grip and pointed a finger at his face. "Walter Baucom! Don't you ever say some shit like that to me again, do you hear me?"

He was still mystified. He had no idea why she was mad at him.

She pointed to the pillars holding the bridge up. Like they were still the imagined Three Brothers of years ago. "They don't get to decide our lives! They don't get to tell me who I marry. They don't get to tell you either. They control every other aspect of our lives—a tax for this, a subsidy for that, and don't ever do what we don't want you to do or we'll turn you out into the cold. But not this! I won't let them have this! I won't let them ruin my one good thing!"

It was strange. Love can be so one-sided. You know how you feel about a person, but you have to take their word on how they feel about you. But sitting there, staring into the eyes of the woman that he loved while she shouted angrily at him, he heard the truth of what she was saying.

He was her *one good thing*.

And she was his *one good thing*.

He couldn't let her go. He couldn't just offer her up like that.

He grabbed her and held onto her. Held onto her like the world was space, and she was the only handhold keeping him from flying out into the endless void. Like catching the edge of a cliff before you plummet to your death.

"I'm sorry," he said, shakily. "I don't want you to go. Please don't go."

———

Driving home from his father's duplex at night, with that box of medicine still nestled in the front passenger seat beside him like a quiet little hitchhiker that he'd picked up, Walt thought about the years gone by, and how they were not so many, but they felt it sometimes. He felt it in the hollow places inside of him. He felt it in the heavy shell of himself, the exposed parts of himself callusing over and over and over again until he felt very little, and maybe that was best.

But this, this bright little possibility in his future, it shone through the stone-skin of his regular self. It was the thing he allowed himself to feel strongly about. It was a secret thing. And secret things could not be touched. The CoAx couldn't touch them. The Fed couldn't touch them. The resistance in all its multiple facets and autonomous branches couldn't touch them.

He had saved every penny that he'd earned doing this filthy work—the only work he could find outside of driving tractors and occasional over-time on the maintenance lines. But overtime didn't help his cause, because that was paid to Walter Baucom, and it would go to bills and scratching out his subsistence.

This money, no matter how dirty, went to John Tapper. And he hadn't touched any of it. Not for overdraft fees. Not for special things that he knew Carolyn deserved, but he couldn't afford. He was more than two-thirds of the way there, and by this time next year, God willing, he would have enough money saved, and he and Carolyn would be able to afford to have a child.

Just thinking about the surprise of it made him grin foolishly in the darkness of the cab of his truck. The little sliver of road in front of his headlights—a simple pathway in the immense expanse of darkness stretching out to either side, like a road through an abyss—turned into the mile-long dirt stretch that cut through the fields of just-planted corn to the little house where he and Carolyn lived.

He looked out the window briefly as he drove. The late-night moon cast a silver glow over everything and it ran alongside of him as he drove down the road, keeping pace with him as it slid effortlessly across the tractor rails and hydroponics lines.

The house they lived in—the house that Walt had grown up in— was small for the Baucom family when things had started. When it had been Grandpa Clarence, and Mom, and Pops, and Roy and him. They fit tightly into the three bedrooms and two bathrooms.

Now, with only Carolyn and him, it was ample. But still cozy.

They had no property to speak of. They were hemmed in on all sides by hydroponics, just about ten feet off the house in any direction. The orb weaver spiders loved to build their giant webs between the tall corn when it came up and the corners of the house. Carolyn couldn't stand them, so it was his job to clear them out every few days when they showed up in late summer.

Secretly, he couldn't stand them either. But it was a labor of love.

As the dirt drive leveled out and straightened up, and he could see ahead of him, his house amongst the fields. It was a pleasant effect. He felt the monotonous troubles begin to peel off of him as his truck rumbled down the drive towards the quaint white box of plastic siding and black shutters. The lights burned yellow inside.

Most of the troubles, anyways.

Things still whisked around in the back of his mind, like debris caught in a cyclone.

Who the hell were the Eudys?

Were they the ones kidnapping New Breed soldiers? And why?

And of course, the white box of Chinese cancer meds that did him absolutely no good at all, they were in his mind too.

He shook his head to get the thoughts to leave him alone.

No. It was his day off. And it was Carolyn's day off.

Finally. They had time to spend together. He wasn't going to screw that up with a bunch of hand-wringing and mental enigmas that, ultimately, had no effect on him.

He didn't give a shit who the Eudys were.

He didn't give a shit who was kidnapping New Breeds.

He didn't give a shit about dead men in plastic tarps.

It was a nice evening. Maybe Carolyn would like to grab the jar of lemondrop and sit outside with him for an hour or so. Yes. It was going to be a good night. A relaxing night. Maybe they'd even make love, which was a bit overdue in Walt's estimation.

He pulled to a stop in the driveway, the house off to the right side of his truck. He could see that, apparently, Carolyn agreed with him on how pleasant the night was. The front door was open.

He felt a minor flicker of irritation, the thought of *dammit, woman* that every husband has from time to time.

It was a nice night, but it was also April, which is when the bugs started coming out. And they didn't have a screen door. So he could just imagine the number of things that were hurrying through the fields towards the bright yellow nirvana of his houselights.

He pushed his truck door open and slid out. Slammed the door and locked it behind him.

As if to reinforce his minor bother, no less than a dozen moths, flies and some other winged insects were buzzing around in the glow of his headlamps, wings flashing, bodies reflecting the light like they were luminous themselves.

He swished through them, unconsciously holding his breath.

On the other side, as the headlights of his truck finally shut off, he called out, "Carolyn, you're gonna let the bugs in, babe."

He climbed the steps to their little front porch.

He stopped.

From where he was, he could see the door.

He could see straight into the living room.

The front door was not just open. It was hanging off of splintered hinges.

And there in the center of the living room was the crescent-shaped scorch mark of a diversionary grenade.

CHAPTER EIGHT

Walter stared.

The splintered door. The scorch mark on the floor.

This isn't real. Not real.

But why was a clenched breath beginning to burn in his chest?

Why was his heart snapping like a snare drum, fast and hectic?

He knew what he was seeing. He'd seen it before.

He gasped, pushing stale, fiery, oxygen-depleted air out of his lungs and sucking in new air, and was it him or could he taste and smell the powder burn from that scorch mark?

He realized his hands were shaking. He stepped through the door and found his feet unsteady. There in those brief moments, his mind and his body were disconnected. Unreality was putting him into a stupor. His body was surging, pounding, screaming at him to do something, like fire shut up in his bones.

He lurched. Like that ancient pickup of his teenage years, the gears catching a second or so after he'd already pressed the accelerator, and then *bang*, he was flying forward.

"Carolyn!" he yelled, hoarsely.

And he was almost sure that she would call back to him, that this was some sort of mistake, that she was indeed somewhere in the house with a perfectly reasonable explanation for all of this, and things weren't bad, no, they weren't bad, they would be okay, his heart would slow down and in twenty minutes they would have laughed all of this off and they'd be watching TV together…

"Carolyn!" he screamed again.

There was only silence in the house.

He moved into the bedroom. Buzzing. Twitching. He walked like a man that couldn't feel his feet.

He checked the bathroom, moving slow and deliberate, like he was caught in that sludgy-air of a nightmare, that air that won't let you move your legs, won't let you move as fast as you want to move.

He floated to the back door, mouth slack like a drunkard.

But his eyes were sharp. Wide open. Flying here and there.

He went out onto the porch. Stared out at the fields, just a little bit of them visible in the circular glow created by the lights around his house.

"Carolyn!" he called into the dark fields.

The fields swallowed his voice. There was no echo.

Must be some other explanation.

Must be. Must be. Must be.

He turned, very suddenly, and he staggered back into the house, realizing that his breathing was much faster than it should be. He could feel the cold wetness on his forehead, on his chest, at the small of his back.

But he was managing to move faster now.

He was being sucked into the reality of the situation.

As he stepped shakily back into his house, his hands slid across the jam. He felt the rough wood, which was not supposed to be rough, but he didn't think anything about it. Splinters slid into his skin, but he failed to register them at that moment.

He looked around, forcing cohesion. Forcing logic. Because it certainly wasn't going to come on its own.

He brought an unsteady hand up to his face and wiped cold, greasy sweat from his forehead and temples.

Broken door.

Crescent scorch mark.

He looked up and saw three moths circling the single living room light. Battering themselves against it.

He needed to calm down. He needed to breathe. To think rationally about everything he was seeing. He knew what the signs pointed to, but…but…he had to test every other possibility before he could accept it.

He flipped his PD open, sliding his fingers across the monitor as it hovered in the air above his forearm. He had to call Carolyn. Had to call her. And when he did, she would answer. Of course she would.

He stood there, staring at the monitor.

Ringing. Ringing.

Come on, baby. Answer your phone.

Ringing. Ringing.

Tell me anything but what it looks like.

Ringing. Ringing.

No answer.

A voice that was not hers reassured him that his call would be forwarded to her when she was available again.

He started pacing the living room floor. Feet moving fast. Nervous. Choppy.

He called her again. And when that wasn't answered either, he sent her a message.

Then he called her again, desperate now, desperate for her voice, desperate for that wake-up call in a nightmare, the reason you shout out, knowing it's a nightmare, hoping someone will hear you and pull you out of the dream and back into reality.

He called her work. He asked her manager in the lightest, fakest tones he could muster, if he had seen Carolyn. Walter's voice sounded strange and stale in his own head. A bad actor reading bad lines.

But if the manager could hear the growing insanity, he didn't say so.

"Nah, she left normal time, Walt. Everything okay?"

"Ayuh," he said, the words flat. Two-dimensional. "I'm sure it's fine."

They said perfunctory goodbyes and disconnected.

Walter walked his hollow self to a kitchen chair and sank into it, like his knees were melting. The chair, one of the two wooden ones that sat at the small, round table. His usual chair. The one on the other side was Carolyn's.

He blinked a few times, trying to focus himself, trying to look at the truth. And what was it that he was seeing? He knew. He knew damn well.

Ram mark on the door.

Scorch mark on the floor.

Carolyn.

Disappeared.

He let out a groan and folded over in his chair, putting his head between his knees. He focused on breathing. And thinking. That's what he needed to do. Think. Please think. Please, brain, start working. Figure something out. Come up with something that you can do. Something that isn't just pissing into the wind. There has to be something. Some solution. Some way…

Why? Why would they take her?

Because they threw rocks when they were kids? Because they said "Fuck the CoAx" a few times? They were adults now. They hadn't said anything anti-CoAx in years.

Why now? Why this?

He sat upright in his chair, all frozen except for his eyes which switched back and forth, back and forth, across the room, like he was reading some words that were hanging there in the dead space.

Is this about me?

He put a hand up to his mouth. "Oh, fuck." His breath smelled like stale cigarettes and sour, adrenaline-sweat coming off his palm. "Oh, no. No. No."

He stood up suddenly. He looked around him.

Shit, shit, shit.

An hour ago he'd been in a rundown trailer tucked back in the woods. And in the dilapidated bedroom of that dark safe house, there'd been a body rolled up into a plastic tarp. A New Breed. An officer. And there'd been gunships prowling the skies. And guntrucks rolling in force through the town center.

And here he sat like a dolt with his thumb up his ass, wondering why they'd come after his Carolyn.

But maybe they hadn't.

Maybe they'd come after him.

He clawed his hair.

Of course they'd come after him!

"Sonofabitch!" Walt shouted into the stillness of his house.

Walt started looking around his house now. Not just in shock. There was something else now too. There was fear. What if they weren't gone like he thought? What if he was standing around in the bear trap, prancing around on that pressure plate, and any second it was about to snap closed?

Goddammit, Virgil, what the fuck have you gotten me into?

He would've never done any of this shit if it hadn't been for Virgil popping up after years of virtual silence, acting like they were buddies, acting like Virgil was doing him a goddamned favor by offering him a job, when the reality was that he would've never come knocking except that he *needed* something!

Just like he and Roy would've never dragged him to all those stupid poker games, except that they *needed* something.

Walter was just a means to an end.

The concept of being used was a black little seed that settled into the soil of his mind and immediately began to send out crawlers, vines, roots.

Walt snapped open his PD again and tried to focus on the glow of the monitor. He realized everything was blurring. He blinked rapidly, felt hot tears come out of the corners of his eyes, felt a hitch in his breathing.

Blame all you want, but Carolyn's gone because of you.

But that bitter little seed, and the angry things that came out of it just continued to grow.

He ripped through his contacts with shaking hands and unsteady fingers and stabbed the air where Virgil's contact hovered. It rang. Walt waited.

Every ring, every warbling little electronic tone pushed him like a dozer blade, edged him closer and closer to completely losing it.

He eyed the kitchen chair he'd been sitting in. He had a brief image of picking it up and dashing it to pieces. He wasn't sure whether he was angry, or sad. Wasn't sure whether it was directed at Virgil or himself.

Blame all you want, his mind told him again. *But you did this. You did this, not Virgil. You thought you were slick. You thought you were gonna be the one that got away with it. But you're just an idiot. You let them use you, and now you're the fool. And now Carolyn's gonna pay for it. Now Carolyn's gone. She's gone.*

Your one good thing.

His PD spouted the same message that it had given him when Carolyn hadn't answered his call.

The urge to break something was almost insurmountable now. Why wasn't anyone answering their phones? There was a goddamned reason why you had that shit strapped to your *FUCKING WRIST!*

There was another option.

One that Virgil had told him very coldly was only for emergencies. *Only for emergencies*, he'd said, while the look on his face said *don't go calling it every time you get a wild hare about something, you inexperienced, non-resistance civvy.*

But fuck Virgil.

If anything counted as an emergency, it was this.

Walt accessed the encrypted file and sent out the ping through the ether of invisible signals.

It only rang once.

Virgil's voice, cold as a slab of concrete in winter: "How'd you get this?"

Walter stared at the monitor, mystified for a moment. "You gave it to me!" he said, a little louder, a little angrier than he'd intended.

Virgil started to speak.

Walt blurted over him. "They hit my house. They hit my house, and they took Carolyn."

Silence on the line.

Walt stared, his mouth open. What was next? What should he say next—

"Get out," Virgil said, flatly. "Don't take anything with you. And don't drive your truck. Go on foot. Go to the bridge. Go now."

CHAPTER NINE

Get out.

Go now.

The words clanged around in a mind about as blank as a white canvas, which is not truly blank at all, but rife with terrible potential.

Anything was possible at that moment, and those possibilities swirled in a maelstrom around him, and he waited for something real to coalesce from it.

He realized he was still staring at his PD screen, and he snapped it shut, hard.

Get out.

He looked around him, and found that suddenly, very suddenly, this house had become a hostile place. Like a murder scene, it had bled into every other aspect of his thoughts, turning them dark, tainting them, coloring them.

This place screamed to him of Carolyn.

The memories poured out of the walls all in a single instant, all at once, like a right hook that you didn't see coming and it sends you reeling into vivid dreamscapes.

The memories, sweet, but bittered and darkened by his fear, by his panic, by the gaping openness that he felt in his chest.

She was hanging the old horse collar that she'd used to decorate the blank wall of the entryway. Getting frustrated with the mounts in the polyboard wall, and then telling him to back off when he tried to help, telling him she could hang the damn thing just fine by herself, brow scrunched in concentration as she zeroed in on the offending mount.

Get out.

And when the frustration was gone, she touched his arm and kissed him and told him that she appreciated his offer to help, but she wanted to do some things for herself. And Walt looked at her work and nodded and told her that it looked good.

Go now.

She was in the kitchen, paring apples for a holiday dessert, because she swiped some extras from the messhall. He moved up behind her, put his arms around her waist and kissed the spot on her neck, right there at her shoulder. She smiled and tilted her head, letting him closer, the curlicue hairs that she could never quite gather into her ponytail, tickling his face.

Don't take anything with you.

He saw himself sitting at their tiny table, bitching about this deduction or that bill, as he stared at the blue glow of his PD monitor and felt that old familiar feeling of *It's Not Fair!* And Carolyn slid him a jar of lemondrop and told him, "So the wind blows, cowboy. Drink with me and we'll talk about it later. We'll figure it out. We always do."

Go…

Walt drew a breath and felt it hitch, halfway in.

This place was haunted.

The flood of memories took no more than a second or two.

He went to the back door and threw it open, and he took a moment to close it behind him, gently.

That was how he and Roy had always snuck out of the house when Grandpa Clarence had passed out in his chair, a bottle of whisky on the coffee table next to him. The two boys would edge out the back door, gently closing the door behind them, pulling the latch so that the sound of it falling into place would be quiet.

The heat at their backs, the sun pulling the air-conditioning from around their skin.

And then they would turn, as Walter turned in that moment, and they would run, just like Walter was running now. And when he was a young boy he would watch his brother, just a few paces ahead, and

Roy would look over his shoulder with a daring half-grin that knew that trouble was just around the corner.

All around them the corn would be summer-tall and the bugs were sun-lit meteors in a hazy July afternoon sky, and they would run, they would run into the fields, and away, and the hard, sharp leaves of the cornstalks would lash at their arms, but they didn't care, they were escaping through it like a portal into another world, leaving war behind, leaving real life behind, seeking adventure.

But in Walter's present, there were no bright fields of green corn.

No promise of adventures misbegotten.

There was only darkness and God-knew what else.

There was only fear of what lay ahead of him, and no excitement at all. He was still escaping, but this time he wasn't escaping into childhood mischief. He was escaping to survive. He was escaping to get away from a thing that was gobbling up his existence, and it was just right behind him, like a black hole, chewing everything up into nothing...

Into the darkness.

Go to the bridge.

Which bridge?

There was only one that mattered.

To Roy and Virgil and Walt, it was The Bridge, and had been since childhood.

The Baucom house sat in the middle of a 270-acre tract. While a great many of the trees in the Agrarian Districts had been razed to maximize the farmable land, they'd left strands of them in place to prevent soil erosion, and also to serve as a visible delineation between tracts.

These lines of trees, usually no more than twenty yards thick, with pines and a few hardwoods in the center of it, and junipers and black-berry brambles on the edges, served as a highway for creatures that did not want to be seen.

Deer. Foxes. Coyotes.

Also, packs of errant local kids that didn't want to be spotted by the gunship patrols.

Walter remembered turning it into a game, as children have the incredible ability to turn almost anything into a game, even when the world around you is at war.

They would run along the deer trails, and they would pretend in that moment that they were freedom fighting commandos, on their way to a secret location, to blow up a CoAx ammo dump or perform some other daring task.

If they heard the sound of gunship rotors approaching, they would take cover in the leaves and brambles. And in those moments when the gunships were just overhead, and the little bit of rotor wash hit them, they would be perfectly still, their breath frozen in their throats, not a muscle moving except for their hearts beating spastically, excitedly, feeling the danger of it, relishing the tension, lying so perfectly still that the urge to pee would nearly overcome them.

These little strips of woods, thin highways for things and people on foot, they were like a whole other world for those young grower kids. And someone could follow them from one end of District 89 to the other, if they had the time and the mind to do it.

But always, before they traipsed these lines of woods and went where they pleased in the secrecy of their forested paths, they would meet. And there was only one place to meet.

It was a place where you could hang out, maybe smoke a cigarette that you'd swiped off of your pops, skip stones on water, and generally be left alone by the looming adulthood that would eventually consume you in a future that was both distant and absurdly close.

And that place was The Bridge.

The Rocky River Bridge, in longhand, but no one really called it that anymore. Only if you were being interrogated by an adult and they asked you where you'd been. If you were of a mind to be honest, you might say, "The Bridge," and if they pressed for clarity, you might say, "The Rocky River Bridge."

Just as long as you didn't dime out *who* was there with you.

The Bridge.

The very same one that Walt had gone to with Carolyn. Where they'd thrown rocks and realized, as they'd refused to admit when they were children, that adulthood was no longer oncoming, but it was, at last, upon them. And it was just as harsh and unyielding as they'd been led to believe.

Walt knew the way very well, even now, even years after the last time he'd ever gone. The paths were still worn well in those woods, by new generations of children and wildlife.

It was dark, but his feet found the path.

He moved along it at a jog for a while, and then slowed.

The way was easy, and it had never changed. These lines of trees, untouched for generations. It was out the backdoor of his house, about three hundred yards to the nearest woodline. Then left. And then you kept going, and after a while, there would be an intersection. Another line of trees meeting at a right angle, and that was the place he needed to find.

He stopped and looked behind him. Shifted his position to find a small hole in the branchwork that he could look out of like a window, out to the rolling fields of cropland, trying to see if he could still see his little house. But there was nothing. Only darkness.

What am I doing?

In the sudden stopping, it was like everything had been chasing him and now that he wasn't running anymore, it managed to close the gap and tackle him. His hands flew up to his head, raked his hair back, pulling the skin of his face tight, pulling his eyelids open wide.

"Shit, shit, shit," he whispered to himself.

Probably there was no one else around to hear him, but when you are in the woods at night there is a sepulchral feel to it that tells you to be respectful, and if nothing else, stealthy.

He bent over slightly, put his hands on his knees. Stared at the forest floor, breathing deep and smelling the pine, the vegetation around him, not that dank summer smell, but a light crispness, a freshness of new growth.

He just had to get to The Bridge.

Would Virgil be there?

Well, it had been implied, at least.

Go, Walt told himself. *Just go.*

He kept moving. Not at a jog anymore. But keeping a good pace. Plowing forward, pushing branches out of the way and wincing when ones he hadn't seen whipped him in the face, or snarled his legs.

The nerves gave him energy he didn't actually have. He started running again, because now it was twofold—now he was thinking about search parties, looking for him, fanning out from the house. But he was also thinking about whether or not Virgil would wait for him at the bridge, and if he waited, how long? If Walt took his time getting there, Virgil might decide to leave him.

He spat out gummy saliva that tasted very faintly of the cigarette he'd had earlier. *Just get to the bridge. Get to the bridge, and you can decide what to do from there.*

So he focused on that. That, and—as much as he could—nothing else.

In the background, his memories, his thoughts. Carolyn. She swirled through it all. She was attached to everything.

Carolyn.

Just get to the bridge.

Time did funny things in his brain. But he knew on some objective level that it had only been about a half an hour since he'd ran out of the back door of his house. And eventually, after a short eternity, he heard the rush of the water through the trees, and felt the ground begin to slope down under his feet.

He suddenly dreaded the prospect of sitting under the bridge, waiting.

Waiting? At a time like this?

Walt was not a patient person by any stretch.

This might be more than his sanity was capable of handling at this time.

Walt picked his way down the embankment. The trees were thinning out now. More hardwoods as he got closer to the river. The sound of it was beginning to fill him up, to surround him like a stifling blanket, and once in his life it might've been soothing but at that moment it was maddening and it hid the world from him so that he couldn't hear anything over the sound of his own breath and heartbeat.

He only went down the embankment as far as he needed to in order to get under the bridge. Then he made his way along a small dirt path that was cut into the slope by years of passing feet, and finally came to the bridge.

He immediately slipped under it. It smelled dank and muddy down there. Like wet concrete and rusting steel. It was even darker under the bridge than in the woods. He sat in a slab of darkness. To either side, the slope created a triangular opening that was slightly lighter than where he was. Down below him, the river rippled in the moonlight, and disappeared into nothingness as it passed under the shadow of the bridge, only to reappear on the other side.

Walter sank into a squat. There on the concrete slab, amongst cigarette butts pilfered from parents, and broken liquor bottles and smashed beer cans that had been purchased with fake IDs, he felt that he was in an abandoned place. A dead place.

It was easy to think that kids didn't come down here anymore. That no one came down here anymore. And it was a cold and lonesome feeling, like a boarded up church or a shopping mall that has gone out of business.

He was sweating from his run. The air was cool. It was supposed to get into the forties that night. He was starting to feel it as it wicked the sweat off his brow, touched the wet shirt at the small of his back, drew gooseflesh from his forearms.

A few cars passed over the bridge. He couldn't hear their engines when they came, but he could hear the *thump-thump* of their tires going over the joints in the bridge. One car would pass and he would look up at the substructure of the bridge that he knew was there, could picture in his mind, but couldn't see in the darkness. And he would listen without breathing for the sound of the tires to slow, or for some sort of signal, for someone to call out to him, but no one did.

Silence.

Another car thumped across.

And then it was gone.

Walter's knees were beginning to ache. Reminding him that he wasn't as spry as he'd been even ten years ago. He muttered a string of obscenities and lowered his butt to the ground. The concrete was cold through his tans.

There had to be a way out of this, right?

Wasn't there?

Somebody he could talk to?

Something he could do?

No, buddy. You fucked it up. You fucked it up good. Because you didn't listen to Pops. You couldn't just keep your head down and do what they told you to do. You had to try to get that extra money. You had to have your secret. Your little personal rebellion. And you didn't even do it smart! You got your money from the resistance!

What were you thinking?

And with Carolyn gone, he couldn't argue with that.

Oh, it was so easy when you were doing it to come up with a justification.

It was only when the consequences came that you realized you were rationalizing it the whole time.

Another car.

He heard the thumps.

Slower than the others that had passed.

Silence for a long moment.

Then a horn blared out into the night and made Walt flinch hard.

He sat there for another few seconds, looking up at the dark things over his head and wondering what the horn was supposed to mean. Was that Virgil? Was he just honking a horn to get him to come topside? Like Walt was his teenage date?

The horn sounded again, insistent. The car-horn equivalent of *Let's-fucking-go!*

Cringing, clenching his jaw, Walt rose up and moved out from under the bridge. Up onto the slope. Above him, he could see headlights on the leaves, making them glow green in the darkness. He kept moving forward. Now he could hear the gentle hush of a small-drive vehicle.

He peered over the top of the bridge abutment.

Dark highway stretching in both directions.

One gray car, sitting in the middle of all that darkness, like a single candle in a dark house.

Walt couldn't see the driver, but the backseat window was rolled down.

Virgil's face, sterner and harder than Walt could ever recall seeing it, stared at him from over the top of the reflective glass. When he called out to Walt, it was surprisingly calm: "Come on, Walter. We need to move quickly."

CHAPTER TEN

Walt sat in the car and there was no hesitation—it rocketed off down the dark backroads before he could even close the door. The sudden forward movement closed it for him.

He sat in the backseat on the passenger's side. The car smelled new. The readouts offered a crystallic, bluish glow over the driver's face and Walt thought that it was the man who had been dressed in the deputy's uniform earlier that day.

The one that had given him a cigarette and asked him why he kept on doing the things that he was doing.

Walt turned to Virgil, sitting directly behind the driver.

Virgil looked straight forward, his left hand perched over the door controls. His index finger stabbed the window button and it scrolled up resolutely against the wind. The sound of the air through the gap made its final pleas and then cut off with a final *shoop*.

Walt wanted to scream at Virgil, to shake him, to tell him, "They took Carolyn! They took Carolyn! Do something!"

Instead, he clasped his hands in his lap.

One iron grip in the other, they writhed and twitched subtly in the darkness like two fighters caught in a deadlock, but Walter's face was stony, his body was still.

Something bad had happened. Something outside of Carolyn's disappearing. Walter could see this in everything that Virgil and his driver did. The way Virgil sat there stiffly. The set of his jaw. His balled fist sitting on his lap. He looked stolid, but then Walt could see the way his eyes jagged around, searching the ever-present darkness for threats.

And the driver, the relaxed man with the cocksure attitude, now cold and silent, gripping the steering wheel with two forceful hands like they were at that very moment, being pursued.

"What happened?" Walter said.

Virgil's jaw flexed, catching the blue lights from the dashboard. "This was a mistake. I told them this was a mistake, but they didn't want to listen."

"Who's 'they'?" Walter asked.

Virgil dodged the question. "We shouldn't have tried to capture a New Breed. For all I know, the CoAx thinks that we're the people that have been kidnapping all the other New Breeds." He shook his head bitterly, then looked at Walter in earnest. "They're coming after us, Walt. They've pulled the big red handle and they have no intention of letting us get away."

"Oh, fuck," Walt almost reached his hand up to clutch his head, like a sudden headache was coming on. But he kept them clamped in his lap. He felt heat rising, spreading like a stain out from his chest, up the back of his neck and prickling across his scalp.

"They took Carolyn," Walt said, shakily, staring at Virgil. "They took her because of this shit."

Virgil didn't respond. He looked right back at Walter. Then opened his mouth. Then shut it. Then looked away with a tiny shake of his head.

"Virgil!" Walter nearly shouted, and out of the corner of his eye saw the driver glance at him and readjust his grip on the steering wheel. "Is that why they took Carolyn?"

Virgil snapped back to Walt, angry now. "What the fuck do you think?"

"Ah, Jesus…" Walter couldn't restrain his hands. Together in a ball, they came up to his face, pressed hard, callused knuckles against his forehead while he clenched his eyes closed and pressed himself back into the seat. "Ah, fuck," he groaned. "I shouldn't have done it. I shouldn't have helped you."

"Hey," Virgil reached across the seat and batted Walt's hands down away from his face. His voice and expression had turned condescending and irritated, the way a tired father might handle an overly-dramatic toddler. "Now's not the time to freak out, Walter. Save that shit for another time when we're not about to get a flight of gunships up the ass."

Walt whirled in his seat. He half-punched, half-shoved Virgil off of him, and suddenly felt so small again, felt ten years old, with big-bad Virgil and Roy hovering over him, telling him to man-up, telling him to quit whining and moaning it was time to come with them.

There is no worse feeling than when someone shrinks you back to your childhood size. It made him want to pummel Virgil's face, but he restrained himself. Just barely.

"Don't tell me not to freak out," he grated. "It's my *wife*, Virgil. I'll goddamned freak out if I want to. Put your hands on me again and we're gonna have problems."

Virgil frowned. "Oh, we're gonna have problems?" He pointed a finger at Walter, very close to his face—not quite touching him, though. My, my, how quickly we regress. "Let me explain something to you, y'knocker. This shit happens. You knew that it could happen. You knew the risks when you got involved. But you wanted the money. And I wanted your help. I promised your brother I'd look after you, and that's what I'm doing."

"Oh, cut it with that shit!" Walt snapped. "You don't do anything that doesn't benefit you."

"No?" Virgil's eyebrows shot up. "And coming down here to pick up your panicky ass benefited me how?"

Walt had no response, except to grind his teeth.

Virgil pointed to Walt's door. "You want out, give me the word, brother. I'll pull over and let you out. I promised Roy I'd take care of you, but I ain't gonna fight you over it."

"I'm not a fucking kid," Walt said, and realized how horribly lame that sounded only after the words had already left his lips.

"Well, then act like a man."

Walt let his breath come out like a hiss of steam through his clenched teeth. *You motherfucker. I should kill you right now. I don't even care anymore. I should throttle you in your own self-important backseat. I should beat you to death right here and now.*

Walter couldn't beat him in a fight. And they both knew it.

But there was something else that Virgil also knew: Walter didn't care.

Virgil had seen Walt fight men that were bigger than him, and he knew that Walt didn't care about whether or not he was knocked out, or lost a few teeth. All that mattered to Walt was opening up that little cauldron of bad temper that he had lurking down inside of him. And if he woke up on his back after taking a hit to the jaw, he'd buy the other guy beer and tell him "good fight."

But until you knocked him out, he wouldn't stop swinging.

And that was the worst type of person to fight.

Because it wasn't victory they wanted.

It was the fight itself.

They both knew this.

So when Walt said, low and serious, "Stop fucking with me, Virgil. I'm not in a good spot right now," Virgil sneered and raised his hands in mock-surrender, but there was a flicker of relief in his eyes, and he did not push Walter any further on that subject.

There was a moment of silence between them, and the spiking temper subsided to a low boil. Still there, just not quite so volatile.

"We're all fucked," Virgil said finally. "It's not just you, Walt." He looked at him, and this time, his eyes were true, and they had softened, just a bit. There was veneer, of course, as always, but behind it, Walt could see true regret. "I'm sorry about Carolyn. I don't know what else to say to you about that. But we're all on the losing end today."

"How do I get her back?" Walt asked, and he heard the child in his voice again.

How do I fix this?

Someone tell me what to do!

Virgil didn't respond. But Walt saw the tiny, subconscious shake of his head.

"Do you want out?" Virgil asked him.

The car seemed unearthly silent.

Virgil didn't look at him. He watched the road. The driver watched the road, too.

It was like no one had spoken. Like the question had been a figment of Walt's imagination.

Virgil nodded ahead of them. "All the ways out are road blocked. They got drones and gunships circling." He shook his head bitterly. "I shoulda figured when they responded like they did. Shoulda known that they knew. Shoulda cut losses and run."

"How did they know?" Walt asked.

Virgil shook that question off. "Answer me now, Walter. Because in five minutes we're gonna be where we're going. And at that point, I need to know if you're walking, or if you're staying." He finally looked at Walt. "If you stay with me, then you're in. You're in, and you can't go back. You have to leave everything behind. We'll have to wipe you. Give you new ID. And at that point, you work for me. Because that's the only way. There are no free rides, buddy. I can't afford to just extract you out of the goodness if my heart. If you want out of the Agrarian District, you're going to have to go with me. That's the path."

"And if I decide that I don't want to work for you?"

Virgil shrugged. "Then we pull the car over, and you can get out. Take your chances with the CoAx." He leaned toward Walt, just slightly, his eyes burningly intense. "I can't promise you Carolyn, Walt. I need you to understand that. I can't tell you that we're going to get her back. But I can tell you that if you stay behind, the implausible becomes the impossible. If you go with me, if you decide to be a part of the resistance...you'll have a chance. A small chance, but—"

Walt shook his head, closed his eyes, and waved a hand at Virgil, like the man was trying to push a spoonful of bitter medicine into his mouth, and Walter wasn't having it. He wasn't ready for that yet. He'd digest truth on his own. He didn't want it crammed down his throat.

He didn't want Virgil telling him how unlikely it was that he'd ever see Carolyn again.

And suddenly, very suddenly, things crystallized for Walt. Things realigned out of the detritus of his life. The paths were not familiar, but at least they were there.

When you're lost in the woods and you find a road, it doesn't matter whether you know what road it is, or where it's taking you. All that matters is that you aren't lost in the woods anymore.

Walter started nodding. Eyes still closed for a moment. Then he opened them. Looked at Virgil. "Okay. You get me out of here. You get me out of the District and I'm your man."

———

In the early years of the CoAx occupation, back when it was more than just the Chinese and the Russians—British, French, Spanish, Israeli, they'd all been there too—there wasn't much going on in the Agrarian Districts. At that time, the Districts had been around for almost a generation, and the newness of them and the ensuing outcries against them had mostly died down to a murmur.

When the resistance sprouted, it came out of the cities. Tight-packed urban areas where the compression of close-quarters spiked everyone's temperatures and that was where the riots began.

From the riots were born quiet backroom meetings. The smarter folks gathering while the angry ones yelled and got beaten back by harried and confused cops and national guardsmen that didn't know whether they were in the right or the wrong, and platoons of foreign troops that didn't care because they were playing an away game.

So the resistance milled about in the confines of the cities.

But then something happened.

When they got serious, when things began to get more organized, the resistance saw that the city was betraying them. Nearly every instance of a resistance cell being captured and sent to DTI had something in common.

They'd been caught because of a citizen reporting "suspicious activity."

Tough lesson for the resistance.

A boon for the Fed and the CoAx.

But eventually, as with anything that exists outside the boundaries of legal society, the resistance had to adapt and overcome, to figure out a new way. And the new way was a great pointing finger, like an age-old placard imploring wild-eyed youth to "Go West, Young Man." Except for it wasn't "West" it was "Into the Agrarian Districts."

Because there were no neighborhoods in the Agrarian Districts. The Agrarian Protection Act had razed the neighborhoods that were there, and forbade the formation of new ones. And without neighborhoods, there were no neighbors. And without neighbors, there was no one to peek out of their shuttered windows and think to themselves, "Well, that doesn't look very legit. Maybe I should call someone..."

And so the resistance fled to the Agrarian Districts, and that was how it had been for a while, for a very long while, as Grandpa Clarence became an old man, and Pops became a man, and Walt followed Roy and Virgil as they became young men.

Oh, yes, the resistance branched out. They perfected being the cautious, underhanded people that they were. And these days, there was very little delineation between the black market and the people that ran the resistance. It all just happened under everyone's noses, with everyone that painted outside of the lines splattering their colors just as fast as they could, while the Fed and the CoAx raced to white wash over them.

But the resistance would always have a place in the Districts. Like it was home. Like they were some wild, vining plant that had gone off in a million different directions. But if you traced the little stems back you'd find a lot of roots in the Agrarian Districts.

And Agrarian District 89, Walter's Home Sweet Home, had been the bitch of the bunch for the CoAx for quite some time.

So it wasn't all that surprising to Walt when they pulled up to a cracked black-top driveway that had been repaired with sealant so many times that it was a complicated cross-hatchery of black-on-black, probably more sealant now than the original black-top.

The house itself was an unkempt box with a gray roof and white siding. The railing was ancient wrought-iron that was beginning to rust now, and the closer they got to the house, slowing to a stop in the sealant-predominant driveway, the more mold and dirt Walt could see clinging to the poly siding. The gutters were filled with leaves, the downspouts hanging askew. The few scraggly landscape bushes were gasping their last breaths, muscled out by big weeds that were choking them to death.

On the small front porch, an older man stared at them suspiciously from a sun-bleached plastic chair that had once been green. He was gray-haired, but his face was hard. His forearms lean and muscled. He wore tans.

The driver pulled them to a stop, then shoved the shifter into park.

He glanced, through the rearview mirror, up at Walt, and then Virgil.

Virgil caught the glance. He worked his jaw—a flash of annoyance, perhaps.

"Walt," Virgil motioned to the driver. "This is Getty. He's one of my guys."

Walt nodded, slightly bewildered at the sudden introduction. "We've talked."

"Right," Virgil said. "Just thought you should know his name." Virgil unlatched his door and pushed it open with a knee. "Come on. Quickly."

They were like mice in hawk territory.

They shuffled out of the car, and though all three of them tried to hide it, Walt noticed that they all did the same thing—they glanced up at the sky, looking for that little hovering speck that might be a drone, watching them. Listening for that low hum that might turn into the roar of a flight of gunships closing on their position.

Virgil had his hands shoved into his pockets. Getty took up behind him, and Walter trailed them, around the car, down a concrete walk, and up to the brick steps of the stoop.

Virgil stopped at the bottom step. He pulled his hands out of his pockets and ventured to put one foot on the first step. He seemed unwilling to push the ornery man on the stoop any further than that.

"Hey, Merko."

The old man—Merko, presumably—looked at Walt. Then he sniffed, and looked out, away from them, over their heads at nothing in particular. "Can I help you gentlemen?"

Virgil cleared his throat, tensely. "I'm supposed to meet Tria here."

"Meh. Heh." The old man rubbed under his nose, wiped snot on his tans. Walt noticed that his right hand was staying very close to his side. There was a weapon there. "I don't know you gentlemen, and I ain't buyin' whatever you think you're sellin'. Hop on, road gear, before I call the cops."

Virgil shifted his weight hastily. Glanced up at the sky again. Then back to Merko. His voice came out as a hiss. "Come on, y'knocker, we ain't got all day. You want to bring the whole shit show down on our heads?"

Merko was unconvinced. "Don't know you. Never met you. Don't know who—"

The front door flew open.

A woman stood there, leaning out. She was tall, and lean to the point of being skeletal. That was really the only impression that Walt got from her in that instant—that she was a skeleton. An angry skeleton. With white hair and cold, hateful eyes.

"It's fine," she snapped at Merko. "Let 'em in."

Merko shrugged, then gestured to Walter without really looking at him. "Don't know who that guy is."

The woman in the doorway glared at Walter and danced on her feet a bit, a fury of impatience. She didn't like being out in the open here anymore than they did. Who wants to dive into water with chum floating all around them?

She thrust a hand out at Walt. "Who's that?"

Virgil glanced at him, and Walt didn't miss the resentment in the look.

Little tagalong, screwing shit up again.

"He's with me," Virgil declared, as though he was doing something noble on Walter's behalf. Then, as an afterthought, he said, "Four-by-four."

The woman in the door rolled her eyes and didn't waste another second hanging out of the door. She threw up a hand, shook her head, and then disappeared inside, her voice trailing after her: "Well, get inside then."

CHAPTER ELEVEN

The interior of the house made no pretenses.

Once you made it past the angry old man named Merko, it didn't even try to hide what it was. There were no pictures on the walls. No decorations. The furniture that was there was compact and collapsible and largely made of plastic—there today, possibly gone tomorrow. There was a sense of the temporary to everything about it. A sense of hastiness.

There was logic to that. To not bothering with disguises. This was not a house for hosting parties. Your friends weren't going to come over for some beers to watch the game. This was a place, owned by a person that didn't exist, and if you were standing in it, you knew damn well what it was because you were there on underhanded business.

Virgil followed the woman into the house, with Getty trailing behind. Walter went in last. Getty sidestepped him and closed the door behind them all with a last suspicious look up into the night sky.

Inside, the windows were covered with dark curtains. They might've been sheets. No light fixtures on the ceilings. Rough openings in the polyboard were visible—openings that fixtures were supposed to cover up, but there was nothing there but bare bulbs, and only a few of those.

The place was dim almost everywhere, and then starkly bright underneath the cold white glow of the bulbs.

The tall, skinny woman swept her way into the main room—what Walter would have guessed was the living room. She stopped there and turned to them. Walter stood behind Virgil for a moment, then didn't like the sensation of that, so he stepped forward and stood beside Virgil.

To their left, there was a gray folding table with three computer units and several monitors dancing around in the air. They were controlled by a man with large, dark eyes, and heavy, dark circles under them. He had a face that would have been sallow if it weren't for his substantial beard.

Walter could see him through the projections of the monitors, could see the intensity and focus of a man who spent all of his time with computers. But the man didn't see him. His eyes flicked back and forth across whatever it was he saw on those monitors, and his hands swiped around, moving this window there, this application here.

The woman snapped her fingers in front of Walter's face. "Earth to you, fuckhead."

Walter looked at her, taken off guard. "What?"

She jabbed a bony finger at his PD. "Take it off."

He looked at it. His fingers went to it and then hesitated.

It wasn't a pleasant sensation to remove something that was biometrically attached. These PDs that the Fed handed out like hotcakes to every fifteen year old upon entrance into high school, they were supposed to be "easily detachable." But people rarely did. They were small and unobtrusive. They were completely water-proof and ridiculously durable.

For most people, they were like wedding bands—you pretty much just left them on and got used to it.

And wasn't that an apt comparison, Walter thought. *Do you, Walter, take the Fed, and all of their propaganda, to be infused into your daily life, to fill your mind with entertainment, to keep you from thinking for yourself, to hold them closely on your body 'til death do you part?*

"Walt," Virgil prompted.

Walt clutched it between his forefinger and thumb and ripped it off. The skin underneath was pale and moisture-wrinkled and vaguely unpleasant smelling, like a creature that had just crawled out of a cave, blinking and hissing at sunlight that it's never seen before.

The woman snatched the PD from Walt and took two steps away from him to hand it to the man sitting at the table with all of the computers and monitors. She thrust it through one of the projections and the man reared back, surprised to be yanked from his digital world by this intrusion.

"Wipe this," the woman commanded. "Quickly."

The man frowned at it, then grabbed it, resolutely. "Ayuh. Sure. Road gear." He snatched up a cord and plugged it into the datajack on Walt's PD. He spoke without looking up. "Hey, Tria, if you were curious, there are no drones in the area. Because I can do things like that, you know. So…you're welcome."

Oh, so she's Tria, Walt thought, and then realized with the sudden flash of someone waking out of an unpleasant daydream that his PD had been taken and was currently in the process of being wiped.

"Hey, whoa," Walt reached out a hand. "That's my shit! That's got my whole life on it!"

Virgil put a hand on his chest to stop him from approaching the man at the computers, who didn't seem terribly concerned with Walter and spared him only the barest of glances while he worked.

"Price of doing business," Tria said, coldly. "Price of freedom."

Tria ignored him again. She looked at Walter. "Don't question me, okay? That will make this all go a lot smoother. Right now, you're on the ragged edge of disaster. I'm the only thing keeping you from a short trip to a long stay in DTI. You want your PD back? Then take it and get the fuck out of here. Otherwise, it's getting wiped."

Virgil still had his hand on Walt's chest. He waved Tria off. "It's fine. He's fine."

Tria looked to Virgil. "Who is this guy anyways?"

"He's an old family friend," Virgil said. He gestured quickly between the two of them. "Tria, meet Walter Baucom. Walt, this is Tria. One of my uncle's lackies." A sneer crept over his lips at this last, quiet statement.

Tria didn't bother to extend her hand to Walter, and Walter hadn't expected her to. She had looked him up and down during the introduction, and he'd returned the favor.

Stick thin woman. Fashionably dressed, but understated. She was an urby, no doubt about that, but unlike most urbies, she was not dressing for attention.

Walter figured that was a byproduct of her shady career.

Tria was already ignoring Walter again, back to glaring at Virgil. "Thanks for the warm intro. But what I really wanted to know was why is he here right now? I was sent to extract you. Not an entourage of yokels."

Virgil removed his staying hand from Walter's chest and stood there, his posture forward-leaning, his jaw jutting, the fingers of both hands rubbing together. Walter knew the body-language well. It wasn't just that Virgil was pissed, it was that he was about to Make A Stand on something.

"Tria, you see a leash on me?" his voice had devolved to a low, grating sound. "You might feel the need to cow to whatever my uncle says, but I don't. If he is pulling me out, then he's pulling us *both* out. Otherwise I'll find my own goddamned way."

Tria was unimpressed. "Good luck with that, Cowboy." She shook her head and turned away from him. "Fed's looking the other way on Eighty-Eighty-Nine. CoAx is on the warpath. Chicoms in particular. Every exit out of this shithole is blocked by a squad of New Breeds and there are flights of gunships taking off from CoAx County every five minutes."

As Tria spoke, Walter's eyes had wandered to the man at the computer. He had placed Walter's PD off to the side and his attention had been drawn away, to the monitors on his right. And whatever he saw on those monitors was making him frown in a way that Walter did not like.

Walter couldn't see what was on the monitor. But he could see a flashing red glow reflecting off the man's pale skin. Something like a warning beacon.

The man at the computer turned fully now, just as Tria was finishing telling Virgil every reason why he wasn't going to get out of the District by himself.

The man at the computer leaned into the monitor, then looked up at Tria.

"Uh…" he said.

Tria was taking a breath to say something else.

Virgil was standing, hands on his hips, eyes looking at the ceiling like a petulant teenager.

"Uh, hey," the man at the computers said. "Tria."

She looked at him. "What?"

"Drones," he said in a strange monotone. "Incoming."

Virgil took a step towards the man. "How close?"

Tria took a bigger step, intercepting Virgil and poking him in the chest with a bony finger. "Check your dick, Cowboy. You're not running shit." She turned to the man at the computers. "Hank, are they coming here, are they armed, and how long do we have?"

The man named Hank frowned, swiped at his eyebrows with a hasty finger, then leaned even closer to the monitor while his fingers flew across the projected controls.

Virgil stepped back away from Tria and spoke quietly to Walter. "We may need to leave."

Virgil turned more and made eye-contact with Getty. He gave the man a little nod, and received one back.

Walter took this in, then returned his focus to Hank.

Tria had moved around the desk now and was looking at the monitors over Hank's shoulder. She jolted up and looked to the man that was still standing at the door, strapped with a battlerifle that there was no way in hell it was legal for him to own. "Get Merko inside," she snapped.

Hank extended a finger and traced it across the monitor. "Two drones. Small munitions. Hard to tell if they're heading here, but they're certainly not heading *away*. We'll know for sure in about three minutes."

Virgil cleared his throat. "Small munitions is still enough to level this house. And in three minutes, we're not gonna have time to get out."

Tria stood up straight and glared at Virgil. "You said you weren't followed."

Virgil was angry in a flash. "I *wasn't* followed, Tria. I'm not just a weekend warrior, I do this shit for a living, unlike you. Don't you think I know when I'm being followed?"

Tria took another glance at the screen and Walter could see she wasn't watching those two incoming drones peel off course to another apparent destination. She was watching them get closer and closer. She shook her head, her eyes slightly wider in her gaunt face. "How'd they know where to find us then?"

"How do they *ever* know where to find us, Tria?" Virgil actually laughed. "It's kind of their fucking job. Now are you going to get us out of here or not? Time's a-wastin'."

The old man Merko came through the front door and slammed it behind him. "What's goin' on?" he demanded.

"Two drones inbound," Tria said.

"For us?"

"Don't know yet."

"Shit."

Virgil started snapping his fingers and stamping his foot to the same rapid beat. "Let's go, Tria. No reason to stick around. You wanna be the leader of this clusterfuck, then make a decision."

Walter watched Virgil's words pass over her face like a violent summer squall.

She's gonna refuse to move, just to screw with Virgil, Walter thought. *I think they hate each other that much.*

"Oh." Hank jabbed a finger at the monitor again. "Flight of gunships. Same bearing. One mike behind the drones." He craned his head to look at Tria from where she was still hovering over him. "You know what that means."

Any sign of anger with Virgil was suddenly stricken from her face. She was moving. "We need to go now."

The words were no sooner out of her mouth than Hank started grabbing the computer modules that surrounded him and shoving them haphazardly into a bag, the components clacking together heedlessly. As he grabbed them, the projected monitors winked out of existence.

Walter realized that the small of his back had begun to sweat. "What are we doing, Virgil?"

Virgil ignored him. "Tria," he called, but she was hauling a big black pack out from a corner and yanking out what looked like three sets of soft armor and two battle rifles. She wasn't listening, and she didn't respond.

"Tria!" Virgil repeated, louder.

She looked up, white hair hanging in her face. "What?"

Virgil spread his hands. "We can't take the cars."

Tria checked the chamber of one of the battlerifles, then twisted and smacked the thing down on the table where Hank had already cleared most of his computer equipment. "We have to."

Virgil's face contorted. "Oh, come on, y'knocker!" he nearly shouted. "Don't be a fucking idiot! We've got less than two minutes and we got five miles to the nearest road. There's no way they won't know it's us! We get in those vehicles they'll send a missile straight up the tailpipe. We gotta run, Tria."

Tria was shaking her head. "We have a roadblock," she was saying, almost like a litany, almost like it was an incantation to ward off evil spirits, and Walter could hear the doubt in her voice, he could see the tremble in her features, those tiny micro-expressions that told him everything he needed to know.

Tria knew damn well if they got in those cars they were dead, but she was mentally stuck on the plan.

"We have a roadblock we can bribe our way through," she continued. "But only until shift change, which is in two hours, which means we can't hike it, we have to drive, it's the only way, it's the only way we can—"

"Fuck that." Virgil spun away from her. "Getty, Walt, let's roll."

Tria stood up, halfway into a set of softarmor that swallowed her small frame. "Virgil! Don't you walk out on this! Your *uncle* is calling you back."

Virgil didn't even turn back. He had his hand around Walter's upper arm and was pushing him for the back of the house, and Getty was close behind. "My uncle's syndicate is on life-support, Tria. I'm not going down with the ship. And unless you want to die or DTI in the next two minutes, I suggest you follow me."

Virgil stopped as they entered a defunct kitchen. There was nothing in it except for an old stovetop that looked nearly a hundred years old. Walter looked back into the living space they'd just come from, and saw Tria yanking her softarmor into place as she stared balefully back at them. Merko was appropriating one of the battlerifles, and Hank was latching his go-bag shut.

Walter looked at Virgil. "What's going on here, Virgil?" He hissed under his breath. "How'd they know where to find us?"

Virgil shook his head. "We don't have time to figure it out." He looked right at Walter. "We're gonna hit those woodlines, Walt. Just like when we were kids, okay? They're gonna come after us, you understand that?"

"Yes."

"We don't stop."

"Okay."

"We keep moving. I can get up with my team when the air clears a bit and find a way out of this place. But right now, we need to get out." And then, quite suddenly, as though he was remembering something he'd forgotten, Virgil raked his fingers back through his short, graying hair and swore loudly. "Un-fucking-believable."

Like his brain had just finally reached out and touched the fear that was already coursing through Walter.

"Virgil," Walter said.

"What?"

"I need a gun."

Virgil looked him up and down, quickly. Then he shook his head. "I don't have one to give you right now, and you wouldn't know what to do with it if you had it. Best thing you can do is stay on my ass and do whatever I say, understand?"

Walter felt his blood rising, a steady warm sensation creeping up his neck.

That feeling of being a kid again, which ran into the reality of his adulthood like a car smacking into a concrete wall. *He still thinks you're a kid. He still thinks you don't know what you're doing. He thinks you're a knocker.*

"Just don't get in the way," Virgil said, as though to rub salt in the wound.

Tria leaned into the defunct kitchen, armored and slung into a battlerifle. "Virgil, don't run. These are your uncle's *orders.*"

Virgil leaned into her and, for the briefest of moments, it seemed to Walter like he was leaning into give her a kiss. But he put his mouth close to her ear and he spoke, just loud enough that Walter could hear his words.

"I know about what you've been doing, Tria. So let's cut the shit. You're not loyal to the man, and neither am I."

She stared at him. Her face moved, just slightly, and then was stony. But in that slight movement, Walter perceived the look of a person who has been caught with their hand in the cookie jar.

Virgil didn't wait for a response. He turned and stalked for the back door. "Let's go," he said. He opened the door and took one glance out into the night sky, and then to the woods that lay just a few yards off the old concrete back patio.

He didn't waste any time. He hit the ground from the back porch, and then started running. Walter hurried to keep up. He could hear Getty's footfalls keeping pace behind him.

The backyard was dark. The woods beyond were a sea of pitch. Walter heard the wet swish of the grass as he ran through it, the smell of the dew, and the spray of it hitting his face as Virgil kicked through the grass just ahead of him.

They hit the woods. Virgil slowed just enough so that they didn't plow into a tree. Now inside the woods, Walter could see just enough of the trees that he could dodge around them.

After maybe fifty yards of running, Virgil came to a sudden stop.

Walter stuttered to a halt, nearly slipping in the forest leaves. "What?" he breathed. "Why are we stopping?"

Virgil dropped to the ground and started pulling leaves and vegetation over himself. "Get down!" he snapped.

Beside Walter, Getty was doing the same thing. Like two animals bedding down for the night, except there was nothing quiet and sleepy about it. It was fast and hectic and panicky.

Walt dropped and mimicked. It was all he could do.

Grab giant armfuls of leaves and scoop them over his legs.

Squirm into it all.

An errant thought about spiders and who-knew what else, crawling through those leaves, but it was peripheral, a not-so-real concern when compared to the monolithic fear they faced.

"Stupid bitch is gonna get herself killed," Virgil was griping as he covered himself.

"Why are we stopping?" Walter repeated.

In the darkness, he could just make out Getty's face, smiling back at him.

Smiling? Really? What the fuck is wrong with this guy?

"Don't wanna be moving when the drones get visual," he said. "They'll scan thermal, but if we were moving it'd make it that much easier. Cover yourself and put your head down."

"Shit," Walter dove further into the leaves and loam.

"Ayuh," Getty mumbled, and his voice was teetering on a chuckle.

"Stay still!" Virgil said from the lump of leaves about a yard to Walter's right. "Don't fucking move."

Both Walter and Getty stopped moving.

The rustling of the leaves quieted.

But there was another noise.

More rustling. But further out.

"Oh, you stupid bitch," Virgil whispered to himself.

Getty made a noise back in his throat. "She better get down."

Walter craned his head up, despite Getty's advice, and he looked through the night-darkened forest and he could see the dark shapes, darker than everything else, moving towards them through the woods.

Tria and her crew got close enough that Walter spied her pale hair in the darkness of the forest, and then Virgil called out in a strangely high-pitched whisper-yell: "Tria! Stop moving!"

Tria, who was in the lead, trotted to a stop about five yards from them. She looked around in the darkness, not seeing them, perhaps expecting them to be standing, and not nestled into the leaves like animals. "Virgil! Where'd you go?"

"Get down!"

Tria lowered herself, slowly.

Her team followed suit.

But only to their knees.

And then a new sound hit Walter's ears, one that was both familiar and strange, and he knew what it was the second that he heard it, but he'd never heard it like this, he'd never been this close. It was a ripping sound, like the air itself was being rent.

And then, far back through the woods in the direction that they'd come from, he watched a small sun being born in two pulses.

Those pulses rumbled through the ground, through his chest, and as the light bloomed, he watched the house that they'd just occupied inflate like a balloon and then *pop* into a million shards and pieces.

Then a *whu-BOOM* smacked him in the face.

His ears buzzed and his sinuses tingled and his eyes watered.

Tria and her group were no longer interested in being on their knees.

They toppled to the dirt almost the second that the shockwave hit them.

Sprawled out on her belly Tria's eyes stretched wide. Her gaunt face lit up with the white light of the explosion, almost like a lightning strike, and then for a flash, it was orange, and then it was gone totally, plunging them into light-dazzled blindness.

In the few seconds to follow, Walter remained plastered to the dirt, balancing on a chest full of air that he'd not bothered to exhale just yet, blinking in the darkness, and listening to small pieces of debris rain down into the forest around them.

They didn't even bother with a strike team, he thought. *They weren't even gonna try to take us to DTI. They just hit the house with two mini bombs.*

What the fuck have you dragged me into, Virgil?

Overhead, the distant whir of a drone passed by. It must've been passing at low altitude. Usually you couldn't hear them.

Then there was another noise, and this one Walter was intimately familiar with. It was the aggressive, choppy sound of rotors, of gunships. The distinct, machine-gun sound of them as they pulled up into a hover.

Walter thrust himself to his knees. "Virgil, they're putting boots on the ground," he said, numbly, and he was glad that his voice sounded so calm, because inside, his stomach felt like it was on fire, or frozen, he couldn't tell which. "They're coming after us."

Tria and her team were already on their feet.

Virgil launched himself out of the leaves and stomped towards. "Tria! What the fuck were you thinking?!"

Tria squared up to him. "I was thinking I didn't want to get a minibomb up my tail pipe."

Virgil stopped in front of her, hands shaking in the air. "You could've given us away!"

Walter couldn't take any more of the two of them. Surely they could put aside their dislike of each other enough to keep themselves alive.

"Virgil! Tria!" Walter strained, his voice somewhere between shouting and trying to be quiet. He jabbed a finger back towards where the house had just been disintegrated. "They're going to fucking come *after us.*"

"No shit, Walt!" Virgil snapped.

But finally, they started moving again.

Walter stood there for a moment more as Virgil stalked passed him, and then Getty, and then Tria, who shouldered him out of her way, and then her crew. And at that point, Walter started moving with them.

He fell in alongside Hank, the computer guy, who was looking back over their shoulders with a shell-shocked expression on his face and mumbling, "I don't fucking believe it," although Walter wasn't sure what about it he couldn't believe.

CHAPTER TWELVE

What time was it?

Walter's hand went to his wrist without thinking, and he felt his finger slide over the soft, hairless skin where his PD used to be. He glanced down at his wrist. In the darkness of the trees, his arm looked naked.

"Stop, stop, stop." It came out a wheeze.

Walter guessed it was from Virgil, but couldn't be sure. Virgil was a few paces ahead, and he'd pulled to a halt and had his hand up, gesturing the others to stop with him. The group compacted from a strung-out line into a tight gaggle in the middle of the woods.

Seven of them. They were all breathing hard at this point. Walter's legs ached, knees and ankles and quads, and he had a stitch in his side. He was glad for the stop, but his animal brain was still pressing for movement—*keep going! Keep going! The danger is still behind you!*

In the cool night air, the seven chestfulls of breath huffing in and out created a thin fog around their group.

Walter bent over slightly and spit gummy saliva into the leaves.

Someone swore and it sounded like Tria.

"How much farther are we running?" That was definitely her, although the exhaustion of the run had taken the edge out of her voice. Maybe she didn't have the energy to be pissed anymore.

Walter straightened, winced at the side cramp, and looked back behind them through the silvery-lit forest, the moon just a half of a pie, hanging bold and blank and watchful above them, like the unblinking eyes of a man on stims.

Somewhere in the distance, just barely audible over the huffing of their breaths, Walter could hear the chatter of gunship rotors. They were back there. Circling around. Scanning through the woods. Looking for them.

They were being hunted, right now.

The CoAx was pulling out the stops.

They weren't messing around.

Someone had poked the wrong thing, had pressed the wrong button, had messed with the wrong person, and now the CoAx had decided they'd had enough of it.

Sickness roiled in Walter's stomach.

Back in those woods, in some far-off field that was just barely visible to him, he saw a searchlight pan through the darkness, turning the black fields to neon green verdancy, and then flashing away just as quickly, like it'd been a hallucination.

"Aigh'," Virgil said, breathlessly.

In the stillness, Walter felt the sweat beginning to accumulate on his arms, cold and greasy. When he looked around to Virgil, he could see beads of it glistening down the sides of his face, and down his nose. They were all tired. All sweating. They had to have run at least three miles, Walter thought. Which was the farthest he'd run in a long, long time.

"Aigh'," Virgil repeated. "We need to figure out where we are. Try to get into contact with someone. Try to figure out what's happening. Does anyone have a clean PD?"

Everyone looked amongst themselves, waiting for someone to volunteer.

No one did.

Whether or not their PDs were listed to their real names or some fake accounts that they'd jacked into, it didn't matter. What mattered was that those PDs were strings, and those strings currently tied them back to the house they'd just run from.

Everyone had deactivated their PDs when they'd known the drones were coming. But if they turned them on again right now, they might as well set up a neon sign.

"Your buddy," Hank said, still doubled over, still trying to recover from his run. The words came out as a cough.

Walter glanced at the computer guy and realized that Hank was looking at him. Then Hank raised a hand and wagged a finger in Walter's direction.

"I wiped his PD when we were at the house. It shouldn't have any location history at all. It'll be blank."

"Will it still get service?" Virgil asked.

"I can put a clone chip in," Hank said, and dropped his go-bag full of computer equipment to the forest floor. He was eager to have it off his shoulders.

"Wait," Tria said, holding up a hand. "Who are you planning on calling?"

Virgil wiped sweat from his eyebrows. "My team. They'll know what's going on. They'll be able to lead us back in. And I just want to know where the hell we are."

"Thought you growers knew these woods by heart," Tria commented.

Virgil sniffed. "Been fifteen years since I been in the woods."

Hank was still squatting over his bag. He looked back and forth between Tria and Virgil. "You want the PD or not?"

Tria said nothing.

Virgil nodded and made a "gimme" gesture with his hands.

"Hold on." Hank dove into his bag and rummaged around in the darkness. He came out with the little square that had so recently been attached to Walter's wrist. He worked a panel open on the back and delicately drew out a small piece of something that glinted metallic in the moonlight. He stowed this item in his bag and produced another one that looked identical. He replaced it. Replaced the panel. Checked his work. Then held out the PD—not to Virgil, but to Walt.

Virgil made to grab the PD, then looked at Hank questioningly.

Hank pushed it towards Walt. "It's still bio-linked to him."

Virgil and Walt looked at each other for a moment. Then Virgil nodded.

Walter took the offered PD. He looked at it. Wasn't quite sure what he was expecting. He supposed there wouldn't be anything different about it. But it *felt* different. Heavier, somehow. He turned the inside of his wrist upwards to the moonlight, saw the pale square of skin where the thing had sat undisturbed for a dozen years. Walter oriented the PD to the patch of whiter-than-white skin and pressed it down.

At first, nothing, and he wondered if it would fall off.

And then a strange sensation, almost a *sucking* as it adhered to him again.

Like a leach, Walter thought to himself. *Like some sort of life-sucking parasite.*

"You sure it's safe?" Virgil asked of Hank.

Hank snorted. "Nothing's safe."

Virgil eyed the man, working his jaw. Then back up to Walter. "We'll do this quick. I have the contact memorized. You'll activate it, then we'll make the call, then we'll deactivate and move to another location. Clear?"

Walter nodded.

Getty intoned: "Clear."

"Hey," Tria said. "How do we know it wasn't one of them that dimed us out?"

Virgil turned his head to her, but without the irritation that had marked their interactions all night long. Walter was surprised to see that this was a legitimate question, and Virgil was treating it that way.

"None of them knew where we were going."

Then Virgil nodded to Walter. "Activate it."

Walter put his thumb against the underside of the little black panel that now clung to his skin. A bead of sweat trickled out from underneath it, cold and slick. He had the very clear feeling in that moment that he was just floating along. He was just floating along, letting everyone else make all these decisions for him. Letting them tell him where he was going to go and what he was going to do. The bewildered grower boy. The young tagalong.

The knocker they all thought he was.

I don't have to do what he says, Walter thought, still staring at the PD. *He wants my PD now. I could use that. I could use that to...to...*
What?

To force Virgil to give him a gun? That wouldn't change anything. Virgil was right—Walt knew his way around the old-fashioned fire-arms that the law allowed them to have, but not a battlerifle. Nothing that they could actually use to defend themselves.

Could he use it to force Virgil to make him false promises about getting Carolyn back?

Wake up! Something screamed at him from the back of his head. *Wake up and smell the coffee, smell the nightmare, smell reality. Get a great big wiff of it, Walt. Taste it. Accept it.*

He watched his thumb, still poised there over the PD, and it had begun to tremble.

"Walter." Virgil's voice.

Walt glanced up.

He felt sick again.

He swallowed, his mouth sweating. "Ayuh. Okay."

He flipped the PD and the monitor sprang into the air, casting them all in a blue glow.

The second it came into being, Walter saw them all flinch.

In the darkness of the woods, this muted light seemed strong enough to summon gunships from twenty miles away. He could almost feel the target locks, zeroing in on him, scanning him, priori-tizing him.

A shudder worked up Walter's back.

The unexplainable feeling that the gazelle gets when it knows it's being watched by something in the tall grass.

Virgil leaned in quickly and swiped and tapped his way through the monitor, pulling up a call screen and entering a contact number that he appeared to know from memory. "Turn it more towards me," he said. "If they see your face, they're not going to answer."

"Hurry up with that thing," Tria whispered, looking skyward. She motioned to the old man of her group. "Merko, scan those skies for me. Let's make sure we're not being watched."

Merko pulled an optic from a pouch on his softarmor, grumbling, "Probably shoulda done that 'fore we activated the PD."

Walter guessed that Merko was probably right.

On the line, there was the muted, intermittent buzz of the waiting tone.

Waiting.

Waiting for a connection.

Virgil scrunched in closer to Walter, trying to make sure that his face was visible to the people on the other end of that line. Maybe they were there, looking at their own monitor, looking at an image of who was calling them and deciding whether or not to answer.

And then, abruptly, the waiting tone vanished.

But it wasn't replaced by anyone that Virgil knew. No sound of connection.

Instead, the call screen went blank, and made a little funny tone, one that Walter knew meant *something's wrong*, and then a passably sympathetic female voice stated into the dark quiet of the woods, "We're sorry, but a network was not detected at this time."

Hank was on his feet in a flash, drawing his fingers rapidly and repeatedly across his neck in a *kill it* motion. "Shut it off! Shut that shit off!"

Walter jerked like he'd been cattle prodded and snapped the PD closed.

The blue light disappeared.

The after-image of the screen danced in darkness.

"What?" Walter breathed. "What happened?"

Hank was already bent back over his bag, swearing to himself as he stuffed things back in place and zipped it up. "Not good. This is *not* good."

Standing beside him, Virgil somehow looked paler than he already had. Walter saw the deep exhaustion suddenly become apparent in his face, and Walter then felt it, like a germ that had somehow passed between them, he felt it seep into his joints, his legs, his feet, his head.

What had the clock on his PD said when he'd opened it?

Sometime after eleven, Walter was sure. Sometime just before midnight.

"They shut the network down," Virgil said, and his voice was toneless, emotionless. And the lack of feeling seemed to make it that much worse to Walter, though he barely knew what Virgil meant by it.

He could tell by the words, and by his expression that the situation had very suddenly changed.

"Is that for real?" Tria questioned. "Does that actually happen?"

"Oh, it happened," Hank said quickly, swinging his pack onto his shoulders again. "And now it's happening here."

Virgil nodded, dazedly. "They're doing it. They're doing it here."

"I don't…" Walter was shaking his head, bewildered. "Someone help me out here."

Virgil looked skyward, with a spark of suspicion in his eyes. "They shut the network down," he repeated. "Which means they don't want anybody in this District calling out, or messaging, or taking pictures or videos. It means they have Eighty-Eighty-Nine on lockdown and they don't want anyone to know what's happening inside." When his eyes came back to Walt's they looked glassy and crazy. "They're purging the District."

"I thought you said that shit wasn't real!" Walter exclaimed.

A flash of annoyance across Virgil's face. "I told you what you wanted to hear."

Merko and his younger counterpart—Walter still hadn't caught his name—exchanged a glance and shifted uncomfortably in their armor. Then Merko stepped forward and touched Tria's arm. "We're not getting out of here tonight. We need to get indoors." He looked at Virgil. "Anyplace you know of that we can get to—"

Merko's outstretched arm, his fingers still lightly touching Tria's, simply separated at the elbow with a sound like someone taking a swipe at dense jungle foliage with a machete.

Walter stared, the image and the sound not yet processed in his brain.

Merko's separated hand hung there against Tria's arm for a millisecond, and then began to fall to the ground. At the same moment, the sound of a heavy, solid impact, like a strong right hook into a heavy bag, and Merko grunted and stumbled sideways.

Behind Merko, the young man with the long hair who Walter still had yet to get a name from, was watching Merko fall with wide eyes and a word half-formed on his lips, maybe a swear, maybe a shout of warning.

And then his face was simply wiped from his head.

And then the woods came alive.

CHAPTER THIRTEEN

Several things in the same instant.

A blur. Each a microcosm. Each separated. And yet all one hurricane of movement.

Merko, hitting the ground, his face changing from shock to pain and then to fear.

Tria dropping to her knees, so fast that her white-gray hair billowed up like it was in water, spread out around her head like a halo. Her hand hooked under the chest piece of Merko's softarmor, and she strained to pull him back upright, and Walter wondered how in the hell she was going to haul a man nearly twice her size.

Help her

Hank was already running. His eyes wide, his mouth a gaping "O" in the center of his face, his arms pumping, his head ducking as a tree flew into splinters just next to him.

All around them, the *thud-d-d-d-d* of suppressed battlerifles.

To Walter's right, Getty was swearing and diving for the ground.

And directly beside him, Virgil was reaching down to his dropleg, ripping the pistol out, his eyes narrowed, his teeth bared like he was moving a great weight.

All in an instant.

"Merko!" Tria yelled.

The instant fractured and everything collided into the mish-mash of reality.

Virgil's pistol was up, and he was stepping *through* Walter, shoving him out of the way, shoving him backward, his pistol firing rapidly, *POP-POP-POP-POP*, back into the woods. Walter tried to backpedal.

He felt himself hit Hank as the man scooted by, yelping like a dog. Walt tried to correct.

Felt his feet slip out from under him.

Fire blooming from the muzzle of Virgil's pistol, strobing his grim face.

Walter hit the ground on his back.

Do something!

"MOVE!" Virgil bellowed out.

A rapid, clacking sound pounded Walter's eardrums. He rolled, kicked up leaves, scrambling for his feet. He could see Tria still trying to haul Merko from the ground while the older man gasped and gaped like a fish with no water.

Beyond them, Getty had one leg sprawled out over the corpse of the no-named-man with the long hair, and the other knee was on the ground, and he had already snatched up the dead man's rifle and was firing it back into the woods.

"Peel!" Getty was shouting as he fired. "Peel! Peel!"

Walter clawed across the forest floor.

"Somebody help me!" Tria screamed.

Walter watched Merko's body jerk. He couldn't tell where the round had gone in, but he watched it pop out of Merko's throat. Tria didn't notice. Was still yelling for help.

Merko's eyes rolled up and fluttered closed.

Do something do something do something!

Virgil appeared and swooped down and grabbed Tria by the collar of her softarmor. He yanked her roughly to her feet like she weighed absolutely nothing and propelled her in the opposite direction.

"Leave him! Move!"

Getty was still firing into the darkness of the woods, the red-orange muzzle flares lighting his face with a mad strobing effect.

Walter flopped onto his belly, right there beside Merko's dead and bleeding form.

Something smacked the dirt with a hard, angry sound just in front of him, spraying debris into his face. He scrabbled desperately behind Merko's body, using it as a sandbag.

"Walter!" Virgil's voice yelled at him. "Walter, get out of there!"

But Walter's brain was stuck.

Do something do something do something

And

I DO NOT HAVE TO FOLLOW YOU!

He didn't recall the moment with any particular clarity when Virgil had told him to not get in the way, but all the same, the way that it had made him feel was suddenly there, and it made him hot and angry in that place, wherever it was, somewhere in his chest, in his gut, in the part of him that you might call his "heart."

I'm not obeying.

I'm going to DO SOMETHING!

Because he hadn't done anything. He had never done *anything*.

He had sat in that pot of boiling water and he had let it cook him into paralysis.

He reached forward across Merko's dead body.

He was face to face with the man, but he didn't see him.

He listened to the bees buzzing over his head.

Bullets.

They were very close.

He kept reaching across the dead man's chest, waiting for that moment when one of those bees would hit his hand, magically separate it from his arm just like it had done to Merko, and he prayed that he would feel what he was reaching for, *please, let me have it…*

"Hey!" it was Getty this time. He had stopped firing, was lurching to his feet, his wide eyes fixated on Walter. "The fuck're you—?"

Walter saw one of his pants legs twitch like an invisible finger had just reached out of nowhere and plucked it like a harpist's chord.

Just *pluck*, and then a little cloud of blood, and the leg went wonky underneath Getty and he staggered.

A battlerifle fired close behind them.

Tria was yelling this time: "Set! Getty! Peel!"

Getty caught himself on a tree.

Something else *whumped* into him.

He arched his back and cried out, then squirmed his way behind the tree.

Somehow, on some instinctive level that Walter was not so very proud of, he knew that Getty was the target, and not him. He knew that the next bullets would be directed there, and not be whistling by so close to the top of his head. So he lurched forward. Onto Merko's body. All sense of propriety gone, there was no purpose for it here, no time to think like that, his crotch was in Merko's dead face, he was crawling over him like he was nothing more than fallen branches and dirt.

Walter seized the dead man's rifle. Ripped it up.

It caught.

The strap the strap the strap

His adrenaline-stupid fingers fumbled about the rifle.

He found the detent. Pressed it. Felt the rifle sway out of the grip of the strap.

Getty yelled: "Hit! I'm hit!"

Walter pushed himself up off of Merko's body. He brought the rifle up, firing blindly. He thought, *You're open now, you're exposed now, they're going to shoot you.*

Then the rifle was bucking violently in his hands and he remembered that he should shoulder it, he should put it against his shoulder, brace it there, just like he would with that old hunting shotgun—the physics weren't any different.

He was up. Up on his feet. Firing. Backpedaling.

The tree with Getty slouched down behind it. One leg bracing him, the other hanging awkwardly out in the open, asking for another bullet, but obviously Getty was having trouble controlling the damaged muscles.

Something split the air very close to Walter's head.

He stopped firing. Turned on his heel. Almost felt his legs go out from under him.

"Hey!" Getty reached for him.

Walter tucked his pilfered battlerifle close to his side, the stock of it under his armpit, and he reached out and snatched Getty's wrist and hauled him up in one smooth, strong motion. He might not be a soldier, he might not know what "peel" meant or how to hit anything with a rifle, but he had strong arms. Strong arms that were used to hauling heavy things. And Getty was nothing but a faulty tractor component that needed to be hauled from Point A to Point B.

He slung Getty's arm over his shoulder in a smooth, hip-tossed movement, and he started pumping his legs. He could feel them hitting hard. He could feel the unsteadiness of the leaves shifting under his feet, but he knew these woods, oh yes he did, and it came back quick, it came back like riding a bike. All it needed was a little spark, a little something to bypass all that adult forgetfulness and access all that childhood knowledge that was hiding in the deep parts of his brain.

Up ahead, he could see the forms of Virgil and Tria, crouched behind a tree.

Tria was still firing. The rounds came out in bursts. The red glare pulsed in the night like a beacon.

Get behind that. Get behind that and you will be safe.

He realized his breath was rattling in his throat again.

Getty was groaning, trying to help by pistoning his one good leg, but the movement was doing more harm than good, working him out of his grasp.

"Stop moving!" Walter yelled hoarsely. "Let me carry you!"

Getty either didn't hear or didn't care. He kept working that one leg.

Walter didn't have the air available to yell again, so he just kept moving.

They were abreast of the tree now.

Walter threw Getty like a sack of seed. The man tumbled into the cover of the tree, just a pace or so behind Virgil and Tria. Walter slid in behind him like a runner going for home base. He came up on his belly, looking at Tria's silhouette, framed in red-muzzle flash.

Virgil was locked on him.

He was furious.

Then Tria ducked back behind the tree.

"Empty!" she screamed, seemed to scream it at her rifle, like it had done something to offend her. Smoke lifted from a vacant, locked-open breach. She had the rifle braced against her side and her other hand scrambled across her softarmor until it found a magazine and yanked it out. "Reloading!" she screamed at the rifle again.

Virgil bent forward to Getty. "Gimme the rifle!"

Getty gave it up without a fight. He was too busy trying to find that tiny little spot behind the tree where he was actually protected. But the tree wasn't thick enough for four people.

Virgil swept the rifle to his shoulder. He pressed his back against the tree. Pressed himself up into a standing position, standing over the three of them. "Y'all get ready to move."

Tria wiggled herself further into cover, yelling and cursing. The magazine was not cooperating. Then she finally got it in the well and it clicked into place. She fumbled about for the bolt-release. Found it. Sent it home. "Okay." She said. "Okay, we're ready."

"Help me with Getty," Walter said.

"Where the hell did Hank go?" she demanded.

A round slapped the side of their tree, sent a spray of splinters into the air.

Virgil twitched. "Shit! Who gives a fuck about Hank? Get ready to move!"

"Help me with Getty!" Walter said again, working his knees under his body, trying to stay small, trying to stay in that tiny little safe area that seemed to be shrinking. His right arm throbbed unpleasantly.

"Ready?" Virgil called. "Get ready!"

"Hold on!" Walter called out.

Tria was barely on her feet, barely had her hands on Getty yet, and they certainly didn't have the man in a position to start carrying him.

"Move!" Virgil wasn't waiting. He leaned out of cover, just enough for the muzzle of his weapon to clear the tree and the hammering started again, although now it wasn't so offensive, now it barely hurt against Walter's ear drums.

They were going numb to the sound. Or deaf.

Walter yelled a curse that he couldn't even hear in his own head.

He hooked his arm under Getty's armpit.

Tria let her rifle fall to her chest again and grabbed Getty with both arms. "Let's gogogogogo!" she urged.

Walter put his back to Virgil and started running again. He got about two paces before he realized that just hauling Getty to the tree in the first place had taxed his legs to the point of failure and now they felt slow and unwieldy.

Not good. Not good. I need to go faster.

I don't wanna get shot.

Don't wanna get shot.

Need to go faster!

Everything was blurry blacks and reds. His vision darkled at the corners. Fear like fireworks in his mind. The thing that lit in your brain like an overloaded circuit and it sparked violently inside of you and the only message your brain received was *run like a motherfucker!*

Somewhere in the run, somewhere in the sludgy thoughts, a clear one came out.

You need to cover Virgil.

CRACK-CRACK-CRACK!

CRACK-CRACK-CRACK!

Virgil was still shooting.

He was still alive.

Still stuck at the tree.

"Stop!" Walter gasped.

Tria was hurting. He could hear the breath coming in and out of her in ragged gulps.

He wasn't any better.

Getty was groaning.

They staggered to a tree.

Too small.

Didn't matter. It was all they had.

Exhaustion and adrenaline clashed in his muscles.

He thrust himself against the tree, because it was the only way he could hold the rifle steady. He took one great big breath of air and belted it out: "Set!" and his abdominal muscles roared with the effort. And then another big breath and: "PEEL!"

Not that he knew what any of that meant.

But monkey see, monkey do.

And he started firing.

Oh God, what if I hit him?

But he could see Virgil running towards him, his mouth wide open, like the big intake port on a gunship, just below the nose, just sucking in as much air as it could. Virgil ran quick. He ran smooth. His body was better trained for combat than Walter's.

Walter's wasn't trained *at all*.

He kept pulling the trigger.

He looked out into the night as he did, hoping to see the muzzle flashes of whoever was shooting at them—*New Breeds, oh my God, they're coming for us*—but he could see nothing.

New Breeds.

Gunships.

Drones.

It was just a matter of time, right? Just a matter of time before…

"Go!" Virgil bolted passed him, reaching out a hand and slapping Walter hard on the shoulder. "Let's go! We broke contact! Move back!"

CHAPTER FOURTEEN

Walter ran through the woods. Through the darkness.

Virgil had taken hold of Getty after a few steps, and he and Walter now hauled him along with them while Tria trailed them, constantly checking behind. But they all knew that there would be nothing to see. If the soldiers were there, they would be shooting at them, and they would not be seen until that happened.

Just ahead, the trees ended abruptly. They'd run into the edge of this strip of forest, and out beyond those trees stood the endless hydroponics lines and tractor rails.

The wide open.

"Shit!" Virgil slowed their pace, looking up and down the line of trees. It was like a cliff, that line of trees.

Hanging between Walter and Virgil, Getty let out a strangled groan.

Tria bumped into Walter's back, then stumbled around to the front. "We gotta keep running. They won't be far behind."

"Where are the gunships?" Virgil said, looking skyward again, huffing hard.

"Who cares where they are?" Tria snapped at him, edging impatiently towards the open ground of the fields beyond the trees. "We can't just sit here!"

Walter found himself nodding. "She's right. Virgil, we need to keep going—"

"Don't tell me what we need to do!" Virgil shouted at both of them. "Neither of you know what the fuck you're talking about! So shut the fuck up!" he looked around hastily. "Where the fuck did Hank go?"

Walter wanted to feel angry, but he just didn't have the oomph in him at that moment. He was too busy sucking down air. Too busy readjusting his grip on Getty so the man wouldn't fall to the ground. Too busy trying to ignore the ache in his arm from clinging to the battlerifle. Because he certainly wasn't going to let *that* fall from his hands either.

"Hey, guys!" a voice hissed out from somewhere in the trees around them.

Tria jerked like she'd been stung and brought her rifle to her shoulder, swinging it in broad, rapid arcs across her field of fire, searching for who had spoken.

A dark shape coalesced out of the rest of the shadows and then emerged into a skein of moonlight that was leaking through the canopy of trees.

Hank's panic-driven, sweat-glistened face stared back at them, wide-eyed, a half smile on his lips that looked incredibly ridiculous sitting there on him, and in that moment, all of the sudden Walter wasn't too tired to get angry.

"Where did *you* go!" Walter snapped at the man. Not even a question. It was an accusation.

Walter's mind went rolling back, taking a break from reality in the span of just a second or two—just the time that Hank stood there with his mouth working for words, blinking in the darkness like a faulty computer trying to perform a command.

As Walter's mind went back, he came up with some pertinent questions, like, *How in the hell were you running when the rest of us were standing there staring at Merko's arm?*

Hank pointed out into the field, his arm bobbing up and down to the rhythm of his rapid breathing. "There's a house out there. I saw the floodlights."

Virgil shook his head violently. "I don't wanna go out in the open."

Tria looked surprised. "I don't hear any gunships."

"There could be drones."

"If there were drones, they're looking at us right now!" she pointed skyward. "You think that canopy is covering all this movement? Not a chance."

"We can't just run through the woods all night," Walter said.

Virgil whipped his head to look at him. "You shut the fuck up!"

If there hadn't been a wounded man hung between them, Walter would've taken the fight right then and there. His chest hitched with mad animal breaths, his blood ran hot like it was filled with molten lead, and he wanted that fight, he didn't care about the consequences, he just wanted to hit Virgil, wanted to take him down a few pegs.

"Listen, motherfucker—"

"Guys!" Getty interrupted.

His voice somehow managed to cool the two of them. Like water on hot coals, turning a fire to charred black.

"We need to get inside, Bossum," Getty said. "I need help. You can't help me if we're runnin'."

Virgil looked at his friend, then bent forward slighty and looked at the man's leg, as though he was, for the first time, coming to grips with the fact that Getty was injured, had taken a bullet to the leg, and was bleeding.

Walter followed his gaze down to the pants leg. From the thigh all the way down to about mid-calf, his light-gray pants were glistening black.

"Come on, Virgil," Tria said. "We need to get in that house."

"We don't know who's in that house," he said, but didn't sound as staunchly opposed as he had moments before staring at his friend's blood.

Tria shook her head. "It doesn't matter who's in that house. Loyalists or supporters, we're the ones with the guns. We're gonna use that house and there's nothing they can do about it. Desperate times, Virgil."

Somewhere in the distance, a gunship growled through the night. That decided him.

Virgil started moving forward. "Okay. Let's go."

———

The house was on the other side of a slight rise in the field. The moon hanging overhead cast the hydroponics lines and tractor rails like veins of mercury exuding up from some rich basin of ore somewhere below the dirt.

The five of them struggled through loose-packed soil that squelched beneath their shoes as though it was just from a hard rain, but it was just all the soil conditioner they'd pumped into the fields. Walter could smell it, a smell like metal and bleach and fertilizer.

Hank took Walter's spot at Getty's side to give him a breather. They stepped over the hydroponics lines easily, but the tractor rails were higher off the ground and they stumbled over them and grunted and breathed heavily as they got Getty over.

Getty tried to stay quiet as his leg banged the side of the rail, but sometimes he would clench his teeth and hiss, sending a fine mist of spit spraying into the air.

Virgil asked hurried questions as they went: "Did it hit the bone?"

"I dunno."

"How bad are you bleeding?"

"I don't know!" Getty was irritated. "Haven't had time to look at it!"

"Aigh'," Virgil was patient with Getty. For the briefest of glimpses, Walter saw the respect the Virgil had for him, and along with that respect, a deep fear of losing him. That fear brushed the corners of Virgil's eyes and mouth, like a filter on a photo, subtly changing the colors.

Watching Virgil in that moment, Walter saw a level of fondness and mutual respect that surpassed anything that Virgil had ever felt for Walter. Virgil had had those feelings for Roy, too. But never Walter. Despite all the time they'd known each other. Despite everything that had happened in the last decade. Despite all of that, Virgil would never have any respect for Walter.

And Walter had to wonder, even in the breathless, terror-drenched moments as they ran through open fields like exposed antelope in lion country, and they heard the far-off rumble of gunships like threatening storms on the horizon, he had to wonder if it really was because

Virgil couldn't see the real Walter, or was it because Walter was truly flawed in ways he himself could not see?

Perhaps Walter was weak.

And maybe Virgil saw that weakness, and disdained it.

"There it is," Tria whispered loudly.

They were at the top of a slope. Walter huffed hard and cast a knowing eye over the wide-open space that was set out before them. It had to be a section of about a hundred acres. The land dipped down from where they were, down to a little swale, and then up again onto another hill, and on the peak of that other hill was the house. It was a small farmhouse, not unlike Walter's.

From where they were, they could not see the highway due to a skein of blocking trees, but they could see the dirt road that led off of it, cutting a narrow swath across the fields straight to the house. It branched once, off in a direction further away from them, and Walter assumed it was probably to another nearby house.

The house was dark, except for a single set of floodlights on the corner of the house overlooking a gravel parking pad where sat a battered brown truck and a small, solarcar that had seen better days.

Walter felt his stomach sinking as he looked at the two vehicles. He wasn't sure why, but after a moment and two more breaths standing there and looking at them, he thought that maybe he had hoped they were third-shifters. Farming was a 24-hour job in the Districts. And if they'd been third-shifters, then Walter and the sweating, blowing, injured group he was with would be able to hole up there without conflict until at least five in the morning.

But that was not the case.

Someone was home.

Probably, everybody was home.

Two vehicles?

Who owns two vehicles?

Families with lots of incomes.

Probably five adults in that house.

He realized that the others were moving out towards the farmhouse. None of them had looked over their shoulder to tell him to come on with them. He started and trotted after them, his tired legs protesting.

He wasn't weak.

He'd simply made choices. He made the choice not to fight. He'd made the choice to have a family instead, and be left alone. And Roy had been a fighter, but look where he had ended up. And Getty was a fighter, and look at him! Was that the price of Virgil's respect?

And why do I care in the first place? It was an indignant scream in his own mind.

I don't care about his respect.

Some people had that power over you. Like being around them drew you back, inexorably, into some previous version of yourself. Maybe a version that you were not fond of. And when you were apart from them next, you looked at yourself with a measure of disgust, as though you'd been drunk and not thinking clearly. Why had you let them drag you back?

Walter shook his head as he jogged after them towards the house.

No more. He needed to start thinking clearly.

His wife had been disappeared. The CoAx had their District shut down. His life was hanging by a thread. A clash of personalities was so low on the totem pole of things to consider, that he almost laughed at himself, but didn't have the wind for it.

"What are we going to do when we get in there?" Tria asked between gulps of air.

"We're gonna hope they're friendly," Virgil said.

"What if they're not?"

"Then they're gonna have problems."

As they got closer and closer to the house, Walter had the increasingly uneasy feeling that all the lights would come on, and out of the house would pour a platoon of New Breeds, and that would be the last thing he saw before a bullet crunched through his skull and obliterated his brain.

It's not a trap, he told himself. *That's ridiculous.*

They shied from the lights on the corner of the house and they moved for the front. A big, oak door, painted white. No screen door.

No windows in it. There was a small porch, a series of brick steps leading up to it. A window looked down at them from the left side of the porch as they approached. It was black and empty. Walter kept staring at it, kept expecting to see a face in it.

"Hank," Virgil whispered. "You hold onto Getty when we get inside, okay?"

"Okay."

"Tria, Walter, we're going to need to clear."

"I don't..." *know how to clear*, but Walter bit himself off with a clack of teeth and just nodded. "Okay. I'm ready."

They hauled Getty as quietly as they could up the steps to the front door.

Walter had his rifle to his shoulder, pointing at the window.

That window.

Was someone watching him from the other side?

Virgil shoved Tria at the door. "I'll breach. You're first through. Okay?"

Tria just nodded, her mouth open, lips tense.

She squared herself to the door, rifle pointing at it as though it wasn't there and she was already aiming for a target just beyond it.

Virgil put his back to the side of the door where the knob was. He nodded to Tria, then gave Walter a cold evaluation that seemed to say, *I wish you were someone else*, and then he reared one foot back and slammed it into the door.

The impact was loud and jarring.

The door rattled in its frame, but didn't open.

Virgil didn't miss a beat, almost as though he had expected it. He pulled his leg high again, knee almost to his chest this time, teeth bared white in the darkness and he hit the door again, and this time it splintered inward and the second it was open, Tria started moving forward.

Somewhere in the house, someone was already screaming.

"Daddy! Daddy!"

Tria went through the door.

Virgil twisted, brought his rifle up. He rolled his shoulder across the jam, then through the door.

Walter's legs moved underneath him, carrying him through the door. He took a glance over his shoulder and saw Hank standing there with Getty draped over his shoulders staring at them with that same expression of wide-eyed and wondering fear that had invaded his face and occupied it ever since the mini bombs disintegrated their safehouse.

"Mommy! Daddy!" A child's voice.

Then just screaming. A high-pitched wail.

Walter moved into chaotic darkness.

A stranger's house.

No lights.

Furniture in places that Walter didn't think it would be.

He saw a living room ahead of him. Wasn't sure where the hell he was supposed to go, so he just kept going straight, his cheek pressed so hard to the stock of the battlerifle that it smarted, but he was barely able to process all of that, it was just a background of pain.

He cleared the entryway. Into the living room.

Tria was cutting left. Virgil was to his right.

The sound of a door slamming open.

Walter spun.

A bedroom door, with a light on.

The silhouette of a figure standing there, and Walter could see the big long gun in his hand, the hunting shotgun, the only weapon people were allowed to own anymore, and it was sad in comparison to the firepower that it faced.

Virgil had already peeled to the left of the open bedroom door.

The stranger whose house this was stood there, barechested, skinny, white legs protruding from the flared bottom of a pair of rumpled boxers. The man's hair was wildly askew on his head, his eyes were wide, his teeth bared like a startled dog. The man said nothing, didn't challenge them, didn't yell. Walter didn't think he could.

Across the house there was still the sound of screaming, but now Tria was also shouting, "Shut up! Shut the fuck up!"

The man in the doorway locked eyes with Walter.

Walter realized, just a bit too late, that he was standing stupidly in the center of the living area, standing there with his shins up against a coffee table, and he just stared back, and he realized that he still had his rifle up, it was still pointing at the man, right at his chest.

"Drop," Walter gasped nonsensically.

Drop your weapon was what he wanted to say, but it didn't come out.

"Drop!" Walter repeated.

Virgil was out of the man's line of sight, and he was edging forward as the man stood there in the doorway, his skinny legs beginning to prance with indecision, and behind him, in the bedroom, Walter saw the flutter of covers and another face, a woman's face.

The man started to bring the shotgun up.

Why? Why are you doing that?

Virgil hit the man from the side. He had his own rifle tucked in tight with one hand, and with his free hand, he stiff-armed the shotgun, slamming it into the wall, and simultaneously buried the muzzle of his battlerifle in the man's neck.

The man jumped back, but found only doorway to meet him.

Virgil pressed him hard into the doorframe. "Don't you fucking move! You drop that fucking weapon! Drop it or I blow your fucking head off!"

The woman in the bedroom started screaming.

Not like the kid was screaming. Not a long, siren-like wail.

The lady was gasping out shouts: "Ah! Ah! Ah!"

Virgil kept his pressure on the man, but Walter saw his head stray just a bit to the side, taking in the bedroom and the woman who was flying across the bed and clammering for something, clammering for one of the dressers…

"Walter!" Virgil shouted. "Get her!"

Walter jumped forward, barked his shins on the coffee table but didn't feel it. He pressed passed Virgil and into the doorway.

As he passed, Virgil kneed the man hard, grunting out, "Drop that thing!" as he did, and a second later, as Walter made it through the door, he heard the man cry out and the shotgun rattle to the floor.

The woman.

The woman.

Get her!

She was at the dresser now.

She wore a shirt that hung down below her hips. Walter wasn't sure if she had anything else on. Just two people, asleep in the middle of the night, and now she was here, in the middle of a nightmare, trying to get to something in the dresser and Walter found himself shaking his head and saying, "Don't don't don't" as the woman ripped open the top dresser drawer.

"Stop!" Walter said, but it came out a plea, rather than a command.

She didn't stop. She was reaching into the drawer.

He couldn't shoot her.

It wasn't words that entered his brain. He didn't consciously think them. It was just a heart-knowledge that was indisputable, didn't need language to articulate itself. Walter launched himself forward and did the next best thing he could come up with, which was to kick the woman hard in the gut and send her careening off the dresser and blessedly away from it.

And then Walter said the most ridiculous thing. And as the words exited his mouth, he realized how ass-backwards they were, standing over this woman with eyes the size of dinner plates, hair tossed into her face, bare legs pushing her backwards against the edge of the bed, her hands uplifted as though to ward off blows.

Walter stood over her, pointing a rifle at her face, and he said, "It's okay, it's okay, ssh, we're the good guys!"

CHAPTER FIFTEEN

The man in the hallway was screaming at them, making wild animal sounds, and Walt heard what sounded like the hardened polymer end of the battlerifle hitting a face, and then the man was silent.

"Shut up!" Virgil shouted. "Just shut up!"

"Frank!" the lady shouted across the bed, scared eyes tracking between the muzzle of Walter's rifle and the man who Virgil had just shut down temporarily. "The kids! My kids!"

"We're not gonna hurt your kids," Walter said earnestly, but he didn't know if she heard him over her own shouting.

Outside of that bedroom, somewhere on the other side of the house, the children were still audible, but gone was the siren wail, and it was replaced by loud crying, and Tria's voice, still telling them to be quiet.

Then the scuffling of feet from somewhere near where Tria was.

A man's voice that Walter didn't recognize shouted: "Who the fuck are you?"

And then Hank yelped out, "Virgil! Help! She needs help!"

Virgil was halfway out of the door by the time Hank called for him. He pointed quickly to the man on the ground that he'd just laid out. "Watch him!"

And then it was just Walter, standing there in a stranger's bedroom, a room that smelled thickly of sleep, of other people's skin, other people's breath, and it was oddly, eerily intimate, and Walter felt like he had perverted this room, he had tainted it by being there, like he had *violated* them…

Walter took a step back from the woman, instinctively putting his back to the corner of the room. The man named Frank was on his bottom, just in the doorway, his back against the wall, holding his face, his nose, which was red and bleeding down in sheets that covered his upper lip.

Two to one, Walter thought.

He gripped the rifle tighter and swung it back and forth between the two of them, the woman and the man, who looked at each other secretively, knowingly, even in their panic, and Walter did not like that look.

"Y'all don't move," Walter said shakily. "You hear me? Listen to me. I swear to God. I will kill you both. I don't...I don't want to hurt anybody, okay? But I will kill you."

He wasn't even convinced of the words that he was saying.

He wondered if they were.

"Don't hurt my kids," the woman said. "Don't you do it."

It was a warning. Not begging. *Demanding*.

"Nobody's gonna hurt your kids," Walter said.

Out beyond the bedroom door, there was a giant crash, a grunting growling sound like two beasts locked in combat, and the children started screaming again. Something shattered. Something cracked. Something broke into pieces. Virgil and Tria and whoever it was they were fighting were all shouting, but Walter couldn't hear a goddamned word anybody was saying.

The woman was crying.

Walter watched her, trying to think of something else to say, something that would make everything just so abundantly clear that everyone would throw up their hands and say, "Oh, well, if you'da told us that sooner..."

His eyes jagged to the right, to the man at the door.

He saw the man's eyes, lingering on the floor just outside the door.

Then they jerked back to Walter, guilty.

What was on the floor?

The shotgun.

Walter started shaking his head. "Don't do it," he said. "Don't, mister. No one needs to get hurt."

Movement out of the corner of his eye.

The woman.

Walter jerked back to her, saw her fingers perilously close to her PD, the little black square on her otherwise bare arms. "No!" he shouted. "Don't touch that!"

Back to the man.

"Sir, I'm telling you not to reach for that shotgun. You do it and... and..."

Peripherally, the woman's hand, getting closer to her PD.

Walter put the rifle on her, indignant now, speaking through his teeth: "Lady! You wanna kill us all? What the hell do you think is gonna happen if you call? Do you have any idea what's going on out there? 'Cause it ain't gonna be the police that show up. It'll be the New Breeds, and they'd just as soon wipe this whole house out as filter through the bad and the good."

Walter switched the rifle back to the man. "Do you know what's going on out there?"

The man was still holding his face. He didn't seem to be planning a go for the shotgun. But Walter's brain was so frazzled in that moment, there was no telling how much of what he was interpreting from their body language was accurate and how much was just wishful thinking.

"We heard the shots," the man said, unsteadily, his voice slightly muffled behind his hand, slightly nasally. "Was that you?"

Walter nodded quickly. "That was us. Okay? That was us. And we are in a world of shit. Not just us. But everyone in Eighty-Eighty-Nine."

"Wha...what's going on?" the woman stammered.

"They're purging the District," Walter said. "They've blocked all the roads out and they've cut off the network." He nodded to her PD. "If you tried to call any number but emergency services you'd get a message telling you the network was down."

"Are you resistance?" the woman asked.

"Beverly!" the man said sharply. "It don't matter who they are, they're not supposed to be here!"

"Listen…" Walter tried.

The man was raising his voice now. "You're putting us all in danger!"

Walter felt the rising tide of his anger getting the best of him. Patience wasn't his strong suit, and his faculties were so worn thin at that precise moment, that even if he'd had a conscious mind to control his anger, it probably wouldn't have worked.

He shook his rifle in the man's direction. "You a loyalist?" he demanded. "That what you are?"

The man flinched away, but didn't answer.

Walter was feeling hot. All that hot lava in his bloodstream again.

"You like the Chicoms and the Russians here?" he shouted at the man, stepped closer to him. "You like the CoAx? You okay with everything they do? Huh, motherfucker? You okay with the fact that they can do whatever the fuck they want? You okay with the fact that they could swoop in here right now and kill everyone in this house and never have to answer for it?" Walter wanted to kick the man, just barely restrained himself. "You think it's okay that they disappeared my wife?"

"Walter!"

The shout obliterated his anger like a wrecking ball through old, moldering brick.

Walter jerked himself back from the brink and blinked rapidly. He looked first at the woman, saw the fear in her eyes, fear of *him*, and he did not like that, it soured in his gut.

Then he looked to his right and he saw Virgil standing there in the doorway. He raised his chin and clenched his lips down to a thin line and met Virgil's judgement with defiance. "What?"

A few seconds passed. The two of them staring at each other.

Then Virgil looked at the woman and the man, and he stepped into the bedroom and he waved his rifle. "Get up," he said, sternly. "Go into the living room. Your children are waiting for you."

The woman got up eagerly. She shuffled her way out of the corner of the bed, struggling a bit and Walter caught himself before he leaned out to offer a hand to her. Maybe it would have been nice, but they were passed nice, weren't they? He hadn't forgotten the anger. It was still down inside. It was there. It would always be there.

The woman edged passed Walter, who refused to make room for her to get by him. She slid across the corner of the bed, flinching away from him like he was a six-foot saw blade whirring away, and whatever piece of her accidentally touched him would immediately get lopped off.

Walter stared at her as she went. The man rose up and followed his wife. He cast a look over his shoulder and caught Walter's eyes for a moment. Walter stared balefully back at him and the man looked away. He and his wife shuffled themselves into the living room like beaten sheep.

Walter shifted his hot gaze to Virgil.

The other man stood there directly across from him, his rifle hanging in his grip.

"What was that about?" Virgil said.

Walter took an aggressive step towards him, closing the distance, entering that portion of airspace that you might call "personal." He stuck his chin out and looked down his nose at Virgil, and the feeling of revolt was uncomfortably addictive.

At this distance, Walter could smell Virgil. He could smell the sweat and the body odor, and the woody, dirty smell from running through the forest and the field, and hiding beneath it, the floundering remnants of Virgil's cologne which seemed so strange and out of place in that moment, like it should have belonged to someone else, not this dirty bastard holding a rifle.

"Who do you think you are, Virgil?" Walter said, barely more than a whisper between them.

Virgil's jaw worked, indignant. "I'm—"

"Listen to me!" Walter spit at him. "You walk around like you can barely support the weight of your own swinging cock, but do you wanna know the truth, Virgil? The truth is that you *rely on me*." Walter shook his head so hard that sweat flung off his nose. "You can pretend all you want that you're doing me a favor, looking out for me because that's what Roy asked you to do before they got him. But you and I both know that you couldn't interrogate your way out of a paper bag. So don't stand there and act like I'm still the tagalong kid. You're not doing me any favors. I don't owe you a goddamned thing."

Virgil's face had gone beet red. His eyes like embers. He opened his mouth to retort, but Tria yelled at them from outside the bedroom.

"Virgil! Can we get some help here?"

Virgil gave Walter one last, hard look, and then turned and stepped quickly out of the bedroom.

Walter took a deep and shaky breath, and he wasn't relieved, didn't feel good. Felt angrier than ever. He stalked out of the room after Virgil and entered the living room.

The living room was a small square of space with an ancient couch and a few chairs that were no better. The chairs were empty, but on the couch was huddled the entirety of a family: The mother and father, a man who seemed too old to be one of their children, and was possibly a brother, and then the two children themselves—a boy and a girl.

A boy and a girl, Walter thought, absently as he looked at them and they looked back at him.

A boy and a girl, because that is what you are allowed to have.

Maybe.

If you're a "match."

What a lucky couple.

Directly behind the couch was where the kitchen and dining room began, all one room, it seemed. The dining table was a small, square thing, and Tria and Hank were pulling Getty laboriously onto the table, Tria madly swinging her hands across the table surface, sweeping off placemats and a cup that had been left there from an earlier dinner.

Walter watched the cup fly off and crash to the floor. He expected it to shatter, but it held and simply gonged thoughtlessly across the floor and rolled into a corner.

Halfway onto the table now, and then being laid down, Getty looked horrible. His entire leg, from the point of the wound and nearly down to his ankle, was soaked. His face had the tired expression of someone that wants to grimace, but doesn't have the energy for it. For all of that, he still looked like he was mentally with it.

Virgil was almost to them when he turned and pointed harshly at Walter where he stood. "You! Watch them!" he pointed to the family. "Nobody moves."

Virgil stalked to the table and did all but throw Hank out of the way. The smaller man staggered back and caught himself before he hit the couch where the family was sitting. He stared back at Getty as they laid the wounded man down on the table and started working.

Hank looked washed out. He gasped for air, and sweat profusely, and he looked shaky and feverish.

Hank backed himself into the living room. He seemed to realize that he was in front of a new audience, and tore his eyes away from Getty to look at the people sitting on the couch. He looked flummoxed, as though he couldn't remember how they got there, or how he had come to be in their house.

He raised both of his hands up, a sign of harmlessness. He didn't have a weapon.

Hadn't Tria given him one? What the hell had he done with it?

"Everyone just stay calm," he said, in a voice that was distinctly un-calm. "We're just…we're not here to hurt anyone, okay?"

Walter looked the family over. He shifted his weight.

He wanted to agree with Hank. He'd said the same words when he'd spoke to the woman in the bedroom. After he had kicked her to get her away from that dresser, and before he had threatened to kill her husband.

On the table Getty thrashed and cried out.

Walter glanced up, saw Virgil holding Getty's shoulders while Tria violently tightened down a tourniquet high on his leg, nearly to his crotch. They mumbled reassuring things to him, and in the living room, Hank mumbled reassuring things to the family, and Walter stood there with a gun in his hands, wondering when they were going to die.

When was the spotlight going to illuminate the windows? When was the sound of rotors going on bear down of the house, and the doors go flying in, and the diversionary grenade come rolling across the floor to leave its crescent-shaped scorch mark?

On the kitchen table, Virgil was hanging over Getty, speaking to the man face to face. "Hey, Buddy, our medkit's super basic, alright? I need to see if it clipped an artery."

"What're you gonna do?" Getty's voice wasn't exactly slurred, but the clarity had gone out of it. He was getting lost in the pain, and for the first time that night Walter looked at the man and realized with some distance, as though he was watching a documentary of the moment and not being a part of it himself, that Getty could die.

Virgil hesitated, then shook his head. "I don't think I should tell you."

"Tell me."

"It's just gonna freak you out."

"It'll freak me out worse if you don't tell me."

"I have to put my fingers in there."

"In the hole?"

"Yes."

"No!"

"I have to."

"Come on, man!"

"I need to see if it hit an artery."

"Fuck!" Getty took a shaky breath. "It's gonna hurt."

"I know."

"It's gonna hurt like a motherfucker."

"I know, Buddy."

"Gimme somethin'."

"I don't have nothin'."

"Gimme somethin' to bite before you do it."

Virgil had already laid his rifle out on the table next to Getty. He grabbed the strap of the rifle, folded it over on itself, and then placed it next to Getty's lips. The man leaned forward and took it into his teeth.

"Okay," Getty said around the mouthful. "Okay. Okay."

Virgil nodded rapidly. "Alright." He looked to Tria. "Gimme those shears."

Tria stood off to the side of the table, watching this unfold with something like morbid fascination. She twitched when Virgil spoke to her and then hesitated, but then caught up with the request. She had a pair of shears attached to her softarmor, along with a small black pouch with a gray cross on the front of it. She ripped both the shears and the pouch from their mounts. She handed the shears to Virgil and opened the pouch and started rifling through the contents.

Virgil set to work cutting a long slit up Getty's pants, all the way from the ankle to where he could shear no further without taking off the tourniquet. The bisected pant leg flopped away, soggy and limp with blood, and underneath, Getty's pale skin was rosy with blood, and it collected the hairs of his legs together in reddish clumps and small rivulets.

Tria removed a gray, metallic package from her small pouch and held it out to Virgil. "HSA," she announced, grimly.

Virgil glanced at it, then nodded. Then he looked at Getty, who was watching him back, waiting for the moment with a shade of terror in his eyes.

"You ready?" Virgil asked him.

Getty let out a small, low whine, but nodded.

Virgil stared at the red hole on his friend's leg.

Then he slipped his fingers in.

Getty's body stiffened on the table, like someone had connected electrodes to him and given him a jolt. But he made no noise. Not yet.

Virgil grimaced and kept probing around in there.

Getty still didn't scream. His right hand balled into a fist and he started pounding the table to a rapid rhythm. His face was turning red, then was past red, nearly purple, the creases of his face turning white with the pressure he was exerting.

"Hang on," Virgil mumbled. "Almost done."

It started in Getty's throat like a groan, like someone lifting a heavy weight and struggling with it, but then it quickly spiraled out of Getty's control and came out, only half-muffled by the rifle strap in his mouth, a painful, ragged howl.

Virgil closed his eyes. Kept his focus.

Tria's hand, still holding the pack of hemostatic agent, was visibly shaking. The metallic packaging caught the light from the fixture over the kitchen table and it flashed in Walter's eyes like a signal. Like someone with a mirror trying to message their desperation.

Getty spit the rifle strap out of his mouth, and his voice came out high-pitched and staccato: "Stop stop stop! Please, Virgil! Fucking stop!"

Virgil withdrew his finger only a second or so after Getty made this request.

His bloody fingers hovered there in the air.

He looked at Getty and nodded with the shade of reassurance on his face. "I don't think it hit the artery. I think it just went straight through."

Tria rattled the HSA at him again. "Here. Take it."

Virgil took the package in his bloody fingers, leaving little red slime trails behind on the metallic packaging. He held it with some consideration. "Getty, I don't know how long until you can see a doctor."

"Okay."

"I can put the HSA in the wound. But it might be in there a while."

"Okay."

"It can get infected."

Getty seemed woozy for a moment. His voice came out strained. "Well, what else were you gonna do? You can't leave the tourniquet on me forever."

Virgil stared at him for a breath or two. "We could...uh...we could cauterize it."

"Aw. Fuck man..." Getty laid his head back. His chest jumped up and down. "Lemme have a cigarette."

Walter blinked. Realized that his eyes had become over-focused, and that the rest of the world around him had started to bleed into unreality, into a hazy, black-and-white nothingness. He looked away from the kitchen table and looked at the family. They all stood there, not looking at Walter, not looking at Hank, not looking at anyone.

They huddled together, the small children in the center, all their arms around each other, like a family in a storm shelter, ducking their heads while a tornado rips their house apart just feet above their heads.

Walter glanced up at Hank.

The man was backed even further away from the kitchen. He was nearly at the living room wall. He looked into the kitchen with a pale face, and open, quivering lips. His left arm was crossed to his body like he had a stomach ache. His right was tucked in there. And Walter could see the movement. He could see the fingers moving deftly.

"What are you doing?" Walter said.

In the kitchen, no one heard him, and they kept hovering over Getty.

Hank jerked. Looked at Walter. "What? I'm not doing shit. Why don't you pay attention to these people."

Walter glanced at the people. Then back to Hank.

Hank was staring at him. His eyes were feverish.

What was that look?

The concept rolled around in Walter's head. It rolled around the outside, and then began to spiral inward, into the center of him, like those old candy machines that his mom would bribe him and Roy with to get them to behave during a trip to the store. The one where she would swipe her PD, and the gumball would come out and roll, roll, roll around, while he and Roy watched in eager anticipation, rolling, rolling, rolling, into the center of a funnel, and then—*plunk!*

The idea rolled, rolled, rolled.

Guilt. That was the expression on his face when he looked at Getty on the table, Walter thought. *And now his expression, his body language, the little twitches in his face, they are screaming "caught red-handed."*

Roll, roll, roll.

Plunk.

Walter's gaze narrowed at Hank. He adjusted his grip on his rifle. "Hank, what happened to your gun?"

CHAPTER SIXTEEN

"Walter," Virgil griped from the kitchen. "What the hell are you doing?"

Walter didn't bother to respond to Virgil. Didn't even bother to look.

His eyes tracked down to Hank's left hand, his arm still pulled across his body, his hand hovering about the PD affixed to his inner left forearm. But it had stopped twitching about. The tendons and muscles of his right hand had stopped their movement. And Hank was staring back at Walter with eyes that both pleaded and threatened all at once.

Walter raised his rifle. "Take your hand away from your PD."

Hank's face seemed to writhe. His skin looked greasy and moist. He slipped a glance at the woman who was his nominal boss. "Tria. Help me out here. This fucker's crazy."

Walter could see out of the corner of his eye that Tria was facing him fully. Her head ducked to Virgil for a bare moment. "What's this asshole doing now?"

Again, Walter ignored them, and focused on Hank. There was no mistaking it now—he was definitely pointing his rifle at the man. Threatening him with it. "Take your hand away from your PD."

Hank jerked his hand away. Stammered, but got no words out.

He stood there with shaking hands half-raised.

Walter advanced a half-step. "Where's your rifle, Hank? What happened to it?"

"I don't know," Hank said. "I lost it."

"How did you lose a rifle?"

"I dropped it."

"Where?"

"In the woods."

"You didn't grab it again?"

"I was running," Hank blustered a bit, seizing upon some modicum of indignance to try and make himself seem right, but his wrongness was a billboard sign so brightly lit on his face that it astounded Walter that the others couldn't see it.

"What were you doing on your PD?" Walter asked, not giving an inch now. He knew the truth. He'd latched on like a fighting dog onto a jugular. He wasn't letting go now. Not with so much at stake. Not with his own life on the line. Not with Carolyn hanging in the wind.

"I wasn't on my PD," Hank said flatly, almost quietly.

Virgil spoke again, but this time his voice was hovering on that balance beam of incredulity and suspicion. "Walter, what are you doing?"

On the kitchen table, Getty let out a low wheezy noise and coughed.

"Let me see your PD," Walter said.

Hank shook his head. "Why would I show you my PD?"

"You lost your rifle because you didn't wanna get shot," Walter suddenly asserted. "They knew where we were because you'd called them in on us. That was why you were ducking for cover when the rest of us were still trying to figure out what was happening. And you didn't have your rifle then, either. You'd ditched it because you wanted them to know you were unarmed. You knew they were coming and you didn't want to get shot."

Hank made blustering noises, but said nothing.

Walter went towards him another step. "You just signal them? Huh?" he could feel the anger in him, very rapid, very sudden, as his mind decided that he was right, yes, he could not be mistaken, Hank was guilty, guilty, guilty and every second he sat there was a second of their lives ticking away.

He jabbed the rifle at Hank. "How much time do we have, Hank?"

Hank tore his eyes from Walter. He seemed to know that what he was peddling was not being purchased. He threw it at Tria, in desperation. "You don't believe this motherfucker, do you? Come on, Tria. It's me. I wouldn't do that. We don't even know this guy. It could be him! It's him! He's the one that's betrayed us..."

Virgil took a step out of the kitchen space and into the living space and Hank jerked at the movement, as though he expected to be hit. But Virgil stood there looking down at the smaller man, and his jaw was working and his fingers were twitching around the sidearm in its holster.

"Hank, quit fucking around," Virgil grated. "Show me your PD. That shit shouldn't even be on. We all shut our shit off. Show me that your shit is off, Hank. Just show me that."

Hank made a sound. A huffing, chuffing sound.

Eyes darting.

Tria.

Virgil.

Walter.

Tria.

The backdoor.

"He's gonna run," Walter blurted suddenly, and no sooner had the words stumbled out of his mouth than Hank jumped like a rabbit scared from the brush and he seized on the backdoor and yanked it open.

Virgil was charging across the living space at him.

He wasn't going to make it there in time.

Hank was halfway out the door.

Walter pulled the trigger.

A flurry of gunshots shook the house.

The children started screaming again.

Both men and the woman shouted in surprise.

Virgil skidded to a halt.

The frame of the backdoor splintered in several places. One foot inside, and one foot outside, Hank's pant legs twitched like a sudden gust of wind had caught them, and his legs went tumbling out from under him like all the bones had gone out of them in an instant.

Everything exploded into chaos.

Virgil was shouting. Tria was shouting. The entire family was screaming. And yet somehow Walter still managed to pick out the individual sound of each brass casing hitting the old and battered hardwood floors of the living room.

In the doorway, his legs folded under him like a broken marionette, Hank hitched in some air, filled his lungs, then started shrieking loudly. One of his legs was jerking and flopping about. The other was locking out like it was in the throes of a vicious cramp.

"He fucking shot me!" Hank's voice split through everything. It had gone up an octave or two.

Walter moved quickly through the living room. There was a feeling in him at that moment, something that he couldn't deny, something that was very dirty, very panicked, very jittery. He'd never caused someone this type of harm before.

Had he really done that?

He grabbed Hank with both hands, the rifle swinging loosely between his knees. He hauled the man backward into the house, grunting, "Shut up, just shut up, you're fine," though the words had almost no conviction to them.

No sooner had he cleared Hank from the doorway than Virgil slammed the door shut again.

"What the fuck?" he yelled into Walter's face.

Walter looked up and met Virgil's eyes, just for a moment. Just for a drawn out moment that wasn't much time at all, but in which many volumes were said.

Tria was at Virgil's back, looking mad to get herself at Walter, but Virgil was stiff-arming her easily into the living room wall, even as he held Walter's gaze. Tria spit and scrabbled like a cat caught in a trap and cursed Walter up and down.

But Virgil knew.

Walter could see it in his face.

He fucking knew.

Walter took Hank and slammed his shoulders back on the floor and put the rifle to his chest.

"How long do we have?" Walter demanded.

Hank mewled noisily, but there was no guile in his eyes anymore. The mask had fallen away. "You fucking shot me!"

Walter shook him. "How long!"

"I don't know!" Hank blurted.

There was a moment of silence.

Just a thin little stretch of time where the admission—so much as it was—was processed by those that had heard it. Tria had stopped scrapping to get past Virgil, and Virgil's shock and attention went away from Walter, and fixed on Hank's sweating, paling face.

Tria was the first to break the silence, only a second or so after it had been born: "You son of a bitch!"

Walter stood up quickly, looked at Virgil, looked at Tria. "We need to get out."

"I need help!" Hank bawled.

"You sonofa-BITCH!" Tria lurched forward and kicked him wildly before Virgil extended a restraining hand and pressed her back. It didn't stop her from screaming at the man on the floor: "Fucking Merko! Fucking Pete! You fucking killed them! You sonofabitch!"

Walter reached and grabbed Virgil, who seemed momentarily lost, and Walter realized that he was disappointed that he—the worthless grower who had never fought in the resistance—seemed to be the only one using his head in that instant.

"Grab Getty! We need to take one of their vehicles and *get out.*"

Walter realized that somewhere in the movement, somewhere in the scuffle, Virgil's eyes had gone to cold marbles, and he'd drawn his pistol. Walter stepped over Hank's body, tried to drag Virgil back towards Getty, but Virgil just shrugged him off and stood over the man on the ground.

Hank looked up at Virgil. Eyes watering. Lips quivering. "Your uncle has my family," he choked out.

Virgil's lips twisted around unpleasantly.

He pointed the pistol at Hank's head.

Hank didn't even seem to notice. He looked right past the muzzle. "Virgil," he said, quietly. "This was Richard. He knows. He knows about both of you. You and Tria and what you've been—"

Virgil shot him in the head.

The body slackened into so much meat.

By now the family had screamed themselves out.

Oddly, at this last, they simply gasped, no more emphatic than if they'd been surprised by a jump scene in a film. The children whimpered a bit. But that was all.

Tria said nothing.

Walter stared at her, his fingers tingling with the sudden terribleness of it all. But somehow—disgustingly—he felt relief. Relief that Hank's death wasn't going to be on his shoulders. It was Virgil that had killed him. Right? Virgil's bullets. Not his.

Tria's eyes were wet. She was shaking her head. "Oh, man. Oh, Jesus…"

"Guys," Walter managed. "We gotta go."

Something shot back and forth in Virgil's brain, Walter could see it in his eyes, and he knew—or maybe just guessed, but it felt like the right guess—that it had something to do with Hank's last words.

This was Richard. He knows.

Who the hell's Richard?

And what does he know?

Questions for other times.

Virgil swung his pistol up and pointed it at the woman on the couch. "Keys," he said without much emotion. He sounded like a man that would exterminate an entire family to find a set of keys. Walter almost believed it himself. But Virgil wasn't capable of that.

Was he?

Any one of us is capable of anything right now.

The man half-stood, waving his hands in a desperate gesture for mercy for his wife. "They're in the kitchen drawer! The top drawer! On the left! Both of the keys. Just take them. Please. Take whatever you need."

The man extended his arms out, hovering them pathetically over his family, as though those arms could stop bullets.

Virgil swung away and holstered. "Tria, you drive. Me and Walter will bring Getty."

Tria moved, but stumbled like she was drunk. She couldn't take her eyes off of Hank's corpse lying on the ground. Lying there emptying the contents of his head onto the ground like a broken pitcher filled with red-wine.

"Tria," Walter said, gently.

Maybe it was the gentleness in his voice.

So out of place.

She snapped up and looked at him.

"Come on," he said.

A flicker of irritation still managed to show itself. Even here and now. Even in this moment. She had a stubborn, prickly soul. Headstrong as a mule.

"Yeah," she said, then moved past him, into the kitchen. She ripped open the drawer. Something from inside, some scrap of paper, went flying, and then she started snatching things out.

The rest of it became background noise. Walter could hear Tria asking something of the family, and he heard one of them respond. But he was looking around now. Looking at the windows.

How long?

How long until the spotlights hit us?

Maybe they wouldn't even use the spotlights. Maybe they'd just hit the building like they had with the safe house where Tria had been holed up. Maybe they didn't care about the family inside. In fact, that was pretty damn likely, wasn't it? They'd already shut down the District. They weren't playing by the rules.

Walter almost laughed at himself.

What a ridiculous thought.

"Walter!"

He turned.

Virgil was at the table with Getty. He'd sat the man up and was getting the wounded man's arms draped over his shoulder. He jerked his head at Walter. "Come on. Help me out."

The man in the living room stared, horrified, at the body on the other side of the couch. He began shaking his head and standing slowly, his arms waving in a *no way* gesture.

"You can't just leave the body…"

"We ain't takin' him with us!" Virgil snapped.

Walter got to them, got his arm under Getty. The man was awake, but breathing hard and looking pale. They hauled him up off the table.

"I got the keys," Tria announced. "Let's *go*."

And they went.

Stumbling out the door. Virgil and Walter both trying to keep an eye behind them at the family, wondering if one of them would go for some secret firearm hidden away in the house. But no one made a move, and then they were gone.

Neither Walter nor Virgil bothered to close the door on the way out.

They hauled Getty to the pickup truck, Tria ahead of them opening doors.

Walter strained to hear the sound of rotors coming, or perhaps the sound of a team moving through the woods, but the woods were too far away and the New Breeds didn't make that much noise.

CHAPTER SEVENTEEN

The pickup truck rocketed down the long gravel road to the main highway.

"Slow down, Tria," Virgil said from the backseat.

Tria had both hands on the wheel, her rifle cradled in her lap, and she was leaning forward over it, like a paranoid driver.

She *was* a paranoid driver. She was checking mirrors. She was fearing exactly what Walter was fearing.

Were the last seconds of their lives ticking down even now?

Tria let off the gas a bit.

Walter felt his heart beating hard. He was stuck now. Stuck in a car. Stuck on the road. Their headlights were a bright burning beacon. This was bad. So bad.

"Where am I going?" Tria said.

"We need to get Getty to a doc," Virgil said.

"We can't take him to the hospital," was Tria's reply.

"I know we can't take him to the hospital."

Tria was reaching the point where the gravel met the highway. She shook the wheel. "Well, where, then?"

"Fuck!" Virgil yelled suddenly. "I don't know! Everything's fucked!"

"Go to Pecan Avenue," Walter said, silencing Virgil.

Tria eyed him in the rearview. "Who's there?"

"A guy I work with," Walter said. "He lives in a house off of Pecan Avenue. He's not exactly resistance, but he ain't no loyalist either. And his wife's one of the SoDro field medics."

"I don't know that guy or his wife," Virgil said.

Walter looked at him. "Well, then come up with someone, Virgil. Tell Tria where we're going if you got a better idea."

Virgil shifted in his seat.

Walter looked down at Getty. He was awake and responsive, but his skin was taking on a waxy sheen.

"Guys," Tria prompted.

"Fine," Virgil said. "Pecan Avenue."

Tria held her hands up as they reached the main highway and she was forced to pull to a stop. "I'm not a grower, guys. I'm not from the District."

"Left," Walter instructed.

She made a quick left. Accelerated. Backed off a bit. Nervously checked her mirrors.

"I want a cigarette," Getty announced with a weak voice that was nonetheless determined. He slapped a pocket on his coat and drew out a pack of them. His hands were a little shaky. Virgil watched him for a few seconds, then helped him get one out, get it into his mouth, and lit it.

Getty took a hitching drag, winced like it was hurting him. He spoke on the exhale and his voice had that muted, cloudy quality as it came through the smoke. "What about the others, Bossum?"

Virgil nodded, glanced up at Walter and Tria. "I'm gonna need to contact the rest of my team. See how they're doing and where they are. If we can hook up with them, we might have a chance of making it out of the District with our asses still attached."

Walter shifted in his seat. The rifle in his arms was beginning to feel uncomfortable and unwieldy, but he still didn't want to put it down. His gaze narrowed a bit at Virgil, then at Tria, though she was looking forward at that moment.

"We need to talk about who we can trust," Walter stated. "Because y'all have some issues, and if it was issues between you, then that's one thing, but it's my life on the line here too." *And Carolyn's*, he thought, but didn't say.

He didn't say it because he didn't want them to tell him that she was gone. He didn't want them to know he was still holding out some forlorn hope. He didn't want them to take that away from him. Not just yet.

"I can't believe Hank," Tria mumbled from the front. But that was all she said.

Virgil looked pensively out the window at the blackness beyond. He said nothing at all.

"What did Hank mean about Richard?" Walter asked, leaning forward a bit as though to put his face into Virgil's line of sight and gain his attention that way. "Who's Richard? Is that your uncle? The guy you work for?"

Virgil didn't answer immediately.

"Yes," Tria said from the front seat. "Richard Honeycutt is Virgil's uncle. And his boss."

"Yours, too," Virgil said quietly.

Walter looked quickly between them. "Still not making sense to me. Your uncle is resistance, isn't he? He's on our side. Hank said that Richard had done all of this. He said that Richard had sold us out. It couldn't be your uncle. Right?"

Walter didn't get an answer.

There was an uncomfortable silence in the car.

Just the sound of the engine at a steady fifty miles per hour, and the blacktop thrumming beneath the tires.

Getty twisted a bit to flick ash on the floorboard, then grimaced painfully and swore.

"Someone?" Walter said, growing irritated. "Anyone?"

"Everything's factioned off," Getty announced, tiredly. He cleared his throat and swiped greasy-looking sweat from his brow with trembling fingers. "You wanna know why a majority of the people in this country can't kick a foreign power out, even though we outnumber them a thousand to one?"

"Because of the New Breeds?" Walter guessed.

Getty shook his head, stuck the cigarette back in his lips. Spoke around it. "No, it's because none of these people in the resistance can agree on the time of day, let alone how to proceed with taking our country back."

"Getty," Virgil said with a warning tone.

Getty's generally-calm eyes flashed angry for once. "Well, y'all ain't speakin' up, so I am. Walt's right. We're in this shit together right now, we're gonna have to find our way out together. He needs to know the truth of how things are. They got the District closed off, Virgil," Getty said, pointedly. "We don't have the luxury of playing games anymore."

Virgil's jaw worked.

"You don't tell him, I will," Getty said quietly.

Virgil kept staring at his friend for a long moment, but then after a few slow, steady breaths, he spoke: "My uncle's policies are shit. He's playing a cautious game at a table-full of cautious players. You remember that, Walt?"

Walter nodded. Playing cautious at the poker table was the best option. Unless you were playing other cautious players. And then you were in for a marathon poker game where no one's pot ever grew or shrunk.

Eventually somebody had to nut up and do something daring.

"The resistance has been in a stalemate for years. Not moving forward, not going back. And my uncle's syndicate..." Virgil shook his head bitterly. "He's more concerned with gathering intel now to increase his cash flow than he is in actually fighting a war and getting the CoAx out of here."

And here, Virgil stopped and exchanged a moment's glance with Tria. The look ended with Tria making a derogatory snort and turning back to stare out the windshield.

"I've been working against him," Tria said, her voice heavy-laden. "You knew, Virgil. So I guess it's no big shock that Richard knew as well. And you were doing it too. Both of us. Shit. Having us together must have looked like a winning opportunity to stabilize his syndicate again."

Walter shifted his gaze between Virgil and Tria. "What were you doing? How were you working against him?"

"He's got a network," Virgil said. "A valuable network, and he's squandering it right now. Doing nothing with it but hording information and leaking it out to the highest bidder. I couldn't abide it anymore. I was—we *both* were—undermining him. Trying to turn his top people against him. Trying to make them support me instead of him. So that I could take control of the network, force him to step down, and actually do something for a change." A sidelong glance at the woman next to him in the front seat. "And Tria was doing the very same thing. I'm assuming because she learned what I was doing and didn't want to work for me if I succeeded."

Tria nodded resentfully. "You got that right."

Walter blinked in the darkness. "Jesus," he said. "You people really *can't* get along." He felt a flash of temper, flaring up like a dying flame that gets a breath of oxygen. "How do you people expect to unite this country against the CoAx when you can't even work with the people on your own damn team?"

Getty smiled a painful-looking smile and let out a phlegmy chuckle. "Haha. Ol' Walt here ain't quite the knocker you make him out to be, huh?"

Virgil gave Getty a harsh look. "Stop talking. Focus on not bleeding."

Walter looked at Virgil. "Who are the Eudys?"

Someone without Walter's talent would have been blind to it.

But Walter saw it clear as day, like turning on an ultraviolet light and seeing the things that you couldn't see with the naked eye. He could see the stillness in the car that the name brought. Like walking into a room and knowing that the sudden awkward silence was because the conversation had been about you.

Everyone in that car knew something about the Eudys.

And they all thought that it was something Walter *should not* know.

Walter felt that little hot ember flare up inside of him again. It never took much to clear off the ashes and give it a little air to start burning again, but this was stoking it with a bellows. This was adding kindling to it.

He jerked irately in his seat. "What is that? Huh?"

Virgil glanced at him. "What is what?"

"What is this?" Walter jabbed his hand at them. "What is this thing that just happened? I ask about the Eudys and everyone gets quiet. What aren't you telling me? I asked you before and you wouldn't tell me then either. Who are these people and why is it that I can't know, huh?" He pointed a finger into Virgil's face. "You *specifically* questioned that Chicom captain about who had been busted out of DTI. You wanted to know. It was important to you. And you weren't happy when he said it was the Eudys. I saw it all over your face." Walter smiled hazardously. "Yeah, Virgil. You forget why you hired me in the first place. How do you think I knew what Hank was up to when the rest of you had your heads up your asses?" He pressed a finger to his temple. "'Cause I see that shit that you don't see, or can't see, or won't see."

Virgil sniffed. "Why don't you calm down."

"Don't tell me to calm down!"

"Heads up," Tria called from the front, her voice tense.

Both of them snapped their heads forward.

On the long, lonely highway, ahead of them, a trail of large headlights were speeding toward them, going the opposite direction. Walter felt the truck slow down just a bit, almost like the vehicle was suddenly cringing, just like every single person in the car.

"What is it?" Getty mumbled, trying to strain up to see.

Virgil pushed him back down. "Guntrucks. Stay down. Look normal."

Walter had just a moment to glance down at himself. The strap of the rifle across his shoulders and chest. The battlerifle itself sitting their plain and obvious in his grip. He shoved it down at the last second.

The convoy roared by, going twice the speed they were going.

One-two-three-four-five of them.

Walter refused to look. Pressed himself back into the seat.

"They're gonna know," Tria said. "They're gonna fucking know."

"Where do you think they were going in the first place?" Virgil ground out.

Walter broke from his paralysis. Turned his head to look out the back glass of the truck.

Red brake lights bloomed in the night, almost all of them at once, and the snake of them compacted in on itself, and then the lead gun-truck jigged right just a bit, just enough to give it room to pull its bulk into a U-turn.

"Comin' after us," he tried to say, but his voice caught.

"Oh shit," Tria mumbled.

Walter coughed, and said it louder. "They're comin' after us!"

"I can see that!" Tria yelled back.

"Then go!" Walter kicked the back of her seat. "There's a farm trail up here on the right. Go fast. It's right after a curve, you can cut off visual."

"What if they got drones on us?"

"Then they got drones! There ain't shit we can do about it now! Go faster!"

Tria stomped on the gas. The truck lurched forward. "I'm going! Don't fucking yell at me!"

"Turn off the lights!" Virgil yelled at her.

She switched them off.

They were in darkness.

Lights coursed across their rearview mirror.

They hit the curve and the lights disappeared.

Walter peered into the darkness. "It's comin' up, it's comin' up, *right there! Right-right-right!*"

The brakes groaned under the load. The tires chirped impatiently. Walter felt the truck list to the left a bit.

Tria yanked the wheel hard to the right. They hit gravel and the forward momentum kept carrying them through it, grinding, crunching, and Walter watched the sides of the forest rush at them.

And then Tria had the truck righted, and she hit the gas again. Virgil hit his head on the front seat. Getty nearly toppled into the floorboards, groaning with effort and then yelping with pain. Walter pressed himself against the door.

"Where are we going?" Tria asked.

"This ain't Pecan Avenue," Virgil griped, righting himself in his seat, only to be undone again by a vicious pothole that made a sound like a mine had exploded under the truck.

"Jesus Christ!" Tria gasped.

"Hit the field," Walter said, pulling himself with significant effort so that he occupied the space between the two front seats. He thrust an arm out across Tria's body pointing to the left. "Cut along those trees right there."

Tria didn't hesitate.

The truck lurched left. It departed gravel and went into soft dirt. The sound of hydroponics lines being ripped apart beneath their chassis was a steady *thump-thump-thump* as the truck pulverized them in its path.

"Do I just keep going?"

"Hold on," Walter blurted, trying to peer through the darkness, trying to magically create some better nightvision for himself through sheer focus.

Tria slowed.

"No, keep going!"

"You said 'hold on'!"

Walter pumped his hand in a forward direction. "Go that way!" Then he turned to Virgil. "Get ready to run. We're gonna have to carry Getty, okay?"

"Where are we?" Virgil looked concerned.

"We're not far from Pecan. There's a cut through the woods. We can be there in a little bit."

Virgil nodded vigorously. "Okay. Ready."

"Tria, bury this shit in the trees."

"What?"

"Pull it hard into the trees and bury it in. Don't let up."

"Ah, shit," she cringed. "Hold on back there!"

She pulled the wheel to the left and the truck bounded obediently out of the field and into the woods. The green branches enveloped them and for a wonderful moment it seemed like nothing was going to obliterate them.

Then something slammed-scraped the side of the truck and a half a second later they rammed into a tree.

Walter flew forward, but his legs in the backseat kept him from flying violently out of the windshield. His hips hit the center console with a vicious jab, and his face hit the dashboard with a dull *crunch*. He felt Getty's body tumble down onto him and a moment later, Getty's voice trying very hard to hold back a scream. And Virgil's voice along with him, alternately cursing up a storm and gently telling Getty that he was going to be okay.

His hips and his guts still aching from the blow, Walter pushed himself up and shoved open the passenger door. It caught on something—some brambles or a small sapling—but he managed to get it open enough that he could tumble his way out. He stood in the dark forest and he listened for the sound of the guntrucks, but all he could hear was the ticking of the engine and something sizzling that sounded like bacon in a pan.

He let the rifle hang loose against his chest and he reached back in to grab Getty.

CHAPTER EIGHTEEN

Why am I the one telling them what to do?

This was the question that kept circling around in Walter's head as they hauled Getty through the woods, the man hanging between Walter and Virgil, limping along and holding onto consciousness with some apparent effort.

Perhaps he was expecting too much from them. It shouldn't be a shock that they didn't know the backwoods of 8089 like Walter did.

Maybe it was a mark in their favor that they were willing to stand down and let him take control in the name of expediency.

But despite his reasoning, he found himself resenting Virgil, and even Tria by proxy. Tria's only defense was that she seemed to be shitty towards everyone. But Virgil had acted as though Walter was a drain, a drag, a leech.

Hadn't even trusted him enough to give him a weapon.

And now, when his ass was to the fire, he was suddenly more willing to respect Walter.

And it made Walter wonder if perhaps he hadn't been deserving of that respect the whole time.

Up ahead of them, Walter could see the twinkle of a light through the trees. He slowed, and Virgil slowed with him, and then Tria, who was a few paces ahead, stopped and looked back at them.

"What is it?" Tria whispered through her heavy breathing.

Walter pointed skyward. "Virgil, you got the scanner?"

Virgil nodded, adjusted his grip on Getty, and fished around for the scanner. He pulled out the monocular. Gave the sky a good look up above them. Then all around. He brought the scanner down and shook his head. "Nothing that I can see."

Walter nodded his head toward the lights beyond the woods. "I think that's Merl's house. You guys stay here. Don't move until I tell you the coast is clear, got it?"

Virgil and Tria both nodded. They accepted it.

"I'll whistle," he said, and turned away from them.

He pushed through the woods, to the edge of it.

The house began to materialize. The light wasn't from the house itself. The light was from the pale glow of the lamp that hung on the power line that fed the house from the street, which was almost a quarter mile away. It cast a hazy, bone-white palor over everything, and a cloud of moths and gnats hovered madly around it, wanting something they would never get.

He stood at the edge of the woods for a few minutes, staring at the house.

He wondered if it really was Merl's house. He had been to Merl's house before. He knew what it looked like. But he'd never looked at it from the woods. Never looked at it like this, in the dark, sleeping and quiet. It felt disorienting and dreamlike.

He also looked all around him. Tried to see if there was anything, maybe even just a sound, that was out of place. He didn't put it past the CoAx or the Fed to know who Walter Baucom was, and who he knew on this stretch of highway. They knew everything. That was their power.

It was just a question of whether they could connect the dots faster than Walter could take advantage of them and bounce to the next.

In the disorienting, cold-sweat stillness of the night, Walter wasn't sure how long he sat there. He felt like it had suddenly been too long, and then felt that maybe he was just impatient and it had only been thirty seconds or so.

He floated out of the woodline. That's what it felt like for a few moments. It took him about five steps to actually start feeling his feet again. He knew that the battlerifle was still strapped to his chest. He considered ditching it, but then thought, *What if there's an ambush?* So he clung to it and tried to shake the exhaustion out of himself.

New Breeds didn't get exhausted.

The could be on their heels right now, tracking them relentlessly. Like machines.

They could be in the woods right now, slitting Virgil and Tria and Getty's throats.

He took a wary glance over his shoulder, back into the woods, but it was just quiet blackness beyond the dimly-gilt shimmer of leaves.

He went to the back door of the house.

He hesitated at the door, feeling a nonsensical feeling of *It's so late and I'm going to knock on his door,* but this was beyond convenience and general manners. This was life and death.

He knocked.

There was silence.

He could almost picture Merl inside, leaning up in bed, frowning, wondering, *Did some asshole really just knock on my door?*

Walter glanced around him again. Then he knocked a second time, louder than the first.

This time there was a noise from inside. A rustle. A grumble. A few curses.

Walter turned his body slightly, looked back towards the woods. Still nothing. Just...nothing. He pictured Virgil and Tria and Getty, lying on the forest floor, throats cut, or perhaps a neat incision at the base of their skull—yes, that would be quieter then all the gurgling...

He shook his head, took a breath and felt his dry mouth.

He needed water.

He heard footsteps from inside.

A light came on.

"The hell is this?" Merl's voice said from inside.

Walter turned to face the door.

Merl peeked out from behind one of the curtains that covered the door's window panes. He stared at Walter for a long moment, his expression in a sort of neutral state, like he wasn't fully awake, and perhaps still believed this to be a weird dream.

He slowly opened the door.

"Merl," Walter said, quietly.

"Walt?" Merl seemed like he still couldn't believe it. He looked down at the rifle that was strapped to Walter's chest. Still just confused. No surprise just yet. He frowned at it. "Why do you have a gun, Walter?"

Walter leaned forward just slightly, looked at his partner earnestly. "Merl, is there anyone in your household that might sympathize with the Fed or CoAx?"

Merl blinked several times, then rubbed the corner of his eye were sleep had crusted. "Fuck no, man."

Walter nodded. "I need help, Merl. I'm in a bad spot. I have a friend that's been shot."

"You have a friend that's been…?" Merl shook his head rapidly. "Take him to a hospital, Walt!"

"We can't *go* to a hospital," Walter said urgently. "Do you even know what's going on out there, Merl?"

Merl's face was slack, but the eyes were starting to show some recognizance. They were starting to pull back the blanket of warm, hazy sleep and the mind was reacquainting itself with the chill of reality.

"They have the District closed off, Merl. No way in, no way out. We're being hunted down. I need Ann to help my friend, Merl. Can she do that? Can you help?"

"Oh, Walter…shit…" Merl whispered, flummoxed.

Then a woman's voice spoke up from behind Merl.

"I can help."

Walter looked past Merl, and Merl turned slightly, surprised.

Ann stood in the entryway, just a pace or two behind her husband. She was wearing a tank-top and a pair of sweat-shorts. Her blonde hair was a frizz of nighttime mess, barely strangled into a ponytail that hung haphazardly off to the side. Her worn, tired face looked at Walter, and her eyes, though bloodshot and weary, were very clear.

"I'll help," she said again. "Bring him in."

———

They brought Getty into the house and pulled him into the kitchen.

Walter was relieved just to see the three of them alive. He'd feared for a moment when he'd whistled back that nothing would respond to him except perhaps a barrage of bullets from a squad of New Breeds in the darkness. But then he'd seen them stumbling along, Tria's small frame struggling to keep up with Virgil, and Virgil plowing thoughtlessly forward, and for a very brief moment he forgot that he had been angry with them.

In the kitchen, Ann hovered her way behind Getty and told them to bring him to the kitchen counter. Breathing and huffing, Tria and Virgil complied. They didn't say anything else. There was no introduction between anybody.

Ann touched Getty on the shoulder and got his eye contact. "Can you sit up straight?" she asked him.

"Yeah," he said. "I can sit up."

"You feel faint?"

"A little."

"If you feel like you're going to faint, let me know."

"Okay."

Ann nodded to Tria and Virgil. "Help him up onto the counter. Let's check out that leg."

Walter stepped in to try and help Tria but she shouldered him out of the way. Her white-blond hair fell into her face as she gave him a irritable sidelong look. But she was gassed. Pride or no pride, she'd given what she had to give physically and she struggled to help Getty up onto the countertop.

Even Virgil's big, well-muscled bulk was slouched, sweat-stained, chest heaving.

Ann tapped Virgil's shoulder. "Watch him," she said, indicating Getty, and then she was gone in a flash.

Merl was standing there, out of the way of all the movement, frowning at Virgil. After a moment or two of silence, Virgil realized he was being stared at, and he looked up at Merl with a questioning glance.

"Aren't you the sheriff?" Merl asked. "Sheriff Honeycutt?"

Virgil shifted his weight, sucked a few breaths as he prepared his answer. "Probably not anymore."

Merl ran a hand over his head, through his short, gray-brown hair. For the first time shock was showing itself on his features. His eyes were widening a bit at this stark new reality. He made a gentle, bewildered raspberry noise. Then his eyes found Walter. And then they hardened a bit.

"Can I speak with you?" he said, stiffly.

Walter didn't really say yes or no.

Merl crossed the kitchen and caught Walter by the arm and half-dragged, half-guided him out of the kitchen and back into the entryway of the back door.

The back entryway was also the laundry room and mudroom. The smell of clean laundry battled with the swampy smell of muddy workboots.

"What the *fuck*, man?" Merl said, shakily.

Walter stood there, then slouched himself against the wall.

Behind Merl, he saw Ann trot back into the kitchen, this time carrying a big red case with a white cross on the side of it. Her field medic kit. Hopefully it would be enough to fix the wound.

What then?

Where did they go from here?

"Hey!" Merl snapped his fingers in front of Walter's face. "Are you even listening?"

Walter blinked a few times. He looked around like he wasn't sure where he was. "What time is it?"

"It's two in the morning, jackass!" Merl hissed. "And you drag me into this shit? I got kids. They're sleeping in the other room…"

A small voice from further in the house. "Mommy? Daddy?"

Merl grabbed his head like it ached. "Oh, Jesus Christ…"

The small voice was joined by another one, and they crowed and cooed like little chicks in a nest wanting the worm, two voices, and Walter could tell that one was a boy and one was a girl, but then again he knew Merl's kids, so it wasn't hard to pick their voices out.

"Mommy? Daddy?"

"What's going on?"

"Is everything okay?"

Merl shook his hands furiously in the air, a silent fit of rage, and then he stepped out of the mudroom. From the kitchen, Walter heard Ann raising her voice: "Merl, I'm a little tied up here, you mind taking care of that?"

Merl ignored the spouse request—he was already kneeling down to address his children. "Hey, guys," he said gently, kindly. "It's nothing. Everything's okay. Mommy and Daddy are just having some friends over, okay?"

Then an adult voice, thick with sleep and bluster. "What the hell is all this?"

That would be Merl's brother, George.

Walter sank back against the wall again. He blinked. It seemed that his eyes stayed closed for longer than he'd intended.

He heard Merl's voice: "Watch your mouth in front of the kids."

"What's going on? Who are these people?"

The children whimpered, disturbed by the concern in their uncle's voice.

"George," Merl said sternly. "Why don't you make yourself useful and get these kids back into bed. Everything is fine. Thanks. It's all just fine and dandy. Hey, you kids go with Uncle George, okay? He's gonna tuck you in nice and tight. We're just having a little party out here, okay? Everything's just fine. Okay. I love you. Go to bed."

He came back around the corner and into the mudroom. He was very awake now. He put a finger up into Walter's face. "Tell me what's going on here," he hissed.

181

"They have the District closed off," Walter said again, but that wasn't what he was thinking. That wasn't the thing that was burning a hole in his brain like molten metal going through thin plastic.

Merl stared at him, like he knew that there was something else Walter wasn't saying.

Walter stared back, and he watched Merl's face warp into a watery mirage.

He felt his chest hitch. His throat tighten.

"They took Carolyn," he choked out suddenly. "They disappeared her and I don't know why."

"Oh, shit," Merl mumbled.

"I don't know why."

"Oh, shit, man."

Merl suddenly grabbed him. Pulled him in. Hugged him.

It was ridiculous. Walter didn't need it. He didn't need any of this. But then he felt himself falling apart.

He threw his arms around Merl. Buried his face in the other man's shoulder, smelled his night-sweat, his sleep, like a father figure, like a friend. He gasped for air, but it wouldn't come. Like someone had punched him in the gut. He tried to speak, but he couldn't. All that calm, all that logic, all that *Let's figure out the next step* evaporated like dry ice in a flame.

When his breath did finally come to him, he let out a horrible noise into Merl's shoulder, but it was quiet. In the kitchen he could still hear Ann talking fluidly with Getty, as though this was a normal thing, to treat a gunshot wound in the middle of the night. Just as normal as anything else.

Walter pulled back from Merl, suddenly ashamed of himself.

"I don't know what I'm doing," he said, not thinking much, just opening his mouth and the words seemed to already be there.

"I don't understand," Merl said, shaking his head, still holding Walter by the shoulders. "They took Carolyn. But what happened? What happened to you? Who is that guy and why is he shot in the leg?"

"I think it was because of me that they took Carolyn," Walter said, his face wet and red, but otherwise suddenly slack of expression. "I'd worked with them. The people in there." A glance at Merl. "With the resistance."

"Holy Jesus, Walt!" Merl hissed. He released Walter and rubbed his face with both hands. "I mean…shit…I don't know what I mean. I can't fault the resistance. But shit. I didn't know. I had no idea."

"That's kind of the point," Walter said bitterly. "But *somebody* knew."

"And they took Carolyn and left you?"

"They took her before I got home. She was gone when I got there. I don't know."

"How do you know she got disappeared?" Merl asked.

Walter looked at him like it was the most obvious question in the world. "There were ram marks in the door and the scorch mark from a diversionary grenade in my living room. That don't sound like a burglary to me."

Merl only nodded to concur, his face newly troubled.

Walter told him how he'd fled the house. How he'd met up with Virgil. And then most of what had happened. He didn't tell it all. He left out the unnecessary parts. He left out the parts where he watched a man's hand separate from his body like an invisible knife had divided it. He left out the part where he'd kicked an innocent woman in her own house because he was afraid of what she was reaching for in a dresser drawer. He left out the part where he'd shot the man named Hank to keep him from running away. He left out the part where he watched Virgil execute him.

There were lots of parts that weren't really worth talking about.

But the big points.

The big picture.

He relayed that.

"We crashed the car in the woods a mile from here to get away from a convoy of guntrucks that had turned around on us," Walter said. "They had to've gotten our description"—*from the family we home-invaded*—"They were coming after us."

Merl looked incredulous. "And you decided it would be a great fuckin' idea to lead them here? Jesus H. Christ! Walter! My family is in here!" As he spoke, his own words riled him. He drew a fist back, clenched it hard, his lips tightening. "I should beat you out of my damn house."

Walter just shook his head. "We lost them."

"What about drones?"

"We scanned for them."

"Shit."

"I know."

"I can't believe this."

"I know." Walter took a swipe at his eyes, felt shame anew. Not for *feeling* it. But for *showing* it. "If I had anywhere else to go, I would have gone there, Merl. And if you need to kick us out after Getty's leg is patched, I understand. But this isn't just me. This isn't just an *us* issue. They have the whole District on lockdown. They're going to find us. And not just us. They're going to find *everyone*. They're going to exterminate every bit of resistance out of this place, and don't think it's gonna stop there." Walter shook his head bitterly. "It won't stop there. We can't call out. We can't message out. We can't even take a video of what they do to us in here. We are completely at their mercy. And they have none. And they would've come for you and your family whether I'd come here tonight or not. Because we drive in the same tractor. Because they don't need any more reason than that."

Merl put his hands on his hips and looked at nothing in particular. The wall.

The floor.

"We shoulda said 'no'," he mumbled, almost dreamily.

Walter almost laughed at him. Almost, but there wasn't enough humor in it. "Yeah, well. We shoulda thought about that a long time ago. That ship has sailed. We can't say 'no' anymore. We're not citizens anymore. We're *subjects*. And subjects can't say 'no.' All subjects can say is 'so the wind blows.'"

Abruptly, Walter felt like putting his fist through the wall, but he thought that he'd done Merl enough damage for one night, best not to damage his property as well. But he felt every year, he felt every injustice, he felt every goddamned single thing that they'd slowly, so

184

slowly and sneakily, taken away from him, and not just him, but his family before him. How they'd taken it all away like a masterful magician, and no one had any idea where it all went.

All those years of thinking that he could get by.

All those years of thinking, "If I just play by the rules, they won't bother me."

So the wind blows.

And the seasons go.

And the seeds grow.

But they should have fought back.

He should have fought back.

He should have done it a long time ago and not waited until every possibility to defend himself was stripped away. His *father* should have fought back. His *grandfather* should have fought back, rather than just speaking out, because words are words and amount to nothing but their own physical weight.

They all should have fought back when they had the means to do so.

But it was too late now. They'd pissed that chance away on the hope and prayer that perhaps, maybe just maybe, unlike every other government in the history of governments, that theirs would be benevolent.

What a crock of shit.

And he understood. Walter understood in that one instant of fury, why it was that for all these years Virgil had looked down on him.

Walter had dug himself into a hole of complacency, and Virgil had watched him do it.

Virgil had known the truth long before Walter had wanted to admit it to himself. But Walter had been afraid of the truth. Afraid of what he'd lose. Afraid for the safety of his family.

But now his family was gone anyways.

Virgil had been right all along.

They should have fought back.

More of them.

Everyone.

Back in the days when they were still *citizens.*

Back in the days before they became *subjects.*

Walter shook his head, wordlessly, and felt every inch of him the fool that he knew he was.

And what now? To say "It's too late anyhow," and then raise up his hands in defeat?

No. Not now. Not after they'd taken everything. Now there was no reason *not* to fight. Now there was no reason *not* to die.

In his panic he had put his friend's family in the line of fire. He'd been a coward.

You've been a coward all your life, he roared at himself inwardly.

For all the fist-fights and all the anger that made him feel like he was an animal not to be messed with, now he came to find out his true place in the order of things. Except that it did not sit well with him.

He'd grown mentally fat on the comfort of society.

But that did not define him.

He would define himself.

"Virgil!" he suddenly barked.

Merl jerked.

Walter moved around him. Out of the entryway and into the kitchen.

Virgil and Tria were looking at him. He realized that he'd shouted probably louder than he'd intended to. But one cannot simply swallow an explosion. Sometimes it needs out. Sometimes it simply has to release. Sometimes you can damage yourself trying to keep it in.

Tria was holding Getty's right hand. Virgil was holding his left.

Ann was between them, putting staples into Getty's red-stained, red-flushed leg.

Getty himself was sitting with locked jaw and bared teeth, watching it happen. There was a gray box strapped to his upper left arm, and a set of clear tubes ran down from it and into a catheter on the interior of his elbow. Probably the standard medley that the SoDro field medics pumped into every knocker who got a limb caught up in some machinery: pain meds, blood boosters, and stimulants.

Club-clip went the staple gun, violent in the silence.

Getty let out a strange noise, but didn't take his eyes away from the process.

Finished with that staple, Ann looked over her shoulder at Walter. "What?" Virgil said.

Walter cleared his throat to get the fire out of him. Composed himself marginally. "We need to talk."

CHAPTER NINETEEN

Virgil met him and they sidestepped away from the group and into the living area. Walter had his eye on Getty, judging their progress, but then he looked up at Virgil, and Virgil was looking at him, not with the great contempt he had expected but with a stern sort of focus.

"What's wrong?" Virgil asked.

"We can't stay here," Walter said. "We're putting Merl's family in danger."

Virgil glanced around him. Then he nodded without speaking.

They were on a ticking clock. It was just a matter of time before the CoAx came for them here. Before they started indiscriminately kicking in every door within a five mile radius of where they'd ditched the stolen truck.

"How close is Getty to being done?" Walter asked.

Virgil rolled his shoulders like he was working a kink out. "She needs to staple the back side. Finish his IV. Then he'll be mostly okay. Still can't move good, though." He looked at Walter with genuine worry on his face. "How are we getting out of here? We gonna borrow their car?"

"Where are your guys? Your team? The snatchers?"

"Various places," he said, enigmatically.

"They don't have a rendezvous point or anything?"

Virgil's tongue worked against his teeth, as though deciding what to say and what not to say.

"Christ, Virgil!" Walter flung his arms out, frustration spooling up. He kept his voice lowered, but it was all intense and grating. "This isn't the time. You held back before because I wasn't a part of this shit.

But I'm a part of it now, okay? I'm in it. I'm with it. Stop holding back."

It wasn't a challenge. It wasn't conflict. Not like before. Not like it would have been only hours ago. Maybe it was the fear. Maybe it was the exhaustion. Perhaps a bit of both. But if Walter had said those exact words eight hours ago, Virgil would have stared down his nose and not said a goddamned thing.

Now, he stared at Walter for a long, undecipherable minute, and then nodded once.

"We have a safehouse in the Town Center," he said. "They should've gone there when shit hit the fan, but it's just a rally point. There's no telling whether they're still there or not."

"Can they help us get out of the District?"

Virgil bobbled his head—yes and no. "That's the purpose of the rally point. To meet up and find a way out. But I can't promise you that they've found a way out. I can't promise you that we'll discover one at all."

"Nobody can promise shit right now," Walter said. "Are our chances better with them or without them? Loyalties and friendships aside. Answer that question."

Virgil considered it, and to his credit, he did it earnestly. Then he nodded. "With them. We've got equipment to fight back. Even with the comms blackout, we can worm our way in to the network, figure out a weak point, try to exploit it. They'll be working on that. If they haven't already gone for it."

"How long are they supposed to wait for you?" Walter asked. "They are supposed to wait for you, right?"

Virgil didn't even glance at the clock. He already knew. "We've already passed that window. The noose closes fast. We know that. I instructed them to only wait four hours if things got hot."

"They're definitely hot."

Tria appeared at their side. Her thin face was thinner. Like the hours had bled her. "What's going on?" she asked.

"We're going to try to get to Virgil's team," Walter said. "In the Town Center. You got any issues with that?"

He half expected her to argue just because she disliked Virgil. But she nodded shakily. "As long as they got a way out of this shit storm, I'm in."

"Maybe, maybe not," Virgil said. "But the chances are better than by ourselves."

"How are we getting there?" Walter threw the question out.

"Can't walk," Tria said. "Not with Getty's leg like that."

Walter agreed. "We're at least five miles from the Town Center. It'd take us the rest of the night if we were carrying him along with us."

"No, we need to get there sooner rather than later," Virgil said. "Our only chance is to catch them before they find a weak point and exfil this place. Otherwise we're back to square one."

"How sure are you that they're going to find this weak point?" Walter raised his eyebrows at Virgil.

Virgil sniffed. "They're snatchers. It's their job."

"So...drive," Tria said.

And then they were all silent.

Walter shook his head slowly. "I can't take Merl's car. On top of everything else."

"Oh, you're gonna take my damn car."

Walter turned and looked behind him.

Merl was standing there, arms still crossed over his chest. In his rumpled shirt and boxers, he looked out of place in this gathering of sweaty, dirty, exhausted individuals with rifles and softarmor strapped to their bodies.

These unfortunate revolutionaries. Fugitives. Hunted animals.

"Merl..." Walter began, but didn't finish. He didn't finish because he wanted the car. He just didn't want to accept it from Merl.

Merl shook his head, waved off any further words. "It's not a charity act and I'monna kill you if you get that shit shot up, I swear to God. But you're doin' more harm than good sittin' in my house. Not that I don't love you like a brother, but you need to get the hell out of here, and soon. And if that means my car, then take it."

"How you gonna get to work?"

190

"Work?" Merl scoffed. "I don't think there's gonna be work tomorrow. But if there's fields to be planted tomorrow morning, I'll report that my car got swiped by a band of idiot revolutionaries and have SoDro send the van around for me. I'll be fine." He smiled. Then stopped smiling. "But seriously, you guys should leave."

"How you feelin', Buddy?" Virgil was in the driver's seat of Merl's old pickup truck.

Getty was propped up in the back, just behind his friend. He looked clearer now, but still not well. Drawn. Expended. Like something disposable that had already been used up and left on the side of the road.

"I'm better," Getty mumbled. "Pain meds and stims are fighting it out in my head right now. Okay if I smoke?"

Neither Virgil nor Tria cared.

Getty got a cigarette into his mouth and lit it. He enjoyed a big draw and exhale, then looked across at Walter, who was in the back with him. He offered Walter the pack. Walter took one and Getty lit it for him.

The four of them drove along tensely, off of Pecan Avenue, which harbored only two other residences, and onto the main highway that would take them straight into the Town Center.

Although the Agrarian Districts were rural and relatively unpopulous, farming had become a twenty-four-hour business. Plantings didn't stop. Pumping the chemicals along the hydroponics lines didn't stop. Harvesting didn't stop. What could be done in the day could largely be done at night. And so it never stopped, a ceaseless machine.

Even at this early, dark hour, there should have been other cars on the road. SoDro vans taking workers back to their residences at points across the District. Those that owned their own cars getting off of work, or racing to check into some odd-hour shift, or possibly to try and put in some overtime before their actual shift started.

But the roads were empty.

Merl's words held a certain weight now in Walter's mind: *I don't think there's going to be work tomorrow.*

Off to their left, he watched three gunships, far out over the dark countryside. They didn't run with lights when they flew over the district, and their metal hides were black on the black sky, but each of the three was burning their spotlights. Searching for something.

Me? Us? Walter wondered. *Or some other element of resistance that they've managed to rout out?*

There had to be others. Others besides Virgil's snatchers, and Tria's crew, and Richard Honeycutt's syndicate.

It wasn't so long ago that the Chicom commandant had called these Districts "dens of rebellion." Or had it been? Yes, it had been nearly a decade. My, how time flies. Walter wondered whether it was even the same commandant these days, or if he'd been replaced by another?

I wonder what my great, great grandfather would have said about that question? I wonder what ol' Walter Baucom The Original would have thought about multiple generations of foreign military commandants being in charge of this so-called sacred dirt?

But a piece of dirt is only so sacred as the blood that has pledged to defend it. Eventually rain and time washes out the blood that is already there, and if no one new steps up, then that dirt is just dirt once again.

Well, he would have ate his hat and fought back.

But then, in his great, great grandfather's time, they'd had the means to fight back. That was before they'd been turned into *subjects*. That was back in the day when the word "Rights" wasn't just some term ascribed to the things in life that made men comfortable, but rather the things in life that made men free.

What do you know about freedom?

And Walter had no answer. He'd lived his life here, in these Districts. And he'd thought that being left alone was all the freedom that he needed. But that wasn't really freedom. That was just avoidance. And avoidance only took you so far.

"You see that shit?" Virgil called from up front.

Walter leaned forward, taking the cigarette out of his mouth. "What?"

They were headed straight north up the highway. Still a few miles out from the Town Center, but it was dead ahead of them, over the woods and through the trees. Now the highway was dark and black and it stretched out with its two concurrent lines, into the darkness, where it seemed to disappear into a wall of trees.

But beyond that seeming-wall of trees, the night sky was not so dark. It glowed. It burned. The outlines of gunships in the sky flitted back and forth. Something like the tail of a comet jetted over them, and Walter knew it was fast-movers.

They watched and drove on.

"Flyovers," Virgil said, very serious. "They're engaged with someone over there."

"You think that's the Town Center?" Tria asked, worried.

Virgil glanced into the rearview mirror at Walter. "I can't say. Walt?"

Walter was still transfixed by the sky. A stream of tracers, like little lightning bolts all in quivering disorderly line, burst from one of the shadowy gunships and arced towards the ground.

Walter felt his heart pound suddenly in his chest.

"Yes," he said, quietly. "I think it is."

"If they're not dropping bombs yet, that means they're in house-to-house," Tria observed.

Virgil nodded.

Tria let out a string of curses.

Walter continued to stare.

Getty laid back in his seat and smoked the last of his cigarette. When he didn't have it in his mouth he regarded the shrinking stick's red cherry with a certain romance, like the touch of a lover he knew he would never feel again. Then all at once, he drew out the last little bit of smoke from it and pitched it out the window and looked very serious, very focused, very clear.

The clearest he'd been since getting that bullet in the leg.

"If that's the Town Center," Tria noted. "It's gonna be blockaded off."

Virgil just shook his head. "If it's an actual firefight, they ain't gonna have time for blockades."

"It's gonna be a shit show."

"This whole night's been a shit show. What else is new?"

Tria leaned and looked into the back, first at Getty, and then at Walter. She didn't say anything for a moment. Then she said, "Are you guys gonna do this?"

Getty nodded. "Ayuh, I'm gonna do it," he said, as though it were a silly question.

Walter just stared back at her. But eventually he nodded as well.

I'm in it. I can't not be in it.

I'm in it for me. I'm in it for everyone.

For Carolyn. For Roy. Even for that drunk, Grandpa Clarence.

I'm all in.

And the truck drove on, as though it were not even in Virgil's control. Like one of those amusement park rides that makes you feel like you have control, but you have none, you are always being inexorably drawn into the center of the action. You will experience everything that it has to give you, and there is nothing that you can do about it. You are strapped in. You can go nowhere.

Your free will doesn't mean shit.

"You need to tell him," Tria suddenly said into the introspective darkness of everyone's looming mortality.

Walter looked at her, confused, thinking, *tell who what?*

He looked at Virgil.

Virgil was eyes-forward, both hands on the steering wheel.

"We might not make it out, Virgil," she pressed.

The man who'd been sheriff of Agrarian District 89 up until only hours ago growled breathily, but didn't respond.

"He has a right to know," she said.

Walter was frowning now.

He realized that Getty was watching him in the stillness, calm as Getty was always seemingly calm, and that was when he realized that it was him they were talking about. It was the subject in which everyone stopped talking when he walked into the room. It was the thing that everyone else knew, but didn't want *him* to know.

"Know what?" Walter demanded, edging forward in his seat.

Virgil stayed silent.

Tria let out a disdainful huff of air through her nose. She turned away from Virgil. Faced the road. Adjusted her position in her seat. "The Eudys," she said, flatly and suddenly, like she'd made a decision. "The Eudy Clan. You ever heard of them?"

Walter looked at her, then at the windshield and he could see the ghost of Tria's form reflected in the angled glass, but only her rifle, and her legs, and her hands on top of the rifle, and how they were squirming together, nervous.

"No. Not before tonight. Why? Should I?"

"They're terrorists," Virgil remarked bitterly.

Tria snorted reproachfully again. "We're all terrorists according to the CoAx. If you wanna be free you're a goddamned terrorist, and that's how it's always been."

Walter had moved now so that he was almost hanging between the two front seats. He felt unwell. It came on him very suddenly. One moment he was just feeling his pulse skyrocketing, and now, all of the sudden, there was nausea that went with it. Was it the exhaustion? Was it his body rebelling against everything he'd put it through? He was no trained warfighter...

"Okay," he said, irritation coming through, the type of irritation that accompanies someone whose patience has depleted along with their feeling of well-being. "What does this have to do with me? Why do I care who the Eudys are?"

Virgil drove.

Tria watched him.

Waited for him.

So did Walter.

Say something, goddammit!

He cleared his throat.

Walter was aware of the way he glanced over his shoulder, as though to measure how close Walter was, and the way that he then shifted, just slightly, just an inch or so away from him, as though he was preparing to fight Walter off.

This is serious, isn't it?

Why don't you just tell me—?

"They're Carolyn's parents," Virgil said.

CHAPTER TWENTY

"No," Walter said. His voice was calm. Matter-of-fact.

His chest felt achey. His vision worn down to just what was in front of his face.

"No, Carolyn's last name was Hartsell," Walter asserted.

He wasn't sure what was happening. Was this a misunderstanding? Were they operating on bad intel? What made them think this ludicrous thing?

Walter knew his wife. They didn't know her. Virgil did, kind of, but Tria didn't. Getty didn't. None of them knew her better than he did.

He fully expected Virgil to look surprised and say, "Oh, all this time I thought she was a Eudy."

Virgil didn't say that.

Neither did Tria.

They both exchanged a glance with each other, but didn't look at Walter.

"She was a Hartsell," Walter repeated, a little more insistent. And with that insistence, a little more unsure. And with that unsurety, a little irritation, a little indignation, a little *how dare they…*

"She was a Hartsell *after* the state took her," Virgil said stiffly. "After they disappeared her parents. The Eudys."

Walter sat there, wordless.

Perhaps his lack of words was perceived as an invitation for more explanation, but really, he didn't want anything else. He wanted them to shut up. He kept thinking, *they don't know what they're talking about, this is bullshit.*

But Virgil didn't perceive that. Virgil perceived silence, and he forged ahead, relieved that Walter was taking it so well, when in fact Walter was simply frozen, his hands clenched together at his knees, and his brain was only half listening to what Virgil said, while the other half ran around in circles with its hair on fire, denying everything and trying to find a hole to hide in.

The *sanctum sanctorum* had been violated.

His memories had been deemed *unreal*.

Everything he knew about the most important person in his life was suddenly stamped with a big, fat, red, FALSE, or at the very least, QUESTIONABLE.

And Virgil was still talking.

"The Eudys started their shit back in the day, back in the beginning. They were the motherfuckers that DTI was designed for. They were the original *Domestic Terrorists*." He put heavy import into the words. "When they were caught, the state took Carolyn, gave her a new name, and shipped her to this District. Gag-ordered and all. The Eudys have been sitting in DTI for over a dozen years. Until recently, anyways."

Walter sat.

That's about it.

There wasn't much else to do.

He could be angry. But that felt pointless. He could rage about it. He could deny it. But here he was, getting this entire pile of shit laid on him while he was hurtled into the storm.

It all felt very pointless.

He stared out the windshield at the distance, where the night was heating up into orange fire light, and dark shapes moved across the sky like wraiths and spit out tongues of fire that chewed through cement and life.

There were people out there. People that those big bullets were obliterating. Someone, down there on the ground, dying right now, dying for something, some *thing*, and Walter was having trouble remembering what it was.

He was about to be there. He was about to be there in the middle of all that, and he couldn't even remember why.

She would have told me, he wanted to say.

But really. Would she have?

If they had taken her parents to DTI. If they had told her what would happen if she spoke about it. If they had told her how very easy it was for secrets to get out.

Oh, Walter could almost see it happening. He pictured some Fed hovering over a little girl version of Carolyn, saying, "Don't ever tell anyone what happened, because three people can keep a secret if two of them are dead, and if we ever find out that you told anyone, and we will, you can bet your pretty pig-tails we will, then we'll execute your parents on national television and we'll throw a goddamned parade about it."

No. Carolyn would not have told him.

In the front of the car, back into his hellish reality, them this doomed meteorite, planet-bound, unstoppable, they were going into that fray, like a gravity well that was sucking them in, and Virgil was driving them in, and from his seat of control he looked in the rearview mirror and he made eye contact with Walter, who was suddenly feeling a little woozy, and he said, "her name's not Carolyn, either."

Walter looked back. Didn't blink. His eyes got dry. Hazy. Everything turned to black and white. He still didn't bother to blink.

"Oh?" he said.

"It's Stephanie. Stephanie Eudy is her original name."

And that was strange. People's names became somehow their embodiments. She didn't look like a Stephanie to Walter any more than she looked like a Robert. She was Carolyn. Carolyn Hartsell. Carolyn *Baucom*, actually, and thank you very much.

Whoever she was, she'd married *him*. She'd married him and she'd taken his name. Which meant that she was a Baucom. Walter knew that. And Virgil couldn't take that away from him.

But then there was something else.

"You knew," Walter said.

Again, his voice was calm.

He was calmer than ever right now, miraculously. He stared at Virgil, and then looked away, out the windshield at what was ahead of them. Along the edge of the visible horizon, there was a light that flashed white, and a rumble that they felt.

Virgil looked away from the rearview mirror.

He didn't respond.

"You knew," Walter said again. "And you let me think that it was my fault."

Tria fidgeted in her seat.

To Walter's left, Getty was sitting, looking out the window as though none of this conversation pertained to him. And Walter supposed it didn't. Getty was wiser than he appeared at first interaction.

"Why did you keep this from me?" Walter asked, earnestly.

Virgil's jaw worked violently. "Because I didn't want you running off."

"Running off?" Walter coughed out a laugh.

"I didn't want you getting it into your head that you were going to run off and ally yourself with Carolyn's parents. They're *Not To Be Fucked With*." He looked at Walter and his expression was that of the person who believes they are finally pulling themselves up to the moral high ground. "I know you, Walt. I know you would have tried to find them."

Virgil started to say something else, but Walter cut him off, his brow knit together. "Wait. Wait. I don't understand. Why did the CoAx come for Carolyn? Was she working with the resistance? Was she getting in touch with her parents or something?"

Virgil shook his head slowly, unsurely. "We don't know."

"You don't know?"

"We don't know. From everything we can see, I don't even think that Carolyn knew the Eudys had been broken out. Why do you think the CoAx and the Fed kept the break-out such a secret? They didn't want to fan the flames. They knew that the entire organization that had gone to weeds would start coalescing again if they found out the

Eudys had broken out. Besides that fact, I don't think the Fed wants to advertise that their DTI had a hole poked in it."

"She didn't even know?" Walter leaned back in his seat. There was a weight on his chest. Somebody had put a cinderblock against his sternum. "She didn't even know."

Virgil shook his head.

"I don't understand why they took her," Walter said, listlessly.

"I don't either," Virgil admitted. "But it has something to do with the Eudys. I guaran-fucking-tee you that."

They can't do that, Walter thought, inanely. *They can't just take her because her parents got busted out of internment…*

And then

Of course they can. They can do anything they fucking want.

What are we?

We're just the people.

We're just the subjects.

So the wind blows.

But no more.

You don't have to go whichever way the wind blows.

You can run against it, if you choose.

But you have to choose.

Walter stopped slouching back in his seat. He sat up fully. Gripped his rifle a little tighter.

How strange. How very strange this all was.

How was it that someone of his historically shitty temper could be so calm right now?

"Tria, you got any more ammo in that bag of yours?" he said.

Tria hesitated, then she dove into the satchel that was between her legs and she came out with extra magazines for their battlerifles. "Good idea," she said. "Everyone top off. Keep your partial mag in your pocket. But this is all we got, okay? This is all we got."

We are going to die today.

They are going to purge us.

They are going to purge this whole District.

Walter took his magazine from Tria's small, pale hand. He swapped it out with the one that was already seated into his rifle. Then he took the half-emptied one and he found a pocket in his pants that it fit nicely into—the left, back pocket. Hopefully it would stay there.

"How far are we right now?" Getty asked.

"Not far," Walter said, looking out his window. "Virgil, what's your plan?"

Virgil took a deep breath. "I'm going to drive as far as I can drive. And then we're gonna bail. And we're gonna fight our way in. And we're gonna hope that my group is there. And we're gonna hope that they have some resources to help us out, and maybe even a way to get out of the District. If not, then I suppose the plan is just to shoot to the last round. Save one for yourself."

"Better dead than DTI," Getty intoned.

"Fuck that," Tria mumbled to herself. "I got a knife."

No one spoke for a full minute after that.

Looking out of his own window, Walter broke the silence: "Virgil."

"What?"

"If we get out of here alive?"

"Ayuh?"

"We're gonna hafta talk."

By which he meant that he might have to throw a few blows.

And though Virgil didn't acknowledge this, Walter thought that he understood.

CHAPTER TWENTY-ONE

Union Highway—the highway they were driving north on—was the main road that ran north-south. It meandered on in a relatively straight line for miles, sometimes with little offshoots that harbored a few old houses.

In the approximate center of Agrarian District 89, Union Road intersected with Town Center Boulevard. These crossroads created four quadrants. If viewed from the air, the first three quadrants—northeast, southeast, and southwest—would show wide, flat, square patches of concrete that extended out from the crossroads.

This was the industrial section. The area where all the hangars were located, all the parts were warehoused, all the machinery was kept and upgraded and recycled and repaired. A miserable-looking grid of metal buildings, usually done in tan, sometimes in gray.

What was known officially as the "Town Center" was in the last quadrant. That one slice of the pie to the northwest of the crossroads. Here, there were no metal buildings and hangars and Quonset huts. Here it was thousands of three-story brownstone buildings, 90-percent apartment buildings, 10-percent bars and stores and entertainment.

The intersection of Union and Town Center was a natural high point in the land. There, sitting at the traffic light nearly every day of his adult life as he drove into work, Walter could see most of the Town Center. In the early mornings sometimes fog would shroud it in a sleepy sort of haze.

Walter had seen the view many times.

But he had never seen it like this.

They were sitting at that same traffic light. And it had caught them now, just as it always caught Walter. And he was leaning forward to tell Virgil to run the light, there was no reason to stop for it now. But then he looked out from that intersection and he saw the Town Center and the words died in his mouth.

But it was the scene.

And it was probably the same reason why Virgil was just sitting there, idling at a red-light like a good citizen when he should have been trucking through it.

To the northwest, the Town Center had been wrecked.

Walter stared at all the building fronts that ran along Town Center Boulevard. It seemed like there was not a single glass window left intact. The sides of the buildings twinkled with smoldering fire-light. Smoke had blackened some areas. Bullet holes of various sizes stitched random patterns across the walls.

Cars stood in wreckage, in various positions, like corpses of men that have been shot and killed and fallen to the ground. One car was up on the curb. One was crashed into a telephone pole and was burning. A third was parked neatly on the side of the road, but it looked like a giant dog had chewed on it.

There were bodies in the streets. Disguised amongst the rubble.

"I can't believe this," Virgil whispered to himself, dumbfounded.

This was where the fighting *had* been.

But it was not here anymore.

To the west, gunships circled over a different section of the Town Center, like flies buzzing around roadkill. Their spotlights would blink on in the darkness, searching for something, and then wink off again. And when it was off, tracers would lance out like gouts of fire from a dragon's mouth and Walter knew that they were obliterating everything they touched.

He could hear the small concussions of all those explosive-tipped rounds shredding wood, stone, metal, and flesh. He could hear them even with the windows up.

They could not see the streets where the gunships circled, but they could see the glow of the fires. They could not see the details of the destruction, but backlit against those glowing fires, they could see the columns of oily smoke spewing into the sky from a dozen points.

Half of the Town Center lay in darkness, the power gone out.

In the other half, it seemed that every single light was on.

Here and there, one of the brownstone buildings was blazing.

"We're going into that," Virgil stated, thickly.

Ahead of them, the light had turned green.

Virgil accelerated. He started rolling windows down. "Everybody get a gun in a window."

There was no point in subterfuge at this point, Walter realized. They were the only civilian car that would be driving *into* that shit. And in the Town Center, in the middle of the purge of District 89, Walter knew that the CoAx troops would not show restraint.

Guns in or guns out, they were going to get shot on sight.

They crossed the intersection.

Walter's window came down and the night wind rushed in. It smelled of diesel fumes and burning rubber, and spent munitions. A drift of low-hanging smoke huddled in the center of the intersection and it stank like death, like smoke should not, and it chilled Walter to the bone and made him start sweating all at once.

The engine thrummed. Almost timidly.

The tires hummed, and they too sounded cautious.

Walter shifted his hips in the seat, facing himself to his door, and his open window. He propped the battlerifle up in the window, looked over the sights. The little reticle hovered in the air, glowing mutely red, adjusting itself to the darkness. Mindlessly it assisted him in killing more efficiently.

For a moment, he wished that he was any other place in the world.

His thoughts were tethered dogs barking and yapping and wanting to run in a million different directions at one time.

He could not afford it.

He pulled them back.

He yanked them violently. His mind. His rabid thoughts. He kicked them into submission.

Live, he told himself. *Fight. Survive. Get out of this alive.*

205

The truck slowed, approaching a road on their left that would lead them into the heart of things. When Walter breathed, he felt the air tremble in his throat.

"Let's be heads up," Virgil said. And then he made the left hand turn.

Walter watched the darkened, smoke-filled world spool by in a great panorama as the vehicle swung wide. Several hundred yards further up Union Road, a group of people scrambled across the nighttime blacktop, lit in the ghostly light of a streetlamp. A family, it looked like. And then another. And then a steady stream of them. Running away.

They straightened out onto the new street—Fraternity Street, so it was dubbed. About a half mile down, he could see roaring fires, and he could see more people trying to get away from the fighting.

Except that some of them were fighting back.

He could see that. He could see them bolting between cover, between stoops of apartment buildings, hunkering behind blown-out cars, firing blindly over their shoulders with weapons that likely stood no chance against the armored dreadnaughts of the New Breeds.

Walter couldn't see the New Breeds they were shooting at. But he watched the return fire—something bigger and more powerful than just the battlerifles, maybe a Lancer—and it hit one of those hopeless rebels as he or she sprinted across the street, and Walter watched the legs of that person come off and tumble across the roadway, and then the torso split, spraying its contents wide, and Walter was glad that he was far away from that sight.

Another fighter fell to the ground and curled up into the fetal position and then was chewed to pieces by a flurry of tracer rounds.

Walter felt his heart thundering as he watched this.

"Oh, shit, shit, shit," Tria uttered.

Virgil accelerated. His eyes looked hooded and dark.

Tria gaped at him. "Don't go straight into that!" she barked. "Go around it!"

"I'm *gonna* go around it!" he said.

A side street loomed up quickly in the firelit dimness.

Virgil slapped the steering wheel rapidly to the right. The truck shook and shuddered and the tires chirped desperately as he took the turn. A street sign that Walter couldn't read whizzed by outside and nicked the back fender with a sharp metallic *BANG*.

Another row of apartment buildings.

People were pouring out of them. Shuffling children out of the doors, the fathers and mothers hauling armloads of precious belongings that would be dropped when their arms tired and they realized that those belongings were not worth their lives.

Virgil skidded almost to a halt while a man and a woman scrambled across the road. The man held a child, a little girl. They barely paused, less than a half-second, to regard the truck that was bearing down on them. Walter looked at the man carrying his daughter, and it seemed that he looked back, and then they were across.

Virgil swore at them, accelerated passed.

Walter looked out his window, watching them as they roared by.

The man frowned at him, and that single look caught Walter off guard. He'd somehow expected those people to see him, to see his gun, and to perhaps be confused, but to feel something akin to relief, relief that someone was out fighting for them.

But the look was just a pragmatic mystification. It said, *who do you think you are, idiot? You think you're gonna make a difference? You should be running like the rest of us. Run, while you still have a chance.*

And then the little family dropped out of sight.

Virgil turned left again.

"Uh…" was all Virgil said.

The truck decelerated rapidly.

Walter was jostled in his window, bumped against the back of Tria's seat.

"I got two," Tria said, her voice suddenly high and stressed. "Three! Four!"

Walter pushed away from the window, looked out the windshield.

He could see their shapes, fifty yards down the road.

The shapes were big. Heavy. Thick. Armored.

New Breeds.

Two on the stoop of an apartment, guns addressed to the door.

Two on the sidewalk.

One was looking at them.

"Virgil," Tria leaned into her window, brought her rifle up. "Virgil! Reverse!"

The truck was still rolling.

The dark, hulking figure of the New Breed raised his own weapon at them.

"Hit 'em," Getty said quietly from his seat.

"Ayuh," Virgil grunted.

The truck engine roared.

The acceleration slammed Walter back into his seat.

Tria shouted something that Walter couldn't hear. There was a burst of flame, and abruptly the sound of gunfire was not a distant thing, it was hammering their heads in the enclosed cab, as Tria leaned out the window and her rifle spat metal in a steady stream.

"Duck down!" Virgil shouted. He'd hunkered down behind the engine block, but his hands were still on the wheels, aiming the vehicle at the soldiers in the road.

Walter ducked. He smashed his face into the seat cushion beside him, but not before he saw a tongue of flame leap out from one of the New Breed's weapon, and he didn't hear the report of the rifle, but he damn well heard the *SMACK* as the rounds hit the engine block, and then stitched holes across the windshield, rapidly tracking towards Tria.

Tria screamed, still firing.

She tried to pull herself in, tried to pull herself down.

Out of the corner of Walter's eye, he watched her jerk, hard.

She gasped.

Jerked again.

The rifle tumbled out of her hand but caught on the retention strap.

"Tria!" Walter shouted, reached up for her, got a hand on her shoulder..

She curled into a ball.

They were still accelerating.

The windshield disintegrated into nothingness.

Walter's mouth was open, sucking in air.

He felt pieces of glass and little bits of plastic dashboard pepper his face, his eyes, his open mouth.

BOOM

The truck lurched

Swerved

Jumped

The distinct *thu-THUMP* of something rolling under the tires.

The roaring, ripping sound of automatic weapons.

And then

CRUNCH

They came to a sudden halt.

CHAPTER TWENTY-TWO

Walter was on the floorboard.

They were being shot at.

He could hear the rounds hitting the car still.

He was struggling hard. Struggling to move. Like being eight years old, caught in the couch cushions, pinned there by Roy who was laughing uproariously, and Walter was panicking, needing to get out, but couldn't move, restricted movement only making him panic even harder.

He was staring at dark, dirty carpet.

Pieces of glass and plastic tumbled around like sand in a harsh current.

Everyone was shouting, and so Walter couldn't really hear what one person was saying.

His ears were ringing, adding to the cacophony of confusion.

Someone grabbed him by the collar of his shirt, and it was like the physical contact focused the dial of his hearing. He looked up, saw Getty's lips moving, and suddenly could hear again.

"Out! Out! Out!"

Getty's wounded leg was dangling semi-uselessly out of the open side door, his good leg was braced against the floor and pressing him backwards, and he was holding his rifle in one hand, and holding onto Walter with the other, hauling him backwards out of the car.

Dimly, Walter perceived that out of the door was the safe side of the car.

The bullets were coming from *his* side, and a little to the rear.

They must have gotten turned when they crashed.

"OUT!" Getty screamed.

Walter plunged forward, almost like diving through water, and suddenly inertia was gone, and he and Getty were both flying out of the car. He watched Getty's face turn to surprise, and then scrunch into a cringe, and he watched black concrete coming up at them as they tumbled out.

Getty hit first.

Walter on top of him.

A bullet skipped off the pavement with a horrible, seeking, whining sound, and it skimmed across the surface of Walter's back, and at first it felt like a slap, but then it felt like a cat had clawed its way across his skin.

"AAGH!" he shouted in Getty's face.

Getty shoved him off, leaned up into a half-sitting position, but still low enough to fire underneath the clearance of the truck, and he let out a burst of rounds, three rounds, six rounds, directed at something, and then a haphazard dozen that he intentionally splattered along the concrete, like skipping rocks over the surface of water.

Those rounds pinged and whined and moaned through the air.

But Walter noted that the return fire had ceased for a brief moment.

Walter thought about saying that he was hit, but then thought, *Now's not the time. I need to get out of here. Just get out. GET OUT!*

Walter struggled to his feet. He felt clumsy and unwieldy. In his mind he wanted to flow like wind, lithe like an animal, with some innate, athletic, predatory grace. But his muscles were overtaxed, and his movements were drunk and desperate and nightmare-slow.

Getty had propped himself up and was reaching a hand for Walter, needing help.

Walter grabbed him up, didn't waste time trying to yoke him, but simply held tight to the man's forearm and started dragging his ass away, away from the vehicle.

Virgil had Tria at the front tire well. She was on her side, legs so horribly exposed, hanging limply out of the relative cover of the tire.

But her eyes were open. And her chest was moving. *Shot. She got shot. She took one through the chest.*

Virgil was crouched by her, maneuvering to get her arm around his shoulders so he could move her away from the vehicle. Her mouth gaped, eyes rolling. Were her lips turning blue? Or was it just the light?

"Go for the stoop!" Getty said as Walter dragged him along, his voice shaking with their tumbling footsteps.

Walter was already going for the stoop. He didn't need to be told. The gunfire had come from behind them, and directly ahead of them was a set of stairs with a neat little inlet, a little concrete alcove, and Walter couldn't think of what the hell that was for—it was actually for trash cans—but he knew it looked safe.

Walter hesitated as they passed Virgil and Tria.

Getty tumbled into him. "We'll cover 'em from the stoop! Go!"

A new crash of gunshots struck at them.

Walter hauled for the stoop. Almost there.

He glanced behind them. Bullet holes were sprouting out of the truck, those hard, heavy rounds from the New Breed's battlerifles punching cleanly through, the thin metal and plastic and vinyl guts of the car not offering much resistance. One of the tires let out a *pop* and a *squeak* and went abruptly flat. Virgil and Tria huddled like two people caught in a sandstorm.

Walter told his body to move faster and it did not comply.

Rounds chipped gouges across the face of the stoop, made it seem momentarily less safe.

But forward momentum was a bitch. And changing their decisions now would surely get them killed.

Walter put his head down. Went for it. Like running into a driving rain, hoping not to get to wet, hoping to run so fast that the raindrops don't hit you…

He slid. Intentionally. Feet first.

His knees hit the ground, then the sides of his legs. He felt the rough concrete simply remove the sides of his pants like they weren't there, and when the concrete had chewed through the pants in that single instant, it got started on his flesh, but it didn't matter, because roadrash seemed a welcome thing when compared to a hole in the head.

Walter hit the wall.

Getty came tumbling after him, collapsing flat and holding his hands over his head while a flurry of intense gunfire hit the stoop and threatened to chip it away to nothing.

The fire abated just a bit over their head, the rain of grit and concrete shards died.

Walter could already feel sticky wetness growing on his right pants leg where he'd slid. The raw sensitivity of excavated sub-dermal layers.

He thrust himself up. For the briefest of moments, the thought, *Am I about to catch a round? Did I choose the right time to raise myself out of cover?*

He slammed his rifle flat on the top of the stoop and started firing and screaming, "Virgil! Tria! Move!"

His rifle roared.

Bursts, he told himself. *Bursts because you don't have much ammo.*

Someone far ahead of him, some dark, hulking shape on the other side of the truck fired back, and the rounds hit close, and Walter felt the rock sting his face, embed into his cheek, but it didn't get in his eye, and he could take the pain, so he just kept firing back and screaming.

Virgil and Tria were moving.

Slow. Too slow.

Actually, Tria wasn't moving. Virgil was dragging her.

Burst. Burst. Burst.

From out in the darkness beyond the truck, there came a *thu-PUNK* sound, and then a hiss, and then the truck lit up like someone had set a strobe in it.

Walter watched with eerie fascination as the vehicle lifted into the air, fully off of its tires, and a thick cloud of gray-white smoke suddenly billowed up from it.

The shockwave hit them.

Walter could feel himself being lifted up and backward, roughly, and the air being scooped out of his lungs while at the same time his chest compressed, stomach compressed, and weird, hot pressure rippled across his skin.

He didn't hear a thing, though.

Felt a pain in his eardrum, in his sinuses, in his brain. But it was dull.

He tumbled. Painlessly, and he had the conscious thought that it should have hurt, *you're tumbling over pavement, this should definitely hurt*, but his limbs were just insensate rubber at that moment.

I've stopped.

I've stopped.

Eyes open.

Night sky.

His body moved. Was being tugged.

Have I given up?

Am I dying?

Getty's face loomed over him. Screaming at him, but his voice was on mute.

Walter frowned at him. Mystified. He should have learned how to mute people's voices a long time ago, it would have in handy—oh, shit, *there's my hearing*—

"Run motherfucker! Run!" Getty was pulling him savagely, then slapped him hard across the face. "Let's go let's go let's go!"

thu-PUNK-sssssSSSSHHHH

Getty heard it. So did Walter.

Getty shrouded Walter's body with his own.

Hunkered down over him, and Walter could only think, *I can't believe he's doing that for me.*

Walter could see over Getty's shoulder. Watched a comet with a bright phosphorescent tail slam into the apartment building fifteen feet above them. Smoke billowed. An avalanche of rocks plumed out, arced down, tumbled.

Walter watched a hefty chunk of blown-apart cement bounce off of Getty's head. Walter looked at Getty, saw the hair parted and the pale skin underneath for a half-second, and then blood welled up out of it with a peculiar suddenness and immediately began dripping.

"Getty?" Walter shook him. "Getty, you okay? You alive?"

Getty twitched on top of him, then righted himself woozily, his eyes crossed for a moment. He blinked rapidly, then managed to focus on Walter. "Lezgo," he mumbled.

Chattering gunfire. Walter couldn't tell what direction it was coming from.

He rolled Getty off of him and the man found his hands and knees, and then his feet, with some effort, everything seeming to take glacially long while the rest of the world spun rapidly out of control around them. At the same pace, Walter found his own feet.

Idiotically, he stood up in the middle of everything.

Bees buzzed around him, angry, very angry, like he'd disturbed their hive.

He felt one of them bite his ear.

In another world, on another mental plane, he knew that they were bullets. He knew that he was an idiot for standing up. So he started to move his feet. Move away from the truck, that's what they'd been doing in the first place, right? Moving away from the truck?

He looked behind him, saw Getty limping with his bad leg, and he felt bad, so he stopped and extended a hand, "Come on, Buddy…"

Another voice: "Walter-get-your-ass-in-gear!"

Walter peered up. He could see Virgil, two stoops down from the one that Walter had hid behind, and he was poked up above, just his head and his rifle, and the rifle was burping out its fiery opinions on things, and as far as Walter could tell, it was the only one speaking.

"Oh, shit," he said aloud.

Something clicked back into place. Like a faulty electronic that needs a good rap to get that loose wire back in contact.

He tightened his grip on Getty's arm and became horribly aware of how exposed he was. He started running towards Virgil. Then past him.

That was the technique, right? To bound over each other?

Past Virgil was another street. It was the end of the block.

Walter and Getty got there as fast as their shambling bodies could get them there. Getty's face was a sheet of red, but peering out of that crimson skein, his eyes were clear and sharp and lucid.

They hit the corner and came skidding to a stop.

Getty collapsed backward against the wall.

Walter found it took an enormous effort to change his direction and grab the corner. He needed to provide covering fire for Virgil and Tria to make it back. Was Tria even still alive? It was all a bunch of nonsense right now.

None of it mattered. Just do the job.

He posted his elbow roughly against the side of the wall and took a half second to make sure that he was aiming clearly over Virgil's head, and then he started firing.

Virgil, ever clear in the face of this shit, immediately got up and started moving. He was supporting Tria, whose head was lolling about like she was on the verge of passing out.

Walter gave two bursts and then he took a moment to look.

He squinted, frowned.

The truck sat there smoking violently, as did the side of the apartment building that had been hit with the other munition—whatever it was. Through the screen of smoke, he couldn't see shit. But there was something he'd heard about smoke. And that was that smoke works both ways.

Virgil and Tria scuffled around the corner.

Tria landed on the sidewalk like a boxer that was down for the count. Her chest was still moving but she was making wretched wheezing sounds. Virgil had barely cleared the corner before he was shouting, "Help me with her, help me!"

"I'm watchin' the corner," Walter called out.

Virgil didn't respond.

Walter wondered if he should help or watch the corner, but he knew there wasn't anything that he could do for Tria, and someone had to watch the corner.

Still, he kept looking back over his shoulder.

Virgil laid Tria out on the sidewalk. She looked like a child in the oversized softarmor she wore. Her chest was working overtime to get air, but Walter didn't think any air was getting in. She tilted her head back. All the way back. She was looking at him. Her mouth open. Her eyes wide. Upside down, she could've been a little girl hanging from monkey bars.

Walter stared at her. She stared back.

Then he looked back at his corner.

Smoking truck. Smoking building. Nothing moving.

"Unnnnngh," Tria's voice, small.

Walter tried to focus. Then he found himself looking back again.

Tria was still staring at him. But his eyes darted away from hers. Virgil was on his knees next to her, with his hands up underneath her softarmor. He worked his hands around. Trying to find a bullet hole. Getty was on the other side of Tria, undoing the straps of the armor so they could get it off.

Is this the best time to do this? Walter wondered, but then he looked at Tria again, and he confirmed, yes, it wasn't just the light, her lips were turning blue. What was that on her neck? Was that…?

"Walter!" Getty yelled.

Walter jerked. Looked at the man.

"Watch that corner!"

Walter nodded. Looked back to the corner.

Nothing. Smoke, and nothing.

He couldn't help himself. He looked back around.

Getty and Virgil, hunched over Tria. Her back was arched. Her head still inclined all the way back, her eyes still fixed on Walter, and he was thinking *why me? why is she looking at me?* And what was that on her neck? What was that right there in her clavicle?

Her hands grasped desperately at Virgil. He kept pushing them away, trying to find the wound under her softarmor, but Walter knew he wasn't going to find the wound there. The bullet that had struck her armor had been stopped by the same. But it hadn't been the only bullet that found her.

"Her neck," Walter tried, found his voice a quiet croak.

Virgil snapped up. "Watch the *corner!*" he shouted angrily.

But Walter wouldn't. He pointed emphatically, angry now. "Her neck, Virgil! Her fucking neck! She's got a goddamned hole in her neck!"

Virgil's eyes jerked down. He stared. Then he yanked his hands out from under her softarmor, almost like he was embarrassed that they'd been there, and he let out with a string of curses, but that was all he did. His hands hovering there.

Walter took a step towards them. He was looking down now. Tria was no longer looking at him. Her eyes were on Virgil. Her body wanted air. Her mouth worked desperately and spittle started clotting up along the corners of her mouth.

Walter stared at the hole in her neck. Such a tiny thing. Not bloody at all. It was surrounded by something that looked like mucous, and every time Tria tried to take in a gasp for air, it would wheeze a bit, and then it would issue out another bit a phlegm.

She'd grabbed ahold of Virgil now. Locked with him.

"It's okay," Virgil said stupidly. "We're gonna fix you, okay? Just... just..."

"Fucking do something!" Walter cried out.

Getty seemed the only calm one. He looked up at Walter. "Hey. If you don't watch that corner they are going to get us." Then he looked at Virgil. "What can you do? What can you do? She needs to breathe."

Virgil said nothing. He only stared down at Tria while she stared back up at him, her mouth blabbing soundlessly and spitting, and the hole in her neck wheezing mutely and coughing up thick yellow clots.

Virgil shook his head. "She's not even bleeding," he said, as though it mattered. Then he looked up at Getty, even while Tria clawed at his neck. "I don't..." he trailed off.

Walter peered around the corner. Two dark shapes moved with the grace of prowling animals, skirting out from around the smoking truck, across the street.

"Shit," he said. "They're coming."

A glance over his shoulder. Tria's efforts were growing weak.

Couldn't someone figure out how to get some air into her? There was some way to fix her. There had to be. They just didn't know what it was, and that was the pinnacle of frustration.

"They're coming," Walter repeated.

The concrete wall that he hugged exploded.

He cried out, flinching away as the sound of gunfire hit him and the shards of concrete sprayed the left side of his face.

He rolled away from the wall. "We need to go!"

Virgil was on his feet, but Tria was still clinging to his legs.

Getty was on his feet as well, and he was trying to pull Virgil away, pull him into cover, but Virgil wasn't about to leave Tria. The two of them hated each other, and yet in this moment, with bullets flying, they'd found out that they would die for each other.

"Help me with her—" Virgil started, trying to drag her by one arm further into cover behind the wall.

Walter watched the words come out of Virgil's mouth as he pleaded for help moving her, and then any other words were cut off.

A bullet hit him in the side. He had just enough time to jerk from the impact, before another one struck his face, and it rearranged his features into something ghastly. Walter watched and saw that Virgil was still alive, his eyes still pleading for help…

Then the back of his head burst.

That was it.

He collapsed instantly.

Fell directly atop Tria's dying form.

She struggled beneath him briefly, weakly.

It wasn't enough. None of it was enough.

Holy shit. Holy shit. Holy shit.

The concrete sprouted dust motes.

Little volcanoes of gray.

Walter felt rough hands on him. Pulling. But they weren't very strong.

He looked, and he saw that it was Getty pulling him, and poor Getty with his eyes wide open, he was no longer the calm one, he just happened to be one of the ones that wasn't dead yet, and with his busted leg he couldn't pull Walter very hard.

But Walter got the point.

Run.

There wasn't any deep meaning. No poignancy. He didn't look back at the bodies. He didn't feel a welling of emotion, though perhaps it would drive him to dust later. He just ran. He ran, pulled by Getty at first, but then overtaking him and going past him, and then Walter was pulling Getty. He ran to save his life. He ran, he ran.

His muscles roared for more oxygen that he simply wasn't capable of giving them.

Everything ached for rest, and he couldn't give it that either.

They ran down the streets, and Walter felt it was mindless, but somewhere in the intervening blocks, as he pumped his legs and hauled Getty along with him and gasped for air that was thin or thick or too smoky with destruction, he realized that Getty was shouting at him, telling him where to turn, and as absent as his mind felt in those moments, somehow he was obeying.

CHAPTER TWENTY-THREE

A flight of gunships went overhead. So close to the tops of the apartment buildings and shops that Walter could feel the downdraft as they went. They came upon them quickly, and the second he and Getty heard the rotors, they froze and plastered themselves to the side of the building next to them.

They knew that if the pilots were looking through their thermals, they would see them. They just hoped that if they weren't seen running *into* the fray, they might not be taken as combatants. So far, either the pilots were too busy, or their luck held.

A family of five passed them on the opposite side of the street. Dirt and smoke-streaked faces. Walter didn't think they even noticed them. They were moving quickly, but they had a dazed, zombie-like look on their faces. A man and a woman, an older boy, and a younger girl who trailed in the back, hanging onto the hand of an old man. Single-file they fled mindlessly away from the Town Center.

Ahead of Walter and Getty, there was a hole in a building that still smoked like a crater in a volcano. Strewn all around the hole, little lumps in the street. Not soldiers, Walter didn't think. Too small. Too lightly clothed.

They stopped at the recessed entrance to a small hardware store.

Walter looked inside. It was dark. There was a bullet hole in the glass door. He had been to this hardware store many times. He knew the owner. Didn't know him by name, strangely enough. They'd never exchanged names, but they talked the latest news in a friendly, fluid manner. Walter had last been in there to buy wood glue for a broken kitchen chair. The man that had owned it had helped him find it.

He breathed, breathed, breathed.

Getty's chest went along with his.

Neither spoke for a moment.

In the background, the gunships roared over the sky. Small arms fire *pop-pop-popped* and echoed around and punctuated everything and then was responded to. Sometimes a hiss of rockets. Sometimes a muted explosion. The fighting had largely moved to another section of the Town Center.

"Who are they fighting?" Walter asked.

Getty had his head back against the wall of the hardware store, looking skyward at nothing and working his mouth as though trying to moisten it. "There's more resistance out here than just us." He lolled his head to look at him. He looked horrible. Beaten. "You think they did all of this just for us?" He shook his head. "Eighty-Eighty-Nine has been a problem for them since day one. They're just cleaning house."

Cleaning house, Walter thought.

Just cleaning house.

Just the two of them now, huddled in the sunken entrance to the shop.

They had purged other Districts.

"Cleaned house," as Getty had put it.

Fed-run media had little to say about it, though.

They'd straighten up the mess they'd made. Make it all sound like the resistance's fault. That was their go-to move. Then they'd just stop talking about it altogether.

Construction would patch things back together. For every few people that were fighting right now, there were a hundred that just didn't want to be bothered. And they would go back to work when they were told to go back to work, and all of this night would be squashed down and compartmentalized in their brains and it would simply be "That night that the CoAx did that round-up and a few buildings got shot up, yeah, that was crazy, fuck the CoAx, wanna go grab a beer after work?"

That had been him, in fact.

It was so many of them.

But it wasn't him anymore.

He could never be that way again.

He was fighting now. Just like the others that were fighting, deeper in the Town Center. And a for moment Walter felt a spaced-out, unreasonably emotional connection with them, and it nearly caused his eyes to water, and he bitterly wondered at the incredible ridiculousness of it all—that these resistance fighters knew so little about each other, that they refused to band together, that they stayed divided over small differences, and so would resign themselves to death and defeat.

Dear God, if they could just decide to work together, Walter thought with frustration. *Then we could win. If they could stop arguing over small shit, then my Carolyn would still be here. Or at least I could have a chance at getting her back.*

We should know who that is down there fighting the CoAx. And they should know us. And we should be working together.

Too late now. They were separated by ignorance.

They were all going to die tonight.

No, he thought to himself fiercely, feeling that angry fire in his gut. It was tempered by exhaustion, but it was there. *That's not what I'm going to think. I'm not going to resign myself. I'm never going to resign myself. I don't care how tired, I don't care how broken, I don't care how many of my friends they slaughter. I'll make them regret coming after me and mine.*

"We're close," Getty said, after a while of breathing.

"To what?"

"To the safehouse."

"Oh."

"How are you?"

"What?"

"How are you feeling?"

Walter looked up at the other man. Getty's eyes were rimmed with tears. He blinked rapidly as though to ward them off, but they only spilled over. He made no sound. He didn't sob. His voice didn't even constrict, nor his face contort with grief. It was like his eyes had simply grown a mind of their own and begun to weep.

"I'm sorry," Walter said.

Getty nodded. "Just fight."

"I will."

"Come on," Getty said.

They moved on through the intersection.

The gash on Getty's head had slowed itself to a trickle. He limped along, sometimes with Walter's help, sometimes leading the way. Occasionally he would hiss or curse at a random pain, but mostly he was quiet and they walked to the soundtrack of the apocalypse around them.

They reached the corner.

Getty nodded to the right. "Keep your eye on the right and behind us. I'll clear the corner."

Walter put his back to the wall, his shoulder to Getty's back and he scanned with his rifle up. He wondered if he looked like he knew what he was doing, or if he looked as awkward and clumsy with the rifle as he felt. He wondered how many rounds were left in the thing. He wondered, of the rounds he'd expended, had a single one of them found what he was aiming for?

"Looks clear," Getty whispered, and Walter wasn't sure why he whispered. Maybe just the tension. "And the building looks intact. Which is a good sign."

They slipped around the corner. As they went, far back through the Town Center streets, Walter saw movement, but it was brief, and he couldn't tell in that single glimpse what it was, or whether it looked like it was heading in their direction or not.

Getty was very circumspect as they moved to the stoop of the apartment building. He looked around manically, up and down the street, up and down again, then again, then again. It seemed every time he took a few steps closer to the entrance, he was re-worried about being watched. But that was good caution. The safe house would not be so safe if two resistance fighters were observed going into it.

Walter wished he had Virgil's thermal scanner to see if drones were watching them.

He looked upward again at the thought and realized that it was getting light out. Night was over now. A gray sky hovered over them, shot through with menacing contrails and pillars of black smoke that diluted themselves into the sky like ink in water. To the east, the sky was blood red, like history's greatest massacre had occurred there, and the sun was simply reflecting off the sea of gore left behind.

"Red sky in the morning, sailor take warning," Walter mumbled.

Getty looked over his shoulder at Walter, then the sky, then sneered at it stubbornly, not in the mood for ill-portents. "This ain't the sea. We ain't sailors. Come on."

With a final, desperate look around, the two of them plunged up the stoop and into the entrance to the apartments.

The vestibule was open. Dark. The light fixture that usually lit the small space was dead. The door to the staircase and elevator that led to the rest of the apartments was locked. Walter wondered if the power had gone out.

Getty moved to a call board. Its projection flickered, but was still active. That was lucky. All the lights were out, but apparently that was by choice—the building still had power. Getty tapped one of the apartment registers twice with his finger.

In blue, glowing letters that cast a cold hue to the vestibule, Walter read that the apartment was registered to a Mr. and Mrs. Furr.

No one that he knew.

There was intimate silence for a moment.

Muted explosions rumbled the ground underneath them.

A speaker on the wall made the tiniest pop, almost polite, and then there was the very slight hiss of an open line, but no one spoke through it.

Getty stared at the register, as though it was staring back. "It's Getty," he said quietly. "Four-by-four." There was a pause. He frowned at the register. "What about you?"

Silence.

Open line.

Getty shifted, glanced at the way out.

Then a man's voice: "Ayuh, Carolina blue. Come on."

The door to the stairs and the elevator made a light, electronic unlatching sound, and Getty pulled it open and limped through, Walter in tow.

Walt remembered Virgil saying "four-by-four" when he'd brought them to the other house, the one where Tria had been operating out of. Had that been considered a safe house? It hadn't been so safe in the end. Now it was a pile of cinder and splinters.

He supposed "four-by-four" was some sort of safe-word. "Carolina blue," apparently a good response.

Getty didn't take the elevator. Walter wondered if it was a tactical consideration, or if Getty was just a glutton for punishment, and had to conclude there must be a reason for it. The explosions were still going off out there. The power grid was going down in certain areas. The last thing they wanted was to be stuck on an elevator.

They ascended two flights of stairs to the top floor.

Out of the stairwell, they walked into a dimly-lit hallway. The doors were evenly spaced and numbered and lettered. They were on the third floor. All the doors began with the numeral 3, and then on down the alphabet.

There was nothing special about it. It looked very institutional. Almost like a dormitory. SoDro only needed to house their workers. They didn't need to surround them with aesthetic appeal.

They walked through this drab but spacious tunnel. Walter heard voices that sounded like a newscast coming from behind one of the doors. Perhaps that apartment was still occupied. Or the resident had left the TV on when they'd fled. Otherwise, there was no sign of life.

Still, Walter couldn't help looking behind them guiltily as they made their way down the hall. Expecting someone to be watching them, these two men battered and dusty and bleeding, lugging half-empty battlerifles along with them.

They weren't CoAx, that was for damn sure. No one would make that mistake.

If they were seen it would simply come down to that person's political leanings.

Maybe Walter would have to shoot that person.

He didn't think it was so far outside of the realm of possibility.

Things had changed a great deal, and quite literally overnight.

The hall ended. Before them stood a door, right smack dab in the center of the wall.

3-K

It was a third floor end unit. As private as an apartment could be.

Getty didn't even knock. They were stepping up to the door when the sound of latches being flung open rattled from inside and then the door was yanked wide, and Getty took a half second to look at the man that stood there, and then he went in and Walter followed.

The apartment was dark.

The door closed behind them. Slammed, actually.

Walter wanted to feel safe, he wanted to feel suddenly relaxed, but he didn't. He kept remembering running out of Tria's safehouse. Kept remembering the mini bombs hitting that structure only seconds later and deconstructing it into its jumbled molecular parts.

There were no furnishings here. A familiar theme. Straight ahead was a room that Walter supposed was the living area, and there was a large window. Next to this window was a folding table. On the table was a long, mean-looking rifle with a bulging protuberance of an optic on top. Behind the rifle was a woman.

Walter recognized her from the safehouse where they'd held Captain Kuai Luo. Then, she'd been dirty and face-paint smeared. Now, she was cleaned, and she was wearing normal clothes.

She turned to look at the newcomers, and she fixed Walter momentarily with those placid eyes of hers that Walter remembered so well.

She was…what was the right word for it?

Prim.

Yes. Prim.

The security latches on the apartment door went clacking back into place. Walter turned and looked at the one doing the clacking.

It was the man with the rat-face. The one that had stood next to the woman that was now seated behind her monstrous rifle.

With the door secured again, the man turned and put his back up to it, his arms hanging limply at his side. He regarded Walter for a moment, then shifted his attention to Getty, who was fishing his cigarettes out of his pocket.

"You okay?" the rat-faced man said to Getty.

Getty just nodded. "Already been patched," he murmured. He lipped a cigarette out. Lit it. The flame quivered. So did the cigarette.

Walter's nerves were no better. His legs felt watery. His brain muddy. Everything in him jittery and jumpy and hellaciously pessimistic.

But the panic was gone. Strange enough.

Fear was there, yes. But a hard, sludgy kind. Like the panic had been cooked down and now it just clung to the insides of Walter's soul like burnt grease. It was a livable kind of fear. The kind that you simply cohabitate with. The kind that you can manage to have sitting on your chest for a long, long time.

Later on, you'd pay, your heart would pay, it would eventually just quit, so many of its beats robbed from it by this calcification of dread. But in the meantime, at least you could think clearly.

When he had his cigarette lit, Getty looked around. He spotted the woman at the table and he nodded to her. "Bobbi," he said, and there was relief there, but it was hard to hear under the utter lack of feeling. A few more glances into shadows and open doorways that led to empty, uninhabited rooms. "Anyone else?"

"We're not enough for you?" the rat-faced man said, and it was so preposterous that Walter knew it had to be a joke, but the rat-faced man didn't smile, and neither did Getty. Nobody smiled. There was nothing to smile about.

The rat-faced man swallowed thickly. "Virgil?" he asked, but there wasn't any hope in his voice.

Getty sucked in smoke and blew it out. His rocksteady calm quavered, just a bit. His eyes tightened around the edges, like they might contort, like they might water again, but they didn't, and his face went dead again. "Nah, brother."

No one spoke.

From the window came a loud, wet sniff.

Walter didn't want to look. He did anyways. Just a glance.

The woman—Bobbi—had her back turned to them, looking out the window. Her shoulders shook once, but she made no other sound.

The rat-faced man straightened up off of the doorway and looked at Walter. "We never got introduced. I'm Porter, but everyone calls me Rat."

How appropriate, Walter thought, and then, *That's pretty fucked up.*

Rat had his hand out.

Walter shook it. "Walt," he said. "I haven't been around long enough to get a name."

Rat just nodded, gravely. "Walt works." He shook his head as though exhausted with the triviality of all their words, and then he walked passed them and motioned them to follow. He pointed to one of two empty folding chairs. "Getty, why don't you pop a squat and get off that leg."

Getty did so.

Walter took the last remaining folding seat.

Rat stood.

After a moment, Bobbi turned back around and smiled sweetly to Walter. "I'm sorry. I'm Bobbi. You're Walter."

Walter nodded. "Yeah. I'm Walter."

"It's good to meet you," she said.

Prim, Walter thought, somewhat dazedly. *What the hell is she doing here behind a rifle?*

She didn't look like she belonged. She looked like she should have been some upper-crust urby. She looked like she'd lived a life of privilege. She looked like the type of person that should have been touting the benefits of the Three Brothers, not out here fighting them to the death.

Walter wanted to dislike her, but she seemed very kind, and he couldn't.

Then he remembered how she had jeered at Kuai when they'd made him piss his pants.

He almost laughed at the memory. The absurdity of it all.

Everyone's got their secret sides, don't they?

Rat let out a half-hearted chuff, and indicated Bobbi with a nod of his head. "Impeccable manners, this one. Even to the very end."

Getty took the cigarette out of his mouth sharply and glared through a thin veil of smoke. "Don't talk like that," he said quietly. "It's not the end."

Rat's mouth twitched. Like he was about to argue or apologize. But he decided to do neither. He looked out the window. "Any change?"

Bobbi settled into the rifle with the practiced ease of someone who has spent a lot of time there. "No," she said. "I don't have a good angle on the fighting anymore. There were ten of them last time I saw them. There's a building in the way now. But the gunships have been pounding it for twenty minutes now."

"Ten what?" Walter inquired.

"Resistance," Rat said flatly. "Don't know who they are, or who they're with."

Walter's eyes coursed over the window, taking note that it was closed, and it was whole—Bobbi hadn't shot through it. And there were no shell casings on the ground. He evaluated all of this with speed that even surprised himself, and he felt a little welling of indignation.

"You don't know them, so you're not gonna help them?"

He immediately regretted saying it. Sometimes exhaustion wears our filters away.

All three of them looked at him.

Bobbi spoke quietly, like she shared his shame in it. "There's gun-trucks with anti-sniper cannons down there. If I fired a shot, this place would be smoking rubble in about a half a second." She shook her head and looked back out the window. "There's nothing we can do for them now."

"I need water," Getty said, a little louder than was probably necessary.

"Yeah," Rat said, happy for the change in topic. "We got water."

"You need water?" Getty asked, looking at Walter.

Walter nodded. "Sure."

Rat walked away, into the kitchen, which had the only sign of life, and that was a refrigerator unit. He left them there. The three of them, in a triangle. Bobbi looking out the window. Getty smoking down the last of his cigarette straight to the filter, and Walter, just watching him, not sure what to do. Not sure what to say.

He felt confused. He felt the beginnings of that old familiar anger. He wanted to do something. He wanted to be *acting* on something.

But they needed to sit. For just a damn minute. They needed to think. They need to drink some water. Try to clear all the blood and smoke and loss out of their heads and see if they could come up with something logical. Because just a lack of emotion didn't mean that you were being logical. One could be unemotional and still make horrible decisions.

Why am I not feeling anything? Walter wondered, and it almost frightened him.

He felt the frustration. He felt the anger. But those had always been easy for him. They came easy to his nature, and they came easy to the life that he'd led.

But there was a muted quality to everything else. A washed out version of what he knew he *should* be feeling. And it concerned him. Frustrated him again. Round and round it goes, mirrors looking into mirrors, but the feeling never really spiraled into anything more, it just kind of hung around like shitty weather that would neither pour itself out nor break up and go away, but just lurked around and occasionally issued a meek pissing.

A lack of catharsis, he thought, remembering the word from half-assed English classes sometime in high school. He wasn't dumb by any stretch, but what use does a grower have for a word like catharsis? There is no such thing. Not in their life. They simply muddled.

And that's what he was doing now. He was muddling.

Muddling through it all, and clinging to that little word, almost obsessively, the way your mind fixates on something, sometimes a song, and you wake up with it looping in your head, never the whole thing, usually just a little snippet and it nags you to death like a rock in your shoe.

Catharsis
Catharsis
Catharsis
Your life
Everything
All of it
Everything you've done
It all LACKS CATHARSIS.

Walter bent forward, braced his elbows on his knees. The battle rifle hung awkwardly on him. He disliked it and he loved it all at once. It was an uncomfortable lover. Its strap chafed his neck, but he wouldn't take it off. You couldn't pay him to take it off.

"Can I bum a cigarette?" he muttered to no one in particular, and to Getty specifically.

Getty pulled out his pack as his own dwindled to nothing. He extracted one. Lit it off the nub of the one he'd just smoked, and he passed this to Walter. Then he did the same for himself. He dropped the butt on the carpet of the apartment and stamped it out.

Walter was momentarily offended.

Then he laughed.

Getty smiled, knowingly.

Walter took a drag on his cigarette and he thought the thoughts that he knew he shouldn't be thinking, but which came to him nonetheless: *Enjoy it. Revel in it. Really experience that cigarette. Taste that smoke. Feel that dumb haze settle on your brain, that makes you feel just a little bit lighter, just a little bit less compacted. Enjoy it because this might be your last.*

He looked out the window at the sky. He couldn't see the sunrise, but he could see the effects of it. He could see the way all the black and navy blue was melting away like colors in a wash. He could see the pink sun reflected in a few errant clouds, and they looked quite nice, even though they were picketed off by pillars of black smoke.

Yeah. That's nice. That's not a bad way to go.

He tried a second time to feel something, but it wasn't there. And what was there to feel anyways? Fear? Oh, he had that. He wanted something better. He wanted to feel the richness of his loss, he wanted to feel the depths, explore them like a deep-sea diver, really get his hands in there and analyze the nooks and crannies of watching Tria gasp her last breaths and watching Virgil's face get wiped from his head.

But there was nothing but dim shapes. Sharp things that would come for him and jab at him, but not now. Not in the waking hours. If he made it to another day, if he ever made it to a point where he could sleep again, they would come to him there. He would feel them there. And he would feel every bit of them, stripped away, naked and intimate he would feel them in a sensuality of terror and grief.

But now?

No. Not now.

Now there was a cigarette in his mouth and a sunrise in the sky.

Now there was nothing but nothing.

Rat returned from the fridge. He held two bottles of water. He had been gone an inordinately long time. Walter registered his eyes, which were red, but he decided not to look in them. He didn't want to shame the man.

Would there be shame? No, there wouldn't be. They all felt it. At least Getty did. And Bobbi did. And clearly now Rat did. He could not shame them. He envied them. Still, he didn't look in Rat's eyes, and he thought perhaps that Rat was relieved not to be seen.

He drank from the bottle of water and then held it, condensating and almost painfully cold in his hands. He felt it drip through his pants leg, and the cold kick-started the nerves in his leg, and he remembered how a good portion of his skin he'd left on the pavement several blocks east of them. He looked down at his blood-soaked pants and winced at the sight of his raw flesh peeking out from behind the shredded cloth.

He sat back. Looked at Getty. Then at Bobbi, who was fixated out the window, but looked listless, and he thought maybe she was just hiding her eyes. Then he looked at Rat. Didn't react from the red-rimmed wateriness that he saw there. Just held the gaze. Man-to-man.

"What's the plan?" Walter asked.

CHAPTER TWENTY-FOUR

Rat walked over to the table. He leaned back against it and crossed his arms over his chest. He looked at Bobbi. The woman looked back like someone who had forgotten her lines while in the bright lights of the stage.

Then she pulled back from the rifle and faced Walter and Getty with a sigh.

Her eyes were dry and clear now.

A coldness had settled over them, but it was a *polite* coldness. It was coldness directed inwards, not outwards. She was numbing herself, the very way that Walter was doing.

"Well," she began, and then said nothing for several beats, her eyes falling to a spot on the floor that seemed to be the invisible center hub of their little circle of four. "We can't get any sort of connectivity out," she said finally. "We can't connect to them. We can't connect to friends outside—"

"We have no friends outside," Getty said, evenly.

They all looked at him. They were confused.

Except for Walter. He knew what Getty meant.

Getty inspected the burning end of his cigarette, flicked ash rebelliously on the carpet. "We got hit at Tria's safe house, on the other side of the District. One of her guys dimed us out. Except he wasn't really working for the Fed or the CoAx." Getty met their gazes now. To drive the point home. So they would know that he was serious. "Richard's turned his back on us. The man that dimed us out at Tria's safe house did it under Richard's orders. He did it because Richard found out

---

about Virgil and Tria's…extracurricular activities. Subverting his little empire."

"Virgil was his *nephew*," Rat said numbly.

Getty nodded. "Money over everything," he said, almost like a well-known litany.

Rat sneered and mumbled it back: "Money over everything."

Silence then.

Walter didn't need it explained. He was intelligent enough to piece it together on his own.

That was what Virgil had been talking about, what Tria had been talking about. The Linklaters and the Honeycutts and several other resistance groups had found a home in the black market. They'd made plenty of money on the underbelly of this war, and eventually the interest in the cause took a backseat to the propogation of more money.

Wasn't that the story of everything?

Follow the money, Walter's Pops used to say.

Theories would abound for everything. But always the answer seemed to be *follow the money*.

Money over everything.

Money had supplanted freedom.

"So," Getty said with finality, "We are very alone."

Bobbi processed this for a time. But then she nodded. "I don't suppose it makes much of a difference," she said, but she was quiet, and Walter could tell that it did make a difference to her. Her hands were in her lap, wrestling nervously with each other.

"We can't get a signal out anyways," she continued. "Even if we broadcast a pirate signal, they'd see where it was coming from. And, apparently, we've no one to call."

Walter stirred in his seat. Leaned back. Then forward again.

He was usually so in tune with body language that he kept his own to a minimum. There was no legitimate reason why he did this except for that he himself could read these things in others, and so doing them felt like he was broadcasting his thoughts, and he did not like that feeling.

But in that moment he was too distracted with a tumult of thoughts to really pay much attention. His brow was furrowing itself deeply, his feet were bouncing peevishly. His gut was doing flip-flops over itself and part of him was looking at what he was conjuring up in his consciousness and it was thinking, *stupid, stupid, stupid, you'll die for nothing.*

But there was another part of him that was nodding along with it and thinking, *You'll probably die anyways. At least this way you did something. You finally did something. It took you your whole life, but you finally did SOMETHING.*

"Can you broadcast from here?" Walter asked her suddenly. "The pirate signal?"

Bobbi eyed him. "No. We would need to hack a local connection." She gestured out the window. "That network hub, right there, the one with the tower coming out of it."

Walter had to lean slightly in his seat to catch sight of it. It looked like a long way off, but he was familiar with the building, and tower. In the morning dimness, he could see the long, thin spire rising up out of the Town Center, red beacon lights pulsing languidly.

"So how does that work?" Walter asked. "I thought they shut down the network."

"Well, yeah, but it's a misnomer," she said. "You can't really *shut down* the network. They just deny service for a geographic area. Which happened to be the entirety of District 89. Any wireless signal still goes through, it just gets intercepted and blocked. The tower says 'no' before the connection to the outside can be made."

"But if it wasn't wireless…" Walter gathered the things together in his mind.

"Right," Bobbi nodded, once. "We'd have to physically plug in. That's why we would have to be there. At that network hub."

"But you could do it."

"I could do it." Bobbi frowned. "But then they'd find us."

"How long?"

Bobbi shrugged. "No idea. Lot of factors there. I'd guess they'd see us and know what we were doing and where we were doing it probably within a minute. Maybe even less. How long it would take them to wipe us out after they found out, I don't know. Depends on the elements they have that are unengaged and ready to deploy. We could last ninety seconds. We could last for thirty minutes. There's no telling."

Flip-flop-flip went Walter's stomach.

Well, now you gotta choose. You've questioned your way out of all the excuses, now it's just whether you have the sack or you don't. So what's your choice, Walter? What is it that you choose? Because it's always a choice, no matter what. No one can decide for you. You can always decide what you are going to do, you just have to except the consequences of that choice.

Which would be his life.

And Getty's. And Rat's. And Bobbi's.

"Would we have time to establish a live-feed?" Walter asked quietly.

Getty stamped his second cigarette out on the carpet and leaned forward, billowing smoke. He looked irritated. "I know what you're thinking, Walter. But let me take this a different direction for a moment, okay? What if we don't actually need to get out of the District? What if we can hole up somewhere until the borders open back up? Obviously not here. But there are other places."

No one spoke.

"Live to fight another day," Getty said. "We drop all this shit here and walk away like the rest of the peasants. Then when shit cools down, we can get back to fighting."

But all at once, he realized that it wasn't relieving the twisting feeling in his gut. In fact, it only seemed to twist his gut in the other direction. *There you go, Walter. There's your excuse. There's your "out." You can just agree with Getty, and I'm sure the others would agree too, because no one wants to die, and then you can be safe, just like you've always been. You can do what you always do, Walter. You can do what you're best at.*

Running and hiding.

"No," Walter said.

Getty looked at him. He didn't seem offended or irritated. Just curious. "No what?"

"I can't run anymore." Walter cast his eyes down. "I won't. And besides, by the time all of this blows over, the propaganda machine will be churning. You know it. I know it. We all know it. And everything that happened here in Eighty-Eighty-Nine will just be some bullshit rumor that no one really believes."

Getty sniffed. Worked some saliva around in his mouth. Took a sip of water.

Bobbi and Rat remained silent. It seemed to Walter that they were the neutral parties in this, but he also didn't know if they knew exactly what he was thinking, although Getty seemed to think that he did. That was okay. It wasn't really a discussion any more. It wasn't a discussion because Walter had *decided*.

He straightened up. His gut was no longer in knots. That was the beauty of committing to a course of action. It removed the angst of analysis. Suddenly the world seemed clear and polarized, no longer as confusing as it had been before.

Still unpleasant. Oh yes, very unpleasant.

But clear.

"They shut down the network," he said simply. "They shut it down and they sealed the exits. Like fuckin' cattle, Getty. Like driving cattle along the ramp and into the slaughterhouse. All the stupid cows too damn dumb and panicked to figure out that they could just trample those fences down if they really had a mind to. That's what we are. We're peasants. We're cattle. And they're just driving cattle right now. They're gonna do whatever they want to do." Walter smiled and it was odd to smile there, but he couldn't help himself. "I never understood how the guys with the cattle prods could not be afraid of being crushed by all these massive animals, but I guess, after you do it so many times, you know that they're all gonna do the same thing that they've always done, because they're cows. They're not coming up with any new ideas."

He let out a sigh, his first feeling of frustration, but then he knew that it wasn't up to him to convince Getty or Bobbi or Rat. That was not how this worked. They were grown-ass adults and they would make their own decisions.

"They can do this shit because there's never any outrage, never any consequences for it, because no one broadcasts it, no one talks about it, and when people want to know what the smoke clouds were, they just minimize it, say there was a brief scuffle with the rebels, and then they never talk about it again. And the world moves on."

Walter looked at Bobbi. "I'd like to open a live feed, Bobbi. I know you don't know me and there's no reason for you to hinge your life on a hare-brained idea like this. But all the same. I certainly can't do it by myself. I want to open a live feed and I want to broadcast what's going on. I want to broadcast this firefight. I want everybody else to see what's happening in the District right now. I want them to feel it. To understand it."

"You think it'll make a difference?" Getty said, his voice almost incredulous. "There's a fifty-thousand workers in this District, Walter. How many do you think picked up a gun and fought last night? A dozen? Maybe two dozen? Do you really think this would make a difference?"

"I don't know if it would make a difference," Walter said, feeling some frustration in his chest now. "All I know is that no one has done it before. And we can't just keep doing the same things, over and over and over again! We're here. We have an opportunity. Let's use it!"

"If you stay, you'll probably die," Getty said plainly.

"Yeah, probably," Walter agreed.

"What if Bobbi doesn't go with you?" Getty asked.

Walter looked at Bobbi. "Can you tell me how to do the live feed?"

Bobbi looked back at him, and there wasn't much there. She had the look of a host whose guest has uttered something horrifically uncouth and she was determined not to give a reaction for the sake of not making the moment *awkward*.

And he knew at once that she was about to tell him things he did not want to hear, such as, *no, you're too dumb to figure out how to do the live feed*, and *we're all getting the hell out of here, good luck to you, y'knocker.*

"I'll go with you," she said.

They all stared blankly.

Walter, blankest of all.

Bobbi didn't repeat herself. She simply looked at Getty, and in her was a glimmer of the same thing that was in Walter, that same elephantine determination that when the course is decided it is DECIDED.

Maybe Getty understood this too, maybe he knew it about her already or perhaps he just saw it in her eyes just as much as Walter had. He just looked right back at her, steady as a man who holds his finger to flame and doesn't wince. "If you go, we're all going."

To her credit, this gave her pause.

Sometimes it was easy to wager your own life.

It was something else to wager with others'.

Walter didn't know enough about computers for her to explain how to do the live feed and for him to actually be successful at it. And besides his lack of technical prowess, he doubted he could make the mile or so through the war-ravaged Town Center and get to the network hub all on his own.

He needed them. He *needed* them.

Bobbi nodded once. "We're all in it now. What he said was right. We can't keep doing the same things. They might take us out when we do this, but we will at least put what they're doing on display. And they won't have a chance to edit it. They won't have a chance to spin it. It'll just be the truth. And that's something they haven't had to answer for in a very long time."

Getty sniffed. Rubbed under his nose. He didn't look put-off. He seemed to be beyond that. He was simply introspective. Thoughtful of the consequences, as all of them were. All four of them imagining the worst, imagining the bombs, imagining the bullets, imagining bleeding out on a street in the middle of the District Town Center with the orange glow of a new dawn on their ashen faces but no hope of seeing the sun rise any further into the sky.

That's okay, Walter told himself, and maybe he believed it, and maybe he didn't, but he committed himself to it, and that was all that mattered in the moment. Commitment. He was committed. Bobbi, it seemed, was committed. And Getty and Rat were committed to her.

"We may not even get there," Getty pointed out.

"We have to try," Walter said, speaking with a conviction that he wasn't sure was even inside of him, but he needed it, he needed that strength to come out of him, to come from him, and sometimes you just had to act like you could do something, you had to act like you were a certain way, like you were brave and courageous, and then maybe you could make yourself believe it.

Rat was nodding, suddenly and emphatically. "Yes. We need to. We have to. This is the *right* thing, Getty. It's the *right thing*."

Getty nodded. "Ayuh. Okay. But if we get our legs cut out from under us halfway there, hold onto that conviction as you die, okay?" He didn't say this in spite. It wasn't sarcasm. He was deadly serious. He meant what he was saying. "The worst thing you can do when walking into the gallows is hedge your bets on walking away alive. I'd rather fight my ass of the whole way there, so if they do get me on the trapdoor, at least I go with a smile, knowing I gave 'em hell."

Walter was taken aback at the pall of seriousness that fell on them.

No bravado. No chest thumping. No cheering circles.

All four of them were beyond that now.

But Getty was right.

He's right, isn't he?

Shit if I know, it was your idea in the first place...

"We'll give 'em hell," Walter said. "To the very last."

Getty nodded. "Okay then. Rat? Bobbi? Is it settled?"

"Settled."

"Yes. Settled."

Getty looked at Walter. "It's your charge, Bossum. Lead it."

CHAPTER TWENTY-FIVE

The streets were utterly devoid of civilian life by the time they stepped out of that apartment building and onto the street, a single-file line of four. If you had a mind to flee the fighting, you had done it already. The only people left were combatants, and both sides knew it.

If the gunships saw this group of four running along the streets, then Walter and Getty and Bobbi and Rat would be bits of gristle and ground meat, splattered all over these brownstone walls.

Walter took the lead. Not because he knew what he was doing, but because he knew the Town Center better than the rest of them.

He knew the nooks and crannies. He knew the places they could duck and hide when drones and gunships came over.

The majority of the fighting, that tumble of death and destruction that had rolled epically through the Town Center all night, was now to the west of them, and just slightly south of the network hub where they were headed. It hadn't died as the night wore on, or dimmed with the rising of the sun. It had only intensified. But in its intensity Walter sensed the pall of death, the fighting for the last breath, the surge of energy and malice that overcomes one's conscious mind just before it is snuffed out of existence.

He didn't think that rolling battle would roll much further.

He thought that perhaps those resistance fighters that were left had their back to the wall now. Now it was do or die time for the fighters in this District, and that included Walter and his newfound friends that weren't really friends, but strangely, somehow, more, and simultaneously less.

The decision had been made.

Walter was committed.

He was going to see this thing through to the bitter end.

"Walter," Getty's voice whispered behind him.

Walter looked behind him and saw that the column of four had collapsed in on itself and they were all huddled there at the corner this building with him. Getty was sweating profusely and looking pale and tired. His leg was worn, but he was still pushing. He had extra weight to bear now, too.

The safehouse had come with a bounty of supplies. Walter's only regret was that they couldn't take all the weapons and ammunition with them, and didn't have enough people to use them all. They left what must have been thousands of rounds of ammunition, five suits of softarmor, and three battlerifles behind.

Now, they were all suited up, and even the softarmor, made lighter and more flexible than the armor the New Breeds wore—it was the armor of mere mortals—weighed them down. Along with the armor, they each had a battlerifle and three spare magazines for it.

Bobbi wore her battlerifle strapped to her back, and she held the giant sniper rifle in her hands. Her eyes up, always looking for the place where she could build a hide, then down at the streets, scanning for danger. Eyes cold. No longer prim. No room for that now. Like she was two people in one, and the other was gone for the time being.

Rat had his rifle in his hands and a compact launcher strapped to his back. Single use. Five shots. Rat said he'd never used it before. But he seemed confident he could learn.

Walter caught Bobbi's eye. "You see anything good for you?"

She shook her head. "Too far away. You been to the hub before?"

"I've seen it."

"Think of tall buildings. Landscape features. What can you see from the hub?"

Walter considered it. "SoDro offices. It's taller than the other buildings."

"Where is it?"

Walter nodded north. They were too deep between these endless three-story apartment units to see through them, but he knew the

SoDro office building was six stories, the tallest building in the Town Center.

"Three blocks north of us," he said.

Rat looked at her with some concern. "That's a long way to go solo."

She nodded. "I'll be okay."

It had already been agreed. Bobbi was the better with the rifle. Rat wasn't quite as good on the computer, but a brief discussion between him and Bobbi had determined he had the prowess to complete the mission without Bobbi's help. Which meant they needed Bobbi on overwatch.

Getty had made the final, pragmatic decision.

"Go then," Getty said. "Move carefully. Let us know when you're established." He tapped the comm unit that each of them had in their ears.

Walter touched his own comm unit lightly. It felt awkward.

Bobbi said nothing else. She straightened a bit, then looked both ways, up and down the street, then behind them, then up above into the sky. Nothing but smoke and destruction all around them. She scampered lightly across the street, didn't stop at the next corner, and then she was gone.

"How close are we?" Getty asked.

"Five blocks," Walter answered. They could see the red light blinking in the sky, even as dawn washed the darkness out of it. The spire of the network hub lifted blackly into the sky like a needle.

"Let's get closer," Getty advised. "Then wait for Bobbi."

They agreed by saying nothing, and Walter took them out again.

A few times, a flight of gunships roared overhead. They didn't take the time to look at markings—were they Fed or Chicom or Russian?—they just dove when they heard the rotors bearing down, and they squashed themselves into overhangs and rubble and gutters and underneath trucks that had been left in the road. Anything that would keep them from being seen.

The flights passed over.

Always, after about ten seconds, they would hear their guns open up. First the rumble-saw sound in bursts, and then the thunderous tremble of thirty explosive rounds striking within a fraction of a second of each other.

By fits and starts and fast-beating hearts, the three of them made it to within two blocks of the network hub. The sandstone buildings around them were in surprisingly pristine shape, as though the fighting hadn't reached this area.

Still no civilians on the streets, and the smell of things burning still wafted from other areas less lucky.

From where they were, they could no longer see the spire of the network hub, but Walter knew that it was two blocks ahead. Two blocks west. Just a few more minutes of walking. Less, if they ran, which they probably would, and though he was tired, his legs were beginning to numb themselves to the task of it even as they ached and griped.

With the three of them huddled in the inset door of a garage, Getty keyed his comms. "Bobbi, how's it lookin'?"

Bobbi's response came through in Walter's ear: "Making my way to the top of the building now. Haven't seen anyone. Just trying to find a good view of the hub."

Getty nodded. "Copy. Let us know."

Walter peered out at the world around him.

He was suddenly struck by the strange duality of his environs, like two realities had suddenly meshed and he was seeing them both at once. Like having two pictures, one in front of each eye.

This was not his Town Center.

It hadn't seemed like it, not from the point that he'd arrived, when it was still dark, and the gradual unveiling through the dawn's light hadn't changed that perspective. He knew consciously that it was the same place, that these were the same streets he'd walked, the same shops he'd gone in and out of to find this spare part of that tool. He knew it, and yet he didn't know it. His *heart* didn't know it, and it was because this place looked nothing at all like his Town Center.

His Town Center had never smelled so much like smoke. It had never been so devoid of workers. It had never been crumbling and on fire. Its sky had never been clotted with black smoke or crisscrossed with white contrails. It had never existed alongside the soundtrack of explosions and gunships and small arms fire.

This was not his Town Center.

And yet, suddenly, he was looking across this quiet corner of it, and his angle underneath the overhang blocked the smoke-muddied sky, and a gust of wind freshened the air, and none of the buildings in this area had been fought over, not bombed or pock-marked by bullets. This street was not strange. This street was a part of him. It was his home.

Had he ever cowered in this entryway?

No. He had walked through it and passed it a time or two. But he had never taken cover in it.

Had he ever been here with fear in his heart?

No. He had always been busy with the mundanity of his life.

Had he ever stood on this street with a gun in his hand, with comrades packed in close behind him, and knowing that this was the day they were going to die, but that they were going to go anyways, that they were going to make a helluva push, that they weren't going to give up?

Of course not.

The alien and the familiar, suddenly becoming one.

It was a disorienting sensation.

It came and went like the first smell of fall.

He shook his head to clear it.

"You okay?" Getty asked.

"Yes."

Getty had his pack of cigarettes out. He lit one. Extended the pack to Walter. Walter considered, then shook his head. He suddenly didn't feel terribly great. The sun was coming in now, between the buildings. A great, big, clear yellow swatch of it. And it gave him a sense of foreboding where there should have been appreciation.

Didn't things like this always happen on beautiful days?

Of course they did.

He couldn't remember a dark and stormy day when bad things had happened.

They had always been on pleasant days, pleasant evenings, pleasant mornings like this.

Blue skies had the power to terrify him.

He inclined his ear to a low rumble. "You hear that?"

Getty squinted through smoke. "Hm?"

Walter leaned out of the overhang a little farther. It wasn't the sound of gunships. He looked first right—west, towards their objective—and then left.

Then he jerked back, swearing at himself and wondering how dumb he was that he couldn't place *that* sound, the sound he'd been hearing since he was a child. After seeing it, it became so monumentally obvious that he was shocked at himself.

He slapped the cigarette out of Getty's hand. "Get down! Everyone down!"

The entrance to the shop was not only recessed, but sunken a few steps. Why it was built that way was a mystery to Walter in that moment, but it seemed like providence or luck, and he didn't much care which one it was. The three of them squashed themselves down into their shallow concrete foxhole.

Above the rough worn top of the first step, Walter watched two guntrucks scream down the street, roar past about thirty yards, and then abruptly come to a halt.

CHAPTER TWENTY-SIX

"Ah, shit," Walter whispered.

Getty had seized his arm and was tugging it manically. "Did they see us?"

"I don't..." Walter wanted to raise his head to look, but he was terrified of being seen. "I don't know."

Crouched behind him, Getty and Rat saw nothing. Walter was their eyes now, and they weren't going to move, weren't going to try and scramble up for a better look themselves.

"What are they doing?" Getty said, voice barely more than a breath of air from his throat.

Walter strained. He eked upward. His muscles quaked and trembled. The tension sucked the energy out of him, cramped his calf, but he was almost too fear-dumb to care about it. He pushed himself up until his chin was nearly resting on the second step down.

He could just see over the first step.

Two guntrucks. Parked in the middle of the street.

A cacophony of doors opening and closing. New Breeds tumbled out of the guntrucks. Walter couldn't understand them because they spoke in Russian, but their commands were not panicked or shouted. They were not harsh, nor angry. They were flat. Muted. Cold. Very business-like.

"I don't think they saw us," Walter whispered.

The soldiers pouring out of the trucks weren't looking their way. All of their faces were shielded with battleshrouds. They scanned all about them, all of their heads always moving ceaselessly, but they didn't fixate in Walter's direction. They weren't perceiving a threat there.

Still, none of them breathed.

Not for a moment or two.

And then, when they did, it was a cautious, shallow thing.

Like rabbits in the grass when coyotes are about.

Walter sank, melted into the stairs. His eyes jagged to Getty. The only movement he was really willing to make. "Tell Bobbi we're on Market Street. Two blocks south of her. Three blocks west. Can she see the two guntrucks? Can she see the soldiers?"

Getty slowly reached up to the button affixed to the chest of his softarmor and keyed the comms. He whispered: "Bobbi. You there?"

"Go with it," she said after a pause. She sounded out of breath.

"Have you found a hide?"

"Not a good one."

"Make do with whatever you got. We're blocked in, hon. Need an assist."

"Dammit. Okay. Where are you?"

"Two blocks south of you. Three blocks west. You see the two guntrucks?"

"Standby. I'm getting in position." A pause on the open line. "There aren't any anti-sniper cannons on those guntrucks, are there?"

Getty looked at Walter pointedly.

Walter stretched upward again. Surveyed the two guntrucks. Then relaxed. He touched off his own comms for the first time. "Bobbi, this is Walt. There are no cannons. Both have Lancers." Walter peered closer, giving the soldiers a visual inspection for the first time. He could see two of the soldiers had the eyegear on them. He could see the four-barreled Lancers on the top of the guntrucks twitching back and forth on their electronic motors as the soldiers equipped with the targeting eyegear looked around. "Controllers are the soldiers on the curb, the guy furthest east, and furthest west of the guntrucks."

Another long moment of silence.

"Okay. I can't see you guys, but I see the trucks and the soldiers." Her breathing seemed more level now, and on the air she took a deep breath and let it out. "Standby."

The line with Bobbi went dead again.

Walter looked back at Getty. "What do we do now?"

The other man shook his head slowly. "We wait. Keep your head down. Let Bobbi be our eyes."

Walter eased himself down. The cement steps were cool on his face. He pressed himself into them. Wondered vaguely and then poignantly if this would be his last sensation.

He didn't think the softarmor would stop many of the bullets, if any at all. Certainly not the Lancer. The Lancer didn't even have to hit you. If the projectile passed within a foot of you, the shockwave alone had a good chance of killing you.

The comm unit in Walter's ear hissed quietly as the line was opened again.

Bobbi's voice was quiet and calm now. "They're moving into the building that they're parked in front of. Breaching front entry…"

From across the street came a shuddering crash and then the sound of men shouting.

"They're in," Bobbi said. "Keep your heads down. The two Lancer boys are still on the street…stack's moving in…rear guard is in…okay, Lancer boys are moving in. Get ready to move, you guys. Get ready…"

Walter tensed. Got his arms and feet underneath him.

"They're in. Move. Move now."

There was no choice but to trust in Bobbi.

The three of them sprang up at the same moment. Walter half expected to find the squad still standing there, and in the last moments of Walter's short existence, he would see those Lancers coming to bear on him…

But the street was empty save for the two trucks.

Walter didn't spend much time looking, and neither did the others.

They beat feet hard down the sidewalk, the triple rhythm of their feet—with the slightly off-kilter sound of Getty hitching along rapidly—echoing off the walls around them. And Walter didn't look back at the guntrucks. He just kept listening to Bobbi.

"You guys are good," she said. "You're still clear. Keep moving. Take that corner on the right. Break the line of sight to the trucks."

"How's the hub?" Walter panted as they ran around the corner. He watched his shadow prance along in front of him as he went westward again. Dawn sunlight warmed the back of his neck.

"Standby," Bobbi said. "Let me get a sight on it again. Okay. Still not a great vantage—I'm going to shift. But for right now, you look clear. The nearest unit I can see is two guntrucks sitting at an intersection about two blocks up and two blocks over from the hub."

Walter didn't respond. Didn't need to. They all knew. All three of them knew.

They would have seconds to open the live-feed. And then it would be the fight of their lives. And they would likely lose. That was just how the math worked out. You couldn't be mad at the math. The math was simply the math.

Getty cleared a corner slowly, looked both ways down the street. Walter and Rat stacked up behind him. To the south, a building had nearly been brought down to its last standing brick. Oddly, the buildings on either side looked relatively unscarred.

They cut around the corner, headed across the street at a diagonal, heading to the north sector of the block. Walter kept looking this way and that, kept sweeping his rifle, but his body was not conditioned for war. His arms ached. His back ached. They threatened to rebel against him. Mutiny. Pure mutiny. He resented it.

Should have trained, was the new mantra that his panic-brain had seized on. *Should have trained, should have trained, should have trained.*

They stopped at the next corner.

The hub was the next block down.

Walter peered around the corner, and he could see it. The fencing around it. The clearing where they'd installed it. A few squat maintenance buildings set around it. One of those. One of those would be the place they needed to get into.

Walter hit the corner of the building, and Getty and Rat followed.

Before them, the network hub took up the sky.

Was it worth it?

Well, it was too far past now to *not* be worth it.

Walter plunged ahead.

CHAPTER TWENTY-SEVEN

Gunfire chattered fiercely in the distance. It was like standing outside of a stadium and hearing the roar of the crowds, but still being removed from it, a strange sense of under-worldliness, like you were skimming below the surface of reality, unnoticed and unnoticeable.

Brownstone walls streaked passed. Here, not quite so peaceful and untouched as the blocks previous.

Here a car stood, still smoking, crumpled into the side of one of the apartment buildings. The windows were white like privacy glass, shattered into opaqueness by a flurry of bullets, but somehow still standing there, delicately, in their frames. Red painted the interior of the car. It leaked out of the front door and onto the pale sidewalk.

Walter worked around it, didn't look inside.

They skirted a smoke-blacked cluster of debris that still stank of off-spent munitions. It was an acrid, nose-curling stench. An angry smell. He could see blood in the rubble. He could see a hand, and that stopped his breath. Because it was a small hand. Very small.

He stumbled to a halt. His lungs wanted the air, but they were stuck for a moment, stuck in exhale. It was strange how he'd not wanted to look in the car, but this small, pale thing sticking out of the rubble, it had snatched his eyes almost hypnotically.

"Walt," Getty said from behind him.

From worlds away.

The ringing in his ears had returned.

Maybe it had never gone away.

Walter stared. Finally inhaled.

The arm belonged to a kid, of course. Maybe five. Maybe four. It was hard for him to tell. He'd never had kids of his own, so he'd never developed that ability to tell a kid's age that a parent somehow magically possesses, and seems a mystery to the childless. And…it was just a hand.

The rest would be buried in that rubble.

He went to it.

He wanted it to reach for him.

He wanted the voice of the boy or girl that was buried there to cry out for help, to still be alive. He bent down and he grabbed it, and Getty and Rat were saying something behind him and they sounded either angry with him, or scared for him, maybe both, but he wasn't really listening to anything they had to say.

When he touched it, it was cold and stiff.

Like a mannequin.

He jerked back.

"Walter, Jesus Christ, man!" Getty limped up next to him, and he grabbed Walter by the shoulders, but not unkindly, almost gently, almost like you would turn a mourner away from the grave of the recently deceased.

Walter realized that he wasn't hypnotized. He wasn't drawn in against his will, wasn't locked onto staring at this thing by some power that was beyond him.

I want to see it.

And so he did. He looked at it.

What he felt…

What *did* he feel?

Nothing that would well up violently or suddenly and force emotions to be wrung out of him like dirty water from a used washrag. Nothing like that.

No, it was worse than that.

It was something down deep.

Something cataclysmic, but so far down inside of him that all he could do was sense the distant disturbance that it caused. He only knew that he needed to look at that hand. He needed to accept it. He needed to let that inside of him.

Look at it. Remember it. Mark it.

"Hey!" Getty smacked his shoulder, this time roughly.

Walter took another moment to look at the child's hand in the rubble. He blinked a few times, almost like mentally swallowing it, like he was making sure that it was all the way down, that it wouldn't ever be forgotten. And then he looked up.

"Sorry," he said, and he didn't wait.

He looked behind them, ahead of them. Saw the coast was still clear.

He started running again.

Ten yards beyond the pile of rubble with the child buried in it, the street intersected with another. Beyond that intersection, the road ended, and the network hub sat. It was completely encircled by an eight-foot fence with barbed wire on the top. There was a vehicle-entry gate directly in front of them. The road that they were running on turned into the drive that led through the gate.

It was an electronic gate. A small box stood to the right of the entry, requiring key-card access.

None of them would have it.

"How's the skies?" Getty asked over the comms.

It took Bobbi a few seconds to respond.

"Clear over top of you," she said. "There's a whole shit storm going on southwest of you, though."

Walter tracked his eyes over the gate, looking for a weak point. "How do we get in?"

Rat was beside him, breathing heavily, sharing his focus.

Getty grabbed their shoulders, started pulling them back. "Let Rat blow that shit."

"If we leave it up it could deter…" Walter stopped himself. He'd been thinking it might keep soldiers at bay for a bit, but they wouldn't come on foot. They'd come in armored guntrucks. And the chain-link fence was about as much of a barricade to them as a sheet of paper. The fence would be useless as a defensive measure.

Well, then how the hell are we going to defend?

He looked beyond the gate, saw the buildings.

Yes. Short, squat buildings. Small windows. Stone walls. That was where they had to go anyways. So they would go. And they would hope that it took the gunships a while to come. Once the gunships were there, the stone walls would mean nothing. They'd be incinerated and buried in rubble in seconds flat.

Just like that poor kid…

Rat had unslung the launcher from his back. He shouldered it and didn't hesitate. He activated it. Some component in the thing made the very slightest whining noise, and then there was an ominous *kuh-shlunk*—one of the five rounds being auto-loaded into the chamber.

Rat made himself small. "Head's down, guys."

Walter barely had time to hunker before there was a loud *POP* and a vicious, rushing *HISSSSS*. A white smoke trail billowed out of the back of the launcher and something fast and green shot out.

A second later there was a flash and another cloud of smoke and the gate stood in tangled ruins with a gaping hole in the center.

A smattering of things peppered Walter's face and hands and head, but none of them were big enough to cause any real damage outside of a momentary sting.

"Nice," Getty said shortly, and then was hauling himself upright with a groan. "Let's move!"

The three of them ran.

The tangled maw of the damaged gate grew in front of them, but slowly. Walter realized how gassed he was. How his running was little more than a stumbling jog.

The horrific boom.

Jesus, it must have drawn attention, didn't it?

Would someone have heard it? Seen it?

Walter felt it like an iron cord had been cinched around his stomach and was being ratcheted tighter and tighter.

The one currency that meant anything to him at that moment was time.

And his accounts were plummeting towards the red.

They clambered through the ragged gate, trying not to snag themselves on the sharp, smoking ends of the wire fencing that were everywhere, like going through a briar patch.

Walter went for the building directly in front of them. It was the largest of the three that were in the small, fenced in complex that made up the network hub. No one worked in any of these buildings, but occasionally maintenance crews had to get in and fix something, and the buildings were there to house the servers and give the workers enough room to access them.

He turned as he neared the building and looked behind them. He could just see the SoDro Offices looming up, a darker shape than the other structures. Most of the Town Center was made out of brownstone concrete. The SoDro building was black steel and tinted windows. It looked untouched.

Somewhere in those windows, Bobbi was hiding, watching.

He felt a hand grab his shoulder and pull him along. "Come on, Walt! She sees us!"

Then they were at the door to the building.

Rat was already there. He tried the handle. No go. It rattled loosely, and clearly it wasn't turning any tumblers. "Locked," he announced to them.

Walter grimaced. Looked the door over. It was a big ass door. A big metal thing. "Can you blow it?"

Rat made a disconcerted face. "Good chance it'll wreck some components inside. Might be the ones we need."

Which would then render this entire operation purposeless. It was already hanging onto the very edge of being a fool's errand—might as well not shove it over the brink.

"Here," Getty said, and he took a knee, slinging off his backpack.

Walter huddled over him.

The pack opened. It revealed about a hundred things that Walter had no idea what they were used for, and a single thing that he knew quite well. It was a small, two-foot demo bar. He handed it to Walter with a slight smile.

"One doesn't run about these environs without a breaching kit."

Walter snatched up the demo bar. Turned to the door.

Getty shouldered up to it. "Come on. Put the flat-head in, right at the latching mechanism. There. Good. Shove it in. Now press it back and forth. You feel it giving?"

Walter did. He strained at it. Felt the flathead of the demo bar slip in a little more. He pressed back and forth again. Something metal popped. The door gave a little more.

Abruptly they were drenched in a horrible noise.

Walter jerked and almost dropped the demo bar. It was a horrendous screeching and he could actually *feel* it poking at his eardrums like an invisible finger and it was physically painful.

"Christ!" Getty jumped, then grabbed Walter and steadied himself. "It's just the alarm!" he shouted over it. "Keep going!"

Walter was working his hands before his brain. But as he struggled with the door and the pry bar, he wondered if there was anyone monitoring the alarms? Surely if anyone *had* been monitoring things like alarms, they long ago would have called it quits? With a war going on a few blocks away, there's no way that they would send anyone to investigate an alarm.

Right?

Sure.

Pop.

The door gave.

And then, satisfyingly, it simply swung open on well-oiled hinges, and Walter felt a giddiness rise up in him that lasted for about a half second before it was trampled by his need to get the hell inside of the building before they were seen and obliterated by a CoAx gunship.

Automatic lights blinked on as the three dusty, bedraggled men tumbled into the building.

It was a big square, nothing more.

In the center of the square were three rows. These rows were black metal shelving units stacked floor to ceiling with black servers and cables that connected everything to each other and bound together into giant spools and these were fed through ports in the ceiling. The three sections of servers stood there, green activity lights blinking like a confused audience.

To the left, a counter that seemed to be there to provide some sort of place for maintenance crews to work.

To the left, something similar, but with some metal storage built into the wall above, and two dumpy-looking rolling chairs that had been left idly in the middle of the floor by whoever had used them last.

Walter shoved the damaged door closed behind him. It didn't latch, but it did hold.

Strangely enough, the alarm was only on the exterior, and when he closed the door it became just an annoying bleating in the background. But at least you could hear yourself think.

"Okay," he said. "What do we do now?"

Rat was already heading for the service bay to the right. "Over here. This should be fairly straight forward. I just need to hardline in. Looks like they have the cables already staged for maintenance."

He gestured to a series of neon pink cables, all with identical male ends. There were four of them at even intervals at the right service bay. It seemed simple enough to Walter: There was a problem with the system, the maintenance crews could simply plug in directly to the system and do what needed to be done. It was just that easy.

It's never that easy.

Rat scampered to the service bay, reaching back for Getty's backpack. Getty shoved it into his waiting hands, still hanging open. Rat grabbed it, fell into one of the chairs, and rolled to a spot in the middle of the service bay. He slapped the bag down, threw it open, and dove inside, yanking out a gray tablet, which he smacked unceremoniously onto the counter. The he looked up at Walter and Getty.

"Y'all watch the door, not me."

"Bobbi's watchin' the door," Getty said defensively.

But Rat was already back working at the tablet, flipping the monitor into existence, activating a projected keyboard onto the counter-top.

Bobbi's voice: "You guys okay in there?"

Getty keyed back: "Ayuh. Solid. How's it looking outside?"

"Clear for now."

Getty nodded to himself and turned to Walter. "You okay?"

Walter stared back at him, almost disbelieving. "Jesus, man, you're the one with the shot leg. Are *you* okay?"

Getty bobbled his head. "As good as can be expected, I guess." He was rummaging for his cigarettes.

Outside, a series of concussions rumbled the earth.

Walter stiffened.

Getty didn't seem to notice.

"Hm," he said, looking into his pack. "Only one left."

"Go on, then."

"Well. I didn't want to be rude." He lit up. Crumpled the empty pack. Then tossed it, almost resentfully, into the corner. "I could go for some coffee. Or whiskey. You know?"

Walter nodded, because he figured that was the appropriate response.

"Either wake me up or fuck me up, one of the two," Getty said, then puffed at his cigarette.

"What?" Walter asked. "All the shooting and the death not wake you up enough?"

"Ha." Getty glanced up at him. Half smile. Then he frowned at his shoes. "No. No, I feel like I'm sleeping right now. And that's kind of frustrating."

Another series of concussions, slightly farther away than the last ones.

Rat's hands, skittering across the keyboard.

"What do you mean?" Walter asked.

Getty huffed out a lungful of sweet tobacco smoke and shrugged. "I dunno, man. Just...feel like I'm about to bite it anyways. Wished I felt a little more alive. You know?"

Walter felt that thing, that big, monstrous, undeniable, unutterable thing, moving down around in the depths of him, and he nodded, because he did know. He did know what it felt to want to feel.

If you'd have asked him twenty-four hours ago, he would have commiserated as best his limited experience would allow him. Because that was the type of person Walter was. He always tried to share in people's feelings, always tried to commiserate and make them feel normal.

But he wouldn't have truly understood.

He wouldn't have understood that some things that happen to a person are just too monumental for the mind to handle. If the mind had an ocean, then that ocean was also the place where the mind dumped the things that it could not deal with. It dumped them into the deepest place, into the place where the pressure condensed it down as it sank, down, down, down, it went, crumpling into a little ball so that no one on the sunny topside would ever see it, ever even know it was there, except…

Except that it changed everything.

It changed the waters.

It changed the tides.

It changed the very polarity of the earth.

The things that we can't process, we don't just forget them. They change us. They change us deeply. And they either do it in one fell swoop, in one cataclysmic shattering that will leave us raving mad, or they do it slowly, slowly, slowly, like wind and tides tearing down rock over eons and eons.

That thing was down inside of him now.

Carolyn

The crescent-shaped scorch mark

"I want my brother back!"

Carolyn

A child's arm sticking out of the rubble

Virgil

Tria

Carolyn

A child's arm

CAROLYN

Walter shook his head to clear it.

Getty offered him the half-burned cigarette.

Walter took it, took a drag off of it. Then took another, greedily, but Getty didn't seem to mind. He felt the nicotine light off the back of his head, and then he handed it back.

"Alright," Rat suddenly announced, and his voice sent electric sparks down Walter's spine, out his arms, and into his fingertips.

He looked up.

Rat was sitting there with his tablet all plugged in, the monitor queued up, the network accessed. Just like that. Just that fast. He was looking at Walter.

"You gonna say something?" he asked.

CHAPTER TWENTY-EIGHT

"Is it ready?" Walter asked. He swallowed on a dry throat that tasted of dehydration and stale smoke.

Rat nodded. "Gimme the word, I start beaming. It's to a public outlet. I can't promise you that people will see it. But it's the best we can do. I'm not beaming until you're ready." Rat shook his head. "I hit the button and we have minutes. Maybe just seconds. Then they're gonna be on us."

And what Walter heard in all of that was, *You have minutes, maybe just seconds, to live.*

Was it possible to make a difference in the tides of things with only seconds left to your life?

Was it possible not to live for something, but still, in the end, to die for it?

Sure. Yes. All of that was possible.

Just as possible as it was that no one would ever see his message.

Just as possible as it was that his last meager seconds on this earth would amount to nothing. A life of nothing, followed by a death of nothing.

Who was Walter Lawrence Baucom III? No one in particular. Some grower. Another guy that died during the purge of 8089. Died trying to prove something. But you can't just decide at the eleventh hour that you want to be a hero. True heroes were forged over time. Not fashioned abruptly, like field-expedient weapons.

No matter what happened, he was a nobody.

Does it change anything?

Walter looked at Rat. Looked at Getty.

Thought about Bobbi, huddled in whatever shadowy corner of SoDro Offices, staring at a network hub and waiting for it to be surrounded.

And he realized that it didn't matter.

Call it peer pressure, if you like. It was a powerful conviction. It was the conviction that he'd already said something to these three people. He'd already said he was going to do this thing. And they had agreed to come along with him. He just couldn't bale now. Couldn't, and wouldn't.

Which was horrendously stupid in the face of the consequences before him, but still…people in situations like the one that Walter found himself in, they often did stupid things. When the stupid things worked, they seemed like genius things. Brave things. When they didn't, well, then they were back to being stupid.

Hindsight being what it was.

"Okay," Walter nodded. He walked over to Rat. Over to the tablet that he'd hooked and hardwired into the network. Sitting there like a bomb ready to go off in the innards of the Fed's control over them, and that thought gave him a little satisfaction.

Somewhere out there, there was a man or a woman who was watching everything that was happening in 8089 with a callus lack of emotion, perhaps drinking coffee as they coordinated this purge. And in a few seconds, they were going to feel something bind up in their guts and their bowels were going to loosen as they realized that something had gone wrong.

And Walter relished that.

He relished the opportunity to make them feel it.

He stood in front of the console. Straightened himself.

"I'm ready."

Rat eyed him, up and down.

Behind Walter, Getty said, "Bobbi, we're about to transmit. Be ready."

Rat hit three buttons in quick succession.

The monitor of the console turned into a mirror. Walter was watching himself. He was watching the live feed that he was beaming out to whatever public outlet that Rat had found to stick it.

A second ticked by, as Walter stared at himself.

He was shocked at his appearance. His face was not the face that he was used to. This face was worn out. It was cold and on fire all at once. His eyes were raging things. His mouth was pressed tight. His hair stood askew and filthy, and his face was smudged with dirt and soot and gunsmoke and bits and pieces of dark debris clung to his sweaty, greasy skin. He held a battlerifle in knuckles that had all been skinned, and bled, and smeared.

Rat shifted, the first note of panic reaching him. Fear that Walter had frozen at the penultimate moment—*Oh, Jesus, we should have known better than to trust a fucking grower...*

"I'm Walter Lawrence Baucom," Walter suddenly blurted out. As if to convince himself. "The *third*, if it matters. And I think it does. Four generations ago there was a Walter Lawrence Baucom the first. And I think that he was the last man in my family to die free."

Walter didn't know where he was speaking from.

Maybe from that inner-ocean canyon where he had dropped the things he could not process.

Changing tides. Changing polarity.

Time is ticking...

"I'm a grower, and I live in Agrarian District 89. Last night, the CoAx shut down our District and cordoned it off. And now they're purging it. As we speak, they've bombed half of our Town Center to rubble." He looked absent for a moment. Out of the corner of his eye, he could tell that Rat was tapping his wrist—*time, time, time!*—but he didn't pay it any heed. "I saw a kid's arm in the rubble. Not sure if it was a little girl or a little boy." He shook his head and focused on the console, on the camera that was beaming his image, his words out to the world. "This is what they do. This is what the CoAx does. And the Fed—our country, our leaders, our government—they've sold you out. And if you were ever thinking about doing something, if you'd ever considered saying 'enough is enough,' then maybe you should do something about it right now. Because the situation is only getting worse. It's only going to get harder and harder to fight them."

He leaned towards the camera. His face loomed on the console. Haggard. Dirty. Desperate.

"If you're watching this, listen to me," he said. "Please listen…"

And then the feed cut out.

A million important things to say log-jammed in his mind, like a pile up happening on a busy freeway.

"What happened?" he stared at the blank monitor.

Rat snatched his rifle up. He was already out of his chair. The rolling chair went spinning off into one of the towers. "Shit, they're on us. They shut us down."

"But…" Walter stuttered.

I barely said anything important.

What was I thinking?

Why did my mind go blank?

Why was I talking like this was a fucking fireside chat?

You fucked it up, Walter! You fucked up your one chance, you stupid…!

"Let's go!" Getty had ahold of him and was moving for the door. "We might still be able to make it out!"

Rat had his battlerifle in one hand, and the launcher tube in the other. The console and the backpack and all the little tools it contained were still sitting at the service bay, forgotten now in the rush to get the hell out of the kill box that they'd trapped themselves in.

"Run, run, run!" Rat was urging them.

"Bobbi, the feed got cut," Getty was saying. "We're exfilling now."

Walter staggered along dumbly.

You stupid knocker!

You wasted your life!

Now you're gonna die for nothing!

Getty ripped open the door.

The morning sunlight blasted their eyes.

Getty out first.

Walter in the middle.

Rat directly behind him.

Bobbi's voice bursting on the comms: "Get back inside!"

The world started as a narrow rectangle of light, and as Walter's eyes quickly adjusted, it grew, and he could see the brownstones ahead of them, and beyond, the SoDro Offices, and the doorway expanded further. He was now fully in the frame of it and there, far off to his left, he could see three guntrucks roaring in their direction.

And they were close.

Way too close.

He knew in an instant that they weren't going to make it.

"Ah, shit…" Getty tried to stop.

His wounded leg buckled under him.

Walter hadn't taken his eyes off of the guntrucks. The lead one was only a hundred yards away now and nothing between them except for a chain-link fence.

He watched that Lancer shift, watched it stare right back at him like a dead eye.

It spat fire.

Getty hit the ground on his ass.

The doorway behind them exploded.

Walter stumbled into Getty, then felt Rat hit him from behind, and that nearly toppled him. He somehow managed to keep his feet.

Up, up, up! his mind roared at him.

"Move!" Rat shouted.

Walter realized he meant "get out of the way."

The rat-faced man had his battlerifle dangling by its strap from one arm—he hadn't even had time to sling it all the way—but he had the launcher up.

Walter grabbed Getty by the dragstrap on his softarmor and he bent low, knowing there would be a geyser-hot trail of smoke coming out the back of that launcher…

POP-HISSSSSSSSSS

BOOM!

With his hand in Getty's dragstrap, Walter straightened up. With his other hand he held the battlerifle against his shoulder and fired haphazardly in the general direction of the guntrucks.

Then he started hauling. Hauling back. Back. Back. Into the dark, into the building, back behind the stone walls that would last for a little bit, but not very long.

He was cognizant enough to stop firing as his muzzle drew close to Rat, who stood there spread legged as though he was immune to bullets, the launcher still affixed to his shoulder.

Ah, fuck…

Walter didn't even hear the *POP-HISS*.

CHAPTER TWENTY-NINE

He was thrown violently into the doorjam.

He felt the blast of it turn his head to the right, yank it, actually, like he'd taken a hard punch. Felt his body tumble into the doorjam like his limbs were that of a ragdoll. He was only conscious of red light, and a sensation like someone had slapped him across the face with a hot skillet.

Hold onto the dragstrap.

That was what he thought.

Don't let go.

He was stunned. His body wasn't doing much besides flailing, but in his mind he was still pulling Getty out of danger. He could feel the drag strap in his hands, but he was just tugging uselessly at it, crumpled on his side, just on the interior of the door.

Getty was crawling back over him, shouting something.

It was difficult to hear.

Getty's torso was over his face. The dragstrap wasn't in his hands anymore. It had been pulled out. The rough fabric that coated Getty's softarmor rubbed harshly over Walter's head, and all of the sudden it wasn't dull pain anymore. His face was on fire.

The two men tumbled into the dimness.

The world was shattering around them.

It smelled of rocket propellant and dust.

Rat screamed.

Injured?

I think I'm injured too.

We're all injured.

The pain, at first a nuclear explosion through his whole head, now began to recede and center around its true source—the left side of his face.

In a stupor, Walter ripped out a breathless yelp, and his left hand went to his face, his right still clutching the rifle. It felt like there was burning acid on his face and his first instinct was to wipe it off but then he restrained himself. His fingertips touched his face and he felt skin that wasn't his—it was slick and sticky and his touch jumped through him like electric sparks.

He screamed. Tried to articulate something, but for a few seconds the pain was wilting all logic.

Dimly, he could hear Getty's voice.

"Your face is burned," he was yelling. "Stop screaming! Stop! You gotta fight! It's just skin!"

Just skin.

Walter choked off his next scream as he felt it bubbling up in his throat. He forced his eyes to open, though he hadn't even been aware that they were closed. The movement made the left side of his face feel weird, like it was cracking the skin.

Daylight.

From his right eye, crisp.

From Walter's left eye, things were foggy.

He blinked painfully, trying to clear it.

It didn't clear.

Rat was in the doorway, looking at him while the world turned to dust behind him. As he stared in horror at Walter, he was trying to get the door closed.

My eye's been burned.

"Get up!" Getty was shouting. "Shoot back!"

Get up. Shoot back.

But my face…!

Well, you're dead anyways. Who cares about your face?

Walter sat up, and it was like magic. Like a miracle.

The pain didn't leave him. But that sick, panicked feeling that you get when you know that you have truly, badly injured yourself, it fled him like a dark cloud suddenly burning off into bright sunshine.

What did *injured* mean to him? It meant very little.

He was dead anyways.

Somehow he was on his feet.

Rat had managed to close the door.

Three giant holes suddenly erupted in the center of it, spilling shafts of light and making noises like a jackhammer had been put to the side of a car. Rat jumped back.

Walter pulled his cement-block feet into action. Stumbled to one of the small windows. The glass was dirty but he could see the shapes outside. He could see the three guntrucks that had parked themselves about twenty-five yards to the north of the network hub, providing cover while the soldiers emptied out the opposite side.

One of the guntrucks was smoking, and the front tire was gone, and the hood was rumpled. One of Rat's missiles had struck true.

To Walter's left, Getty began to fire out of another window, the battlerifle chattering aggressively, but even in the enclosed space, Walter's eardrums were too rocked to really be offended by it.

This is insanity, he thought.

And he wasn't wrong.

There was a madness coming over him. A rushing feeling of flowing momentum, of knowing that you cannot stop now, you cannot hesitate, you can only charge forward, carried by the flow. It was unstoppable and it was terrifying. Because it did not care about the consequences. It only knew the spirit of a suicide charge.

He knew the end, but the end didn't matter.

He saw a battleshrouded head peek up from around the front of one of the guntrucks, rifle spitting madly. He sighted almost instinctively, like he actually knew what he was doing, and squeezed off a flurry of shots. He saw them shatter across the fender of the guntruck and maybe one or two struck the head—he watched the soldier jerk back.

It probably didn't kill him.

Only struck his battleshroud.

The best he could hope for was some spalling to the face.

It would take more than that to kill these demi-gods.

Another shape, another move, another shift, another squeeze.

The rattle, the rumble, the concussion of it slapping back at him in the small enclosed area, the blast of each cartridge spent, radiating out of his muzzle, bouncing off the wall and coming back at him, but it all just flowed, it all just melted and he was going, going, shifting, shooting—

A Lancer pointing right at him.

Shit

He ducked.

The window blew out with a horrendous noise.

Chunks of concrete and mortar flew in over his head. A fist-sized piece of debris tumbled down, struck him on the side of the head, felt like it nearly ripped his ear off. But he found himself thankful that it was his right side and not his burned left, which was screaming as tiny secondary projectiles peppered it.

"Rat!" Walter yelled. "Blow that fucking Lancer!"

Rat was duck-walking along the wall towards Walter. Behind him, the door was shuddering as a few more rounds went through it, pushing the door open a bit as they passed through, letting in that harsh morning light that should have been golden but was instead bleach-white like a desert sun.

Rat shouted something back.

Walter couldn't hear him.

He stuck his gun over his head and blind-fired out the ragged chunk of concrete that used to be the window. A piece of glass gouged at his hand. He registered the sharp pain, but it was momentary, and it took a number at the back of the line to the rest of the things that hurt.

Three bursts of fire.

Then nothing.

He yanked the rifle out of the space, stared at it dumbly.

"You're empty!" Rat yelled at him.

I know that already, Walter thought, but then why sit there staring at his rifle?

Rat punched him in the shoulder, hard. "Reload your rifle!"

Walter jerked. He stripped the magazine out. Fumbled another one out. His hands were trembling and unpracticed. He tried twice to get it in the magwell and failed. Succeeded the third time—it's a charm, as they say. Then he struggled with the bolt release and finally managed it.

He moved to stand.

Rat pushed him back down.

A scattering of bullets chipped away a bit more mortar from the ragged hole over their heads.

Rat was leaning into him, yelling in his ear to be heard. He could feel the man's hot breath, could feel his voice poking at his eardrums, and yet it was still barely audible for some reason. "Take the *left side* of the hole. The *left side*. Shoot until you're empty. Shoot at everything that moves. Okay?"

"Okay."

A storm of projectiles from the Lancer punched through the concrete wall, caving in a section. More small arms clacked away the bricks and brownstone directly over his head.

Walter cringed and looked up.

The sunlight was caught in a haze of dust. He could actually see the tiny little paths, like wakes left by boats, where the bullets had ripped through the dust. He had no other words to say as he gaped up at this. But he thought, *They're gonna splatter my face as soon as I stand...*

"Ready?" Rat said, shaking him.

"Ayuh," Walter called out before he could really think about it.

"MOVE!"

Walter sprang up.

Too damn slow

He punched his knuckles against the concrete wall. Smacked the rifle down.

He watched tracers screaming at him, around him, but it was too late to do anything but what he had stood up to do and Walter wasn't going to stop, he wasn't going to fail again.

He screamed in the face of the incoming barrage and he sent his own.

The burned left side of his face screeched in agony.

Bullets chewed concrete and spat it in his face. In his eyes. On his burned skin. He felt things hitting him and didn't know whether they were bullets or pieces of debris, and it didn't matter. He was still standing, and whenever he saw any of them move he would rattle out at them as his mouth filled with dry dust and he tasted it and it filled his nose and eyes and everything around him, dust and concrete and gunsmoke.

POP-HISSSSSSSS

BOOM

Walter watched the Lancer disappear in a flash and a sudden cumulus of smoke billowing up from it.

"Down!" Rat yelled.

Hand on his shoulder, driving him back down.

Walter hit the ground hard on his knees.

He was empty again. He reloaded, a little smoother than last time.

"Getty!" Rat was yelling across Walter as he worked. "How's it look?"

Walter glanced in Getty's direction.

Getty was posted on the other window, and his window had fared no better than Walter's. What had been a perfect square opening had now been blasted into some hellish polygon, and Getty fought to just get his muzzle clear of the side of it and let out little bursts of rounds, then duck back in as a hundred more stormed back at him.

This last time he pulled back too hard and lost his footing. He toppled backwards, barely catching himself on the service bay counter, and then, halfway into the fall, seeming to just give up and decide to let himself hit the ground.

Two big, glowing hornets shot through the hole-that-used-to-be-a-window and shattered one of the towers of servers in a shower of sparks and a groaning, sizzling sound.

Getty was cursing up and down, dropping the mag from his rifle and swapping it with an utter fluidity that boggled Walter's mind. He was just now getting his back up. If he'd ever learned to gunfight like Getty had, maybe they'd be in a better situation right now.

Shoulda woulda coulda.

Getty didn't get up when he charged his rifle. He sat there with his legs splayed out in front of him and he touched off his comms. "Bobbi! What the hell we lookin' like?"

Bobbi's voice sounded distant in Walter's ear and he realized that his own piece had come slightly out of his ear in all the tumbling. He pushed it back into place and her voice crystallized like she'd walked into the room with them, midconversation.

"...pulling back right now. They're at the corner of the building at your eleven o'clock. Two blocks north of your pos."

"Fuck," Getty said, untransmitted. Then, to Bobbi: "How many? Did we get any?"

"I see two down right now. There are six at the corner. Three behind the northernmost guntruck. There's still one Lancer battery in commission."

"Any anti-sniper?"

"Negative."

"Can you find the guy operating that last Lancer and take his ass out?"

"Standby." Her voice was strong, but strained. Focused. Like she was talking while trying to solve a puzzle at the same time.

Outside, Walter heard the Lancer bark at them and a section of the concrete wall around them, a section that was about waist-height, and directly between the two windows, abruptly bulged, and then shattered inwards.

Walter cried out wordlessly and scrambled away from it.

He watched the bricks go tumbling and then disintegrate in the onslaught, and he watched the rounds careen off the smooth cement floor and go sparking violently in strange directions with sounds like the moaning of a large animal.

A piece of ceiling collapsed a few feet from Walter.

"Christ!" Rat was huddled against the wall, then pulled himself off of it, as though he didn't want the next piece of wall that exploded to be the one that he had chosen to pin himself to. "They're gonna bring the whole building down on us!"

The Lancer fire abated for a moment.

Getty to Bobbi: "Jesus! Can you find the guy? He's gonna tear our ass out in a second!"

"Hang on, I'm looking!"

Another barrage slammed through the wall, about a foot left of where it'd struck last time. It started working its way left, towards Getty. Walter watched it encroach on him, his safe zone decreasing with every single round that punched through in a thundercloud of concrete dust.

Getty already had his back to the wall. He couldn't back up any further. And yet his legs kept on kicking at the floor, his eyes wide and bright, and he yelled over the comms, "Bobbi! Take him out! Take him out!"

No response.

Walter watched the gap between those horrendous rounds and Getty shrink down to a few yards, then just a yard, and as he watched it, he thought stupidly *maybe he can just jump across it…*

Then the Lancer stopped.

Getty was breathing raggedly, letting out little noises, like he was sliding slowly into water that was either too scalding hot or too ice cold.

There was no audible report this time.

Bobbi's voice on the comms: "I got him, Getty. You okay? You there?"

"Fuck!" Getty screamed out, just a release. Then he keyed up, his voice marginally more controlled. "Ayuh. I'm here. We're good. What's going on?"

"Bad news," she said.

CHAPTER THIRTY

"What's the bad news?" Getty asked levelly.

At Walter's side in the smoking, choking room, Rat was swearing quietly to himself.

Bobbi sounded bracing, almost apologetic: "That squad is still at the corner of the building. They're not maneuvering. They're waiting for an airstrike, I can guarantee you that. And I got a flight of three, inbound towards you as we speak. Less than a minute."

Getty looked up from the pile of rubble that should have contained the parts of his body, and he met Walter's gaze, then Rat's. He sat there for a moment, still perched up on the service bay counter, his hand still on the PTT for the comms. He said nothing. He looked like he might be sick. The first sign of plain and simple mortality that Walter had seen in him all day.

And it drove the point into Walter like a railroad spike.

"They're gonna blow this building down," Walter said. Not much emotion there. Just a statement of fact.

Getty didn't respond.

Rat shifted, his shoes scratching through rubble as fine as sand. "Yeah. That's what they're gonna do."

"We could run for it," Walter said.

"We couldn't get far," Rat said quietly.

"*I* wouldn't get far," Getty said with a ghostly half-smile. He nodded at his leg. "*I* wouldn't. Y'all might."

Rat shook his head fervently. "Banish the thought, Getty."

Getty shrugged. "You could if you wanted to. I wouldn't hold it against you guys. Could give y'all some covering fire."

"We could *all* go," Walter said again. "They're two blocks north of us. That's over a hundred yards. And we'll be running. We've got a good chance of not getting hit."

Getty threw a thumb skywards. "Them birds'll strafe us on the run, just as soon as blow out this building. Die out there, or die in here." He said it calm enough. Peacefully enough. But there was a tremor in his voice.

"Guys," Bobbi said in their ears. "Y'all got about twenty seconds. You gonna get out of there or what?"

"Hold on," Walter said into the comms. He looked frantically between the two of them. "You motherfuckers! *I'm* the grower! I'm the knocker that doesn't know how to fight! Why are you two laying down right now? We can run. We can at least *try*. I'd rather die out there than in here."

Walter was on his feet now.

He was going to run. But he needed them to run with him. Otherwise it would be running *away*. And he wasn't going to do that. They were going to run it together, or they were gonna die in this shady hole like sick animals that have crept under a crawlspace to breathe their last breaths in relative comfort.

Walter was about to start screaming at them, about to start grabbing and dragging as best he could, if that was all he could do.

But then Getty struggled to his feet, a hard glint in his eye and that soft sense of mortality sudden stricken from it like the hard thing inside of Getty had reached up and throttled it, broken its neck, and stuffed it down. "Aigh' then. Let's die in the sun."

They didn't wait.

They ran for the door.

No more talking.

Rat threw the thing open, though there wasn't much left of it anymore.

Bright morning sunlight hit his face. And Walter thought that was good. That was very good. And they ran into the sun, the three of them, Getty limping significantly, but not all that slow, he was giving it a good effort.

Out into the great wide open.

Nothing between them and a dozen guns, cold eyes sighting down hot barrels.

It was a long run, Walter realized. He had pictured a short sprint, but now it looked like miles were stretching between him and the next available piece of cover, and there was the scraggly remains of the gate to contend with on top of all of that.

He was no more than five loping strides into it when he started to feel every muscle in his body give up, hit the wall, nothing left to give.

We're not gonna make it.

Well, you should enjoy this sunshine, then.

Carolyn!

But then everything exploded around them.

CHAPTER THIRTY-ONE

The next few moments were hazy.

They never got processed into his memories.

They simply were, and then they were not.

Just before the entire street in front of them erupted violently like some giant and long-awaited caldera, Walter thought he saw three little gray somethings streaking out of the sky. But then, the explosion, and the earth lifted, like all the world was sitting on a rope bridge and some jackass was bouncing it on the far end. It bucked and swayed under his feet and then a giant, invisible hand smacked him in the face and chest and sent him backwards, and in the moment when the breath emptied out of his lungs and his chest compressed, he saw guntrucks defying gravity, along with great geysers of what had once been the cement street.

Then there wasn't much of anything.

Then there was pain. But it was more just the *concept* of pain, rather than pain itself.

He opened his eyes and the world was white, like it had snowed, white on everything, but that wasn't right, it was just the sunlight. It was just the sunlight making everything so very bright, shouldn't his eyes be dilating, blocking some of that light out? It was blinding...

He felt a wind. A wind that was gentle, hell, almost pleasant at first. It wicked hot sweat from him.

Then the wind turned harsh. Hurricane. Tornado. Ripping. Sending debris into his burned face. He tried to cry out, realized his lungs still didn't have oxygen. Tried to move, but that required oxygen, and he didn't know if his muscles could do it anyways. Everything felt broken and falling apart. Like all the communication lines across his body had been severed.

Oh my God, I broke my back.

I'm paralyzed.

Someone was yelling.

The wind battered him. Beat him. Buffeted him.

Rotors.

Those are rotors.

Shit! The gunships!

He tried to open his eyes. The light was too painful. Too bright. His eyes watered and welled. He squeezed them shut again. His left eye was damaged, he remembered that.

The voice was still yelling at him.

No, not at him.

At *them.*

"...okay? One of you move! Stand up!"

Bobbi. It was Bobbi's voice.

Walter tried to lift his hand, but his arm was approximately the same mass as a small car.

The wind had reached its worst. It wasn't getting stronger, but it wasn't letting up. The sound of the rotors were heavy and panic inducing, but there just wasn't much he could do about it at that moment. He was trying to get the unwilling machine of his body to work, like a man in the driver's seat of a battery-dead car, trying to crank, crank, crank.

"Can any of you hear me?" Bobbi cried out. There were tears in her voice now.

I can hear you.

Then, finally, a connection reestablished in his brain. It remembered how to breathe. So that was good. He felt his diaphragm come out of its shocked, spasming state and all of the sudden acrid-tasting air went avalanching down his throat. He coughed wretchedly against it, and that seemed to be the thing that sparked off the rest of his connections.

All of the sudden his body was moving, curling up like a pill bug around his cough. Then he was rolling. And he could feel his arms and his legs—holy shit, they were moving, *thank God, I'm not paralyzed!*

"Walter!" Bobbi screamed in his ear.

"Ungh," he responded to no one in particular.

"Walter, they're landing right on you! To your left! To your left! I can start shooting but you need to be able to move, do you hear me?"

Walter had managed to roll onto his left side, so when he squinted his sore eyes, he saw what Bobbi was talking about. He was looking out across a debris field, and about twenty yards from him, one of the gunships was setting itself down onto the ground, just inside the fence-line of the network hub.

The other two gunships hovered overhead.

"Can you move?" Bobbi yelled at him. "Can you hear me?"

Walter found the PTT button and pressed it. "Yes. I can hear you."

The gunship's skids touched the earth. The side wall of the gunship was already open. He could see inside. He could see New Breed soldiers looking at him. He could see their armor, but he couldn't see their faces past the battleshrouds.

It was a Fed gunship.

It was his own countrymen come to kill him.

He grunted and reached for his weapon, the battlerifle still tethered to his chest. He grabbed at it clumsily, barely cognizant of what end to point at the bad guys, but determined that he was going to make them shoot him.

Better dead than DTI.

Yes. That's how the saying goes.

Carolyn.

Ah.

Sorry.

The bird settled fully, and as it did, three New Breed soldiers tumbled out.

"If you're ready, I'm ready," Bobbi said in his ear. "I'm ready. I'll take the one closest to you."

Walter stared at him.

This one stared back at him. The one in the front. The one closest to him.

The one that Bobbi would shoot.

He just looked like a man to Walter.

He felt his hand slide into the grip of his rifle.

"I've got him," Bobbi said.

The soldier was about ten yards away now.

"Walter!"

The voice wasn't from Bobbi.

It made him jerk.

It sucked him back.

Like a black hole had suddenly erupted in space just behind him and sucked him through at the speed of light.

Walter.

Walter!

Walter, goddammit! What're you so ascared of?

Walter...

Walter...we could do better but they won't let us.

He blinked, thinking at first that it had come from the soldier that was advancing on him, but then his eyes skidded madly about, and he caught sight of a fourth figure, not a New Breed, not as big or as wide, and he was dressed in softarmor, and he was vaulting out of the gunship and running towards Walter, his battlerifle swinging wildly from side to side.

"Walt!"

Walt.

That's me.

Who the hell are you?

But he knew it. It was something that didn't need logic to calculate. Something that simply was. It was a fiber that ran through him. It was a part of his tapestry. It was a part of the whole of him.

It was Roy.

In his shock, in a sludge of disbelief while his conscious mind told him—*nope, that's impossible, they disappeared Roy, he got sent to DTI, and NO ONE COMES BACK FROM DTI!!!*—he remembered one very important thing, and he snatched at his PTT button and blurted, "Bobbi, don't shoot! Hold your fire! Don't shoot!"

CHAPTER THIRTY-TWO

Bobbi was saying something.

Walter didn't hear her.

He was staring at his brother.

His brother?

Impossible.

But was it?

He had the feeling, like when something is on the tip of your tongue, when you've almost figured out the riddle, but you can't quite articulate it. The connection is almost there, it's just hovering in mid-air, like an arc of electricity from one pole, sizzling, trying to reach the next pole, trying to complete the circuit.

"Roy?" he said in disbelief.

Roy stumbled up to him, and around him, the four New Breed soldiers with their Fed insignia didn't point guns and mow them down, as Walter was sure they would, nor did they charge them with restraints, nor did they throw diversionary grenades at them.

Two of them stood up straight, one looking southeast, the other looking northwest, and the other two plowed past Walter as though he didn't matter, and Walter couldn't see where they were going, but he figured they were going to Getty and Rat.

Oh my God, Getty and Rat, are they okay?

Like a firework in his brain, and gone just as quickly.

"Roy?" was all he could really get out.

Roy bent down with purpose, down onto one knee. It was Roy. It *had* to be Roy. Older, most definitely—he looked shockingly like Pops now. And he had a neatly trimmed goatee that he'd never worn before, and his hair was salted at the temples, and it was shorter than Walter had ever seen him wear it…

But it was Roy.

Beyond a shadow of a doubt.

"Hey, little bro," Roy said, worry scribbled over his surrealistically aged features.

Walter felt an uncontrollable urge well up in him, and he reached forward, bent up at the waist, suddenly filled with strength, and he grabbed Roy and put his arms around him. If it was awkward, Walter didn't notice. He hugged his brother to him desperately and felt a love in him that he hadn't even considered in a very long time, a love that he had very deliberately buried long, long ago. Because he didn't want the loss of Roy to touch him, he didn't want to wake up every morning with that feeling in his gut like he'd been ripped apart.

But here he was!

Here he was, in the flesh.

Holding his brother, Walter smelled him. And he smelled just as dirty as Walter did, but he also smelled like Roy. In a way that was imprinted on the granite bedrock of Walter's consciousness. And it seemed that it could not be true, because here is a face: *no one comes back from DTI.*

Except that someone had.

Roy had.

And whoever had broken out…

"Was it you?" Walter blurted, suddenly pulling away.

Roy looked troubled, confused, hurried. "What?" his eyes traced quickly over Walter's features, not a loving glance, a diagnosing glance.

He think's I've got my senses knocked loose.

"Was it you that got broken out of DTI?"

Roy somehow managed to nod and shake his head in the same motion. "It's complicated. Shut up for now. Are you hurt?"

"No, I'm fine," Walter was struggling up into a sitting position.

"Anything broken?"

"I don't think so."

"Does your head hurt?"

"Yes."

"Can you see okay?"

"No."

"Bright?"

"Yes."

"How old are you?"

"Twenty-seven."

"What month is it?"

"April! Jesus, Roy! What the fuck're you doing?"

Anger mixed with real concern flashed across Roy's face. "You might have some TBI, that shit hit real close. We didn't think you were going to come running out of the goddamned building like that! You should have stayed inside. What the fuck were you thinking?"

A distant part of Walter reared back indignantly.

Somehow that tone never went away.

Little brother. Stupid little brother.

But then the thought was gone, washed away by the flood of love and relief that Walter felt, just seeing Roy in front of him, actually alive, actually well.

"Was that you guys?" Walter asked numbly.

"Fast movers," Roy nodded. "Speaking of, loyalist troops have interceptors inbound and we got less than five to get the hell outta Dodge."

Roy stood up fully, grabbed Walter by the arm, helped him stand. Walter looked about him at the New Breeds. It felt like walking in a pride of lions. He'd never stood amongst them like this when they weren't pointing guns at him, demanding papers. Now their backs were to him, looking out, scanning for threats.

Feds.

Fed New Breeds.

"Are you Fed?" Walter asked as he struggled to keep his feet and the blood rushed out of his head and his vision sparkled dangerously. "What's going on?"

"I told you it's complicated. But they're not Fed. Not anymore. Come on."

Not anymore?

Defected, then?

"El-Tee," one of the New Breeds hollered up. "Both live, one's unconscious."

Walter turned, blinking against the bright light and his own fading vision, fighting the feeling of hot-cold that prickled his scalp, threatening to make him faint. The other two New Breeds were with Rat and Getty.

Getty was awake and alert, though dazed. He was getting to his feet. His eyes were darting left and right, very confused, and Walter saw very clearly in his eyes that he was wondering if he should grab up his rifle and start shooting or not.

"Getty!" Walter raised his hand and made a staying motion. "It's okay!"

Getty locked eyes with him, gave the barest of nods.

"Friends of yours?" Roy asked, working an arm under Walter's and around his shoulder.

"Ayuh."

Roy nodded to the two New Breeds triaging Getty and Rat. Without another word, they both bent and scooped them up, carried them in their arms like children. Getty looked surprised, and slightly indignant, but he let it happen.

"Three minutes," someone spoke up.

"Let's go," Roy hollered loud enough for everyone. "Hustle up! Road gear, motherfuckers!"

Walter and Roy were moving. Roy was moving faster. Walter was trying to keep up. He suddenly felt incredibly nauseas.

TBI, he thought. *Traumatic Brain Something...?*

Did it matter? He knew that the first two words were Traumatic and Brain.

That said enough.

Shit.

As they neared the downdraft of the waiting gunship, Walter heard Rat come alive. He looked left, saw the gigantic New Breed carrying the small man at a jog, and Rat was just coming to, and all he was seeing was a gunship and a battleshroud, and he was starting to freak out.

"Rat!" Walter yelled, groggily, the pressure of the yell making his head hurt.

TBI...

"Rat, it's okay! It's okay! They're friendly!"

Rat struggled for a second longer, eyes wide but unseeing, unfocused, like a sleepwalker.

The New Breed barely seemed to notice his struggle. Walter heard the soldier say something to Rat, and he couldn't tell what it was, but Rat's eyes went to the soldier that was carrying him and frowned, but didn't fight anymore.

They were in the downdraft now.

Somebody else was yelling something in his ear, but Walter couldn't quiet tell what was being said, or who was saying it. *Wait until we're out of the downdraft, moron, no one can hear shit right now*, he thought.

The two New Breeds with Getty and Rat reached the gunship first.

Walter had his head ducked down, his eyes squinting against the wind which dried them and pelted his skin with a hail of tiny pebbles, and he was reminded that the skin on the left half of his face was missing. He realized that somehow he had begun to cry, which was very odd, because he wasn't feeling much at that moment, he was feeling very disconnected, watching his two friends—they were friends now, right? Hell, they'd bled together, they might as well be—as they were hoisted up into the belly of gunship, and that open side door waited for him too, and it was all very unreal that he was going to enter a gunship under his own power, not bound and gagged with the flash of a diversionary grenade still dazzling in his eyes.

Why am I crying?

It's just the wind.

It's the wind and the dust.

But it wasn't that his eyes were watering.

He was crying. His chest was hitching. He was sobbing.

What is wrong with me?

The deep things. The things in the ocean abyss.

Changing tides.

Changing polarities.

Then they reached the open door and Roy was pulling him into the gunship, and he was out from under that downdraft. The cabin was still horrendously loud, but at least the wind wasn't in his ears anymore. He could still hear the voice chirruping at him, and as he clambered aboard, it clarified.

"…you motherfucker!" Bobbi screamed. "Tell me what's happening! Walter, Getty, can anybody hear me right now? What the fuck is going on?"

Walter and Getty's eyes crashed together.

They'd been so caught up in what was happening that they'd forgotten about Bobbi.

Beside Walter, Roy was speaking into a comm unit of his own. "Secure! Let's get the fuck out of here!"

Getty was looking with sudden and uncharacteristic panic at the New Breeds, and at the one normal human being, which was Roy, who the New Breeds had called "El-Tee" which Walter knew meant "Lieutenant."

"Bobbi," Getty belted out. "We gotta get Bobbi! We can't leave her!"

He tried to lean forward.

The New Breed that had carried him stiff-armed him back into a sitting position.

"Sit the fuck down," the soldier barked.

Walter spun to Roy and grabbed his brother by the shoulder. "Roy! Hey, Roy! We got a friend still on the ground! She's in the building…"

Roy was shaking his head. "No, Walter. No."

"We can't leave her!"

Underneath them, the deck rolled, and the bird was airborne, rising rapidly into the sky.

"Sorry," Roy continued to avoid eye-contact.

"Roy!" Walter shook him.

Roy jerked back, cleared his shoulder of Walter's grip, then looked at him. "We got about two minutes to clear this airspace or we're going down in a ball of flames, understand? Our fast movers saved your ass but they can't stick around with the interceptors inbound, and neither can we." He shook his head, managed, somehow, to look put-off. "Everyone on this bird just risked their life for you, *little brother*, just be happy you're alive!"

Walter stared.

Funny, he could feel the tears drying on his skin in the wind that was rushing through the open gunship doors.

Funny, he could feel him*self* drying up with them, like mud in a hot sun.

Funny, how brothers have the unique ability to turn you from love to rage in a hair's breadth of time.

"Put the bird down," Walter said.

Roy took a half-second to evaluate the look in Walter's eyes. Then he shook his head. "I'm sorry, Walt, but we just don't have time."

The gunship was moving now, not just rising up, but tilting, slightly, it's nose downward, but it's forward motion pinning everyone to the deck like artificial gravity. Out of the corner of his eye, Walter watched the world tilt in a disorienting way, but he was crystal clear for the first time in the last ten minutes.

He didn't really want to do what he was about to do.

But he had already decided.

And when you're decided, it is best not to hesitate.

He backed up a half step and snapped his rifle up.

Roy had partially turned away, but at the movement, he jerked back around.

He saw the muzzle of the rifle staring at him, and then he looked at Walter with disbelief in his eyes. At first that was all there was, but then there was a note of fear in them as well.

He had looked on the wounded man that they'd dragged aboard the gunship and he'd seen his *little brother*.

But things had changed, hadn't they?

Walter wasn't himself anymore. He wasn't even the person he'd been the last time the sun rose. He had only just begun to realize these violent catalysts being activated in himself, these cataclysmic shifts, but it seemed that Roy abruptly saw them in their fullness and when he looked at Walter it was not the look that you give a person you are familiar with because you have known them all your life.

It is the look you give a person when you realize that you don't know them at all.

But it couldn't just end there.

Of course not.

Even as Walter opened his mouth to speak, he heard a bark from one of the New Breeds, and out of the corner of his eye, he could see the soldier raising his rifle up to point at Walter.

Walter completely ignored the New Breed pointing the rifle at him. "We got a fighter stuck in a building and we are not leaving her." Walter said, and his voice was cracked and worn and ground to shreds. "She's the only reason we're still alive. Tell them to put this bird on the roof of the SoDro offices."

"You gonna shoot me?" Roy asked, holding his gaze.

Walter opened his mouth to respond.

Then he heard a sound from behind him.

It was the pop and crackle of a stun gun.

And then the sound of someone uttering a cry of surprise.

Walter spun to look behind him, and saw Getty and Rat, slumped into the arms of the New Breeds that had taken them aboard the craft. Stuck to each of their necks was the bolt from a stun gun, still crackling out blue arcs of energy.

The two New Breeds held the stun guns in one hand, and lowered Getty and Rat's bodies to the ground with the other.

Walter already knew the mistake that he'd made.

He knew it as he turned back to Roy.

Turned back to his brother and saw the muzzle of a stun gun.

Behind the stun gun, Roy looked stern, but apologetic.

"I'm sorry, Walter."

The stun bolt struck him in the forehead.

CHAPTER THIRTY-THREE

His mind bobbed in shallow consciousness for a while. A timeless while, like some segment deep in space where time is relative and reality has sped along ceaselessly without you, decades flying by in the span of seconds.

He became conscious a few times.

The first, was a start.

He jolted, gulped air, wanted to fight.

He thought he was still in the gunship. He couldn't feel the wind anymore, and thought that maybe they had closed the doors. When he looked up it was the same dark gray ceiling, the stability joints of the aircraft standing out like ribs, like he was in the belly of a whale.

There was also a New Breed.

He had his battleshroud undone. He was a broad-faced man, which was typical of the body-mods. He had a fiery red beard and Walter thought he looked like some sort of Norse god, with eyes that twinkled with mead and mischief.

The Norse god was applying an IV pack to Walter's arm and telling him to hold still. Walter stared, blinked rapidly, trying to focus, and came to the sludgy realization that this muddling of his mind was beyond what should have happened with the stun gun, and as his vision cleared enough, he realized that the IV pack—just a little black box strapped to his arm—had already been fed into his veins, and what the Norse god was doing was pushing a tranquilizer or an anesthetic into his bloodstream.

He didn't want to go down again.

He wanted to fight. He was very angry.

And then, he just couldn't find the energy to be angry.

He was swallowed in an enveloping warmth, like being sunk into a hot bath, but without the initial, bracing sting.

As he sank again, he tried to look around, and he wanted to ask, "Where's Rat? Where's Getty? What the fuck is going on?" but his mouth wouldn't move, nor his throat make any sound. He couldn't see them at all, but then, he was finding it hard to turn his head.

The last he heard was his brother's voice: "Walter, don't be scared. I'm here."

He thought that someone was holding his hand.

Maybe Roy, but he couldn't be sure...

Walter, don't be scared. I'm here.

Walter, don't be scared.

I'm here.

Walter.

I'm here.

Don't be scared.

I'm here.

I'm here.

I'm here.

Awake again.

Kind of.

He tried to move again, tried to do it with violence. But he was stuck in a place between sleep and awake. And in this nightmare place his greatest efforts garnered him only the slightest twitches of his limbs.

He tried to cry out. He felt a slight moan come out of him. He tried again and got the same result. He buckled down, and this time just tried to scream as loud as possible, desperate to either wake himself up, or have someone wake him up, anything to get out of this nightmare place.

He let out a loud noise.

Roy's voice: "Chill out. You're okay. Don't be scared."

Walter blinked a few times.

Yes, it was sky above them.

Bright sky.

He could actually feel the sunshine on his face.

Or was that the warmth of the drugs?

What are you doing to me, Roy?

"Nothing bad is happening to you," Roy's voice assured him, although Walter could not see his face. "So don't be scared."

What about the others?

Too late, back under.

———

Weird dreams.

He was standing in a barren, shitty trailer. He looked around it. He thought it was the one where Virgil had kept Captain Kuai Luo for questioning.

The same trailer. But different.

In only the way that dreams can be in places that are not the places they are supposed to be.

Walter got the sense that the small cramped living area where he'd stood, banished from the room where Virgil was doing his work, smoking a cigarette with Getty, was much larger, much more expansive than it had been in real life. Something like a ballroom.

And then, of course, it was filled with people. Some sort of social occasion. They were all lounging along the same wall with Getty. They were all laughing and sharing drinks.

Walter didn't feel happy at all.

He felt pissed that no one was taking things seriously.

Getty smoked his cigarette and smiled at him. "Maybe you don't really mind it that much," Getty said. "Maybe you just *think* you should mind it, and you don't, and maybe that's really what scares you. Huh?"

"No." Walter just shook his head.

Getty pointed with two fingers and a cigarette pinched between them, his eyes on Walter's chest. "Look at that."

Walter looked down at his chest.

Which was not a chest at all.

He was looking into muddy waters. But they were deep.

The longer he stared, the deeper he went. The darker the muddy water got. Almost until it was pitch black. And then it was. He was still plunging into them, and he had the crazy image in his mind of his head bowing down and into his chest, delving into himself, some backwards version of a snake eating its own tail.

There was something down there in the dark.

He wasn't *feeling* it necessarily. Just *knowing* it.

Down there in the deep, deep dark.

In the deep, muddy dark that is black.

He was drowning in it.

His lungs were clawing for air.

Too far from the surface now.

He was going to die down there…

———

Blip.

Back to reality for a wakeful second.

Someone was doing something to his face.

There was a great deal of pain.

He heard something beeping manically.

Someone was speaking rapidly, urgently.

Something pushed into his veins again.

Oh well.

———

Carolyn was tied to the chair.

In the trailer that was defunct.

That was a ballroom.

That was filled with people.

Carolyn was in the chair, but she was asking the questions.

She seemed very serious.

"Who's been kidnapping New Breed soldiers?" she asked, seeming to be a little irritated with Walter, as though he knew the answers and was refusing to give them.

"I dunno," Walter answered lamely.

"The Honeycutts?" She prodded. "The Linklaters? The Eudys?"

Virgil's voice from beside Walter: "The Eudys are *extremists*," he asserted.

Walter turned to look at him.

Virgil was looking back at Walter. Half his head was gone. He was smiling. Or was it just that his lips had been ripped off by the bullet? A few teeth were missing, shattered to jagged roots by the path of the projectile. His eyes twinkled merrily.

"*Extremists*," he said again, his gory mouth dribbling blood, loose flaps of skin moving as he spoke. "They're all extremists and they're Not To Be Trusted."

Walter turned back to Carolyn, disturbed.

"Why?" she asked.

"Why what?" he answered.

"Why are they kidnapping New Breeds?"

"I dunno," he said again.

"Who got broken out of DTI?"

"The Eudys," a voice announced.

Walter looked in that direction.

It was Captain Kuai Luo. He was lounging on the wall with Getty. They were passing Getty's last cigarette back and forth. Captain Kuai Luo let out a stream of smoke and nodded at Walter, pointedly.

"The Eudys," he repeated. "Carolyn's parents."

"Extremists," Virgil stated again. "Fucking extremists."

CHAPTER THIRTY-FOUR

Walter came to more evenly this time.

And this time there were no drugs.

He felt himself rising up. Felt the light of reality piercing the deep strangeness of his dream world, but the questions and the images clung to him even as he surfaced and opened his eyes. As he was waking he had the pressing feeling that the dream was important, that the questions raised were important, and that he should not forget them.

He opened his eyes, and he knew he was fully awake, and he stared up at a ceiling of white polyboard tiling, and identical walls. There was a circular light above him, and it was dimmed to a tranquil blue.

The dream was still there.

It still made sense.

The urgent need of those questions still clutched his stomach. He turned them over in his mind like a puzzle in his hands, waiting for them to dissolve into the stuff of dreams—that nonsense stuff that falls apart in the light of reason much like a sand sculpture will crumble when it has fully dried and the wind strikes it.

Who has been kidnapping the New Breed soldiers?

Hadn't Virgil asked that question?

He had. When he'd first begun to question Captain Kuai Luo.

The captain hadn't had an answer.

But…he'd known the answer to another question.

Who was broken out of DTI?

The Eudys.

Carolyn's parents.

THE PURGE OF DISTRICT 89

And who was going to do extreme things, like kidnapping New Breed soldiers?

Why, the extremists, of course.

Carolyn's parents.

But why?

Just to torture and interrogate?

It seemed like much trouble for not much gain.

The resources that would have to be committed to getting multiple New Breeds in custody would be large. The intelligence that they had would likely not outweigh that cost.

Why?

Why kidnap them?

And where was Carolyn's parents now?

And where was he sitting at this very moment?

And most importantly...

Carolyn.

The concept of her like a bone-deep ache.

He heard something stir in the room with him, and he leaned up. He was lying on a bed. It was pushed to the side of a room. The room was small. A sink and a toilet opposite him.

His heart hammered.

Cell, he thought, suddenly. *I'm in a cell.*

And then, with positivity, with conviction that squeezed his innards to mush: *DTI, oh God, I'm in DTI.*

As he came into a semi-sitting position, propped up on his elbows, he saw who else was in the room with him.

"Roy," he rasped, and in the one word there was something like a longing and something like a hatred. But brothers were unique that way. They could have both in equal measure. "What the fuck—"

Roy raised one hand, cutting him off.

He was sitting in a chair, and he looked cleaned. Scrubbed. He wasn't wearing his softarmor anymore. His dark hair, which looked like it was on the shaggy end of being close-cut, looked like it had been wet recently. All the dirt and smoke was scrubbed from his face, but there was a notable cut that ran from the bottom of his left earlobe over to about halfway across his cheek. It was a minor cut, but red and angry.

Roy held his brother's gaze, and Walter pumped anger back at him, and for a brief moment, in the silence of their looks that managed to say so much, Roy looked regretful. But not entirely remorseful.

Roy lowered his hand, and spoke, evenly, quietly. "Don't freak out right now. You're not detained." To make the point, he gestured to Walter's wrists. "You have no restraints on you." Then he gestured to the door—a plain gray rectangle. "And the door's not locked."

Walter forced himself into a more upright position. "You left one of my people—"

"One of your people?" Roy scoffed. "Tell the truth, Walter. How long have you known any of them? Hm? How long?"

Walter burned, but clenched his jaw and no words got out.

Roy propped a hand up on his knee. "You think I don't know that you just met these people yesterday? And yet you point a rifle in my face to save one of them." Roy looked genuinely troubled by that. "We had enemy fast movers inbound on us. If we'da tried to pick your person up, we would've all been blown out of the sky." He sniffed and looked away. "You forced my hand."

Walter frowned at him. "Why were you even there? I don't understand."

Something flickered around behind Roy's eyes. "We were on our way to try and extract a different group of fighters." He paused there for a long moment, and the anger in his eyes melted into something like sadness. "But we lost them before we could get there. Good people. Friends of mine." He gave Walter a pointed look. "Friends that I've known for some time."

Walter felt his own brandished anger wavering as he saw that hollow sense of loss in his brother's eyes. He still knew very little and understood less about his brother's story, but he knew that look. He had lived that look oh-so-recently, and it stung him like a fresh cut.

Roy cracked his knuckles hastily. A habit that Walter didn't recognize. Perhaps a nervous twitch he'd developed after a decade in DTI.

"We couldn't save them. But you broadcast at just the right moment, right before we were about to kick dust. And we were able to save you. And your two...*friends*." A sneer twitched at Roy's mouth. "I'm sorry we couldn't save the other, but we ran out of time. We did what we could do."

"Where are they?" Walter asked.

"They're safe," Roy said. "They're in other rooms, just like this one. You'll see them soon."

"Where are we?" Walter said, casting another glance around him, trying to level his breathing out, trying to disguise the unease and the fear.

Roy considered the question with his mouth open, then shook his head. "No, I can't tell you that. Not yet."

"Roy..."

"You're safe," Roy said, for the umpteenth time, and this time was no more convincing to Walter than any of the other times. "Relatively, anyways. I will tell you this—we are bunking with a lot of Fed troops. So don't be shocked when you see them."

Walter swallowed and realized that his throat was dry, his tongue was pasty, and his lips were like paper. He tried to work some moisture into his mouth. "Defected?"

Roy nodded. "As of yesterday. Do you want some water?"

"Yes," Walter said, trying not to sound desperate for it.

Roy pointed to the ground next to Walter's bed, just to his right.

Walter leaned over and looked and found a white plastic tray sitting there with two bottles of water, a few boxes of juice, and some fruit-cups. Quick and easy calories.

He bent down, grabbed a bottle of water, opened it, and took a light sip.

The water wasn't cold, but it was cool.

It was glorious.

He drank another sip, thinking of not overloading his stomach so soon.

He was hungry though. And when he capped the water, he looked down at the fruit-cups.

"Drink up first," Roy said. "If you keep the water down fine, then eat. How's your face feeling?"

Walter reached up to the left side of his face.

Just before his finger's touched, he recalled in harsh detail, the sound of Rat's rocket launcher going off, spewing hot gasses into the side of his face and knocking him back into the door frame. Remembering this, his fingers hesitated before they touched his own skin, and when they did touch it, they did so lightly.

It surprised him that he felt no pain.

Quite the opposite, actually.

The left side of his face felt numb. Almost like he was touching someone else's face. It felt a little greasy. A little puffy. He couldn't feel any of the beard stubble that had begun to prickle the other side of his face.

"How's it look?" Walter ventured.

Roy's eyes traced it over without much concern, and then he shrugged. "The NeoSkin is still melding. You don't look like a monster or anything. But you can tell something got you. And I don't think you'll be growing a beard anytime soon."

Walter nodded soberly, withdrew his fingers from his face.

His brain reasserted itself to the situation at hand.

The hurricane of questions still blew madly in Walter's mind but he was finding a bit of a groove now, snatching some pertinent ones out of the air. It was causing things to be more linear. It was abating the confusion.

Every question answered took a little more of the darkness away, shed a little more light, made him feel a little less lost.

"What happened to you?" Walter suddenly choked out. "Where'd you go?"

"Where did I go?"

"They took you."

Roy smiled unpleasantly. "They did. They took me to DTI."

"How long...?"

Roy watched his little brother, nodded slightly as he saw the connections being made. "Do you know who the Eudys are, Walter?"

Extremists, fucking extremists.

"Yes. Kind of."

Carolyn's parents.

Fucking extremists.

Roy leaned forward, hunched onto his elbows. "The Eudys and I were housed in the same block of Sweetwater DTI. It's some God-forsaken place in the middle of Wyoming. Even if you found a way out, you'd just be stuck in the Rockies. You wouldn't get far." The smile still hung on his face, almost a rictus now.

"But you did get out."

"We were busted out," Roy said, quietly. "Or the Eudys were. And I managed to hitch a ride along with them."

Walter eyed his brother carefully. "How'd you manage that?"

"I slit the throat of a guard that was about to shoot them during the escape. Then I took his weapon. Then I invited myself along. Maybe they would have invited me along anyways. I like to think that they would have. We'd not talked much—they don't allow much talking in DTI—but I felt that we were good friends after ten years of being in that place together. Can you make friends with someone you barely speak to? It's possible. It's surprising how much you can communicate in looks. Ha." Roy's smile became marginally more genuine. "Just like you, Walter. Like your special skill."

Walter nodded, slowly.

More dots connected.

More light shined into dark, obscured places.

"When did all of this happen?" Walter asked.

"Two months," Roy said. "Closer to three now."

"And are you still with them?"

Roy nodded. "I am. We all are."

Extremists.

"Why would someone call them extremists?"

A twitch of Roy's eyebrows. "Who said that? A Fed?"

Virgil, your old best friend.

Do you know he's dead now, Roy?

"Nobody you know." Walter said.

Roy thought for a second, then gave a half-lidded look as if to say *tom-AY-toe, tom-AH-toe.* "I suppose that some folks view them as extremists. I suppose that to some people their methods, back before they were captured, seemed to be extreme. They didn't differentiate between Fed and CoAx troops, like everyone else did at the time. But who turned out to be right on that one? And some of their attacks took civilian casualties. But how many more has the CoAx taken?"

Roy leaned back in his chair. His feet fidgeted underneath him, then lay still. "It's war, Walter. The best thing you can do is fight tooth and nail, kill everything that might help your cause to kill, and get it done quickly. That's what the resistance has been missing." His eyes thrilled with a devilish light. "For ten fucking years, they've been missing that. But they've got it back. They've got it back, and we have a chance. We're gonna fight dirty. We're gonna fight however we can. And we have a chance now, Walter. A chance against the New Breeds…" he trailed off, as though realizing he was treading into something he should keep silent about.

"The Eudys," Walter said. "They're the ones that've been kidnapping the New Breeds."

Roy looked back, and he didn't answer in the affirmative or negative, but all the same, Walter saw that he'd struck upon the truth.

"Why?" Walter asked, echoing the thoughts of his dream. "Why are they doing it?"

Roy shook his head. "Can't tell you about that. Not yet."

Walter sat up fully in his bed now. Enough light. Enough peripheral questions.

He swung his legs out of his bed and touched them to the floor. It was a steel floor. It had the feeling of something temporary. Maybe it was. Maybe this whole place was temporary, ready to pack up and move on at a moment's notice. Walter wasn't sure how defected troops were keeping themselves hidden from the rest of the Fed military and the CoAx. But that wasn't the thing that he wanted to ask.

His question, the most important question.

His thought, the most important thought.

He cleared around it, like exposing a fossil and brushing away all the dirt around it.

"The Eudys," Walter said again, thickly. "They're Carolyn's parents."

Roy watched his brother. Then nodded marginally. "Yes. They are. I didn't know about that until—"

Walter's heart surged in his chest for a reason he couldn't define. He squared his body at Roy, almost like he was about to launch himself at his brother, but the look on his face was one of desperation, of pleading.

"Are they gonna find her? Are they gonna find where they took her? Are they going to break her out?" Walter could feel the heat rising through his bones. "They have to *want* to find their daughter."

My Carolyn.

My one good thing.

Because Roy is here.

And Roy was sent to DTI.

And I know they always say that NO ONE COMES BACK FROM DTI, but Roy did, and so did the Eudys, so why not my Carolyn? Why not my one good thing?

All of this other stuff he could not find the words to say. His throat clamped up mercilessly on him. He thought to reach for his bottle of water, but his hands were shaking a bit, and he needed to clasp them together to steady them.

And besides...

Besides...

Roy was looking at him strangely.

"Walter," Roy said, very carefully. "Carolyn's not in DTI."

Walter stared back and was so muddled by everything that he couldn't even read the truth in Roy's eyes, and his mind delved into the worst, the very worst, because that seemed to be the thing that Walter had a knack for landing in.

She's dead. He's about to tell me that she's dead.

Oh, fuck...No, no, no...

"She was never disappeared."

Walter's mind immediately attempted to brush that aside—Roy didn't know, he wasn't there, he hadn't seen the scorch marks in the floor—but Walter's mouth said nothing, in the same way that hearing something that makes absolutely no logical sense will somehow strip the words out of your brain for a moment.

Silence. Walter searched his brother's face and saw nothing but confusion and honesty.

Roy searched Walter's face and saw a madness he had never seen before.

Roy spoke, and he spoke gently, like you would to settle a madman down.

"The Eudys knew that Carolyn was going to get disappeared. Their break out of DTI was the reason the CoAx wanted Carolyn in the first place, Walter. They wanted to use her as a bargaining chip against the Eudys. And the Eudys found out about it." Roy peered at him, eyebrows up, almost a hopeful cringe. "That's why my team was there in the first place. They got Carolyn out, but they didn't manage to get themselves out before the CoAx shut the District down. I was embedded with this unit of Fed troops that we knew would collaborate, and when the CoAx shut down the District, we activated them."

Walter didn't care. He didn't care about who was loyal to whom. Not in that moment.

His only concern in that moment was where his wife had been taken.

"Where's Carolyn now?" he choked out. "Where did they take her?"

"Carolyn's with her parents, Walter."

Walter found his head moving, even as his throat seized up and something light and almost effervescent came surging up his chest. Or perhaps it was just the feeling of dropping the brick of cement that he'd been carrying in his guts.

"But the door," he croaked. "The scorch mark…"

"The CoAx still hit your house," Roy said. "But we'd already taken her out."

"You got her?" Walter said, sliding down to the foot of the bed, not really knowing what he was doing until his grasping hands found his brother's shoulder and clutched at his clean, unbattled clothes. "You saved her? You saved Carolyn? She's safe?"

One of Roy's eyebrows twitched upwards. "Safe?" He chuffed. "Of course not, Walter. None of us are safe. Not really. And her least of all. She and the Eudys are going to ground. They're going to be hunted like dogs. They're going to be constantly moving. Never resting. Never in one place for very long. And any communications we get from them are going to be basic commands." He looked at Walter pointedly. "You cannot communicate with her."

Walter realized his hands were clenching and unclenching. "She's my *wife*, Roy!"

Roy's eyes bore down into a scrutinizing squint. "And do you love her, Walter?"

Walter laughed, frustrated, mad, bitter. "Yes! Of course!"

"Then you need to let her go for now, Walter."

Walter felt his frustration turn black. "Let her go?"

"Ayuh," Roy replied flatly. "Every communication between us and them puts them in danger. We'll be straining to even maintain command. We certainly can't afford give you conjugal-fucking-visits."

"Roy…"

"There's a war on, Walt." Roy snapped. "And you're right smack dab in the middle of it. Lives are hanging in the balance. Millions of them. And three of those lives are the Eudys, and their daughter— your wife. You wanna see Carolyn again?"

"Yes," Walter said, like wind in a hollow.

"Good," Roy replied with a stern nod. "That gives you something to fight for."

"What's that supposed to mean?"

Roy let out a growling noise. Abruptly he stood up. Hesitated. Turned to the door, and then stopped himself, and turned back to his brother. He pointed a finger at him. "You fucking stop it, Walt."

Walt sat there, dumbstruck.

"Stop acting like an idiot. We all know that you're not. I can see it in your eyes, Walt. I can see that things have changed. And it's not just the time that's passed. No, *you've* changed. I can see that thing inside of you that you've been denying all this time, for all those years. I can see that they've poked it awake." Roy nodded. "That's good. You can use that. You'll *need* to use it.

"You want Carolyn back?" Roy asked him, leaning forward, both angry and earnest. "You want things to go back to the way they were?" he laughed, harsh and bracing, like a winter wind had suddenly come in and chilled Walter to the bones. "Then you better help us win this war. You better help us fight."

Walter felt his hands. They'd already curled into fists. They ached, the knuckles, the split skin, where bullet fragments and concrete chunks had gone into him, or had taken the flesh off of him.

He felt that hot, black something, the burning thing, that catalyst of change buried so deep somewhere in the abyss of him. And he realized that he felt relief that it was still there. He felt relief, because this burning thing was so much better than the fear, so much better than the longing.

This burning thing was a thing that he could have *right now*.

It was already his.

And, magnificently, it could not be taken away.

Changing tides.

Changing polarity.

Summer into winter.

Equatorial heat into frigid poles.

"I can fight," he said.

Roy opened the door to the room and looked back at his brother. Again his eyes searched, again they scrutinized. "I sure hope you can," he replied. "But we'll see. We'll see soon enough."

"Ayuh? And how's that?" Walter demanded hotly.

Roy's face was deadly serious. "They took Pops, Walt."

Walter felt a wash of heat go over his head. A panic sickness. "What?"

"They took Pops," Roy repeated. "They took him because of his connection to you. To *us*." Then Roy raised a finger and pointed it at Walter, and the look in his eyes was one of intense conviction, the two Baucom boys, each watching the other.

When Roy spoke, his voice was quiet, as though he did not want anyone else to hear: "I'm gonna get him out. And you're gonna help me."

WANT MORE FROM DJ MOLLES?

Try the Bestselling *The Remaining* **series:**
The Remaining
The Remaining: Aftermath
The Remaining: Refugees
The Remaining: Fractured
The Remaining: Allegiance
The Remaining: Extinction

Also by DJ Molles:
Wolves

Made in the USA
Las Vegas, NV
26 September 2023

78181321R00177